The Life She Finds

A GRANITE SPRINGS NOVEL

Maggie Christensen

To my wonderful husband and soulmate who proved
to me that it's never too late to fall in love.

Also by Maggie Christensen

Oregon Coast Series
The Sand Dollar
The Dreamcatcher
Madeline House

Sunshine Coast books
A Brahminy Sunrise
Champagne for Breakfast

Sydney Collection
Band of Gold
Broken Threads
Isobel's Promise
A Model Wife

Scottish Collection
The Good Sister
Isobel's Promise
A Single Woman

Granite Springs
The Life She Deserves
The Life She Chooses
The Life She Wants

Check out the last page of this book to see how to join my mailing list and get a free download of one of my books.

Prologue

It was a perfect November evening. Lyn Carter twirled in front of the mirror admiring how the pale blue dress skimmed her body and the fluted sleeves hung from her shoulders to stop just above the elbow. She'd had a hard time persuading her mother to buy it, but the dress, combined with the silver strappy sandals, almost hidden by the gown, completed the outfit. She felt like a princess, dressed to meet her prince.

Lyn shivered at the thought of the evening ahead. She and Ken Thompson had known each other all their lives. Having grown up on neighbouring properties outside the town of Granite Springs, their parents had been friends. He was tall and handsome with the blond curls any girl would envy. Until recently, he'd just been a good mate, but now they were – what? She knew what her parents – and his – wanted, expected, hoped for, and it made her uncomfortable.

She'd always been a disappointment to her dad who'd wanted a boy to carry on working the family farm. When she turned out to be their only child, he'd transferred that hope to the desire she marry the Thompson boy, so the two properties could be combined. But the thought of replicating the life of her mother and Betty Thompson made Lyn want to throw up. She wanted more out of life than to be a farmer's wife. The day to day chores, the routine, the thought of being dependent of the vagaries of the weather and the price of sheep made her want to get as far away as possible. She loved the town of Granite Springs but had had enough of life on the farm. And she didn't want to spend her life at the beck and call of a man the way she'd seen her mother do.

As soon as she could, Lyn intended to travel. From her days in primary school, she'd dreamt of visiting all the places she read about. She wanted to sail down the Nile, climb the ruins of the ancient cities in Greece, wander round the pyramids, lie on the beach in Bali, ski in the Alps, visit the places her favourite authors had written about in London, the Lake District and the Scottish Highlands. And she was determined nothing would stop her.

'You look lovely, darling.' Lyn's mother pushed open the bedroom door. 'You were right. This is the perfect dress for you. It brings out the blue in your eyes. I hope your young man appreciates you.'

'Mum!' But Lyn smiled at her mother's obvious delight. As the daughter of older parents, she'd sometimes felt irritated by what she saw as their overprotection, but she knew they loved her, and only wanted her to be happy. It wasn't their fault she felt constrained by the limitations of this small country town.

She couldn't wait to branch out, to leave Granite Springs and spread her wings. That was why she'd applied to universities as far afield as Sydney and Brisbane, instead of the nearby Canberra which was the choice of most of her peers. She had known from a young age she wanted to become a teacher, a job which she knew could take her to the far-flung parts of the world she longed to visit.

There was the sound of a car driving up and stopping, then a loud knocking at the door.

'That'll be young Ken, now,' her mother said, sounding almost more excited than Lyn, who was having second thoughts about partnering the boy who'd been her childhood friend to the event of the year. Suddenly, the boy she'd shared skinned knees and swam in the dam with had become a young man who made her shiver with feelings she didn't want to experience. Not now when she was on the brink of a wonderful future, when she was about to break free from this place.

She followed her mother through the house to where an unusually bashful-looking young man stood awkwardly in the hallway chatting with her dad. His normally wild curls had been slicked down, he was wearing a wide-lapelled jacket of maroon velvet with matching trousers and a frilled pink shirt and was holding a corsage of three white rosebuds. He looked like a stranger.

'Looking good, Lyn,' Ken said, his smile turning him back into the boy she knew.

Lyn twirled again to give herself time to put an appropriate expression on her face. She could see from her mum and dad's expressions they were envisaging them walking down the aisle together already. 'You're looking pretty cool yourself,' she said, holding out her hand so he could attach the corsage to her wrist.

'Now, you two young ones have a good evening, and bring her home safely, Ken,' her dad said.

'Don't you worry, Mr Carter. I'll take good care of her.'

Lyn followed Ken out to his car – the beat-up old white ute he used around the farm and which they'd both managed to prang more than once when they were learning to drive.

'Whew, glad that's over!' Lyn complained, when they finally left the family property and were heading for the main road into town.

'They love you, Lyn, and just want the best for you.'

Lyn sighed. She knew Ken and *his* father didn't see eye-to-eye. She should be grateful for loving parents. But, sometimes, she just wanted to strangle them, to escape from their clutches. Well, not long now.

*

The car park at the showground was filling rapidly when Ken and Lyn arrived. They joined the groups of Year Twelve students, all dressed in their finery, walking towards the hall where the formal was to be held.

Once there, Lyn excused herself to join the other girls who were jostling with each other at the mirror in the inadequate ladies' room and admiring each other's dresses. The air was filled with the scent of perfume and a sense of anticipation.

'Love your dress.' Lyn turned to see two of her classmates standing arm-in-arm. She'd known Jo Freemont and Alice Jordan since primary school, but they were townies and she didn't see much of them outside school. They seemed happy enough to stay in the town they'd grown up in, but Lyn knew the future that was in store for them, wasn't for her. She had no intention of getting tied down to a man, any man, no matter how attractive he was.

'Thanks,' she replied. 'You both look great, too.'

The other two smiled their thanks.

'You with Ken tonight?' Alice asked. 'I saw him as we were coming in. He's looking sharp.'

Lyn gave her a faint smile. She didn't need Alice to tell her how Ken looked in his formal gear. She'd felt like a film star sitting next to him in the ute which for once didn't smell of sheep. If only… But her mind was made up, and no handsome guy in his flash outfit was going to change it.

The evening passed quickly. Some of the boys had sneaked a keg of beer into one of the adjoining rooms and they would disappear in ones and twos only to return in a more cheerful frame of mind. The company became louder and louder as more and more alcohol was consumed. Lyn even found herself, on a trip to the ladies', being offered a drink from a bottle of vodka by a classmate she barely knew. Although she'd have welcomed something to blur the proceedings, she shook her head.

It wasn't till they were on their way home again, that she and Ken had time to talk. He stopped the car on the track leading up to the farmstead and, knowing he'd had at least his share of the beer – she could smell it on his breath – Lyn geared herself up to refuse any attempt to seduce her.

Lyn wouldn't have objected in principle but didn't intend to lose her virginity in the front of a ute on a dirt road.

She needn't have worried.

'Look there,' he said pointing to the heavens. 'I love this time of night when the sky is so clear you can see all the stars. It's as if we're the only ones alive in the world.'

Ken took her hand gently. Her fingers curled in his, and they sat in silence, gazing up into the sky, united in a moment of wonder more intimate than any act of passion would have been.

It would be so easy to accept his evident affection, to fulfil her parents' expectations, but Lyn had bigger dreams.

As Ken tentatively stretched an arm around her shoulders, she slid across the ute's bench seat and moved away from him.

One

45 years later

'Raise your glasses to an exceptional woman and a much-loved headmistress.'

Lyn Hudson blushed as the room, filled with her colleagues and friends of the past twenty years, toasted her, then broke into strains of *For She's a Jolly Good Fellow.*

Having chosen to take early retirement at sixty-two, she'd have much preferred to leave quietly, without any fuss, but the staff at Irene Longman College for Girls had different ideas. After today's celebration – which followed a full school assembly – there would be the requisite dinner with the parents which would also serve as a fundraiser for the school.

Then, finally, she could get on with her life.

She smiled and raised her own glass, her eyes scanning the room to encompass friends and foes alike. Being headmistress for over twenty years had not been without its challenges and Lyn had made a few enemies along the way. But they were all here today to send her off in style, the leather-bound collections of her favourite Jane Austen and the Bronte sisters' books a testament to her love of English literature.

'You're really going to do it?' Gail, her long-time friend, trusted deputy of the past ten years and natural successor asked.

'I sure am,' Lyn replied. 'I can't wait. My tickets are all booked, the apartment's rented out. All I have to do is pack my case, have

Christmas with the family, and in two weeks' time I'll be off, and you won't see me for dust. I'll be travelling to all the places I've only dreamt about – the places the rest of you saw when I was married with a small child.'

'Half your luck.' Gail gave a wry grin. 'But enjoy yourself. Just take care – a woman on her own…'

'Rubbish! I'll be fine. And you'll make a great Head next year. It's time for a change. I've been here too long. The place needs some fresh blood, a new outlook.'

'I hope so.' Gail emptied her glass and looked around for another. 'Hell. I suppose I'll need to be more circumspect when I'm Head. You always seemed to balance everything so well – your personal life never intruded on your school one.'

'What personal life?' Lyn chuckled. When her marriage dissolved seven years earlier, she'd thrown herself into her work. Or had she done that before then? Her ex-husband had accused her of neglecting her family. Was that why he'd looked elsewhere, found himself a woman who was the complete opposite of her?

In her own mind, Lyn had been doing what needed to be done to help pay the mortgage and all the expenses their small family seemed to generate. Her life hadn't turned out to be what she anticipated when she left Granite Springs all those years ago. But it had been a good life and, when her daughter had been born, she fell in love with the tiny bundle. Now that daughter had two of her own and Lyn loved them so much, too. She'd miss them – probably more than they'd miss her – while she was gone. They all had their own lives now, even her granddaughters.

For the first time since she left Granite Springs determined to see the world, to build a different life for herself – different from that of her parents – Lyn felt a growing sense of anticipation. She couldn't wait for the next phase of her life to begin.

*

Lyn was glad to reach home that evening. The dinner had been entirely as demanding as she'd expected, with numerous speeches and well-wishes, topped off by the presentation of a monstrosity of a silver tea service she knew she'd never use. Her jaw ached from smiling, and her shoes were killing her.

Slipping off the offending footwear, Lyn padded barefoot into the kitchen to pour herself a much-needed glass of wine. Given the nature of the event filled with parents, she'd chosen to limit herself to one glass of champagne, and now was in dire need of something stronger to sustain her than the coffee she'd drunk two cups of at the end of the dinner.

She turned on her playlist of blues music and curled up on the sofa with a glass of merlot, the lights of the city shining on the ribbon of the Brisbane River far below. The music helped her relax and forget the day. She had finished the wine and her eyes were beginning to close when her phone vibrated. Tempted to ignore it, Lyn saw her mother's number. She sighed and answered.

'Lyn!' Her mother's broken voice immediately forced her alert. 'It's your dad, he's dead!'

Two

It was Christmas Eve and Ken Thompson steeled himself for the Christmas dinner at the old family home, the home that should have been his. He didn't resent the fact his father had chosen Alec to manage the property instead of him. They'd never seen eye-to-eye and the argument they'd had when Ken was in his early twenties had put paid to his inheritance.

He didn't begrudge his younger brother; he loved the guy – the little fellow who'd followed him around as a child. And Ken had made a success of the business he'd created in town – he was now a well-established and popular real estate and stock and station agent – but it still rankled that his dad had seen fit to cut him out that way.

It didn't matter that he was now a local councillor, and the previous year had been invited to stand as a member of parliament. He didn't have truck with any of the major parties and he was too old for that lark. Politics was a young man's game. Though Ken didn't feel old. Inside, he was still the young man who'd wanted to change the world.

'Everything okay, Dad?' Neil asked, walking into Ken's glass-fronted office in Granite Springs Realty. At least his own son had joined him in the business. Granite Springs Realty would carry on when he retired. It hadn't all been for nothing.

'Fine, son. Just thinking about tomorrow.'

'Uncle Alec was on the phone to check we'd be there for lunch. I said we would, but I'd have to leave early. I…'

'Other fish to fry, have you?'

Neil blushed. 'I said I'd join Sal and her dad for dinner. That okay with you?'

'Sure, son.' But Ken felt a twinge of regret, as Neil walked off, whistling. He knew Neil couldn't stay with him for ever. It was only natural he should find a new love to replace the one who'd left and taken his daughter with her. But Ken had become accustomed to having him around. Neil might not be home often, but he took away the sense of isolation Ken tried to ignore, the loneliness he'd experienced since his wife left all those years ago. The thought of growing old alone in this big house sometimes scared him.

Ken gave himself a mental shake. What was he thinking? Neil had only said he had a date for Christmas Eve, like any other young man his age. There was no need to get gloomy about it. Maybe this thing with Sally would work out, maybe it wouldn't, but he wasn't one to stand in the way of true love, if that's what it was.

Suddenly the door swung open to reveal an old friend of Ken's.

'Time for a pre-Christmas drink in the Golf Club?' the newcomer asked. 'I'm heading there now. Would be good if you can join me.'

Ken didn't reply, but Col Ford obviously took his silence for assent. 'See you there,' he said with a grin, and with a wave in Neil's direction, Col was gone again.

Ken checked his watch. 'Time to close up,' he said to Neil. 'We're not going to get any more trade at this time on Christmas Eve. Everyone's either in the pub or getting ready for tomorrow.' He'd let the rest of the staff go early for just that reason. Now there was only Neil and him, and soon he'd be left alone too.

'I suppose you have plans for tonight?' he asked, in the faint hope Neil would offer to spend it with his dad.

'Sal and I are going out to dinner, to The Riverside.'

Ken's face must have registered his disappointment, because he added, 'You could join us.'

'No, son. You have a good time. I have a book I need to finish, and I should get up to date on my paperwork.'

'But…' Ken could see the concern in his son's eyes.

He'd been seeing it there a lot recently, as if the boy thought he was getting too old to cope. He didn't feel old and didn't want anyone to pity him, least of all his son. 'Col invited me out for a few drinks with him when we finish up here. So I won't be alone all evening.'

'Right.' Neil seemed relieved. It didn't take much to put his mind at rest.

Ken hadn't given Col a definite answer, because he knew how it would be. They'd have a few beers, maybe order a couple of pies or sausage rolls at the bar, chat about old times, then Col would head off home to his wife and he'd be left feeling even more alone than if he'd headed straight home from the office.

But as he locked up and said farewell to his son, Ken found himself en route to the club. Any company was better than none, and he was in danger of turning into his father if he spent too much time alone.

*

Half an hour later, he was glad he'd come. It was fun to reminisce about the time when they'd been teenagers and amazing to realise it had been forty-five years ago. Where had the time gone? Col had married in his early twenties, while Ken had taken a few years longer to settle down with Sheila who had stuck with him till Neil was finished school, before telling him she was tired of living in Granite Springs and was moving to Melbourne.

They'd rubbed along pretty well over the years, but it hadn't been the love match his friend had found. He'd missed her companionship, but there was the pleasure of Neil's company during college holidays to look forward to and his work and the various local groups he belonged to kept him busy.

Then Neil had married and there was the added delight of his little granddaughter. But that ended too. Neil had made the same mistake of choosing a woman from out of town, a woman like his mother who couldn't settle in Granite Springs but craved the bright lights of the city. The bonus had been Neil returning to live with Ken and the pair had lived and worked together happily ever since – till now.

The reminiscences about their school formal, sparked by talk of an old photo Col's wife had unearthed, brought back memories Ken had tried hard to suppress – memories of the girl he'd grown up with, the girl his parents had wanted him to marry. He'd have liked that, too. In their last year at school, his childhood playmate had suddenly morphed into a desirable woman, one he wanted to spend the rest of his life with. If she hadn't left town, his life would have been different. Maybe his dad would have seen his point of view, maybe he'd be running the property now instead of Alec.

'Another beer?' Col was holding up his empty glass, one eyebrow raised, and Ken realised his companion had finished his drink while he'd been musing on the past. He nodded and drained his glass.

'What happened to that girl you were dating back then?' Col asked, when he returned from the bar with two more beers. 'She was a Carter, wasn't she?'

'Lyn Carter,' Ken agreed, her image appearing so clearly in his mind, he could almost touch her. 'She left town as soon as school was over. Went to stay with some family in Sydney, only came back for Christmas and didn't want to know me.'

'Weren't they neighbours of yours?'

Ken nodded and took a swig of beer. 'Were they clients of yours?' he asked.

'Sadly not. They always used George Turnbull. I guess they're with the guy who took over his law firm when he retired.'

'How're you enjoying retirement?' Ken knew Col had retired a couple of years earlier to enjoy life with his new wife.

'Good. Speaking of which…' Col checked his watch, 'I should go. I'm meeting Jo at The Riverside. It's a busy night for them and she's agreed to help out. Why don't you join us?'

'I don't think…' Ken began.

'Come on. Jo'll be tied up till later and we can share a bottle of wine for old time's sake. I keep telling her it's time she let it go, but she insists it's a mother's privilege to keep an eye on her half of the investment. What would I know?' He spread his hands and gave a wry smile, but Ken knew that while Col regretted having no children of his own, Jo's had always held a special place in his heart and that of his late wife.

'You've twisted my arm.'

The two men left together and walked across town to where The Riverside restaurant sat on the side of the river, as its name suggested. It was a balmy evening, the moon casting an eerie glow across the water.

'Remember?' Col asked with a chuckle, as they passed the narrow strip of sand on the edge of the river where the branch of a large tree stretched over the water.

'Were we mad, foolish, or just young?' Ken asked. The rope which had hung there in their youth, providing hours of entertainment for their younger selves, was long gone.

'All three, I think. But these days there's so much talk about safety. We never considered it might be dangerous.'

They laughed.

The noise of happy, chattering people and the clash of dishes met them as they entered the restaurant, along with a delicious aroma of herbs and spices. Ken spied Neil and a dark-haired woman sitting at a window table. They appeared to be engrossed in each other, so he decided not to disturb them and followed Col to a table in a back corner.

They had almost finished their meal before Jo joined them.

'Well, have you two finished setting the world to rights?' she asked with a chuckle, then added, 'Thanks, Steve,' as a tall young man set a plate in front of her. 'One of the perks of being an owner,' she said to Ken. 'Instant service.'

Ken smiled.

'Well?' she asked again.

'We've been talking about the old days,' Col said. 'Everything was so different then.'

'Not so different really,' Jo said, accepting a glass of wine from Col. 'The older generation still thought things were better in their day, and the younger ones couldn't understand what they were talking about. Here's to our generation.' She raised her glass and the men joined her in the toast.

'What are you doing for Christmas, Ken – family do?' she asked.

'Yes,' he sighed. 'Alec and Judy want to do the traditional Christmas lunch with Neil and me in attendance. It's a pity they never had children of their own to spoil, but they dote on Neil, always have.'

'A bit like Col and Alice with my three,' Jo said, with a fond glance at her husband. 'And is that Sally Anderson I see with Neil over by the window?' Jo gestured to where Neil and Sally were rising to leave.

'It is. They've been seeing each other for some time now. I hope she doesn't let him down. He's had enough disappointments.'

'Sally's a good girl. She's not to blame for her parentage, and after the initial hurdle, she's become part of our extended family. He should be right, there. I presume he is serious about her?'

'Neil doesn't give much away, but he's having dinner with her parents tomorrow, so I guess it's no flash in the pan, and he tells me she's not like Tina. I knew that marriage would never work.'

'You'd miss him if he married again.'

'I would.' Ken stared down into his glass. 'But it may not come to that. It's early days.'

But was it? And if Neil did remarry and move out, the house would seem even emptier than before. After Sheila left, it had taken Ken years to get used to being alone, then when Neil's wife left and he came back to live in his childhood home, it was as if the place became alive. What would Ken do once he was alone again? It didn't bear thinking about.

He'd never been one to seek out the company of others – men or women – and there certainly hadn't been any women in his life after Sheila. He'd steered clear of the predatory harpies who latched onto any available men in town. But he did appreciate having someone to come home to and enjoy a beer or a glass of wine with at the end of the day.

On the plus side, if there was a woman in Neil's life, he might find it easier to have Daisy to stay. Then Ken could spend time getting to know his granddaughter. He'd like that.

Not long afterwards, Ken left to walk home. He still lived in the house he'd bought only a year after his father kicked him out. It was close to the river and the centre of town, within easy walking distance of everywhere he needed to be. He rarely drove except to show properties to prospective buyers and there were few of those at this time of year. There would be even fewer after Christmas when those who'd stayed around for the festivities cleared out to the coast to escape the Granite Springs January weather, only picking up again when the annual batch of new teachers arrived in town for the beginning of the school year. He'd never felt that need himself. Besides having a business to run, he couldn't imagine what he'd do on the coast. What he did have a hankering for was to visit some of those places he'd only seen on travel programmes on television. Maybe one day.

The heat of the day had subsided, and the air was filled with the fragrant aroma of the lemon scented gums that bordered Main Street. Ken loved this walk. It reminded him of his childhood on the farm. If he closed his eyes, he could pretend he was back there, that his father was in the shed, his mother in the kitchen cooking dinner, and... Lyn Carter was waiting for him by the fence line. Hell, he hadn't thought of Lyn Carter for years, not till Col mentioned her.

Once home, Ken couldn't get the conversation with Col out of his mind. It was years since he'd thought of those days, of Lyn Carter – his first love. When he and Sheila married, he'd determined to forget his lost love and accept the woman he'd chosen, his son's mother.

But now, Lyn's image was as fresh in his mind as if he'd seen her yesterday. He pulled out an old photo album and there they were, all dressed up for their Year Twelve formal. He'd forgotten he had that photo, couldn't remember it being taken. He closed his eyes and remembered.

Three

After her mother's call, Lyn called Amy with the news before booking herself a flight to Granite Springs. Her father was dead. She needed to be there. She was worried about how her mum was coping, alone after over sixty-five years of married life.

And she was beset with guilt. Why hadn't she been a better daughter? Why had she only made flying visits over the years, expecting her aging parents to make the trip north to visit her?

She'd used the excuse that Amy and the girls were there, it was easier for her parents to fly north than for her to travel to Granite Springs. But if Lyn was honest with herself – and perhaps now was the time to be honest – she'd been afraid of what she'd find there; afraid of finding her younger self; afraid of the reminder of what she might have become if she'd stayed. It was easier to remain in Brisbane cocooned in her own little world – the one she'd carefully constructed over the years – to retain the image of the successful school principal and career woman she'd developed over the years, and play the bountiful host when her parents came to visit.

The heat hit Lyn as she stepped out of the plane, reminding her of one of the reasons she'd left – she hated the heat and dust of summer here. The flight had been full, many of the passengers arriving home for Christmas, and there was the usual flurry of hugs and greetings as the new arrivals were welcomed by friends and family.

By the time she'd retrieved her case and organised a hire car, Lyn was frazzled, a feeling that wasn't helped by the line of traffic she encountered on the way into town. Surely Granite Springs didn't used to be so crowded? But, once in town, the traffic eased and the familiar wide main street, cars parked nose to kerb, the lampposts decorated with poinsettia wreaths, and the enormous gaily decorated Christmas tree beside the war memorial in the centre of town assured her she was home.

But the house where her parents lived had never been home to her. It was where they'd moved when her dad could no longer manage the property, when he'd been forced to retire and move into town. She didn't think they'd ever considered it to be home either, even after living there for over twenty years.

The woman who greeted her at the door, seemed to have aged, shrunk, since Lyn had last seen her, only a few months earlier. Both she and Lyn's dad had made the trip to Brisbane to celebrate Maddy's nineteenth birthday. They'd seemed well then, and her dad had joked he'd be around to annoy them all for a few more years. Lyn bit the inside of her cheek as she remembered how they'd all laughed. It didn't seem so funny, now.

'Mum!' She wrapped her arms around the woman whose eyes seem to have sunk into her head, feeling her trembling, her bones sharply outlined under a thin covering of skin. Had she been this emaciated last time they'd met, and had Lyn been too occupied with her own concerns to notice?

'Oh, Lyn!' Her eyed filled with tears. 'What am I going to do?'

Lyn took her mother's arm and led her inside. 'I'm here now. I can take care of things. I think we need a cup of tea.'

Tea had always been her mother's remedy for all their ills, and the mention of it seemed to galvanise her into action. 'I'll make it. You settle yourself. The bed's made up in…' She made a move as if to take Lyn to the bedroom.

'It's okay, Mum. I can manage.' But could her mother? Lyn made her way to the spare room, the one her parents had designated as hers, even though her visits had been few and far between.

Setting her case down on the white candlewick bedspread, Lyn felt her own eyes moisten. This was going to be more difficult than she thought. Of course, she'd known this day would come, that her parents couldn't live for ever. But, somehow, their gradual aging and infirmity had escaped her notice. Lyn sat down on the bed for a moment to collect herself. She would be no use to her mother if she fell apart. She needed to be the strong one, just as they'd been there for her and supported her decision to spend her life in a different town, in a different state.

'Aunt Wyn?' Lyn asked her mother, when she walked back into the kitchen where, true to form, her mother had set out their tea in the fine bone china Royal Albert cups and saucers she'd been using for as long as Lyn could remember.

'She'll be here for the funeral.'

'Good.' Wyn was Lyn's favourite aunt, her only aunt, and her dad's sister. Hers had been the home Lyn fled to when she left Granite Springs. Never married, Wyn had been a role model of sorts for the young girl fresh from the farm with a head full of dreams. The older woman worked in a large law firm, lived alone in a tiny cottage in the centre of Sydney, and seemed to the young girl to lead a magical life.

'She's not getting any younger, either,' Lyn's mother said. 'Your dad's death has hit her hard.' Her hand shook as she picked up her cup and took a small sip.

And you, thought Lyn.

'You'll stay.'

It wasn't a question. 'Of course, Mum.' She'd stay till after the funeral, till after Christmas, then… She couldn't give up her trip, not after all those years, but… She looked across the table to where her mother was holding her cup in both hands and rocking back and forth. How could she leave her like this?

'Amy and Chris will be down with the girls. Chris may have to go back to Sydney for a few days, but Amy and the girls will stay for Christmas.'

'That'll be nice.' Her mother's face forced itself into the facsimile of a smile.

'The funeral, Mum?' Lyn hated to bring it up, but she had to know.

'That's all taken care of. The solicitor has seen to it. The boy who took over from George Turnbull.'

Lyn hid a smile. The boy must be close to her age. Bruce Jenkins had been working for George Turnbull for years and had taken over the practice when the old man retired. That much she did know. 'I'll contact him then, shall I?'

But her mother had disappeared into a reverie. Did this often happen? Had it been happening for long? Or was it the shock of her dad's death? Maybe she could talk with her mother's doctor, find out if she'd been consulting him recently. She could ask about her dad at the same time. Mum had said on the phone his heart had just given out. Did that happen? Maybe it did when you were in your nineties.

*

The funeral was a dismal affair conducted by the local funeral parlour with the body interred in the local cemetery. It all passed in a blur for Lyn, the realisation suddenly hitting her as the coffin was lowered into the grave. Until now, she'd been too busy to grieve, caring for her mother, greeting old family friends, accepting condolences.

The arrival of Amy, Chris and the girls had been a godsend. Their presence had relieved some of the burden on Lyn, but she had still been the one her mother turned to for comfort. And Amy had had to deal with the grief-stricken Maddy and Sophie who'd never encountered death before and who'd loved their great grandfather dearly.

The number of people at the church had been a surprise, though it shouldn't have been. Lyn's parents had lived in this community all their lives and had been well-known and respected. She was the one who'd turned her back on it.

Many of the mourners were strangers to Lyn, but her mother seemed to know them all, accepting their condolences as Lyn stood alongside her at the church door – an archaic custom Lyn could have done without.

'Good to see you back, Lyn. So sorry for your loss.'

Lyn looked up into a face that was vaguely familiar, a face she hadn't seen for over forty years. 'Jo, Jo Freemont?'

'Jo Ford now. Give me a call when you feel up to it.' The woman smiled and moved on, allowing the next in line to offer their words of comfort.

Jo Ford – of course. Lyn remembered now. Although she'd long left Granite Springs, her mother had kept her up to date with local news. She'd even sent her copies of the weekly Granite Springs Advertiser till Lyn asked her to stop. And the scandal of Jo marrying her old friend's widower had been one of the titbits she'd shared. Lyn and Jo had been friends once, though not close. She wouldn't mind catching up with her over a coffee or glass of wine – if she was here long enough.

*

The funeral over, there was just Christmas to get through. The excitement of Lyn's granddaughters helped them make it through the difficult day without too many tears. The two teenagers still felt the loss of their great grandfather, but for them, Christmas was Christmas and a time for presents and celebration.

Fortunately, everyone had prepared early for the festive season, so there were gifts aplenty for the girls to open and get excited over. At their insistence, the entire family went to the Christmas Eve service, held in the same church as the funeral only a week earlier and even Lyn, a staunch agnostic, had to admit to feeling somewhat comforted by the atmosphere pervading this holy place.

But on Boxing Day, life hit them again with a vengeance. Lyn was barely awake when she heard a loud thump, then a cry. Jumping out of bed, she rushed to discover her mother lying on her back in the hallway, one foot at an unnatural angle.

'Help me get up,' Edith said, making an attempt to rise before falling back to the floor again with a groan.

Lyn went to her side. 'Where does it hurt?' she asked. There were bruises on her mother's arm and leg, the hall cupboard door was open, and a small stool was lying overturned beside her.

'My hip,' Edith responded, 'but I'll be fine. Just help me up.'

It was the old stubborn mother she knew so well talking, but Lyn wasn't going to take any chances. She'd heard about the dangers of falls to women of her mother's age, and damage to a hip was nothing to ignore.

'I don't think so.' She looked around to see Amy arriving with Chris behind her. 'Can one of you call an ambulance?' she asked, her heart racing. She'd just lost one parent. She couldn't bear to lose another.

'I don't want to…' Edith objected.

'It's best,' Chris said, taking over. 'Amy's calling the ambulance now. Better make sure everything is all right, and you'll be in good hands.'

At his words, Edith seemed to relax. 'If you think so, Chris,' she said.

Lyn bit her lip. That was so like her mother – to ignore her advice, but be willing to accept it when Chris offered the same. She'd always listened to the men in her life. It seemed nothing had changed in that respect. But Lyn was glad Chris was here. At least it meant her mother would get the treatment she needed. It was likely she'd broken or fractured a hip, not uncommon in an elderly woman. Though what on earth she was doing climbing up there was anyone's guess.

'I just wanted to get out your old high school yearbook,' Edith said, stifling a groan.

'My yearbook? What on earth…?' But she could see her mother was in pain so didn't pursue it. Lyn hadn't seen that book since she left town, had consigned it to her past along with everything else in Granite Springs. She was surprised her parents had kept it, but she supposed she shouldn't have been. Her mother had always been sentimental. Lyn shuddered to think what other things she might have kept tucked away.

She dropped to the floor beside her mother, taking the frail hand covered in age spots in hers and stroking the strands of white hair away from a face that was pale with shock and pain.

Amy slid a pillow under Edith's head, and Lyn gave her daughter a weary smile. Then the younger woman fussed around, wondering about breakfast.

The two teenage girls walked into the hallway, their eyes wide with surprise and fear.

'What's happened?' Sophie asked. 'Is GG…?' Her voice trembled.

'Your great grandma has had a fall,' Chris said. 'Best you girls shower and dress, then help your mum with breakfast.'

'But…' Sophie said.

'Come on, Soph. Do as Dad says. We'll find out what happened later,' Maddy said.

They disappeared again, just as Lyn heard the ambulance arrive.

Chris answered the door, and soon Edith was being lifted onto a stretcher by two paramedics.

'I'll go with her,' Lyn said.

'Like that?' Chris managed to raise a smile.

Lyn looked down and realised she was still wearing her thin cotton nightie. No, she couldn't go like that. 'As soon as I get some clothes on. I'll be with you soon,' she said to her mother, dropping a kiss on her forehead.

Showered and dressed in the pants and tee shirt closest to hand, Lyn entered the kitchen where Amy was cooking breakfast. 'I'm off to the hospital,' she said.

'You've had a shock, too,' Chris said. 'I'll drive you.'

Lyn made a weak attempt to refuse, but knew he was right. Her mother's fall had shaken her. She was trembling. 'Thanks.'

'Are you all right, Grandma?' Sophie asked, moving forward to give her a hug.

'I will be,' Lyn said. 'Your dad just doesn't want two invalids on his hands.'

'Let me know the news, Chris.' Amy turned from the stove. 'Don't forget we're due to fly home this afternoon,' she added with a frown. 'We can always delay our trip,' she said to Lyn.

'Mum!' Maddy remonstrated. 'I have to...'

'Your great grandma's health is more important than your holiday,' Amy replied sharply.

'I'm sure it won't come to that, Maddy. I don't want to spoil your trip. I'll be right once we know what's happening with your great grandma. There's nothing you can do here,' Lyn said to her daughter. But she saw her own plans disappearing. Her dream of bringing in the New Year in New York's Times Square – of spending two weeks ski-ing in Aspen, before heading off to London, then Europe – began to fade.

She was due to fly out in two days' time. How could she do that with her mother in hospital?

Four

It was over for another year.

When Ken awoke on Boxing Day morning, he sighed with relief. What was it about Christmas that brought it all back? He often visited Alec and Judy throughout the year, had dinner and a few drinks without any adverse effects. But the festive season, the time of year when, as boys, he and Alec had vied with each other to see who'd put the star on top of the tree, who'd be first awake on Christmas morning, the years when he'd assumed he'd be the one to take over from their dad…

As he brewed his first coffee of the morning, looking out onto the garden of native plants he'd spent the past few years cultivating, he puzzled over what Neil might want to say to him. After the traditional turkey lunch Judy had prepared, and before he left, his son had taken him aside.

'I have something to discuss with you, Dad,' he said. 'Tomorrow? I'll be back around ten.'

That in itself put Ken's antenna up. He couldn't remember when his son had last told him when he'd be back home. Ever since he'd returned to live with Ken, his tail between his legs when Tina left him, he'd treated this house more like a hotel than a home. But that's perhaps as it should be. Neil wasn't a child anymore; he wasn't answerable to his father for his movements. And these days, he seemed to be spending more time with Sally Anderson than he did at home.

Maybe he'd decided to pop the question to Sally last night, and that was what he wanted to tell him, but surely he'd want to bring Sally along with him if that was the case? Maybe not. Ken had long given up trying to understand the way the younger generation thought, though Neil was more of an open book than most.

It was only eight now, so he'd have to wait. He poured his coffee and carried it with a plate of toast and vegemite into the study. This was his special place, the room he always retired to when things got too much for him and even when, as now, he was alone in the house, it was the one that beckoned him.

Lying where he'd left it the night before, was the Michael Connelly novel Neil had given him for Christmas. His son knew his tastes so well. Ken would love to have travelled to Sydney to hear the great man speak – it wasn't often one of his favourite authors came to Australia – but things had been too busy in the office. Neil must have remembered his disappointment.

He settled himself in his favourite chair by the window and, his coffee and toast on the low table beside him, began to read.

*

The rattle of the front door opening dragged Ken away from the exploits of Bosch and Ballard. Putting an old envelope in the page to act as a bookmark, he rose to greet his son.

'Dad!' Neil pulled him into a hug as if they didn't live together, hadn't seen each other only the day before. Something was up. Ken sometimes found it difficult to believe he'd sired this tall blond muscular man who was more at home on the rugby field or cricket pitch than in an office. But he was glad he'd chosen to be part of the business. It was a comfort to know it would continue when he finally retired, something he wasn't ready to do yet.

'Can I get you a coffee?' he asked, realising he'd been so engrossed in his book, he'd allowed his own to grow cold.

'A beer would go down well,' Neil said. 'Enjoying it?' he asked, picking up the copy of *The Night Fire.*

'One of his best,' Ken replied. Beer? This early in the day? But it *was* Boxing Day so maybe it was only natural, or was what Neil had to say going to be so disturbing, he'd need alcohol to hear it? 'I'll get us a couple of beers,' he said, before going into the kitchen and taking two cold cans from the fridge.

When he returned, Neil was seated on the office chair, spinning around, eyes down, his hands clasped between his knees. He stopped the chair from spinning, looked up at Ken's approach and accepted the proffered can.

'Well, what's this you have to tell me that's so important it can't wait?' Ken asked, popping open his can and taking a sip of the ice-cold liquid.

Neil opened his can, took a swig, and expelled a loud breath before replying, 'I've been talking with Uncle Alec.' He gave Ken a sideways glance, then looked away again. 'He's asked me… he wants… This is hard, Dad. But I know the farm means a lot to you, too. Uncle Alec wants me to join him to learn how to manage the property, to take over when he's ready to step down.'

Ken felt a tightness in his chest. Was he about to have a heart attack? His father had gone that way. He felt numb. This must be how someone feels when his entire life disappears in front of him. He rubbed his forehead, shaking his head at the same time.

This was the last thing he'd expected. Suddenly, he became conscious of Neil gazing at him, his eyes filled with concern. 'Are you all right, Dad?'

Ken managed to nod.

'I know it's a disappointment for you.' Neil rolled the can between his hands.

Disappointment? Disappointment didn't cover it. Ken felt as if his heart had been cut out leaving an angry gaping hole. 'How long?' he asked, his voice shaking. This hadn't happened overnight. Alec must have approached Neil some time ago. The pair had been plotting behind Ken's back. A hot anger began to rise, anger at his son, anger at his brother, anger at himself for not realising it was happening.

Neil couldn't meet his eyes. 'Not long. Since the bushfire.'

Ken remembered how, as members of the Rural Bushfire Brigade, they'd both been called out to the fire in early October. One of the properties Neil helped save had been the one Ken and Alec grew up on, the one Alec now owned.

'It struck me then,' Neil continued, 'that it was where our family came from. I felt a tug – something I couldn't explain. So, when Uncle Alec suggested it, I… I've been spending some time there. I enjoy it, Dad, working outside, not stuck in an office and showing homes and properties to other people. I want my own property. And this one belongs to our family.' He seemed to run out of words and took another long swig of beer, draining the can and crushing it in his hand.

'So that's it?' Ken asked. 'You're going to leave your old man to fend for himself while you play at being a farmer?' He knew he sounded bitter but was too upset to care.

'It's not like that,' Neil objected. 'It's part of the family. It's my heritage. If you'd…' He stopped, as if realising he'd said too much. 'I never did understand what happened. Why you left, and Wooleton went to Uncle Alec.'

'It's a long story, son. And not one for now. I don't hold it against Alec. He did what he had to in the circumstances. I don't think he liked it any better than I did at the time. He was all set to go to the city and become a lawyer. It was all up to your grandfather.'

Ken remembered that day. It was imprinted on his mind. The final argument. He'd returned from Ag College full of enthusiasm, wanting to put his new-found knowledge into practice. But, when he'd shared his ideas with his dad, the old man lost his temper.

'Bring cattle into a sheep property? Have you lost your mind?' the old man raged. 'This property has raised sheep for generations. That's where Wooleton got its name. You want to turn that on its head because of some wild ideas you've come across in Canberra? What do those jumped-up academics know about real farming? Let them try coming out here and getting their hands dirty.'

Ken had tried to reason with him, but it had been of no use. The upshot was that he'd left his home and moved into town. He'd used the skills he'd learnt to help other people find their properties and done pretty well. But in his heart, he'd never completely forgiven his father for robbing him of his birthright.

'You did send me to Ag College, Dad. Didn't it occur to you I'd want to use that knowledge for more than just *selling* land?'

'I guess.' Had he? Ken wasn't sure. But when Neil had suggested he study agriculture just like his dad, Ken had been delighted his son wanted to follow in his footsteps. Now the decision had come back to bite him.

But it hadn't seemed that way at first. As a new graduate, Neil had been keen to join his father, enjoying the variety the real estate job offered him, or so he'd said. Then he'd met Tina who would never have been satisfied living away from the town. When Daisy had been born, he knew Neil had been happy with the nine to five existence that allowed him to spend time with his young family.

Then Tina left taking Daisy with her. It seemed Granite Springs wasn't enough for her, though Ken suspected there was more to the split than a simple dislike of the town. Was that when the rot set in? Had Neil been hankering for a change since then? Had it only taken the bushfire to bring it to a head; or had he been secretly plotting this all along?

Ken drew himself up short. This sort of thinking wasn't going to get him anywhere. And he couldn't go back in time, go back to Wooleton now, even if he wanted to, which he wasn't sure he did.

'I suppose you'll be wanting to move out there, too?' He caught a guilty expression on his son's face.

'Not right away, but… Uncle Alec suggested we could get permission to put one of those demountables in the back paddock. I've had a look at them online. They have some pretty substantial ones these days. Sal…' He bit his lip and crunched the already crushed can even tighter. 'We…'

'It's serious, then? You haven't known each other long.'

Neil looked up to meet Ken's eyes, and Ken recognised that look. It was one he hadn't seen in his son's eyes before. It was one his own eyes had held all those years ago in the photo he'd been studying only the night before. 'I see,' he said. 'Well, as long as she feels the same way about you, I wish you both happiness. She'd be happy out on Wooleton?'

Neil nodded. 'We haven't actually talked about marriage, but she likes it out there. She may have grown up in the city, but she's a country girl at heart.'

'Hmm.' Ken hoped Neil wasn't making another mistake. 'So, when is this move going to take place?'

'You'll have to put up with me for a bit longer. It won't happen all at once. I need to sit down with Sal to decide on a design – there are some nice ranch styles that would fit in well with the old homestead. Then, once everything is open again after the holidays, I can get it all started. There's finance and planning permission to arrange, then we need to place the order. The construction itself should only take around six weeks. So, all going well, maybe Easter?' Neil's voice was enthusiastic as he outlined the process to which he'd clearly given careful thought. This was no sudden decision.

'And you want to start out there when?'

Neil reddened. 'As soon as you can release me. I don't want to let you down.'

But that's exactly what you are doing.

'It might take a bit of time to find someone to take your place, and the beginning of the year can be busy with new staff arriving for the university and local schools. But I can start advertising and asking around. Meantime, maybe you could spend a couple of days a week out there, getting your hand in.'

'Thanks, Dad. I knew you'd understand.' Neil rose and went over to enfold Ken in an awkward hug.

But did he understand? Ken thought about it when the younger man had left, whistling as he went, clearly relieved to have this conversation over. Then he remembered how he had been at Neil's age. *His* father had prevented him from following his dream of living on the land. He'd never do that to his own son.

But that didn't make it any easier to accept that his son had succeeded where he had failed. Wooleton would stay in the family, just not with Ken at the helm. But Alec! Why hadn't his brother talked with him before he'd approached Neil? He must have known Ken would be upset – more than upset. He was devastated.

How could his brother have done this to him?

Five

Lyn walked out of the air-conditioning of Granite Springs Base Hospital into the searing heat of the December afternoon and stood for a moment to take a deep breath. Her mother's fractured hip would take time to heal, time during which she'd need Lyn close by. Lyn's forehead creased. She wished she was a child again and could stamp her feet and resort to a temper tantrum. There was no way she was going to be able to set off on her longed-for trip – the trip she'd eagerly planned over the past year.

The consultant was pleased with the surgery. He said her mother had come through it well, but would need to visit the rehab clinic for four to six weeks and might never regain full mobility. Lyn closed her eyes at the thought of what that might mean. Edith Carter had been fiercely independent all her life and wouldn't take kindly to the enforced inaction and exercise regime she was about to be subjected to.

What it did mean was there was no way Lyn could leave her to fend for herself. She'd have to cancel the trip and stay here in Granite Springs at least until the end of her mother's treatment. After that, who knew what would happen? The thought of having to spend even more time here was difficult to contemplate, but she knew her mother needed her.

The street outside the hospital was almost deserted at this time of day. Anyone with any sense was inside their own home or in an air-conditioned bar or café. As her stomach told her it was lunchtime, Lyn saw a sign she remembered, and wondered who owned The

Bean Sprout Café these days. Back when she was in her final year at school, it was where they bunked off to when they wanted to avoid an unpopular class or a sporting event they disliked. It had been owned by a family called Beattie back then. She thought they'd had a son, but he'd been younger than Lyn. She couldn't remember his name.

Making an instant decision, Lyn pushed open the glass door to be hit with a welcome wave of cool air. She looked around. Not much had changed. Although the place had obviously been repainted and boasted new tables and chairs, the atmosphere was still the same. Lyn ordered an iced coffee and salmon with tomatoes and fetta on flatbread from a cheerful woman and took a seat in the corner.

While waiting to be served, she took out her iPad and, with a heavy heart, logged into her travel account to cancel her bookings. Then she checked her travel insurance to ensure she was covered for death or illness of a family member, sighing with relief to discover she was. It wouldn't have mattered if she wasn't covered, but the knowledge she wouldn't lose her carefully garnered travel budget went some way to console her. This way she could rebook later in the year – or next year, depending on her mother's health.

Suddenly, she remembered Jo, the woman who'd spoken kindly to her at her dad's funeral. 'Call me', she'd said. Did she mean it, or was it just the sort of platitude one offered to mourners on such occasions? No, she remembered Jo Freemont as she'd been then. They'd been good mates all through primary school, but moved in different groups at high school as they were in different classes. Jo and another girl had become friends. Lyn racked her brains. Alice, that was it. The pair had become inseparable.

But Jo had always been there when Lyn needed a friendly ear, a shoulder to cry on. She'd been someone Lyn could always rely on to tell it like it was, never to sugar-coat an unpalatable truth. Maybe she could share her misgivings with her old friend now?

Turning back to her iPad, Lyn opened the White Pages directory. She soon found C and J Ford with an address outside town. To her relief, her meal arrived before she could make the call, giving her time to reflect if it was a good idea. But, when she'd finished the lunch which proved to be delicious, she was still of the same mind.

'Thanks,' Lyn said to the woman who came to remove her plate. She ordered another coffee and took out her phone.

*

Lyn felt better as she walked back to her mother's house. The house would never be home to her. Home was the high-rise unit looking out over the Brisbane River, the two-bedroom apartment she'd lived in ever since Glenn left. Her childhood home outside Granite Springs was long gone, and she felt no temptation to revisit it. Lyn had been happy there and didn't want her memories sullied by seeing other people living in the place where she'd grown up.

Jo had been pleased to hear from her, justifying Lyn's decision to call. From their brief conversation Lyn deduced Jo had lived on her acreage for many years. They'd arranged to meet for coffee next day at a café called Mouthfuls which was new since Lyn left. Half the town was new since then, and Lyn's brief forays back to visit her parents hadn't included any trips around town. It would be good to catch up with Jo.

Once home, Lyn was at a loose end. She'd finished her book and, now she was retired, there was no work to catch up on. She suddenly realised how much of her life had been taken up with issues related to the school. Now all that was over.

Wandering around the empty house, Lyn decided to do some cleaning and tidying. It would take her mind off things and fill in the time till she could visit her mother again that evening. She turned on the radio to provide background music and set to work. She was surprised to find the house less immaculate than she expected. Her mother had always been houseproud, but now there were cobwebs in some corners, and grime on the bathroom tiles. What hadn't her mum been telling her?

All went well, till Lyn reached the hallway where Edith had fallen. The stool her mother had been standing on had been returned to the living room, but when she opened the cupboard door, Lyn noticed everything on the top shelf was higgledy-piggledy, as if her mother had been rummaging around.

With a sigh, Lyn fetched the stool again and, taking care to balance herself sensibly, reached up, pulling everything out and dropping the items on the floor. Once down again, she sat on the floor to look through what she'd found, stopping when she came to the yearbook. Why on earth had her mother been looking for it?

Taking the tome in her hands, she rubbed a finger over the cover bearing the faded school badge and motto, and the slogan *Granite Springs High – Class of '75*.

Lyn was almost afraid to open it. Then, as she turned it over in her hands, a photo fell out. There she was with Ken Thompson, all dressed up for their formal. It brought it all back. The night her childhood friend had stopped being just that, the night she'd felt the first stirrings of desire, the night she'd taken fright.

*

'Lyn!' Jo hugged her. 'I was so glad you called me. It's been too long. I was so sorry about your dad. And now your mum's sick.'

For a moment Lyn regretted arranging to meet Jo. She should have known her old friend would arrive brimming with sympathy. But the feeling soon went, replaced with pleasure in her old friend's company.

As if sensing Lyn's sentiments, Jo added, 'I'm sorry. You're probably tired of people's sympathy. But I am glad you agreed to meet with me today.'

'I'm glad, too,' Lyn said, meaning it. She'd always liked Jo. 'This place is new,' she said, looking around the café.

'Not so new, really,' Jo chuckled, a sound Lyn remembered. 'Mouthfuls has been here for some time. It's very handy, right around the corner from the library. I see you made a stop there today,' she said, gesturing to the books Lyn had placed on the table.

'Yes, I was early, so I took the opportunity to replenish my supply. I didn't expect to be here for so long, but now...' She spread her hands in a gesture of uncertainty.

'Well, I for one am glad that you are,' Jo said. 'But tell me what happened to your mum. On the phone, you just said she had an accident.'

'Oh, it was so stupid. It could so easily have been avoided,' Lyn said and proceeded to describe what had happened, and how her plans had been disrupted. 'Now it seems I'm here for at least six weeks, maybe longer,' she finished with a rueful grin. She'd been tempted to tell Jo what had led her mother to be climbing into the cupboard but decided to keep that to herself.

'Oh dear! The poor soul. On top of having to deal with your dad's death, too. How's she bearing up?'

'Not great,' Lyn admitted. 'She seems much frailer than I remember.'

'She's a hardy soul, but it comes to us all,' Jo said, her eyes clouding.

'You know her? Of course you do. You were at Dad's funeral. But...'

'I volunteer at the library. I deliver books to the housebound,' Jo explained. 'When she and your dad were unable to get out, I'd drop theirs round to them.'

'But... she...they... weren't ill. We talked on the phone every week. I saw them a few months ago. She never said...'

Jo put a gentle hand on Lyn's arm. 'She wouldn't have wanted to worry you. She's very proud of you and what you've done with your life. And your daughter and her two girls. "My four beautiful girls", she'd say.'

'Oh!' Lyn didn't know what else to say.

'Coffee?' Jo asked.

'What?' Lyn was still contemplating how her mother had managed to dissemble on their weekly calls. If she'd lied about their health, what else had she kept hidden from Lyn? She realised what Jo had asked. 'Yes, please. A latte, but I'll get it.'

She was too late. Jo had already risen and was placing their order.

'I ordered a slice of banana bread, too,' Jo said when she returned. 'We can share. I'm sorry if I gave you a shock. It's often those closest to us who we feel we can't be honest with.'

Lyn was about to disagree when she thought of all the things she kept secret from her own daughter. Jo was right. *We always want to protect the ones we love, and they won't thank us for it,* she thought.

'I took early retirement and was planning a long trip,' she confided in Jo, when their coffees arrived along with the promised banana bread. 'I knew Mum and Dad were getting older. Of course I did. But it didn't occur to me... I've been stupid, too. Even when I cancelled my tickets yesterday, I was planning for when I could rebook them and continue my trip. How selfish is that?'

'It's not selfish at all. Your mum wouldn't want you to cancel everything for her.'

'No, but...' Lyn bit her lip. She exhaled. 'Maybe I'm not meant to travel the world. When I do make plans something always seems to get in the way.'

'Do you want to talk about it?'

Lyn gave Jo a wary glance. She didn't confide easily, usually preferring to keep her own counsel. Then she relaxed. This was Jo, the girl she'd shared so much with in her childhood. Being with her was like slipping into an old pair of shoes. She took a deep breath.

'It all goes back to when we finished high school. I knew I wanted to get away from Granite Springs. I had big dreams. I wanted to see the world. I knew that if I gave in to my emotions…' she hesitated, an image from the past rising up behind her eyes. The girl in the photo from the school formal wasn't so very far away. '…I could be stuck here for the rest of my life.' She gave Jo an apologetic look. 'I'm sorry if that sounds disparaging of the choices you made.'

'Not at all. We all have our own dreams, and mine was to remain here. I've never regretted it.' She smiled encouragingly.

'I felt… if I stayed, I'd become a farmer's wife and I'd seen how that wore down my mother. I didn't want my life to be a replica of hers. I wanted something different. I planned to get my teaching qualification and use that as the springboard for my travel. It all seemed so simple.'

'It didn't happen that way?' Jo guessed.

Lyn shook her head, remembering. 'Not at all. I met Glenn in my final year at university. He had already graduated and was just getting started in his career. We married, and going to teach in an underdeveloped country was suddenly off the agenda. We'd save and travel later, we decided.' Lyn sighed and took a long drink of her coffee. She could see them as plain as day, that young couple full of plans and excitement, ready to take on the world.

'I became pregnant,' she said. 'It wasn't planned. I was only twenty-two. But when Amy was born, we both fell in love with our beautiful daughter. All our plans for travel flew out the window.' She smiled. 'She was a beautiful baby, but babies cost money. It took both of our salaries. By that time, we had a mortgage too. Our lives were busy and became busier. Travel was something we talked about only when we watched travel documentaries. It didn't figure in our budget, not then. As my career took off, I became headmistress and the school became my life. Sometimes I barely had time to spend with the family, though I tried to help Amy when her girls were little. But I still harboured the idea that Glenn and I'd travel together – one day.'

'What happened?'

'Cheryl Hopkins happened. Glenn left me.' Lyn felt a bolt of the anger she thought she'd managed to quell. 'Seven years ago, that happened. I began to make my plans again. Amy's married, my granddaughters are growing up. They don't need me anymore – if they ever did.' She gave a wry laugh. 'This was to be my time.'

'Oh, my dear!'

'Maybe it's not meant to be, never was.' Lyn gazed down into her now empty cup. 'Sorry to bore you with all my woes, but it's been good to get it all out, to tell someone. Right now, Mum must come first, I owe her that.'

'She wouldn't expect you to put your life on hold for her,' Jo said, repeating the sentiment she'd expressed earlier.

'Maybe not. But she deserves it. She and Dad never tried to stand in my way. They'd have liked me to stay here, marry the boy they had in mind for me. If I'd done what they wanted, my life would have been different, maybe happier. Who knows? But I wouldn't have Amy and my girls.'

There didn't seem to be much more to say. Recounting what amounted to her life's story had exhausted Lyn, who felt faintly embarrassed to have washed her dirty linen in public, as her mother would have said. But who else could Lyn have told it to? Who else would have listened without judging her or suggesting solutions?

'Thanks for listening, Jo,' Lyn said, as they rose to leave.

'I'm glad I could be here for you,' Jo replied. 'Since it looks as if you're going to be in Granite Springs for some time, you must come out to Yarran – that's the name of our property – for lunch or dinner and to meet Col. We're not all country hicks, you know.'

'Far from it. I remember Col. I'd love to come.' Lyn remembered them all, Col Ford, Gordon Slater, Alice Jordan, Kay Little and that boy who'd arrived late in the school year and made such a play for her, David… Jackson, that was it. And, of course, Ken Thompson. She stifled the urge to ask what he was doing these days. She knew he'd married – a newcomer to town, her mother had been quick to tell her, as if emphasising what Lyn had thrown away. Seeing that photo had brought it all back.

As she walked away from the café, there was a lightness in Lyn's step. It was as if, by unburdening to Jo, she'd found a new hope. Maybe spending a few weeks in Granite Springs wouldn't be so bad, after all.

Six

'I love you, Grandpa.' Daisy's tinkling voice was music to Ken's ears. Neil had managed to prevail on Tina to allow him to bring their daughter back to Granite Springs with him for a week. The week was almost over, and Ken would be sad to see his granddaughter leave, but according to Neil, Tina had a new man in her life and would most likely be more willing to let Daisy spend time with her father and grandfather in school holidays in the future.

'I love you, too, sweetheart,' Ken replied, tousling her blonde curls. She was so like her dad – a female version of what Neil had been like at that age – it made his heart turn over. 'Does Tina keep in touch with your mother?' he asked Neil, who was spreading vegemite on a piece of toast, as the thought occurred to him. He hadn't seen or heard from his ex-wife since she left town, but she was Neil's mother and Daisy's grandmother.

Neil frowned, handing Daisy a plate with two slices of toast. 'She sends gifts for her birthday and Christmas, but apart from that, I don't know. Daisy,' he said, taking a seat beside the little girl, 'does Nana Sheila come to visit you at Mum's, or do you visit her?'

Daisy shook her head, her mouth full of toast. She took a sip of orange juice and asked, 'Is that the grandma who sent me a book for Christmas? She lives a long way away.'

'I guess not then, Dad,' Neil said.

'And you?' Ken had never asked his son this before. He wasn't sure why he was asking now. The Christmas period did strange things to people, brought back memories, some good, some not so.

Neil reddened. 'We're in touch. I call her from time to time. She's happy in Melbourne, has made a life for herself there.'

'She never…?'

'Remarried? No. What's made you think of her now?'

'Oh, I don't know. I was just looking through old photos after Christmas,' Ken said, by way of an explanation, hoping it would satisfy his son. It wasn't photos of Sheila that had caught his attention, but the older ones of Lyn Carter. How he wished he could go back in time, but what could he have done to change things? Back then his life had been tied up with Wooleton where his future lay. He'd had no inkling of the split that would happen when they finished school. 'What are you planning to do today?' he asked to change the subject.

'Sal has the day off, so we're going to spend it with her,' he said. 'She and Daisy are getting on well, aren't you, pumpkin?' he said, ruffling his daughter's hair.

'I like Sally,' Daisy said, taking a bite from her toast. 'Are you going to marry her, Daddy?'

Neil laughed. 'It's a bit too early for that, but how would you feel if I did?'

The two men held their breath while Daisy seemed to consider the idea.

'Could I be a flower girl?' she asked at last. 'My friend Heidi was one last year and she got a pretty dress.'

'I'm sure that could be arranged,' Neil said. 'But don't mention it to Sal just yet. I need to ask her first.' He hesitated, then added, 'We're going to go out to the farm, Dad.' He cast a wary glance at Ken. 'Daisy wants to see the sheep, and Uncle Alec suggested today would be good. It's also a good time to…' He cleared his throat. 'I put in a building application when the council opened up again yesterday. I thought Daisy could see where we're planning to locate the house.'

'The house. Right.' Ken had been trying to forget about it, but the floor plans had been sitting on the coffee table for the past few days.

'Is that where I'll sleep when I come to visit, Daddy? Will Grandpa Ken be living there too?' She turned her bright smile towards Ken.

'Not me, sweetie. But you can still come to visit me here.'

Daisy nodded as if it was all settled.

Neil and Daisy were still fussing around when Ken left for the office. It was nice to have a child around after all those years; made him feel younger. But it didn't change the fact Neil would be leaving him in a few months. He had to decide how he was going to manage. The women he employed were good on the real estate side, but most people looking for an acreage, whether it be large or small, preferred to deal with a man – it took a long time to change the country mindset, and it probably wouldn't happen in his lifetime.

Maybe it was time to follow his old friend's example and retire. But how would he spend his time? He still had good years ahead of him and a lot to offer. Maybe he could find a younger man who'd be willing to learn the ropes, perhaps an energetic new graduate like Neil had been. He was still deliberating on this when he reached the office.

The morning passed quickly, Ken's problem not far from his mind. He was drafting an advertisement, having decided not to wait till Neil actually left before trying to find someone to replace him, when one of his staff popped her head into his office.

'Not having lunch today, Ken?'

He checked his watch. One o'clock already. Where had the morning gone?

'We've all had ours, so we can hold the fort if you want to go out.'

Ken realised he was hungry. He hadn't eaten since the slice of toast at breakfast. He really needed to start looking after himself better. 'Thanks. I'll do that.' He turned off his computer, grabbed his phone and walked outside where the stifling heat hit him, almost sending him back into the chill of the office.

Ken made his way along Main Street, ducking from under one shop awning to another till he reached the club, where he pushed open the door into its air-conditioned comfort with a sigh of relief. Even though he'd lived here all his life, Ken had never become accustomed to the intensity of the summer heat. Maybe it just seemed more so here in the town, away from the open paddocks of the farm he'd grown up on. Whatever it was, he much preferred being indoors these days. He had a vague recollection of his mother closing up the house against the heat, even pulling the curtains to leave the inside dark, then opening everything up again to catch any light breeze in the early evening.

He was surprised to see Col Ford propping up the bar. 'Didn't expect to find you here,' he said.

'I could say the same about you,' Col said. 'Jo's taken the twins into Canberra for the day, making the most of the school holidays. What's your excuse?'

'I eat here most days,' Ken admitted. 'I never seem to get around to making a packed lunch and there's no point in going home. Neil's taking his daughter out to the farm with Sally, so I'm on my own today.' He wasn't sure why he felt the need to explain himself to his old friend.

'I thought I saw the two of you with a little one at the park the other day,' Col said. 'Jo said it must be your granddaughter.'

'Daisy, yes. Not so little anymore. She'll be eight next birthday. I've missed so much of her growing up, but at least her mother's seen sense now and let her come to visit.'

'Join me for a bite to eat?'

Ken ordered a beer and the ploughman's lunch and followed Col to a table on the far side of the room. They chatted for a bit, tossing around their discontent with the way the government was handling the drought, then Col said, 'I saw Alec at a New Year's Eve do. He said Neil was planning to move out there. What's that all about?'

Ken grimaced. Talking about it made it real. 'Yeah, he's decided – with some encouragement from my brother. He wants to become a farmer.' He pushed back a lock of hair that threatened to fall into his eyes. 'I suppose it shouldn't have come as a surprise.'

'But it did?'

Ken took a swig of beer before replying. 'I thought Neil was content working with me, living in town. And now he and Sally seem to be making a go of it...' He sighed. 'But it seems he had a hankering to find his heritage or some such thing. Anyway, as soon as the lad can organise for one of those demountables to be erected out there, he'll be off. It makes me think...' Ken downed another mouthful of beer. 'It should all have been his anyway, things being what they were. Alec and Judy have no children to carry it on, so it's only fair Neil take his rightful place.' Ken had told himself this so often, the words flowed off his tongue as if he really believed them. 'But I had no warning. Alec should have told me.' Ken drummed his fingers on the table. He couldn't let it rest. He knew he had to have it out with his brother.

Seeing the shocked expression on his friend's face, Ken said, 'Sorry,

Col. It just takes a bit of getting used to. I was actually drafting the ad for someone to replace him before I left the office.'

'It can't be easy.'

They sat in silence till their meals were served, then ate without speaking.

'On another topic,' Col said, when they'd finished eating and were drinking coffee. 'Did you know an old friend of yours is back in town?'

'An old friend of mine?' Ken raised an eyebrow.

'Lyn Carter. Jo bumped into her at her dad's funeral before Christmas and they had coffee together the other day. It seems…'

But Ken had stopped listening.

Lyn Carter was back in town.

Just as he'd resurrected her memory.

Seven

Lyn had difficulty controlling her nervousness. Her mother was being discharged today, and Lyn was aware Edith would need a lot of care. She was managing to move using a walker, but it was a slow process and she easily became frustrated at her lack of progress.

It had been a sad New Year for Lyn who'd hoped to have spent it in New York at the start of her world trip. Instead, she sat alone in the empty house mourning her father, worrying about her mother, and trying to work out how to manage Edith's recovery. Lyn had arranged to have handrails installed in the bathroom and had taken up all the loose rugs in the hallway – one of which had most likely contributed to her mother's fall. It had been rucked up by the stool she was standing on.

Glancing around to check everything was in order, that her mother would find nothing to complain about, Lyn set off, glad her parents' car was still in the garage and in good working order. The Holden Commodore was a larger car than she was accustomed to driving; her dad had always favoured the Australian brand.

Sitting in a wheelchair, Edith looked even frailer than she had in the hospital bed. Lyn had to leave her sitting by the doorway, in the care of a hospital volunteer, while she fetched the car, then the two of them had to part-support, part-lift her in. Edith had been offered the use of the wheelchair after she was home, but she waved it away, insisting she needed to keep mobile before she lost the use of her legs completely.

But the way she'd said it, and her accompanying grimace, told Lyn she was still in a lot of pain. She was glad the new walker was sitting in the hallway waiting for her mother.

When they were finally home, and Edith was ensconced in an armchair by the window which allowed her a good view of the neighbourhood, Lyn went off to make a cup of tea. While she was waiting for the water to boil, she fetched the good china and set out two cups and saucers on a wooden tray with a flower pattern – one she remembered from her childhood growing up on the farm.

'Here you are,' Lyn said in what she hoped was a cheerful voice, as she carried in the tray and set it down on the coffee table. 'I bought some of those fig biscuits you like, too.'

'You're a good girl,' Edith said, reaching out a shaky hand for the cup and saucer and accepting a biscuit. 'You shouldn't be here waiting on me. You have your own life.'

Lyn felt her eyes misting. Her mother had always seemed strong to Lyn as she was growing up – as a farmer's wife, she'd had to be. It was hard to see her like this. 'I'm here as long as you need me,' she said. 'I'm retired now, so my time is my own.'

'I don't want to be a burden to you,' her mother continued as if Lyn hadn't spoken. 'Al and I talked about this. He thought he'd go first, but we decided whichever one of us was left wouldn't stay in this house. We checked out the retirement villages and nursing homes. So don't think you need to take care of me. I'll need help in selling this old place, but after that you can get on with your life.'

Lyn's eyes widened in surprise. She almost dropped her cup. This was the last thing she'd expected. 'But, Mum...'

'No buts.' Edith's voice became stronger. 'I know what those doctors said. This recovery is going to be a long haul, and I may never regain the strength I had before I fell. I know it was a stupid thing to do – to climb up there. I brought it on myself. But it would have come to this anyway. I'm too old to live in this big house all on my own.'

'I could...' Lyn found herself saying. She wasn't sure where the words had come from or what she intended to suggest. Surely she wasn't intending to offer to move back here to Granite Springs?

'No, Lynnie.'

Lyn smiled at the pet name she hadn't heard for years.

'I've made up my mind. I want you to contact the real estate people – Granite Springs Realty will do a good job for us – and get this place in order.' She let her gaze wander around the room. 'I see you've made a start. Your dad and I let things go a bit lately. It's time…' She gave a sigh. 'This was never the home the farm was. It's a pity…' She sighed again. 'But things change, and the Thompsons got the place in the end, after all. We never blamed you, Lyn.' She gave Lyn an affectionate smile.

Blamed? For leaving Granite Springs or for not marrying Ken Thompson? Lyn hadn't thought of her childhood friend for years, and now reminders of him seemed to be popping up everywhere.

'I think a nursing home might be best,' Edith continued. 'I want you to contact Eden Gardens and get me on their waiting list. Your dad and I visited all of them and that was the one we settled on. With a bit of luck, they'll be able to take me before the house sale is finalised.'

Lyn couldn't believe her ears. Her parents had not only discussed what was euphemistically called *the next stage* of their lives, but had even chosen where it would be spent.

'Even if Al hadn't gone when he did,' Edith said, 'we knew it wouldn't be long before we had to make the move.'

'Oh, Mum!'

'No need for your tears,' Edith said, clearly seeing Lyn's eyes filling. 'I know my limitations. Your dad and I should probably have moved before now, but we kept putting it off, thinking we had plenty of time. Plenty of time,' she chuckled with a hoarse laugh which descended into a cough. 'Who did we think we were kidding? But it's time now. I know what Al would say if he could see me like this – "You're all used up, Edie." I can hear him now.'

Lyn looked at her mother. She saw an old woman, one who had struggled to accept her beloved daughter had dreams that took her beyond this town, but whose life had taken a different turn from what she expected. It had given Edith a much-loved granddaughter and two beautiful great granddaughters. And she was that daughter. Lyn was grateful that, however much they might have disapproved of her life choices, her parents had supported her decision, and even – if Jo was to be believed – been proud of her accomplishments. Now it was her turn to support her mother in *her* decision.

'If you're sure that's what you want,' she said.

'I am. You'll contact the realty and the nursing home for me?'

'Okay, Mum. But if you change your mind…'

'No, my mind's made up. This house was never our home, and it's an empty shell without your dad. The sooner I can move on the better for all of us.'

But Lyn saw a bead of moisture edging its way out of the corner of one of Edith's eyes. Did her mother really mean what she was saying?

*

For the first couple of weeks Edith was home, Lyn kept herself busy catering to her mother's needs and beginning the massive clean-up Edith wanted. It seemed the damage to her hip hadn't diminished Edith's ability to make her demands known. With that, and ferrying her mother to her rehabilitation appointments, Lyn had her hands full, though she had taken time to visit the nursing home and put her mother's name on the waiting list. She'd been pleased to discover it was a light, airy building with a pleasant outlook over manicured gardens, and the staff she'd met had all been very friendly.

Finally, Edith was satisfied the house was presentable enough to go on sale. 'I want you to see that realter today,' she said, as they sat having breakfast. 'We've wasted enough time. I just want to get on with it.'

So, settling her mother in the armchair facing the window, Lyn picked up her bag and set off. Walking down Main Street, she found the large blue sign in a window which was covered in photos of homes and properties for sale. This must be the place her mother specified. She pushed open the door and walked in.

Lyn blinked, unable to believe her eyes. The man who was walking towards her looked exactly like the Ken Thompson of her youth. But it couldn't be him. This man was only in his thirties, whereas Ken would be her age. Neither of them would ever see sixty again.

'I'll deal with this one, Neil.' The voice was familiar and came from a glass-fronted office in the corner. The man who now appeared was straight out of her past, almost exactly as she'd imagined him. The eyes were the same, and the mouth, though the thick blond curls had thinned and were now closer to white than blond.

Lyn felt like a teenager, as if the intervening years had fallen away and she was eighteen again.

'Ken. Ken Thompson,' she stuttered, trying to remember what her mother had said about him. What was he doing here? There had been something about an argument with his father. He'd married. She'd tried to ignore any mention of him. He was in her past, part of a time she wanted to forget.

'My brother has the farm,' he said, as if he could read her mind. It had always been like that between them, she remembered. It was as if he could see right into her head and knew what she was thinking. 'I heard you were back in town. It's good to see you again, Lyn.'

There was something in the way he said her name, the way it seemed to roll off his tongue, that took her back to her childhood, back beyond the teenage years when their hormones had come into play, threatening to ruin what had been a close friendship.

He knew she was back in town? How could she have forgotten the ubiquitous gossip mill of this place? Since leaving to go to uni, Lyn had been the typical fly-in fly-out daughter, flying in for birthdays and Christmas, then quickly flying out again to continue her life somewhere else. She'd never spent any real time here – till now.

'I was sorry to hear about your dad. It must have been a blow.'

'My mother wants to sell the house,' she blurted out, scarcely aware of what she was saying. 'She's had a fall and… it seems she and dad talked about what she should do.' As she spoke, it suddenly occurred to Lyn that, while *she* had no idea Ken Thompson was Granite Springs Realty, her mother would be very aware of it.

'I'm sorry to hear that. I know how difficult it is when your parents get older. I lost mine quite a few years ago.'

Lyn wondered what had happened in that family. Ken was the elder son, the one old man Thompson had looked to as the next in line to take over when he was no longer able to manage the property. That was why Ken had been heading off to study agriculture. He'd been destined for a life on the farm, the life which was anathema to the eighteen-year-old Lyn.

'It's a long story,' he said, again seeming to understand her thoughts, 'but you didn't come here to hear that. Come through and take a seat.'

Although being confined with him in a small room was the last thing Lyn wanted, she found herself following him into the office from which he'd emerged only a few moments earlier.

Once there, he was all business, describing the service he could offer, stating terms and showing her examples of their marketing. 'But you may prefer to talk to some of the other realtors in town before you make your final decision,' he said at last.

'No. My mother specifically told me to come here.' *The old devil,* she thought. *She knew exactly what she was doing. Is she still trying to push us together? But he's married, and that must have been his son who I saw when I came in.*

'You met my son, Neil,' Ken said, as the younger man popped his head in through the door. 'Neil, this is Lyn Carter – or…?'

'Hudson,' she said.

'Lyn Hudson. She's Edith Carter's daughter, here to discuss selling her mother's house.'

'Hello, Mrs Hudson,' Neil said. 'I was sorry to hear about your dad. It's a pity to see the house go out of the family. But there's always a demand for sound family homes like that. Can I have a word when you're free, Dad?'

'Sure, we're almost done here.' He turned to face Lyn. 'I'll have the contract prepared then, as soon as you sign it, we can arrange advertising and viewings. What will your mother do when it's sold?' he asked, a crease appearing between his eyebrows.

'A nursing home. She's had me put her name down for Eden Gardens.'

'One of the best. You won't be staying around?'

'No.' What was it about his eyes that made her feel uncomfortable, as if she was abandoning her mother when she should be caring for her? 'It's her choice,' she said shortly.

'I'm sure. Your mum always was a tad independent.'

Was she? Lyn hadn't noticed. Back when she was growing up, her parents had been just the two people in her life who provided unconditional love, albeit with what seemed like a lot of restrictions – except when it came to Ken, she realised. Was she being selfish to want to leave her mother to stagnate here in a nursing home, while she got on with her life? It hadn't occurred to her before, and Ken hadn't said anything. It was more what he hadn't said, his expression.

'You'll let me know when the contract's ready?' she asked, picking up the bag she'd placed on the floor and getting ready to leave.

'Will do.' Ken came around from behind the desk to shake her hand. His felt so large as it covered hers, producing a fleeting memory, gone before it could take root. 'It should be ready in a day or so. I'll have someone call you.'

'Right. Thanks.' Why did Lyn feel a sense of disappointment that he'd have *someone* call her, rather than call himself? She quickly stifled it. Of course he was a busy man, too busy to make a call to a new client – he'd have processes for that.

They walked out of his office together. Ken followed her to the outer door and opened it for her. 'I'll be seeing you,' he said, as she walked out wondering exactly what had just happened.

Eight

Ken stood just inside the glass door watching Lyn walk away. She hadn't changed much. She was still the girl he'd fallen in love with when they were both eighteen. But he knew *he'd* changed. He thought of the thinning hair he saw in the mirror each morning, the lines around his eyes and mouth. But, he drew in his stomach, he'd managed to stave off the midlife spread that bedevilled many of his friends, partly due to regular swimming and partly due to good genes. It was only when he looked at Neil he remembered how he'd looked as a young man – the young man who'd failed to win Lyn Carter.

He admitted to himself a regret that once again Lyn seemed intent on leaving Granite Springs, though he wasn't sure why he'd expected anything else. The sixty-two-year-old wasn't so different from the eighteen-year-old at heart. Nor was he, Ken realised, recognising the lurch his heart had given when he saw Lyn walk in.

Surprised that, after forty-five years Lyn Carter still had the ability to send his heart racing and with a sigh for what might have been, Ken turned back into the office where Neil was waiting for him. The sight of the young man who meant so much to him restored his equilibrium and made him count his blessings. His marriage to Sheila might not have been one of his best decisions, but together they'd brought this young man into the world. Ken could never regret that.

'You wanted to see me, Neil?' he asked.

For the next half hour, he listened as Neil detailed the new listings he wanted to share with his dad before he went out to the farm for the remainder of the week.

'Have you found anyone else for the office yet, Dad?' Neil asked. 'I saw the ad you're running.'

'Keen to move on, are you? Don't let me stop you. I can manage,' Ken said, though he wasn't sure how he could, with the sudden influx of new properties on their books, not least the one Lyn had just given them, one he wanted to be sure to handle himself.

But Neil wasn't so easily fooled. 'Don't be daft, Dad. I said I wouldn't leave you in the lurch. I'm happy to do the weekend shifts and the open houses the girls can't manage. I'm sure you'll find someone soon. I've been asking around, too. There are a few guys in the cricket team who could be looking for a change of career.'

Ken nodded, but he wasn't sure he wanted some dissatisfied mate of Neil's who was only looking for a way out of his current job. 'We'll see, son,' he said.

'Uncle Alec said you're coming to dinner tonight,' Neil continued. 'Maybe we can talk more about it then?'

'Sure, son.' Ken gave Neil a pat on the shoulder, before going into his office and closing the door. He wanted to get the contract for the Carter house prepared as soon as possible, eager to have an excuse to see Lyn again. She may not be intending to spend long in Granite Springs, but he expected she'd stay till the house sale was finalised, and he intended to make the most of it. She'd made no mention of her husband, just her married name. Ken wondered if there was still a Mr Hudson on the scene and if he was in Granite Springs, too, surprised how upset he felt at the prospect. Then he gave himself a shake. What there had been between him and Lyn had come to nothing, and it had all been forty-five years ago. No one could carry a torch for a woman for forty-five years, could they?

*

Sitting on the veranda at Wooleton, a beer in his hand, Ken felt the cares of the day slip away. It was strange how, apart from Christmas, he enjoyed being back here. Alec and Judy had done well with the property, probably made a better fist of it than he'd have done. Ken now regretted his irate phone call to Alec berating him for setting all this up with Neil without consulting him. But, true to form, his brother had been very conciliatory, and Ken had relented.

Now he'd had time to consider it properly, he was glad Neil would be the one to carry it on into the next generation. Imagining his grandchildren growing up here, where he and Alec had, of little Daisy playing the same games, in the same yard, brought a smile to his lips.

'Something amusing you, Dad?' Neil joined him, dropping into a nearby cane chair. The chairs had been there since his parents' time and could do with being replaced, but they were comfortable, and he could see Alec and Judy had given them a new coat of paint.

'No. Just reminiscing. I'm glad you decided to come onto the property. Wooleton needs fresh blood, and I can see you and Sally raising a family here.'

'Woah, it's a bit early for that!' But Neil was smiling as he took a swig of beer. 'I haven't asked her yet.'

'But you intend to? You did say the pair of you had talked about the house you're building?'

'Yeah, but it's not like when you and Mum were our age. We're planning to live together. Marriage – that's a whole different ballgame.'

'Maybe Sally doesn't see it that way. In my experience women always think love and marriage go together. You do love her?'

Neil gazed into the distance before replying. 'We love each other. But is that enough to make the commitment of marriage? I've been down that road already, and look how that turned out.'

'You said this is different.'

'Mmm.' Neil rolled his beer can between his hands.

'What are you two looking so serious about?' Sally walked out of the house, carrying a plate of lamb chops and sausages. She looked pretty in her white three-quarter pants and blue top, her dark hair lying on her shoulders, her eyes bright as they fell on Neil. 'Alec is ready to start the barbecue and would appreciate your help. It seems it takes three men to cook for us.' She shook her head in amusement. 'I need to go back in to help Judy with the salads.'

Neil seemed relieved at the interruption, but Ken determined to resume the conversation at another time. Sally would make the perfect wife for his son and would make a good stepmother to Daisy and mother to any children they might have. Ken hoped they wouldn't wait too long.

The two men rose and followed Sally over to where Alec was firing up the barbecue. She reached up to drop a kiss on Neil's cheek before disappearing back into the house.

'You have a good one there,' Alec said. 'She'll make an excellent farmer's wife.'

'Not you, too,' Neil groaned, but he had a smile on his face.

'What's new?' Alec asked Ken, when they'd transferred the meat to the grill, and helped themselves to another beer from the esky Alec had set beside the barbecue.

'Busy time of year with the new cohort of teachers and lecturers arriving in town looking for accommodation.' He took a sip of beer. 'Oh, and Lyn Carter – Lyn Hudson now – came in this morning to put her mother's house on the market. Seems old Mrs Carter's taken bad and will be going into a nursing home.' He held his breath, hoping Alec might have forgotten their parents' plans for his own marriage which would have joined the two properties.

It was a faint hope.

'You two were an item back then, weren't you?' Alec asked. 'Or was it all in the parents' imagination? Well, we did join up the two properties eventually, when the Carters moved into town. The old man died recently, didn't he?'

'Before Christmas. That's what brought Lyn back.'

'And how was it, seeing your childhood sweetheart again, big brother? Still a pull at the old heartstrings?'

Ken gave what he hoped was a derisive laugh. 'Hell, Alec, that was forty-five years ago. A lot of water has passed under the bridge since then.'

He saw a speculative look in his brother's eyes before it disappeared.

'Was that the woman you were with when I walked in, Dad – the one you said you'd deal with?'

What did I do to deserve such an observant son?

'You know our older clients prefer to deal with me,' Ken said, in an attempt to diffuse what was now becoming an awkward conversation.

'Hmm.' Neil didn't appear convinced. 'Anyway, Dad. Uncle Alec and I have been discussing something we wanted to run past you.' He gestured towards Alec with his beer can.

'Oh yes?' Ken asked, glad to have the change of subject.

'It may seem a radical idea,' Alec said, 'but the young fellow came up with it, and I think it's worth pursuing. You explain it, Neil.'

'I suggested to Uncle Alec it would be a good idea to run a herd of cattle alongside the sheep.' He glanced at Ken as if to gauge his reaction. 'You see, Dad, cattle and sheep. It makes so much sense. They eat different things – the ewes eat the short grasses and the cattle the taller ones. It's a perfect mix. Many of the cattle farmers are doing it the other way round; it helps diversity grazing and grassland management.'

Neil looked puzzled as Ken began to laugh, and even Alec seemed surprised.

'You don't know, do you?' Ken asked. 'Neither of you. I guess Dad never said.' He turned to Alec. 'That's what we argued about. I made that very suggestion back when I came home from Ag College. That's what angered Dad so much, why he threw me out. He'll be turning in his grave. So, yes, I think it's a good idea. It's just a pity it's taken so long.' He took a swig of his beer. 'It's too late for me, of course, but I wish you both well.'

'Really, Dad? You suggested it to Grandad? I wish I'd known. I'd have…'

'Dad never said,' Alec interrupted. 'The old devil. It makes so much sense and would have helped out a lot back then. It never occurred to me until young Neil here brought it up.' He slapped Neil on the shoulder. 'A chip off the old block, eh?'

Ken didn't know whether to be pleased, sorry or angry. But it didn't matter. The argument with his dad was water under the bridge, too. And maybe it had all been for the best.

Any further discussion was suspended by the appearance of Judy and Sally carrying bowls of salad which they placed in the middle of the nearby table, and Judy's calling out, 'Isn't the meat cooked yet? What have you men been doing?'

'Ready now,' Alec said, removing the now well-cooked chops and sausages from the grill and piling them onto a metal tray. 'Take these over to the table, Neil,' he said. 'Your dad and I'll be over to join you shortly.'

When Neil was out of hearing, Alec spoke to Ken in a low voice. 'Hell, Ken, I'm sorry. I had no idea what you and Dad rowed about. I thought it was something to do with the Carters. You know – you and Lyn.' He dragged a hand through his hair which, like Ken's, had lost much of its youthful thickness. 'If I'd realised…'

'There was nothing you could have done. It's old news. We moved on. You've made a go of this place – you and Judy – and I've done the same in town. Thanks for taking on Neil. It hit me hard at first, but now I've had time to think about it, it makes sense,' he said, putting his earlier thoughts into words. 'He and Sally are the next generation. It's good to know Wooleton will stay in the family.'

'Glad you see it that way now. I admit I was a bit unsure how you'd take it, and your phone call…' He pulled on one ear. 'I should have spoken with you first. I realise that now. But Neil's like a son to me, the son we never had. And Sal's a good girl.'

'We'd better join them now,' Ken said, seeing the women sending glances in their direction.

'Good man!' Alec clasped Ken by the shoulder, a wide grin on his face.

Thankfully the discussion over dinner was general. There was no further mention of Lyn Carter or their childhood on neighbouring properties. But when Ken was driving back to town, he remembered the last time he'd travelled this road with Lyn. It had been the night of their high school formal. She'd looked so pretty that night. They'd stopped to admire the stars. He'd been such an innocent – they both had. He'd thought it was the beginning of something, but it had been the end – the end of what he'd tried to dismiss as a youthful infatuation. But which he knew had been more than that, much more.

Nine

'I saw Ken Thompson again the other day.' Col Ford was pouring his wife a glass of wine before dinner. 'He's losing that son of his to the farm. His brother took it over after there was some sort of dispute.' They were both sitting outside on the wrap-around veranda they loved on the small acreage called Yarran, Jo's old Labrador, Scout, lying at their feet. 'Maybe we should invite him over to dinner one of these days. He'll miss Neil when he moves out.'

'How is he? I told you I had coffee with his old girlfriend, Lyn Carter that was, didn't I?' Jo asked, smiling fondly at the man she married just over a year earlier. She still couldn't quite believe her luck at having found love with her old friend at the ripe old age of sixty, when what had been a close friendship had morphed into something much stronger and more passionate. When her husband and childhood sweetheart had left her for a younger model, she'd turned to her good friends, Alice and Col for solace. And when Alice succumbed to the cancer that invaded her system, Jo and Col had found comfort in each other's arms.

'He said she'd been into the office. Her mother wants to sell up.'

'Oh, what a pity. I suppose Lyn will be heading off again when it's all settled. I wonder...' Jo pursed her lips, an idea forming in her mind.

'What are you cooking up, now?'

'Maybe we could invite Lyn too.'

'At the same time? Don't you think that would be a bit obvious?'

Jo chuckled. It wouldn't be the first time she'd been accused of matchmaking. 'Maybe,' she said. 'But what could be more natural than to invite two old schoolfriends to dinner. We could ask Kay and Nick, too,' she suggested, naming a good friend of hers, who'd also recently found love again in later life.

'Women!' Col shook his head. 'I suppose you want me to be the one to invite Ken?'

'He's your friend. I can remember…'

'Okay, okay,' he agreed, more, Jo thought, to stop a trip down memory lane, than any real desire to invite his old friend to dinner.

'Good.' Jo felt the warm glow she always did when she could see her plans were about to come to fruition. Of course, there might be no spark between Ken and Lyn. The intervening years might have put paid to any lingering attraction they had for each other, but she had a hunch there was still something there. While Lyn had been adamant her only desire was to travel the world and it was something she'd always wanted to do, Jo gave a lot of credence to fate. And if it wasn't fate that had brought Lyn back to Granite Springs, Jo didn't know what it was.

They sat in silence for a few moments, before Col asked, 'So when do you want to arrange this dinner?'

'Soon.' Then Jo had what she thought was a brilliant idea. 'I know! Next Sunday.'

'Sunday? You mean…?'

'I do! You can't say it'll be obvious if the place is filled with other people.'

'If you're sure, honey. I thought you wanted it to be family only,' Col said, referring to their joint birthday which fell on the twenty-sixth of January, which was also Australia Day, a fact that had caused much amusement over the years.

'I did,' Jo said, 'but I've changed my mind. Kay and Nick were going to be there anyway, and Sally has asked if she can bring her new partner.'

'Isn't that Ken's son?'

'So it is!' Jo said, struck by the way it was all falling together. 'And it's to be a lunchtime barbecue so the littlies can take part. It'll be a lot more casual than a dinner would be.'

'Less of a set-up, you mean?' Col asked, taking a long sip of his wine. 'And are you sure you're happy to have Gordon there?' he asked, referring to his old friend and former business partner who was also Jo's ex-husband.

'He's still your friend,' Jo said with a wry grin, 'and I guess he's finding life difficult with a new baby in the house. He may have strutted about like a dog with two tails when Carol announced her pregnancy, but from what you've told me, the reality of becoming a father again in his sixties is much what we predicted.'

'I don't think Carol's finding it too easy, either.' Col frowned. 'I don't think she was prepared for the realities of motherhood. But, what would I know? Alice and I weren't blessed with children of our own.'

'You were both great with ours.' Jo raised her glass to him in appreciation. 'And you make a great stepdad and step-grandad.'

'Thanks, sweetie.' Col drained his glass. 'Now did I hear something about dinner?'

'You did. It's just so lovely out here this evening. The heat has gone and there's a light breeze. I love this time of day.'

'Wait till our new livestock arrive. They'll keep us busy.'

'Have you decided yet?' Jo knew Col and their neighbour, Owen Larsen, had been talking about the pros and cons of stocking alpacas or llamas on their small acreage. Since he retired from his law practice and they married just over a year earlier, Col had been considering various options to fill his time and utilise their paddocks. It appeared to have come down to those two choices.

'Looks like we'll go for the alpacas,' he said. 'They're a bit smaller and more cautious than Llamas. Owen's been a great help. He's managed to find a guy on the other side of Canberra who breeds them. We thought we could arrange a trip out there to have a look, maybe take in a picnic. You and Fran can come too,' he added quickly.

'I should think so. Sounds like a fun excursion. I'll tee it up with Fran.' Jo liked Fran Reilly who had moved into the neighbouring property with Owen before Christmas. Another instance of a couple who'd found love later in life in Granite Springs, though they were ten years younger than Jo and Col.

'We should invite them to the birthday do, too, if we're going to make it a bigger affair.'

'I'll do that.'

Ten

'It's Col's and my joint birthday next Sunday. We're having a few people over for a barbecue at lunchtime. It won't be a big affair, just family and a few friends. We'd love you to come. It'd be a chance for you to catch up with some people you might remember from school.'

Lyn held the phone to her ear and listened in stunned silence as Jo babbled on. She hadn't come back to Granite Springs to catch up with old friends. She was so ashamed of the way she'd left, without saying goodbye to anyone. And she'd never once sought out her old friends when she'd come back to visit her parents. It had been good to see Jo again, and she'd proved to be a willing ear, but the thought of a whole group of people from her past made her nervous.

'I'm not sure I can leave Mum,' she said to gain time. 'Isn't Sunday…?'

'Australia Day? Yes, it is. I know most people will be having their own celebrations or going to one of the events the council organises. It would be good to see you again,' she said encouragingly, clearly sensing Lyn's indecision. 'Does your mum need continual care? Would you like to bring her too?'

'No!' Lyn said hurriedly, not exactly sure which of Jo's questions she was saying no to – perhaps both. 'It's kind of you to invite me…' She hesitated for too long.

'Good. We'll see you there. Twelve o'clock and no need to bring anything.'

Jo hung up, leaving Lyn with her mouth open ready to refuse.

'Who was that on the phone?' Edith appeared in the doorway,

pushing her walker. 'This damned contraption!' she complained. 'I bet the doctor never tried to walk with one.'

Lyn stifled a smile. It was good her mother was beginning to complain – a sign she was getting back to her old self.

'Jo Ford,' she said, still clutching her mobile. 'She's invited me to her birthday bash on Australia Day. It seems she and Col share a birthday. I didn't know that. I guess, back when I knew her, the girls and boys celebrated separately, and…' she mused, 'I'm not sure I went to many of her birthday parties. Dad always thought it was a waste of petrol to go into town for a party.' Lyn remembered the frustration she'd felt as a young girl, when all the others in her class were talking about the fun they'd had.

'He wasn't a bad man.' With a sigh, Edith took a seat at the kitchen table. 'But there wasn't much spare cash for petrol in those days, and the trip into town and back to drop you off and pick you up again was time away from the farm – time we couldn't afford. We tried our best.'

'I know you did.' Lyn bent over to hug her mother. 'I had a happy childhood and I loved being on the farm.'

'It wasn't as if you were completely isolated. You had Ken living right there, next door,' Edith said with a grin. 'You saw him when you went into his real estate office?'

Lyn bit her lip. She strongly suspected her mother had an ulterior motive for sending her there and had decided not to mention seeing him. 'You knew!' she accused the older woman.

'Everyone around here knows Ken Thompson is Granite Springs Realty, has been for years. There was some sort of dispute with his old man after he came home from college. One day, he was the golden boy all set to work Wooleton and inherit, the next he was out on his ear and young Alec had taken his place. We never found out why. It's a pity you and he didn't make a go of it.' She pursed her lips, as if about to say more.

'That's enough, Mum. I know what you and Dad wanted back then. I didn't. I left and that's an end to it.'

'If Wyn hadn't been so willing to take you in…'

'Don't blame Aunt Wyn. I'd have found somewhere else to go. I needed to get away.'

'And what do you think of him now?' Edith couldn't seem to let it go.

For a moment Lyn was baffled. Did her mother really think that now, forty-five years later, she and Ken could reignite what they'd had at eighteen? 'He's older. We both are. And isn't he married?'

As soon as she spoke, Lyn knew she'd said the wrong thing.

'I don't know why you let that nice Glenn go,' her mother said.

'He met someone else, Mum, I told you at the time.' Lyn felt a spurt of anger surge up at the direction of this conversation. It was a reminder why she'd rarely spent any time in Granite Springs with her parents over the years. She was sixty-two and her mother was still trying to run her life.

Suddenly her mother seemed to grow tired of the topic. Her eyes began to close, and Lyn regretted showing her irritation. Edith was an old woman. She'd never change now. But she was Lyn's mother and she was sick.

'Would you like a cup of tea? And I think there are still some of those fig biscuits you like,' she said, in an attempt to appease her mother. There was no point in getting angry. She did love her mother. It was just so frustrating to have to defend the decisions she'd made for her life – defend Glenn's decision to leave her.

Edith opened her eyes again. 'That would be lovely, dear.'

They'd eaten early, a habit Lyn had forgotten. She was having trouble getting used to things she had taken for granted growing up. Having their evening meal at five o'clock was one of those. It meant she was hungry again before bedtime, resulting in her snacking, usually on cheese and biscuits, or a piece of cake. She patted her stomach, flat now, but it wouldn't be for long with this regime.

Lyn took a few deep breaths as she boiled the water and took two teabags from the cupboard – English breakfast for her mother whose taste hadn't changed in years, and camomile for herself which she hoped would help calm her.

'This is lovely, Lynnie,' Edith said, when Lyn placed the china cup and saucer on the table along with a matching plate containing two fig biscuits. 'You're a good girl.'

Girl! Lyn grinned. She supposed she'd always be a girl to her mother, just as Amy would always be a girl to her. She'd calmed down by now, realising there was nothing she could do to change things. Surely it was time she learned acceptance.

'I hope you accepted Jo's invitation,' Edith said, when she'd finished her tea and had demolished both biscuits. 'You should get out more. There's no sense in you staying cooped up here with me. You need to mix with people your own age.'

Lyn sighed. She thought her mother had forgotten about the conversation with Jo. 'I'm not sure, Mum. I don't like to leave you. I'd hate you to have another fall. I don't need to go. Jo's family will be there. I don't know them and…'

'But you'll know some of them. She and the Little girl were close. She's remarried again too now.' Edith sniffed. 'That Jackson fellow she married when they were young turned out to be one of those… what do you call them?'

Lyn had no idea what her mother was talking about and didn't want to pursue it. 'Maybe,' she said to mollify her mother and gathered the empty cups and saucers together. 'Don't forget you have your physio appointment tomorrow morning.'

'How can I? I'm reminded every time I try to move. It's no fun being my age and incapacitated like this. You young ones can't imagine what it's like to have to rely on other people and to be forced to accept their help. And now I have these screws inside me, I feel like something from one of those science fiction movies your dad liked to watch.'

Her dad liked to watch sci-fi movies? Lyn's surprise must have shown on her face, because her mother added, 'It was after he retired from the farm and we moved here. He had time on his hands he hadn't had before. He enjoyed a good movie. He didn't read like I did.' Edith sounded defensive.

'But the physio is helping, isn't it?' Lyn decided not to continue the sci-fi conversation. It was a side of her dad she'd never seen, never been aware of, one she could scarcely imagine.

'Well, that young man seems to know what he's doing, and at least I'm mobile.' Edith's face creased and Lyn thought she could see incipient tears in her mother's eyes. 'For a time there, I was afraid I'd never walk again.'

Tempted to hug her mother once more, this time Lyn held back. They'd never been the sort of family to show overt affection and two hugs in less than an hour was probably too much for her mother to cope with.

*

Next morning, Lyn saw her mother settled into the rehab section at the Base Hospital before heading down Main Street, her stomach turning somersaults at the thought of what lay ahead. Before they left home, she'd had a call from Ken Thompson's office – not from him. But the woman who called indicated Ken wanted to meet with her in person to discuss the terms of the contract. Lyn wasn't sure why that made her uncomfortable, but she found herself feeling flustered. She'd taken more care than usual with her appearance, choosing a smart flame-coloured linen dress she'd only packed at the last moment, not really expecting to wear it.

She reached the sign for Granite Springs Realty before she was mentally prepared to face him. Taking a deep breath, she pushed open the heavy glass door.

This time, Ken was waiting for her in the main office, his lips curling into the smile she remembered, the one that used to make her insides flutter. Today, it was nerves that were having the same effect. But there was nothing to be nervous about. She was here to pick up the contract, to arrange an open house, and discuss a marketing plan. Deciding she was allowing her mother's veiled hints to get to her, Lyn put a matching smile on her face and moved to meet Ken, hand outstretched.

'Ken!'

'Lyn!'

They shook hands, and Lyn noted how Ken's hands were still as large and strong as she remembered, but were now softer than they'd been when he worked on his parents' farm. The years of office work had made their mark. He was no longer the outdoor man she'd almost given her heart to all those years ago.

'Come in.' Ken led her into his small office which seemed more claustrophobic than ever today, despite the glass walls. When they were seated, he picked up a sheaf of papers and slid them across the desk. 'I have the contract ready. I put in the price range we discussed and can arrange an open house for Saturday week, but I really should take a look at the place before we proceed.'

Now he tells me!

'It's been some time since I visited your mother's house,' he added, giving her a wary glance.

He'd visited her parents' house? Why hadn't her mother said? What else was she keeping from her?

Clearly seeing her puzzled expression, Ken continued, 'I sold the place to them, you know, back when they moved into town. It was a sound investment and should fetch a good price now, as I said when we last met.' He cleared his throat. 'I may have visited a few times in the following months to make sure they were settling in. We'd been neighbours, and my family bought them out. I felt some sort of responsibility.'

'I didn't know. That was good of you.' Lyn didn't know what else to say. She was embarrassed to think he'd been showing his concern for her parents while she'd been pursuing her career in far off Brisbane. It had never occurred to her to wonder how they were coping with life off the farm. They'd seemed happy enough when she made her fleeting visits, or when they travelled north to visit her and Amy. Suddenly she felt swamped with guilt and had an urge to defend herself. Instead, she pressed her lips together.

'When would you like to make your inspection?' Lyn knew her words were more formal than the occasion warranted, but it was the only way she could maintain her equilibrium which had been shattered by his revelation.

Ken seemed unperturbed by her words. He leant back in his chair and removed the glasses which she noted he hadn't been wearing on their last meeting. Their dark rims made him appear more professional, more distant, less like the man she remembered. Without them, his face took on a more vulnerable expression.

'How about tomorrow?' Ken replaced his glasses and checked the large desk diary sitting in front of him. 'I can be there at nine if that's not too early for you.' He glanced up with a smile.

Amused to see he hadn't graduated to an online calendar, while suspecting his staff kept one for him, Lyn smiled back. 'Not too early at all. Mum doesn't sleep well, and I've always been an early riser.'

'I remember.' Behind the glasses, Ken's eyes twinkled.

Lyn remembered too, remembered early mornings during the long summer holidays when she and Ken would escape their respective homes and meet midway between to make mischief. He'd always been the leader, she his willing follower. When had that changed? She guessed it was when they both hit puberty, when their childhood friendship threatened to turn into something more, something that delighted both sets of parents but scared Lyn to death.

'Can I take it home for mum to sign now?' she asked, trying to dispel the feeling the memory invoked.

'If you're happy with the terms. We'd take the usual fee and may require payment if we need marketing beyond our normal limit, which I don't expect. It's a good time of year to put it on the market. I don't anticipate you'll have to wait long for a sale.'

'Right.' Lyn picked up the document and gave it a quick read-through. She knew her mother trusted Ken to do the right thing by her, so skimmed through the small print. It seemed to be a standard contract. She slid it into the folder Ken offered.

'I can pick it up tomorrow, too,' he said. 'Your mother might want her solicitor to look at it, but there's nothing out of the ordinary in there.'

'Thanks.' Lyn prepared to leave.

'Will you be staying around?' he asked, holding the door open for her.

Lyn looked up at him – he was a full head taller than her. 'Until it's sold,' she said.

'See you tomorrow, then.'

*

Back home with Edith, Lyn produced the contract. 'Ken said you might want your Bruce Jenkins to check it over,' she said.

'Pouf! What would he know? If Ken says it's okay, then I'm happy to sign it.'

'But, Mum, Ken's the one who put it together. It might be good to have it looked over by someone who's impartial.'

'Impartial? What rubbish! I've known Ken Thompson since he was a baby. I'd trust him with my life. Why, if things had been different...'

'Not that old saw again! It was over long ago. We've both moved on.'

'Hmph. Well, I need a rest after all that activity this morning. Can you help me to my room?'

Surprised by her mother's request for help – she was usually so independent, even if she did rail at having to use her walker – Lyn hurried to assist. She suspected it was her mother's way of changing the subject.

Once she'd seen Edith to bed, Lyn returned to the kitchen where the contract still lay on the table, Edith's wavering signature clearly visible. She picked it up, returning it to its folder ready for Ken the next day. Then she stood up to make herself coffee, stopping by the window to see her reflection in the glass.

What did Ken see when he looked at her? Did he see the aging woman who'd spent her life trying to get ahead, to please others, who'd put her own dreams aside? Or did he see the shadow of her younger self, the girl he'd once known – just as she saw in him the boy he'd been? She shook her head to dispel the images which threatened to overwhelm her. But she couldn't get out of her mind the fact that, like her, he'd been forced to put his dreams aside, to follow a route he'd never intended.

That was the one thing they had in common.

Eleven

For the second time that week, Ken watched Lyn's back as she marched away. What had he done to upset her this time? And what had happened over the years to change the warm girl he remembered into this cool customer? Maybe, like him, she'd been unlucky in her choice of partner. He hadn't heard anything about her marriage, not much about her at all, after she left. Although he'd seen a bit of the Carters initially when they moved into town, he hadn't been close to them. They were of his parents' generation and he always got the feeling – especially from Alan Carter – that they held him responsible for Lyn leaving town.

Now he stroked his chin wondering yet again if he could have done anything to keep her here. But it was pointless. As he'd told Col, it was water under the bridge. They were different people now. He had the distinct impression she'd prefer not to do business with him, was only there at her mother's instigation. Edith Carter was a wily one. She and Ken's mother had been allies back then, pushing the two young people together. It had been his mother who'd encouraged him to dress so smartly for the school formal. He could still remember how proud he'd felt in the maroon velvet. He'd had a good laugh at the image he presented when he found the old photo. And his mother had counselled him about the corsage, too. What did he know about flowers and such?

'Okay Dad?'

Ken turned to meet Neil's eyes. He'd miss him when he finally left the office and moved out to the farm for good.

'Was that the Carter woman again?'

'Hudson. Her married name's Hudson. She was picking up the contract for the Carter house.'

'Would you like me to take care of it? You seem to be a bit...'

'No, it's fine, son. I can do it. They were our neighbours when I was growing up, and your grandad bought the old couple out when they came into town. It's the least I can do, to see the sale through.'

'If you're sure?'

Ken nodded, but he wasn't sure at all. Seeing Lyn Carter – he couldn't think of her as Lyn Hudson – had stirred up old feelings he'd thought buried for good.

*

'Busy today, Dad?' Neil asked, when he joined Ken in the kitchen next morning for a breakfast which, as usual, consisted of toast and coffee. Ken was always keen to get to the office and had got into the habit of dropping into The Bean Sprout for a snack mid-morning. The coffee was good there, and Marie always had some of her special cakes and muffins freshly baked that morning.

'Mmm.' Ken swallowed before replying, 'I'm going around to the Carter place at nine to check it out, make sure I've set the right price range. I didn't do that before now as I sold them the house in the first place and have a good idea of current values, but it doesn't do any harm to check. I'll pick up the signed contract then too. Thought I'd get an open house set up for Saturday week.'

'I can do that if you like. I'm out at Wooleton again tomorrow. You're still okay with that?'

'Course, son.' Sometimes Ken was surprised by his son's compassion. 'You caught me off guard at first, but I think it's good to keep it in the family. I'd hate to think of the place going to strangers when Alec and Judy get too old to take care of it.'

'Like the Carters.' Neil looked serious, then gave Ken a sly smile. 'So, you'll be seeing Mrs Hudson again? You said you were neighbours. So, you and her? You grew up together?' Neil raised one eyebrow.

Ken had a good idea what his son was asking – implying – but decided not to be drawn. 'On opposite sides of the dividing fence,' he said, before ostentatiously checking his watch. 'I need to go. I have a few things to do before I head out. Need a lift?' He downed the remains of his coffee grimacing to discover it had gone cold.

'No, I'm seeing Sal tonight. I'll take my car.'

'Right. See you in the office.'

Ken was glad to get out of the house. Neil's questions had come too close to home, in his attempt to uncover what had been between Lyn and him all those years ago – or had it? Had there really been the chemistry he imagined, or had it all been on his side? Well, he'd never know now, and what did it matter? But, seeing her again, Ken had felt the familiar leap in his stomach. It was as if he was eighteen again and aching for his first real kiss.

He sighed. He'd been a fool to insist on dealing with this sale himself. What was he trying to prove? He'd just get this morning's inspection over, pick up the contract, and let Neil handle the rest of the sale. Then Lyn would be back off to wherever she'd come from, back to her husband, back to her no-doubt tidy life and out of his hair.

Once in the office, he checked the emails that had accumulated overnight, and found the checklist for the inspection he should have done earlier. Although he'd presented Neil with what he thought was a believable reason for the delay, he really had no excuse. The fact was, Lyn's appearance in the office had taken him by surprise. Although Col told him she was back in town, it never occurred to him she'd walk right into what was his territory. He'd felt like a teenager, hoping their friendship would turn into something else, something more lasting, more… Hell, if he kept thinking like this, he'd need to take a cold shower before he went out.

*

The house looked much the same as he remembered, its red brick exterior perhaps a little more tired, showing signs of the intervening years. He noticed the windows and doors appeared to have been repainted fairly recently, and the roof looked to be in good repair. As was his custom, he assessed the exterior before heading to the front door, up the paved path between two garden beds showing the effects of the long drought. He'd been right. If the inside matched, it should fetch a good price.

Lyn greeted him at the door. She looked even better than she had in the office, more relaxed, casual, wearing a strappy bright blue sundress. He remembered how she'd always loved bright colours. Clearly that hadn't changed.

'Hello,' she said, 'Mum and I were about to have coffee. Will you join us, or do you need to get on with what you have to do?'

Ken hesitated for a moment. Did he want to spend more time with her or just do what he had to and leave? His mind was made up by Edith Carter appearing behind her daughter. The old woman was pushing a walker and looked frail enough to keel over at the slightest breath of wind.

'You'll join us for coffee, Ken, won't you? It's been a while. I suppose you want to make sure we haven't wrecked the place in our dotage?' she chuckled.

'Not at all, Mrs Carter. I'm sure you and your husband took great care of this house. I can see from the outside it's in good shape. You must have had some painting done?'

'Not long before Al died,' she agreed. 'We wanted to be ready for... if...' Her eyes clouded over, then she seemed to recollect herself and realise they were still in the doorway. 'Come through,' she said, leading the way into the kitchen which was redolent of a sweet fragrance mixed with the more pungent aroma of coffee beans.

'Take a seat, Ken.' Lyn was all politeness this morning, the cool manner of the previous day having vanished. Was she feeling more comfortable with him, or did her mother's presence have something to do with it? 'Coffee?' she asked.

'Please.'

'Lyn has been making an apricot and nut loaf, though I don't know why she wanted to have the oven on in this heat,' Edith said, as she sat down beside him and pushed her walker away from her. 'I can't be doing with that damned thing.'

'Mum, you know what the doctor said,' Lyn remonstrated.

'Doctors! What do they know? That young man at the hospital has never been hamstrung with one of those contraptions. I feel like I'm a toddler learning to walk.'

Lyn rolled her eyes in Ken's direction. She placed a china cup in front of her mother and handed him a mug of strong black coffee, then offered him a piece of the delicious-smelling fruit loaf.

'Thanks. Looks good.' Ken picked up a piece and took a bite. 'Tastes good, too.'

'I have to do something with my time,' Lyn said, sliding into a seat opposite and helping herself to a small piece.

'Hmm.' It hadn't occurred to Ken how Lyn might feel trapped here in Granite Springs, the town she'd been so eager to leave.

'Lyn tells me you think the house will sell well,' Edith said. 'It's been good to us. I don't forget it was you who sold it to us. Al and I were fresh off the land, and the whole idea of living in town was strange. But we did it, and here we are, years later.' She coughed, her eyes moistening as if realising anew that she was the only one left. 'It takes a bit of getting used to,' she said. 'We were childhood sweethearts, Al and I, just like…' She paused and her eyes moved from Ken to Lyn and back again before continuing, 'I can't get used to the fact he's gone. I keep expecting him to walk into the room, to ask what's keeping me. Sorry. I'm just a silly old woman,' she sniffed.

Lyn handed her a tissue. 'It's okay to be sad, Mum,' she said, a break in her voice.

'But this young man didn't come to hear me babbling on about the past. I've signed the contract for you, Ken. And what's this I hear about your Neil going out to Wooleton to work with your brother? I wonder what your dad would have made of that?'

Ken wondered how she'd managed to hear about Neil and Alec. The woman was not long out of hospital and practically housebound. The gossip mill in Granite Springs was alive and well. But he saw from Lyn's startled gaze it was news to her.

'Neil's your son, isn't he? I thought he worked with you?' she asked.

'He does, but he and Alec have come to an agreement. He's putting a house up out on Wooleton and will be moving out there permanently when it's finished. You remember Alec, my younger brother?' *The one who was always running after us, trying to muscle in on our games.* 'He and Judy don't have any children of their own, so it's a way of keeping the property in the family.' He knew it was a weak excuse and could see from the expression in Lyn's eyes she didn't buy it.

But Edith Carter nodded. 'It's what your mum and dad would have wanted. It's a terrible thing to see the property you've slaved over all your life going to strangers.' She glared at Lyn as if it was her fault the Carter property had to be sold. 'Though,' she said with what Ken could only call a smirk, 'we'd always intended our two properties to be joined.'

Ken was beginning to feel out of his depth. He was aware there was a hidden agenda here, one over which he had no control, and he could see Lyn was annoyed at her mother's insinuations. He finished his coffee quickly. 'Maybe Lyn could show me around?' he asked. 'It won't take long. I have a checklist here.' He took out the sheet he'd printed off earlier and stood up.

Lyn rose too, clearly as anxious to curtail this conversation as he was. 'Will you be all right here, Mum?' she asked.

'Why wouldn't I be all right in my own kitchen?' Edith asked. 'I'm not ready to topple off the twig just yet. See you show Ken everything he needs.' Her voice followed them out, adding unwarranted instructions.

'It must be difficult for you,' Ken said, when they were out of earshot of the old woman. 'My mum was just the same as she aged, but at least I wasn't living with her.'

'She means well,' Lyn sighed. 'It must be hard to lose your independence. It's her choice to go into a nursing home. She had it all arranged, even before her accident. But…' she bit her lip, '…I don't know how she'll cope.'

'She won't change her mind… about selling, I mean?'

'No. She really couldn't manage here on her own, and I can't stay around.' She bit her lip again.

She didn't say she had her own life to lead, but Ken sensed that was in her mind. He didn't blame her. She'd made her life a long way north of here. No doubt she had a husband to get back to, children, maybe even grandchildren. He was curious but it wasn't something he could ask her about.

'So, that's it!' Lyn said, as they returned to the kitchen where Edith was still sitting where they'd left her.

'Thanks, Lyn, Mrs Carter. I'll be off now. As I've told Lyn, we'll start advertising and will organise an open house for tomorrow week.' He glanced towards Lyn. 'Will you…?'

'We'll arrange to be out. Mum isn't entirely housebound.'

'Good. I've put Neil in charge of the sale, so you'll be dealing with him in future.' Lyn's face was impassive, but Edith's mirrored her disappointment. Surely she wasn't still trying to push the two of them together? If it hadn't worked back when they were young and their hormones were raging, how could she think it would work now? Though Ken had to admit Lyn was looking pretty good and could still raise stirrings of feelings he'd never thought to experience again. That was why it was for the best he stay away from this one.

*

Glad to be back in the air-conditioned office, Ken passed all the necessary information on to Neil and set about the other sales he was managing. The ping of his phone was a welcome interruption, but when he read the message, he sighed. He'd forgotten the annual fundraising cricket match for the under-eighteens to be held that evening on the local cricket pitch. In addition to being a local councillor, he was an active member of Rotary and he'd promised to help at the sausage sizzle.

It was normally an event he looked forward to, but this year, he'd have been happy to give it a miss. Still, he wasn't one to go back on a promise. *I'll be there*, he texted back, mentally rearranging the quiet evening he'd planned.

The rest of the day passed smoothly and, by the time Ken arrived home, he was preparing himself to be sociable. He knew the club needed all the support it could get if it was to remain viable, and it was a good way for the youngsters to release their excess energy. Not only that, with the coaching skills of Jason, who owned Mouthfuls with his wife, Melody, they'd turned out a few good players over the past few years.

'Going out tonight, Dad?' Neil sauntered in as Ken was making himself a quick sandwich to stave off his immediate hunger. He knew the smell of fried onions and barbecuing sausages would be too much to resist once they got going, and could already feel his mouth water at the prospect of unhealthy white bread slathered with tomato sauce and wrapped around a burnt sausage and sliced onions. Events like this brought back memories of his childhood, when a trip to one of the many community events in town was the highlight of an otherwise uneventful year.

'I'm helping with the Rotary sausage sizzle.'

'Oh yes, the cricket. That's tonight? Might take Sal along for a bit. Introduce her to another of the delights of Granite Springs.'

'Let her see what she's up for if she gets involved with you on a more permanent basis? Aren't you playing yourself this season?'

'No,' Neil replied ruefully. 'That knee I bust before Christmas is playing up. It wasn't fair to the team to hold them back. Best I rest up and keep myself for next season. Besides, it gives me more time with Sal, and to get my new place up on Wooleton.'

'How's that going?' So far, Ken had tried to avoid asking about his son's latest project, but it wasn't going to go away, and he should be showing an interest.

'Sal or the house?' Neil grinned.

'I was talking about the house. I presume all is well with you and Sally.'

'It's a slow process.' Neil pulled on one ear. 'Council's just beginning to wake up after the holidays, and I think half the staff must be still on leave. You're on council. Can't you do something about it?'

'You're joking! I may sit on council but don't have anything to do with the everyday running of departments. Even if I did, I couldn't show favour.'

'I guess not.' Neil gave a yawn. 'We'll just have to wait. But we have settled on a design, one that'll fit in with the old homestead.'

'The one that's been lying around on the coffee table for days, you mean?' Ken grinned. 'And what's with this "we"? If you're having Sally be part of your decision making, don't you think she'll have expectations?'

'Dad! I told you. We'll be living there together.'

'But no commitment. Is that fair to her?'

Neil's eyes widened.

Ken could see he was about to speak, to reiterate what he'd said before about his dad being behind the times. He held up his hands in a defensive pose. 'Okay, okay. I know what you said, times have changed.

I'm old-fashioned. But I think you'll find women haven't changed too much. They'll still want a wedding ring.'

As he said it, he remembered Sheila – how she'd made it clear to him she wouldn't settle for less. Then his mind moved to Lyn. She'd been different. He'd never had the impression she was keen to get married – quite the opposite. Maybe he didn't know women as well as he thought.

The cricket ground was a hive of activity when Ken arrived. He barely had time to don the apron he was handed before there was a line of small boys, dollar coins in their sweaty hands, waiting to be served.

'Hey there!' Col Ford said, as Ken joined him. 'Been waiting for you. Jo's over at the drinks tent with a couple of other women. It's just you and me here, till reinforcements arrive.'

Finally, a couple of other members of the club arrived, and Ken and Col took their own bread and sausages over to a wooden bench. 'Phew,' Ken said. 'Where did they all come from? Who'd have thought there were so many small boys in the need of sustenance on a Friday evening?'

'They use up a lot of energy running around, and I think the parents use the sizzle instead of dinner,' Col chuckled. 'Looks like you might be doing the same yourself,' he said, as Ken wolfed down a second sausage sandwich.

'Maybe. Didn't have time for a proper meal before I left.'

'Talking of meals,' Col said. 'Jo wants me to invite you to our combined birthday bash next Sunday.'

'Sunday. Isn't that…?'

'Australia Day. It is.'

Ken had forgotten Col's birthday and the Australian holiday fell on the same day. When they'd been in school, Col had often joked that the whole school got a holiday for his birthday. He hadn't realised it was Jo's birthday, too. Sunday was a day when time hung on his hands. He'd been meaning to use this one to tidy up the garden. 'I guess,' he said, wondering what had prompted the invitation. Col and Jo had a birthday every year and this was the first time he'd received an invite.

Jo called her husband at that point and Col disappeared, saying, 'Twelve o'clock and no presents, but you can bring a bottle if you'd like. You know where we are.'

It wasn't a question. Ken's position both in council and in the real estate business meant he was familiar with just about every acreage around town. And he was also a member of the Rural Fire Brigade – one of the army of volunteers who answered the call when a bushfire threatened the natural bush and properties.

Checking the barbecue, Ken saw the demand for sausages had begun to diminish, and the two men who'd replaced Col and him were now cleaning up. They shook their heads when he offered to help, so he headed for home.

As Ken walked back the way he'd come, past homes he'd sold or visited over the years, he thought again about Col's invite. Had his friend sounded awkward, as if he was hiding something? The words he used, "Jo wants me to invite you". Did that mean it was all Jo's idea? Did Col want him there or did Jo have another agenda – one Col didn't agree with? He shook his head. Maybe he'd been too quick to accept. But what reason could he have given for refusing? It was a birthday celebration for a couple of old schoolfriends, one which coincidentally fell on Australia Day. What could be wrong with that?

It wasn't until Ken was home, seated in his comfortable armchair with a glass of wine and his Michael Connelly novel on his lap that he remembered another school friend, one who had recently returned to Granite Springs. Jo couldn't have invited Lyn Carter too, could she? He felt a thrill at the prospect but was it prompted by fear or pleasure?

Twelve

'How are you feeling this morning?' Lyn helped her mother sit up in bed. 'Are you sure you didn't try to do too much yesterday?'

'I'm not done yet.' But Edith groaned a little as she leaned back against the bank of pillows. 'Though I may stay here for a bit longer.'

'How about a cup of tea and maybe some breakfast?' Lyn asked, knowing how much her mother hated eating in bed, believing it was a sign of slovenliness.

'Maybe. I could fancy a boiled egg with a piece of toast. Then I'll need to get up. This is the day you're off to see those old schoolmates of yours, isn't it?'

'I don't need to go. I can stay here with you.' In fact, Lyn thought she'd be grateful for the excuse. As Jo and Col's birthday event approached, she'd become less and less eager to attend. What did she have in common with them now? Yes, it had been good to have coffee with Jo, but she'd told her more than she intended and the thought of seeing her again, along with all of her family and God knows who else from her past, wasn't Lyn's idea of fun.

Living out of town all of her school years, with a father who despised what he derisively called *townies,* Lyn had spent most of her childhood isolated on the property with only Ken for company when they could both escape their chores – those chores that had made her so determined to escape. She'd be happier to stay home with her mother and a good book.

'No, you go and enjoy yourself. It'll be good for you to see what you've been missing all those years. You had friends here once. You may have moved on, but there are still good people here. You may even find you like them.' Her mother laughed, ending in a cough. 'Now, where's that tea you promised me?'

While Lyn was waiting for the water to boil, she stared out the window at the white and pink oleander bushes in her parents' back yard. She'd always thought it a pity they were deemed poisonous. The flowers were so pretty, and they grew so well here. Her eyes moved across the rest of the garden; the garden that had been her dad's pride and joy; the only piece of land he'd been able to call his after they sold the farm.

It was odd, she thought, how her mother, who'd struggled to establish a garden on their drought-ridden property, had eschewed this one in town. It was as if, now they were on a town water supply, the challenge of making things grow had disappeared. Instead, she'd seemed to busy herself in what could only be described as *good works*, joining various charity and volunteer groups. As far as Lyn knew, until quite recently both parents had been active members of the Granite Springs community.

That was what exhausted her mother yesterday. She'd insisted on attending a gallery opening in aid of the hospital, and a garden fete held in the grounds of a local church. At least it had kept them busy during the open house. True to his word, Ken hadn't reappeared, his son, Neil, arriving at the stated time to welcome prospective buyers.

Lyn wasn't sure what happened next. She'd expected a phone call, some indication of the success or otherwise of the day. But, so far, there had been nothing. She could only hope the house had been inspected by a family who'd fallen in love with it and made an offer. That would enable both Lyn and her mother to move on. It wasn't too late to reschedule her travel plans – and she had nowhere to live back in Brisbane as her unit was already rented out.

A call from her mother brought Lyn back to the present. Edith was looking brighter when Lyn carried in her tea and boiled egg with one slice of toasted white bread and butter, just the way Edith liked it.

'Thanks, darling. No word about yesterday?'

So, she wasn't the only one who was eagerly awaiting news?

'No. I'll give them a call tomorrow when the office is open.'

'You could go in.'

'No need. I can call and speak to Neil.'

Lyn thought her mother was going to say something, perhaps suggest it would be better to speak with Ken. 'I'll make a salad and leave it in the fridge for your lunch,' she said, before the older woman could speak. But she couldn't help wondering why Ken had handed the sale over to his son. He'd appeared to relish their earlier meetings. Or did he prefer to forget the past, like she did?

*

Lyn was wearing a candy-striped sundress with shoestring straps when she drove out to Jo's home towards lunchtime. Despite Jo telling her not to bring anything, Lyn couldn't bear to arrive empty-handed, so had baked an olive, tomato and goats cheese damper from a favourite recipe.

She was surprised to discover how far out of town Jo and Col lived, but it was certainly lovely here, despite the browned grass in the paddocks. A few cars were already parked by the fence which surrounded the house and, when Lyn got out of the car, she could hear the sounds of conversation and the excited yelling of children. Loud splashing noises interspersed with screams of delight told Lyn the pool was proving popular on this hot day.

When she walked through the gate into the yard around the house, Lyn paused for a moment, seeing several groups of people. She wished she hadn't come. What did she have in common with these people? But before she could turn tail, Jo, who was standing on the edge of one of the groups, caught sight of her.

'Welcome, Lyn. I'm glad you made it. You shouldn't have,' she said, as Lyn handed her a platter containing the loaf.

'It's not much. Happy birthday!' Lyn gave Jo a peck on the cheek, marvelling at how elegant the other woman looked with her upswept white-blonde hair, wearing a loose garment in royal blue, her wrist jangling with a couple of gold bracelets.

'Come and meet some of the others,' Jo said, leading her towards a group of people who seemed to be around the same age as they were.

'You should remember most of them.' She laid the damper on a long table which was covered with other platters of food protected by foil and pulled Lyn into the group.

Lyn forced a smile to her face, ready to see people she hadn't thought of for years. They were people she'd never thought she'd see again, and she felt both nervous and shy at the prospect of meeting them again.

She accepted their condolences on the loss of her father, and answered questions about her mother, surprised they seemed to know more about her parents' life than she did. But why should she be surprised? Granite Springs had always been like that. It was one of the things she liked about living in a city – your neighbours didn't know your business. But of course, that had a downside, too. There was no one to know or care if you were in difficulty.

Caught up in her thoughts, Lyn let the conversation flow over her. Her eyes wandered to where another group – mostly younger people – were encouraging a couple of little girls into the pool. Then, her gaze stopped. Was that? It couldn't be! But it was! Ken Thompson's son was standing with a young dark-haired woman. They were chatting to a man who was an older version of the Gordon Slater she remembered, and a woman with blonde hair holding a baby. As Lyn watched, Ken himself strolled over to join them, a beer in his hand, and a smile on his face.

She knew she shouldn't have come!

Thirteen

Ken was enjoying a beer and chatting with Neil, Sally, Gordon and his wife, Carol, when he felt someone's eyes on him. He turned cautiously to see Lyn Carter hurriedly avert her gaze. He felt his stomach turn over. He'd been right. Jo and Col did have another agenda – or was he making too much of her presence?

Lyn was back in town; they'd all been in the same year at school. It was only natural for Jo to invite her to get together with old friends. So why did Ken feel as if he'd been robbed of the opportunity to be the one to bring her back into the group?

Ken was so caught up in his frustration, and perhaps a touch of resentment, he failed to remind himself he was the one who'd offloaded the sale of her mother's house to Neil, the one who'd decided it would be better if he didn't get too involved. But better for whom?

He stole another glance in Lyn's direction. Her back was turned to him now, and he could see she was wearing one of those skimpy dresses which showed off her still smooth skin. Even from this distance, he could tell she was looking good. The few times they'd met, she'd been more covered up. Now, with her bare shoulders, her short blonde hair, she looked like someone he'd like to know.

Catching himself up short, Ken took a swig of beer and tried to listen to the conversation going on around him. But all he could think of was that Lyn Carter, the only girl he'd ever really loved, the girl he'd tried so hard to forget, was standing only a few yards away from him.

'Dad!'

'Sorry, son. What did you say?'

'Sal was asking what you thought of the house.'

'The... oh, you mean that demountable thing you plan to call home?'

'Ha ha. I told her I'd shown you the plans.' He put an arm around Sally's shoulders and gave her a squeeze.

'I think you'll be very happy there – both of you.' He gave a conspiratorial wink.

'I think it's a great idea,' Gordon said. 'I've been helping this young man with the legal aspects of his project. Jo and I loved it here, and our three had a ball growing up. You'd know that, growing up on Wooleton. We townies used to envy those of you who lived on the broad acres. But Neil didn't have that experience?'

His words filled Ken with a sense of guilt. He'd loved his childhood on the farm. Was he to blame that his son hadn't enjoyed the same experience he had growing up in the country? He remembered the hot summer days helping his dad with the sheep, then bunking off to meet Lyn when his chores were over. Had his own pigheadedness deprived Neil of the same fun?

For a moment he pictured how his life might have been, married to Lyn, managing Wooleton. Then the image faded. That wasn't what Lyn had wanted. *He* wasn't what she'd wanted. And he'd married Sheila who would have rather died than live on the farm. And without Sheila, Neil would never have been born. He looked across at his tall son, the image of himself at that age, and knew he had nothing to regret.

'I intend to make up for it, now,' Neil answered for him, 'and any sons of mine will grow up there too.'

He gave Sally another squeeze.

'Dad, isn't that...?' Neil was gesturing with his beer can towards the group on the veranda. 'Aren't you going to join them?'

There was nothing Ken wanted more than to join the other group, but would it be too obvious to move over immediately after Lyn arrived? Hell, he wasn't a young kid anymore and they were *his* friends.

He was saved from a decision by seeing Col making a move towards the barbecue.

'Looks like Col might need a hand there,' Gordon said. 'Ken?'

Glad to have an excuse both to leave Neil's questions and avoid meeting Lyn again, at least for the time being, Ken followed Gordon to where Col was loading steaks, sausages and onions onto a state-of-the-art barbecue.

'This looks pretty upmarket, Col,' Gordon said, picking up a spatula in one hand and barbecue tongs in the other. 'New?'

'Our birthday present to ourselves. The old one was on its last legs, and when we saw this one advertised, well…'

'That old one saw a few good years,' Gordon said with a grin, and Ken wondered, not for the first time, how it was that the two men could have remained friends and, till recently business partners, having been married to the same woman.

'Thanks for asking us along today, Col,' Gordon said, as if reading Ken's mind. 'And thanks for making Jo so happy. I'm sorry I gave both of you such a hard time when you first got together, but I had Jo's best interests at heart.'

'Hmm.' Col clearly didn't want to reply, didn't want to have this conversation. 'Did you see Lyn Carter over there, Ken?' he asked. 'Jo had coffee with her and thought she needed to catch up with some of her old friends. Weren't you and she…? She's still a good-looking woman.' He winked.

'We grew up together and I partnered her to the school formal. That's about it.' Ken exhaled, hoping Col wasn't going to pursue this line of conversation. He drew a hand around the inside of his shirt collar. Was it getting warmer? Maybe it was the heat from the barbecue?

*

'You remember Lyn Carter?' Jo was drawing a reluctant Lyn towards Ken. The barbecue was almost over and, so far, he'd managed to avoid speaking to her.

'We've already met,' Lyn said. 'Ken's selling Mother's house.' She didn't appear any happier to see him here than she had in the office.

'Oh!' Jo seemed surprised. 'Well, I'm sure you have lots to talk about.' She was called away by one of her grandchildren, and Ken was left standing there with Lyn and feeling awkward.

'Neil tells me the open house went well,' he said, searching around for something to say. 'Has he been in touch?'

'No.' Lyn sounded as awkward as he felt. 'I'd planned to drop into the office tomorrow.'

'Public holiday.'

'Right.' She glanced around. 'Is your wife here?'

'Divorced.' It had been a long time since Ken had to explain his marital status. Everyone in town knew his history. Hadn't Edith Carter told her daughter? 'Nearly twenty years now. You?'

'Same. Seven for me.'

'Children?' He had a vague recollection there was a daughter, but had tried not to listen to Edith's stories of how well Lyn had done.

'A daughter – Amy, and two granddaughters.' Lyn's face softened when she mentioned her family, and Ken could see the young woman he remembered.

'They live in Brisbane?'

She nodded and glanced around as if seeking an escape, whether from him or the party, Ken wasn't sure.

'Look,' he said without thinking. 'Why don't we get out of here? Jo and Col won't mind, and the party's liable to go on for hours. We can get a drink somewhere, maybe catch up on old times. It's been a while.'

Ken saw an array of emotions flicker across Lyn's face. She hesitated, then said, 'Why not?'

Fourteen

Lyn made her farewells to Jo and Col, wondering what on earth had possessed her to agree to Ken's suggestion. After trying to avoid him, sure her mother was trying to matchmake yet again, here she was leaving her friend's party with the one person who'd forced her to leave town in the first place. No, that wasn't strictly accurate. Ken had really played no part in her leaving. She'd determined to do that even before the school formal. But the feelings she'd experienced that night had been what precipitated her departure.

As she followed Ken's SUV into town, Lyn's mind veered from one direction to another. On the one hand there was no harm in having a drink with an old friend; on the other, that old friend had already aroused emotions she never wanted to experience again. She grimaced as he drove into the car park behind the golf club. It was a safe bet he was a member here, as conventional as his dad had been. She'd saved herself from a life which followed the same dull pattern as their parents when she left town, even if what she ended up with hadn't turned out to be as exciting as she'd hoped.

When they walked inside, they were greeted by a raucous sound of voices as several groups of people – mostly men – tried to outdo each other in sharing their scores, good or otherwise to their fellow golfers.

'Sorry,' Ken gave her a wry smile, 'I'd forgotten the annual Australia Day tournament. I thought this would be somewhere we could have a quiet drink.'

'That's okay. I presume you play?'

'Not often.' Ken rubbed his chin, in a gesture she remembered. 'It sometimes helps if I play a round with a client, but I'm no golfing fanatic. Don't really see the point of it, chasing a little ball around a field. Though it is good exercise.' He drew in his stomach as if to demonstrate.

Lyn felt her own stomach clench. She wondered what other exercise Ken engaged in. He was in good shape for a man his age – still showing the physique that had wowed all the girls back in high school. But he only had eyes for you, she reminded herself. At the time, until the evening of the formal, she'd explained away their friendship as being that of just a couple of kids who'd grown up together, almost as brother and sister. But the shudders of excitement she'd felt when dancing with him, their bodies closer together than they'd ever been since they'd wrestled together in primary school, told her otherwise. It had scared her.

'What'll you have?' Ken's voice interrupted her.

'A white wine would be good.' Lyn took a seat at the window table Ken had managed to procure, as far from the noisy groups of golfers as he could. While he fetched their drinks, she gazed out at the wide expanse of green and wondered how the club managed to maintain it in the drought. She seemed to recall her dad saying something about sand. Were the greens made of sand? It seemed odd, but she couldn't see them from here.

Ken returned and placed her wine on the table, the glass moist with condensation.

'Thanks.' Lyn picked it up but didn't immediately take a drink.

They sat in silence for several moments, each unsure what to say. What do you say to your old childhood friend after all this time? She should never have agreed to this drink.

Ken broke the silence. 'So, now you're back in Granite Springs, what do you think?' He waved his glass around.

Surely he wasn't asking for her impression of the club?

'The town, I mean. You must admit it's changed a lot over the years.'

'Ye…es,' Lyn replied cautiously. 'I suppose it has. But there's a lot that hasn't changed much at all.'

'Come on, Lyn. When we were growing up, Granite Springs was a small town. Now we have the university, the art gallery, the fruit processing plant, not to mention the housing developments and small acreages outside town. It's become a regional centre. Though,' a crease appeared between his eyes, 'it wasn't enough to keep Sheila here, or Neil's wife, Tina.'

What was Ken trying to do? If he thought he could sell Lyn on Granite Springs the way he sold houses, he was mistaken.

'I'm sorry.' What else was there to say? It seemed the Thompson men weren't lucky with their women. Is that what Lyn had been? Ken's woman? No, but she could have been – if she'd stayed. A shiver ran up her back. 'So that wasn't his wife your son was with at the barbecue?' Surely this was a safe topic of conversation?

'No, but maybe the next one. They're planning to move in together.' Ken rubbed his forehead. 'I'll miss him,' he said with a sigh.

'But you'll still see him every day.' Lyn wasn't sure why she was engaging in this conversation. But she sensed something about him, a sense of loss that made her want to discover what he was sad about.

'No,' he said, and began to tell her how Neil was going to return to the family farm, leaving his dad to take what was his rightful place. 'He's going to be difficult to replace,' he said at last. 'He's a good salesman, and he kept on top of our IT stuff as well. I guess I'll need to have him give me a crash course before he leaves.'

Lyn recalled him saying something similar to her mother, but her mind had been elsewhere, and she hadn't taken it in at the time.

He took a swig of his beer. 'But enough about me. What have you been doing all these years? Your mum said something about your becoming a headmistress?' He chuckled. 'You always did try to boss me around.'

'Did not!' The words flew out of her mouth. Suddenly, it was as if the room disappeared, and Lyn was back in the paddock with the younger Ken. Although almost exactly the same age, she'd tried to exploit her two month advantage and demanded to be the leader in many of their games – rarely successfully, especially when Ken grew taller and stronger and managed to wield his authority over the skinny little girl Lyn had been.

'We had some good times, didn't we?' he asked, as if he'd travelled back in time with her. 'A country upbringing, the freedom to roam around unshackled. That's what I want for my grandchildren.'

They smiled at each other, bound by the shared memories.

'If you like, we could pop into the office, and I can get you the report on yesterday's open house,' Ken said, effectively bursting the bubble that had enclosed them for just a moment.

'Sure. Why not?' Lyn was glad Ken had changed the subject. She didn't want to be reminded of those times, the carefree days before everything became complicated, before their parents' expectations formed a millstone around her neck, before her own emotions threatened to get out of hand.

Once in the office, Ken was all business. It was as if the shared moment in the club had never happened. Lyn was glad. She didn't want to risk anything that might break down the wall of defences she'd managed to erect between her and Ken Thompson, defences that were just as important today as they'd been forty-five years ago. She was older and wiser now, but was aware it still wouldn't take much for her emotions to spill over.

Fifteen

Ken looked through the small bundle of applications. None of them had the experience he was hoping for. There was quite a mix ranging from those disillusioned with their current employment who thought they could make a killing in real estate, to new graduates having difficulty finding employment in their chosen fields.

He sighed and thrust a hand through his hair. Neil's move was going to leave more of a gap than he'd imagined. Damn him! Damn Alec! Damn his dad who'd forced them into this situation! And now there would be sheep and cattle on Wooleton, after all.

Deciding he needed a coffee before selecting who to interview, Ken went into the main office where the Nespresso machine sat in one corner. He preferred the brew from the cafe across the street, but knew he'd have to brave the heat to get there and would return unrefreshed. At least he could enjoy this one in air-conditioned comfort.

Neil was already there. 'Coffee, Dad?' he asked, handing Ken the cup he'd already prepared, before fixing another for himself. 'Any luck?'

Ken shook his head before taking a sip of the welcome caffeine hit. 'Maybe you can give me a hand, if you're not too busy?'

'Sure thing.' Neil grabbed a chocolate chip cookie from the jar the women in the office kept replenished, and followed Ken into his office, closing the door behind him.

'You're not going to be so easy to replace,' Ken said, as Neil twirled a chair around to take a seat, leaning his elbows on the seat back, the coffee clasped in both hands.

'No? I thought you'd find it a cinch. Surely there's someone out there who you can train up.'

'That's the trouble,' Ken said, pulling on one ear. 'None of the candidates have worked in the field before. At least you had the right background when you started out. After your time at Ag College, you could talk to the farmers in their language. This lot…!' He spread his hands.

'Let's have a look.'

Ken handed over the bundle of applications, glad he'd insisted on hard copies. At least it proved they were literate – if they hadn't found someone else to write it for them. He slowly drank his coffee while Neil read through the letters of application.

'How about those two?' Neil asked, handing back two of them. 'They look like possibilities.'

Ken skimmed the two Neil had chosen. He was right. They might not be perfect, but they were the best of a bad bunch. 'Thanks, son. I'll set up the interviews. Want to be in on them?' He knew it would be best to get a second opinion, and Neil knew the business almost as well as he did.

'Can do. Set them up on a day when I'm in the office, and I'm your man.'

'The report on the viewing at the Carter place?' Ken asked, just as Neil was getting ready to leave. 'I bumped into the daughter on the weekend and we called in here to check it out.' He saw Neil's eyes widen, but didn't offer any further explanation. What he did in his private life was none of Neil's business, and there was nothing to know anyway. 'Only two couples through?'

'That's right. It was damned slow. I don't understand it. There are a lot of people looking, but I guess it was a hot day. Maybe that stopped them. Might try another next week. The place looked good. Shouldn't be hard to shift.'

'Okay. Will you let her know?'

Ken saw Neil give him a wary glance.

'You seem to be friends. Why don't you call her? And why did you give it to me in the first place?'

Ken wasn't sure how to respond. He'd asked himself the same question without success. Initially, it had been a knee-jerk reaction, a desire to maintain some sort of distance from the heartbreak of his youth. But now? It had been good to see Lyn again at the barbecue, to enjoy a drink together. What was the problem in managing this sale? They were both free, and older and wiser. There was no danger of their getting into any complicated relationship at their age – or was there? He still had no idea what had scared Lyn off back then, no idea how she felt seeing him again now. But it might be worth finding out.

'Okay, son. Get me the paperwork.'

'Dad! It's all on the computer.'

'Of course it is.' Ken passed a hand over his eyes. What had he been thinking? Maybe he *should* retire. Then he wouldn't have to worry about finding someone to replace Neil. But he loved this business, loved matching people up with their new homes, finding buyers for those who wanted to move on. It was satisfying to receive thanks from grateful customers, and the collection of Christmas gifts – the bottles of wine and scotch sitting in the corner of his office – bore testament to that.

The door swung shut after Neil, leaving Ken feeling as if he'd been dismissed as forgetful at best, an old fogey at worst. It was a feeling he'd had several times recently, and he didn't like it. So what if he preferred the old methods? They'd worked perfectly well for him in the past. But he had to admit the digital images in the window which could be changed at the drop of a hat were a damned sight better than the old printed photographs. Thinking of photographs led him to wonder what shots Neil had done for the Carter place.

Normally, one of the first things he'd do himself, was to arrange for a local photographer to visit a property to take a series of shots both inside and out. He checked the file on the database, seeing only one. It was a good one, showing the exterior of a regular family home with a well cared for garden. But it wasn't a recent one, and where were the others?

'Neil,' he called, stepping back into the main office.

'Dad?' Neil looked up from his computer with a frown.

Ken could read his mind. *What does the old man want now?*

'The Carter place. That's an old photo. Looks like the one I used when we sold it to them. And there don't seem to be any interior shots.'

Neil tipped his chair back and clasped his hands behind his head, his face taking on a slightly shifty expression. 'No… I… You wanted the open house set up. I was in a rush to get out to the farm. I thought it would go quickly and we could save on the…' His voice trailed off as he clearly recognised the glint of anger in Ken's eyes.

Tempted as he was to berate his son, Ken merely turned on his heel. He should have known. The boy was already acting as if he was part of Wooleton. The business of Granite Springs Realty was secondary to what was now his main interest and the focus of his attention.

As soon as he was seated in front of his own computer, Ken sent an email to Jason Leech, the local photographer they used to show their properties to their best advantage, and another to Lyn to apologise this hadn't been done sooner. He'd have liked to call her, to hear her voice again, but decided against it. He was her realtor first and friend second, if indeed they were to renew their friendship. Though it had looked promising over drinks in the club.

Then he re-read the two applications Neil had pinpointed, before composing emails inviting them both to interviews the following week. He didn't hold out much hope. One was a young man who'd been to school with Neil. He sounded keen enough, but his background as a building contractor wasn't exactly what Ken had in mind. The other was a young graduate. Jamie Ferguson had graduated from the local William Farrer University at the end of the year and, determined to remain in town for what he described as *personal reasons*, was eager to try anything. At least both sounded willing to learn the business, but Ken shook his head as he pressed *send*, then entered the interview times into both his and Neil's online calendar and into his desk diary. He knew as he did so, his son would laugh at the dual entry, but he put more faith in his desk diary than in the online one.

That done, Ken checked his watch, surprised to see it was close to three o'clock. Remembering he had promised to view a potential property for sale, he grabbed his iPad and headed out to where his car had become a heat box, having sat in the parking lot all day.

Familiar with the town, Ken had no need to check the map or enter details into the satnav – he didn't even know why he'd bothered with one, but it had come as part of the car when he bought it. All tech features, the salesman had said, when Ken was only concerned with a vehicle that would get him from A to B and handle the dirt roads outside town. But it was a good car and served him well.

Ken drew up outside the redbrick family home and sat for a few moments studying the house. This was something he liked to do. Over the years, Ken knew he'd developed a good nose for the value of houses in town, for those which would sell easily and those which would require more work. Much like the Carter house, this one was of an older vintage, probably a bit tired inside. But, with its four bedrooms and large backyard, it should attract one of the young families on his books.

He walked up to the door and rang the bell.

Fifteen minutes later, he was back in his car, wondering what had happened. Instead of the expected welcome with perhaps a cup of indifferent tea or coffee, the meeting had been brief. The owner had shown Ken around then ummed and ahed before saying he'd have to consider Ken's terms and would be in touch.

Ken scratched his head before firing up the engine. But on the way along the street he noticed two of the neighbouring homes had signs in their front gardens. Like the other houses in the street, they were of the same vintage as the one he'd visited. The signs carried a logo showing the outline of a house and the letters DNS, a company with which he wasn't familiar. Was there a new guy in town? Was he missing something?

A slight detour on his route back to the office, took Ken past Lyn's mother's house and, as he slowed down to check the For Sale sign, he caught sight of her in the garden. Embarrassed at being caught, though there was no reason why he should be, Ken gave a quick wave and speeded up, regretting the impulse that had triggered the detour.

Neil was gone by the time Ken returned to the office, so he noted what details of his visit he could, entered a follow-up date in his diary, and closed up for the day. Then he sat staring into space. Life had thrown him a curved ball when Lyn Carter walked into this office. The question was, how should he play it?

Sixteen

Lyn watched as the SUV drove off in what seemed like unnecessary haste. She'd recognised Ken's car idling along the road minutes before she stood up and wondered what he'd do when he noticed her. She smiled to herself. The drink they had together was nice, almost like old times. Over the years, she'd missed that sense of being at one with someone, someone who knew her inside out, what made her tick, what made her mad, and what made her sad.

But the one thing he hadn't managed to deduce, was the startling effect he'd had on her emotions, and the reason she had to get away before she was caught up in events beyond her control. Keeping control had always been important to Lyn. Maybe it was why she'd been so successful in her career. As headmistress of the prestigious girls' school, she'd been able to exercise her control, her authority. And in so doing had maintained the school's reputation as one of the elite high schools in Brisbane, no mean feat in the light of such great competition.

Sighing with something like regret, Lyn picked up her secateurs and the basket of blooms she'd managed to salvage from the drought-stricken garden. Granite Springs wasn't on water restrictions yet, but it was wise to remain frugal with watering, and she was doing only enough to keep the place looking good to prospective buyers.

Thinking of buyers reminded Lyn of her visit to Ken's office on Sunday. As soon as they walked in, it was as if the old friend she'd had a drink with morphed into the distant businessman she'd met there before. She wasn't sure how she felt about his seeming transformation.

While she had no intention of reigniting any of the feelings her younger self had so successfully stifled, it would be nice to know Ken still found her attractive. Or was she being stupid – wanting the best of both worlds?

'Is that you, Lyn?' her mother's voice, which was becoming stronger every day, called out from the living room. 'Was that Ken Thompson's car I just saw? Why didn't you stop him and invite him in for tea?'

Damn! Lyn had forgotten that her mother, sitting in the window, was keeping her eye on all the comings and goings in the street. Of course she recognised Ken's car. But surely she also saw how it speeded up to pass the house?

'I don't know,' she lied. 'Was it? I wasn't paying attention to the traffic. Look, I found some lovely hibiscus still in bloom. I'll put them in a vase, then make some tea, shall I?' She held up the orange blooms for her mother's attention.

'I remember your dad planting those bushes,' Edith said, her eyes glazing over as they did when she talked about her husband. 'They took so long to come good. Who'd have thought they'd outlive him? They'll most likely outlive me, too. I won't be here to see them bloom next year.' Her lips turned down in a grimace.

Unsure whether her mother was referring to her prospective move or her projected demise, Lyn decided not to respond. 'Tea?' she asked again.

'It's almost time for dinner. Why don't you pour us both a glass of that sherry Amy gave me for Christmas? I think I could handle a small one.'

Sherry? Her mother was full of surprises. Lyn had never known either her mum or her dad to be much for alcohol, apart from her dad's one beer on a Saturday night, and the one-off glass of something on special occasions.

'Will do, but I think I may have wine.' Relieved her mother seemed to have forgotten about Ken and his car, Lyn went into the kitchen, her mother's voice following her with instructions as to which glasses to use. Lyn rolled her eyes. How was Edith going to cope in Eden Gardens when she was no longer able to make demands?

While in the kitchen Lyn slid a casserole dish into the oven. She'd prepared it earlier, adding vegetables to some diced chicken breasts she'd picked up in the supermarket that morning. She'd noticed a distinct improvement in the produce available in town. A lot had changed since she left, and all for the better. Granite Springs could now rival Brisbane for the range of goods available, and the selection of fresh fruit and vegetables surprised her. It shouldn't have, but she was conscious of the difficulties local farmers must be experiencing in the extended drought conditions.

'Now,' Edith said, when she had taken her first sip of sherry, 'when are you going to see that young man again? You let him go once. Don't make the same mistake this time.'

Lyn almost choked on her wine. Was her mum never going to give up? 'If you're talking about Ken Thompson, there's no chance of anything other than a business relationship there, so don't get your hopes up. And I expect it'll be Neil we see again at the next open house.'

Undeterred, Edith continued, 'It was such a pity you left town when you did. I know Wyn was glad to have your company, but it would have been a good match. Your dad and I would love to have seen the farm combined with the Thompson place – old man Thompson was all for it, Betty too. I don't know what happened when Ken came back from his studies, but...' she pointed a finger at Lyn, '...if you hadn't left, I'd be willing to bet young Alec wouldn't have got the property.' She nodded to herself.

Lyn stared at her mother in amazement. She had no idea why the farm hadn't gone to Ken either, but surely it was nothing to do with her? She tightened her lips and took a gulp of wine. But she'd be interested to discover what happened, too. When she left, Ken had been eagerly looking forward to a future on Wooleton, to taking over the property when his parents could no longer manage it, and the younger Alec had been hellbent on becoming a lawyer with premises on Sydney's Macquarie Street. Something had gone awry somewhere along the line.

But Edith hadn't finished. 'He should never have married that flibbertigibbet from the city. I said it wouldn't last. She was never cut out to be a country wife.'

And I was? Lyn realised how little her mother understood her, or perhaps she believed what she wanted to believe.

'He told me he was divorced,' Lyn said without thinking.

Her mother latched onto her words right away – nothing wrong with her mind. 'When did he say that? I thought you just went to the office with him after Jo's barbecue – to find out about the open house.'

Lyn bit her lip, wishing she hadn't been so economical with the truth. Her mother always did have a way of winkling out information from her as a child, but Lyn thought she'd become more expert at hiding things as she grew older. What was it about her mother that made her feel like fifteen again? Did Lyn have that effect on Amy? She hoped not. But there were probably lots of things her daughter hid from her, too.

*

Dinner over, Lyn helped her mother to bed with much fussing and mumbling. Although unable to manage for herself, Edith didn't accept help readily. But, at last, she was safely ensconced in her bed, a glass of water and a book on the bedside table along with a small handbell, and her walker within easy reach. 'Be sure to ring if you need anything,' Lyn said, before going out and leaving the door slightly ajar.

Her mother merely grunted.

Back in the living room, Lyn poured herself another glass of wine. Then she opened her iPad to check her emails, delighted to see one from Maddy. Her granddaughter had been in the Philippines for almost a month and was due back any day. Lyn had seen a few photos on Facebook showing white beaches, blue water and groups of happy young people. But this was the first personal communication.

She scanned the message, then sat up straight at what she saw. Maddy was coming here? She read it again to ensure she hadn't made a mistake. No, there it was clear as day,

I got into the University of Queensland, my first choice, but it's not too late to change my preferences and I've met this guy who's studying education at William Farrer. I thought it would be cool to be close to you and GG. Can I stay with you till I find a place? I'll be back home on the weekend and plan to come down to Granite Springs as soon as poss. Will text you my ETA. Maddy xx

Despite her love for her granddaughter, Lyn's first thought was, *she can't!*

Taking another gulp of wine, Lyn considered the implications. If the sale didn't go through immediately – even if it did – she'd be sharing a house with a nineteen-year-old and a ninety-four-year-old. This wasn't how she intended to spend her retirement. She could feel the bottled-up resentment of years rise into her throat, threatening to choke her.

Maybe this was her karma – something she'd never believed in – her punishment for disregarding her parents' wishes for her; for leaving them without any explanation; for staying away; for ignoring the fact they were becoming older and frailer; for...

No! She was being stupid again. She loved her mother and her granddaughter. This was an opportunity to spend quality time with both of them. Who knew how long her mother had left, and how much longer would Maddy want to spend time with her grandmother? She should look on this as an unexpected gift of time.

Having settled that to her satisfaction, washed down with another gulp of wine, Lyn scrolled down her other emails, deleting the spam and skim-reading a few others, before her eyes settled on one from Granite Springs Realty. Anticipating it being from Neil or one of the admin staff, she opened it to discover it was from Ken.

Her eyes widened as she read that, *due to other commitments*, Neil was no longer able to look after the sale, so Ken would be managing it himself. Lyn took another sip of wine before reading further, unsure how she felt about this. Did Neil really have other commitments or had Ken chosen to do this as a way of spending more time with her? And, if this was the case, was she pleased or... An unfamiliar sensation of warmth flowed through her. She took a breath and continued to read. Ken stated the need for more photos to be taken of the house, apologising this hadn't been done sooner. He was suggesting he and a photographer come around... next day!

Lyn glanced around the room, but there was nothing out of place. There was no reason to refuse the request and, when she read further, she saw he'd asked her to call if there was a problem. Otherwise they'd be arriving at ten next morning. She cursed herself for ignoring her emails till now. But, even if she'd seen this one earlier, there would have been no reason to refuse. Lyn shut down her iPad with a sigh and took her empty glass through to the fridge for a much-needed refill, pleased to see the kitchen was in the same immaculate condition as the rest of the house. It should photograph well and hopefully sell soon. Then she could get on with her life.

But why did she have a niggling feeling things weren't going to be that simple?

Seventeen

'This it?' Jason asked, as he leaned against his car and stared at the old federation home. 'You want both exterior and interior shots?'

Ken nodded. But already he was regretting the impulse that had brought him here. There had been no need for him to take over when Neil pulled out. He could easily have handed the sale to Joy or Cathy. There were other, more pressing, jobs for him to take care of. He could pretend he wanted to see things right for Mrs Carter; that he felt sorry for her having so recently lost her husband; that the Carters had been their neighbours for years and good friends with his parents. But he knew none of those excuses would wash. He was here because of Lyn Carter – he couldn't think of her by her married name.

Seeing her again had resurrected all the feelings he'd thought had gone forever. He was a fool. He was sixty-two, not a teenager. But neither was she. And, when she'd walked into the office, it was as if he *was* a teenager again. Was life giving him a second chance? If so, he didn't intend to let her slip away this time.

He forced his mind back to the present as Jason picked up his camera, tripod, and bag of tricks. 'Let's go,' he said.

'Good morning.' Lyn opened the door, a wary expression on her face.

What was she afraid of? Did she feel it too – this spark that seemed to flare up between them? Or was it all in his imagination? Was he just a sad old man trying to breathe new life into a long-lost romance?

'Morning,' Ken said with a smile. 'This is Jason, who'll be taking photos. I'm hoping to have them in next week's paper, and they'll be in our window then, too. It should drum up some interest for the open house. We'll try not to disturb you.'

'That's okay. I was making coffee. Would you like a cup, or do you have to rush off?'

'Coffee would be great. I need to follow Jason around, but…'

'It'll be ready when you're finished,' Lyn said, now looking amused.

What was it with the woman? She seemed to blow hot and cold, or was he being too sensitive?

Ken and Jason moved through the house, Jason taking shots of the rooms as directed by Ken and adding some of his own which he felt would complement them. Finally, they were back in the kitchen, where the welcome aroma of freshly brewed coffee, and a sweeter smell awaited them.

'I baked some banana bread this morning,' Lyn said. 'Would you like a slice with your coffee?'

Jason was quick to take a seat and accept the proffered coffee and cake. Ken followed more slowly, bending to speak to Edith Carter who was seated at the end of the table. 'Sorry to intrude on you,' he said. 'Neil should have taken care of this last week.'

'No problem,' the old woman said, waving away his apology. 'It's good to see you again, Ken. Isn't it, Lyn?' she asked, with what appeared to Ken to be a sly grin.

Ignoring her mother, Lyn handed Ken a mug of coffee and the plate of banana bread, while he tried to work out what was going on. What was the unspoken message that had passed between the two? He was damned if he knew, but it appeared to be one which annoyed Lyn.

After an awkward conversation, the two men left, Ken promising to see them as arranged on Saturday.

*

There was no sign of Neil when Ken entered the office. He checked his diary, but there were no viewings or meetings scheduled and it wasn't one of his days for Wooleton. He should have been here. Ken was about to call his son, when Alec walked in, his face white.

'What's up, little brother?' Ken asked, surprised to see Alec off the property on a working day. It was most unlike him to come into town during the week. It was Judy who normally did the shopping and made the trips to the Co-op for supplies.

'It's Jude. She's having some tests at the Base hospital. They said it'd take about an hour. I couldn't stand sitting in that waiting room with all the other sick people. I thought...' Alec looked around wildly and thrust a hand through his already tousled hair.

'You look as if you need a decent cup of coffee,' Ken said, thinking a glass of brandy might be more appropriate, but not at this time of day. 'Back in thirty minutes,' he said to Cathy who was the only other person in the office. 'Call me if you need me and try to get hold of Neil.'

'He's at Wooleton,' Alec said, as the two men made their way out of the office and along the road to The Bean Sprout where Ken ordered two mugs of strong, black coffee.

'Now, what's this about Judy?' Ken asked, when they'd both taken their first slugs of coffee. 'What's the matter with her?'

'We don't know, maybe nothing.'

But the expression on Alec's face told a different story.

'She had her usual breast scan the other week, then, yesterday...' Alec exhaled loudly, '...she had a call telling her they'd detected some irregularity and that she should come in for more tests. Some irregularity! We all know what that means.'

Breast cancer! The unspoken words hung between them.

'How's she taking it?' Ken could see Alec was shaken to the core, but Judy always tended to be the calmer of the two.

'Oh, you know Jude,' Alec said, pinching at the skin on his throat. 'She keeps saying they're only being cautious, but I can see she's worried. Her mother died of breast cancer when Jude was in her early twenties. I know it's something she's always been afraid of. Hell, Ken, what am I going to do if...?'

Ken saw a bead of moisture form in the corner of Alec's eyes. He awkwardly patted his brother on the arm – they'd never been a very tactile family. 'It may not come to that. It's just some tests, you say?'

Alec nodded. 'That's why I asked Neil to come out there today. I couldn't let Jude face it on her own.'

'Of course not.'

The two men sat drinking their coffee in silence.

Ken had never seen his brother so worried. Alec was normally the more contented of the two brothers. Despite having to give up his dream of a prestigious law practice, he'd buckled down to life on the farm and made a go of it. Judy had become the perfect farmer's wife, a stalwart member of the Country Women's Association and secretary of the local Quota Club, where she added her voice and actions to promote gender equality and empower country women. She was a voice of reason in what was a formerly male-dominated community.

If anything happened to her, she'd not only be missed by her family but by the entire community. Ken pulled himself out of these pessimistic thoughts. As Alec had said, she was only having tests done. It probably happened a lot. No doubt they'd be laughing over it and celebrating her results later in the day.

'You're probably right.' Alec drained his cup and checked his watch. 'I should be getting back. I want to be there when…'

'Right. You'll let me know?'

Alec nodded.

Ken gripped his brother's shoulder firmly before they parted, Alec striding towards the hospital, and Ken walking more slowly back to the office. Once there, he was able to download the photos Jason had sent through. Ken still marvelled how quickly this could be done these days. No waiting around for them to be developed, simply an email with all the images attached. He scrolled through them, selecting those to forward to the local paper with the ad – a half-page feature, he decided – and which to put on the rolling display in the office window.

But, even as he did this, Alec and Judy weren't far from his thoughts. It had sometimes occurred to him that, apart from their inability to have children, they'd lived a charmed life. It would be devastating if Judy was diagnosed with breast cancer. Though it wasn't necessarily a death sentence, it was a serious condition and she would require careful treatment.

When his mobile rang over an hour later, and Ken saw his brother's number, he grabbed it. 'Alec, what…?'

Alec didn't give him time to finish. 'We just got back. It's bad news.'

His voice broke. There was a moment's silence, then he continued, 'Sorry, Ken. I'm determined to be strong for Jude. They found something and think it's malignant. The doc wants her to go to Canberra for a biopsy. They can fit her in the day after tomorrow. It means that...' He cleared his throat.

Ken didn't hesitate. 'You need Neil out there. I understand. Give my best to Judy – and take care of yourself. She needs you to be strong. Is there anything I can do?'

'Thanks, mate. Be in touch.'

Ken looked at the silent phone. He felt for his brother. But, in an odd way, he experienced envy, not envy of his and Judy's predicament; envy of having someone he cared for enough to be broken up by her illness. Ken had never had a relationship like that. Sheila and he had been...what? Partners in the ship of marriage, a ship that had foundered early on, but had kept floating until it finally sank under the weight of their combined indifference.

Life wasn't fair. What had Alec and Judy done to deserve this? But what had any family done to deserve the ills that befell them?

Alec's news made Ken think afresh about Lyn Carter, about what might have been. It was times like this that made one realise how fleeting life could be. In all likelihood Judy would be fine, would live out her allotted span. But it certainly brought one's mortality closer.

Was there still a chance for him with Lyn? Could they rekindle the embers of the flame that had begun to ignite when they were both eighteen, or had it been extinguished forever?

Eighteen

Lyn gazed out the kitchen window as the much-needed rain poured down, turning the garden into mud and making the gutters overflow. Although welcome for breaking the drought, it wasn't what Lyn wanted to see on the day of their second open house.

'The farmers will be happy.'

Lyn turned to see her mother lurching into the room with her walker. 'Yes, but I hope it doesn't keep our buyers away,' she said with a frown.

'If they're interested, they'll come,' her mother said. 'Didn't you say how impressed you were with that article in the paper?'

'Yes. Ken did a good job. And the photos made this place look amazing. But...'

'You worry too much,' Edith said. 'Are you still intent on going out to your friend's today? It won't be very nice there in the rain.'

'We'll be inside,' Lyn said, as she deftly poured two cups of tea, removed two slices of bread from the toaster, and slid a poached egg onto each of them. 'It was good of Jo to invite us, and you'll enjoy the change of scene.'

'That's true. I'm getting a bit tired of being in the house. It's beginning to seem like a prison.'

For you, too? But Lyn didn't share her thoughts out loud.

'What time's your young man arriving?'

'He's not my young man, Mother. Ken's our realtor, and he'll be here around half nine. We need to be ready to leave then.' But Lyn felt an unexpected quiver of pleasure in anticipation of Ken's arrival.

'Well, it seems you know who I was talking about.' Edith pursed her lips. 'This looks lovely, Lynnie. You're so good to me.' She slipped into a chair and took a sip of tea, giving a sigh of satisfaction.

Lyn felt a bolt of pleasure. It wasn't often her mother praised her. She knew the older woman must be in pain, frustrated at her lack of mobility, but sometimes it was hard to countenance the flood of complaints that burst from her lips on a regular basis. Lyn had to constantly remind herself this was her mother who had recently lost her life partner, who was now incapacitated and dependent on her recalcitrant daughter for help and support. Lyn smiled inwardly at her own assessment of herself.

Despite the rain, the trip out to Jo's was pleasant. Ken had arrived at the appointed time and they'd exchanged only a few pleasantries before Lyn hustled her mother out and into the car, not the easiest task in the heavy rain.

By the time they reached the turnoff to Yarran, the rain had eased. Lyn was glad, though when she left the car to open the gate, she almost slipped on the gravel which was slick from the soaking it had undergone.

Jo came out to greet them, her dog Scout at her heels. She helped extricate Edith from the car and into the house, along with her walker, despite the older woman's objections that she could manage without it.

'You know you can't, Mum,' Lyn said, glancing towards Jo, who nodded sympathetically.

'Col's over at our neighbour's,' Jo explained, when Edith asked after him. 'Owen found a contact for some alpacas. Seems we're going to be adding them to our menagerie,' she said. 'They're supposed to be gentle creatures and easy to maintain. Here's hoping.'

'Sheep were always good enough for us,' Edith said. 'But we had a living to make. You're both retired, Lyn tells me. You'll be one of those hobby farmers?'

Both Lyn and Jo laughed at the derisive tone in Edith's voice, Jo replying, 'I guess you'd call us that, Mrs Carter.'

*

'Why don't you go along to the choir or come to Pilates?' Jo asked, when they were all seated around her kitchen table, Jo's old Labrador at their feet. 'You sound as if you could do with some distractions.' The three were discussing the potential sale of Edith's house and her plans to move into Eden Gardens, and the older woman was chastising Lyn for "spending all her time with me when she should be getting out and about".

'That's kind of you,' Lyn said, touched by the thoughtfulness of her old friend. 'But I don't think so. I don't expect to be here long enough to become involved in anything like that. As soon as the house sells and I see Mother settled in Eden Gardens, I'll be off on my travels.'

Seeing the look of disappointment in her mother's eyes, Lyn felt bad. She'd told her about her proposed trip. Surely Edith hadn't expected her to stay around Granite Springs? She had other things to do with her life, but maybe she could stay a bit longer.

What had she planned to do in her retirement when she returned from her travels? Lyn realised with a shock that she hadn't thought any further. She had Amy and the girls. But Maddy would soon be caught up with her uni studies and friends – she'd have her own life. And if she studied here in Granite Springs as she was suggesting, she wouldn't be close by. There was still Sophie. But she was planning to spend a couple of months on exchange in France later in the year. And Amy had intimated she couldn't wait to be a free agent again and was planning to get back into the workforce on a full-time basis.

That left Lyn with friends or becoming involved in some sort of volunteer work. For the first time, it occurred to her that she had few friends. Her work had been her life.

Glenn always told her the family came a poor second. Maybe that's why he looked for someone less driven. His new wife was certainly that. Cheryl was quick to give up her lowly admin position and devote herself to catering to his ever-growing needs when they married. These days, they lived on the Sunshine Coast where, now retired, he spent most of his time on the golf course, if Amy was to be believed.

Suddenly retirement in Brisbane appeared less attractive. Lyn changed her mind. She'd always enjoyed singing and been told she had a good voice. 'I may take up your suggestion of the choir, Jo,' she said.

Nineteen

The house seemed empty without Neil. Ken felt he was rattling around and had taken to spending more time in the office. But, even there, Neil's absence cast a pall over everything.

Judy was home, having undergone surgery – the biopsy had revealed a malignant tumour – but it would take time for her to recover. Meantime, Alec seemed to have gone to pieces. Ken didn't blame him. It must be a blow to see the woman you loved go through such a traumatic experience. And it wasn't over. There was chemotherapy treatment to follow.

When Ken visited Wooleton, it was Neil who greeted him; Neil who took charge. Ken was proud of his son, but there was still a small part of him that wished it could have been different, that it could have been him Neil was working with.

'I'm sorry, Dad,' Neil said, when they were alone on the veranda. 'But you see how it is. Uncle Alec needs me here. I know I promised to stay on till you found someone else, but…'

'It's okay,' Ken lied. 'Alec and Judy need you here. I can manage.'

'How did the interviews go? Sorry,' he repeated, 'I know I said I'd be there.'

At least the lad was still taking an interest – or pretending to.

Ken drew a hand through his hair, remembering the two young men, both professing it was their one goal in life to work with him. *Had it really been two weeks ago? He should have made it out here before now, but Judy had only come home from hospital on Friday and yesterday had been Lyn's open house.*

Ken pulled his mind back to Neil's question. 'Yeah. It was a difficult choice, neither were going to be ideal, but I ended up offering it to your old school mate. I think he has the makings of a real estate man. His construction background should help, and he'll probably be more acceptable to the farming types than a fresh-faced graduate.'

'Like I was?' Neil laughed.

'You were different.'

Ken thought back to Neil's first few days in the real estate office. He'd taken to it like a duck to water. But that was in the past. Now he was going to have to start again with a new trainee in two weeks' time.

'Ken, good of you to come.' Alec appeared behind them on the veranda, looking as if he'd aged ten years in the past two weeks. There were lines around his mouth that hadn't been there before, bags under his eyes. He was unshaven and his hair seemed to have turned grey overnight.

'Alec!' Ken drew him into an awkward hug. 'How's Judy?'

'Coping. Coping better than I am, I think. Neil's been marvellous. I don't know what we'd have done without him. You did good there.'

Ken felt a burst of pride. Whatever Neil decided to do with his life, he was his son, and Ken could take some credit for how he'd turned out.

Judy was lying back in an armchair when the three men walked into the living room. She seemed to have shrunk, but when she spoke, her voice belied her weak appearance. 'Come to see the invalid, Ken? The reports of my death have been greatly exaggerated,' she laughed, quoting her favourite Mark Twain and sounding like her old self.

'Good to see you, Judy,' Ken said, going over to give her a hug and dropping a kiss on her forehead. 'You'll be back ordering these two around in no time.' But even as he spoke, he wondered if it was true. She'd undergone major surgery and still had the chemo to contend with. How much could her body stand?

'D'you mind if I have a few words with this one?' Ken said, gesturing to Neil, after they'd all enjoyed lunch. Between them, Alec and Neil had managed to cook a roast and put together a salad, proving they wouldn't starve while Judy was out of the kitchen. 'I need to go through a few matters with him, tidy up a few loose ends.'

'Sure. You can have him for as long as you like,' Alec said.

Following Ken out to the veranda, Neil popped open a can of beer and offered one to his dad. Ken shook his head. 'Not now, son. I brought along the folders of the deals you were involved with and need to check a few things.'

'Go for it.'

It didn't take long for Neil to fill in the gaps for Ken, who was about to rise when Neil said, 'Wasn't it the open house at the Carter place yesterday? I saw that article in the Advertiser. It looked good. Pity about the rain. How did it go?'

Ken took off the glasses he'd needed to check the data in the folders, and leant his elbows on his knees. 'The rain didn't seem to stop them. We had a good few through. One particular couple seemed interested. I'll be following up with them tomorrow.'

The young couple who'd expressed most interest were new to the town. The man was newly appointed to the high school and they had three young children. It would do the house good to have a young presence there again. And it would give him another opportunity to talk with Lyn, too, he knew.

'That's good, Dad. And the lovely Ms Carter?' Neil winked.

Ken felt himself redden, as if Neil had read his thoughts. 'I'll be contacting Mrs Hudson to give her my report,' he said stiffly.

'Mrs Hudson?'

Ken hadn't heard Alec arrive behind them.

'Dad's old girlfriend,' Neil said with a grin.

'You mean Lyn Carter?' Alec asked. 'Didn't you say you were selling her mother's house for her?'

'For Mrs Carter, not Lyn,' Ken clarified.

'Same thing,' Neil said. 'I think Dad still carries a torch for her.'

Where did his son get such an antiquated expression?

Ken saw his brother raise an eyebrow.

'No,' he said hurriedly. 'Just another house sale. All that was over and done with years ago – before you were ever thought of, Neil,' he added to his son.

But Alec didn't appear to be convinced. 'From what I remember...' he began.

Neil rolled his eyes.

'...you and Lyn were always in each other's pockets, from when we were little. I tried to tag along, but you'd have none of it. Thick as thieves, they were,' he said to a now interested Neil.

'We were kids and neighbours,' Ken protested. 'You were younger. And Lyn was a bit of a tomboy back then.' His eyes glazed over remembering some of the exploits they got up to, not far from where he and Neil were sitting now.

'Not so much of a tomboy now, Dad,' Neil said with another grin. 'She's quite a looker for her age,' he told Alec.

Ken cringed. If there was one phrase that got under his skin, it was that one. Why was it the younger generation had to have a stereotype for their older counterparts? 'That's enough,' he said. 'I'll just make my goodbyes to Judy and be off.'

He made his way into the house but found Judy dozing in her chair, so quietly left again. 'Tell her goodbye and I'll call out again soon,' Ken said to his brother, giving him another hug. *Had Alec lost weight, too?* Ken thought there was less of him than there had been two weeks ago. 'Take care of yourself, little brother,' he said. 'We can't do with you getting sick, too. You need to stay strong for Judy.'

'You're right,' Alec sighed.

'Good job he has me to keep him on track,' Neil said, giving Ken a hug. 'You'll be right, too?'

'Course.' Ken felt a lump in his throat. These were the two people he was closest to, and this was where he grew up. He was just as bound to Wooleton as they were. But he was the one who had to leave.

It was as Ken was driving home, that Neil's words echoed in his mind. His son may have been joking, teasing his old dad, but many a true word was spoken in jest.

Ken had been unable to dismiss Lyn Carter's face from his subconscious ever since she walked into his office. It wasn't enough to have taken her for a drink, to meet over the sale of her mother's house. He knew he had to see her again, away from the office, away from her mother's house, away from other people. He needed to discover whether they still shared that spark, or if it was all on his side, in his imagination.

He made up his mind with a determined smile on his face. As soon as he reached home, he'd call to invite her to dinner.

Twenty

Lyn gripped her phone wishing she could take back her words. But it was too late. She'd accepted Ken's invitation to dinner; agreed to meet him at the local Italian restaurant – another new addition in her absence – on Wednesday evening. And she had no sooner hung up than she regretted it.

He'd caught her at a bad time, Lyn told herself. Otherwise she'd have had the sense to refuse. But she'd just read a text from Maddy informing her that, not only would the young girl be arriving on Thursday, but she'd be accompanied by a guy called Zac. He was the new man in her granddaughter's life and the reason for her deciding to enrol in William Farrer University.

'Who was on the phone?' Edith called through from her bedroom.

Damn! Lyn sighed. There was nothing wrong with her mother's hearing. She'd thought she was asleep. Now Lyn knew Edith wouldn't rest till she'd found out about the call. She walked into the bedroom, the phone still in her hand. 'It was Ken – Ken Thompson.'

'Ken?' Edith's eyes gleamed. 'What did he want, calling you at this time on a Sunday? Does he have a buyer, or…'

Lyn felt herself redden. 'He's asked me to dinner,' she said abruptly, hoping that would be an end to it. She should have known better.

'About time, too. I wondered when he'd get around to it. I saw the way he looked at you. He's not forgotten you. Mark my words.'

'Mum!' While exasperated by her mother's continual hints – which were becoming less subtle by the day, Lyn couldn't help wondering if she was right. 'I'm sure he only wants to discuss the sale. He did say there was one family who seemed interested.'

'Rubbish! He's not going to spend good money on dinner just to say what he could in an email or in his office. I hope you said yes.'

'I did. And there's something else. Remember I told you Maddy wants to come to uni here?'

Edith nodded, an eager smile on her face. 'She's a dear girl, wanting to spend time with an old woman.'

Lyn forbore to mention the attraction was a young man, not an old woman. 'She sent me a message to say she'll be arriving on Thursday with this friend of hers – Zac. I think she expects us to put both of them up here.' A crease appeared on Lyn's forehead as she tried to work out the implications of this. Would the two young people expect to share a room? And if so, how would her mother react?

It was a big house. There was enough space for them to have a room each, but Lyn didn't want Maddy to feel as if she had to sneak around, nor did she want her mother to be offended. It was her house. Oh, it was all too hard. This wasn't what she'd expected when she came here for her dad's funeral.

Edith seemed to have no such qualms – maybe it hadn't occurred to her to question possible sleeping arrangements. 'That's good news,' she said. 'And it'll be lovely to meet her young man. Seems she has more sense than her grandmother. Turn out the light when you leave, will you, Lynnie.' She turned over and closed her eyes.

Lyn sighed again as she made her way back to the kitchen. What had her mother meant by her final remark? Still, she was right about one thing. It would be good to see Maddy and to meet her boyfriend. They'd no doubt find it too restrictive to stay here for long, and be keen to find alternative accommodation, maybe in a group house with other students.

No sooner had Lyn settled down on the sofa with her book than her phone rang again. This time it was her daughter, Amy.

'What's this about Maddy moving to Granite Springs?' Amy asked, without any preamble. 'She's been very secretive since she got back from her trip and now she tells us she's changed her preferences; she's going to study down there at Willian Farrer; and she's going to stay with you – her and some guy she met on her travels. Were you in on this? Why didn't you tell me?' Amy seemed to run out of steam.

'Steady on, sweetheart,' Lyn said, astounded at the rage in her daughter's voice. 'I haven't deliberately kept anything from you. I had no idea Maddy was being so secretive about her plans. She did text me a couple of weeks ago to say she intended to study at the local uni here and wanted to stay with your gran and I for a bit. It never occurred to me you and Chris didn't know. But is it such a bad thing? From what I've heard there's a brand new school of music and drama at Willian Farrer, and she does intend to pursue her music, doesn't she?'

Amy started to speak again, her voice so loud that Lyn held her phone away from her ear. She seemed to be saying Chris blamed Lyn for encouraging Maddy in her decision.

Lyn refused to listen to anymore. 'Amy, you know that's not true,' she interrupted, doing her best to remain calm. 'Actually, having Maddy here is the last thing I want or need. This house is on the market. I plan to leave as soon as it's sold and your gran's settled, so why on earth would I encourage my teenage granddaughter to come to stay? Have you and Chris met Maddy's new boyfriend?'

She heard Amy groan. 'That's another thing. When we picked Maddy up at the airport, she was with this long-haired layabout. He's from Melbourne.' She said it as if it was the other end of the world. 'He was carrying a guitar, so I suppose he's another muso, but not classical like Amy.'

Lyn could imagine her daughter's disgust. When young Maddy showed an aptitude for music, Amy and Chris ensured she had the best teachers, sending her to a school which specialised in the performing arts and paying for private tuition. Their ambition for her was perhaps even greater than the young girl's own, but Maddy was very talented and had persevered with the hours of practice her chosen vocation demanded.

'She's young, Amy. Try to remember what you were like at her age.'

Lyn thought of herself at Maddy's age. Unlike her granddaughter, she'd been too timid – or scared – to give into her emotions and had fled to the seemingly safer haven of Sydney and Aunt Wyn's comforting harbourside home. But had it been any safer? In her final year at Sydney Uni, she'd met Glenn and the rest was history.

'You will keep an eye on her, Mum?' Amy asked. 'I... we'll miss her.

With Sophie off to France mid-year, I'd hoped to have Maddy around at least until she finished uni.' Her voice broke.

Lyn relented, feeling her daughter's pain. Amy had remained at home all through her university studies. It was natural for her to have expected the same of her own daughter. And it was unfair of Maddy to have sprung her decision on her parents at the last moment. But it did demonstrate a degree of independence Lyn wished she'd had at Maddy's age.

Though, were there similarities? Granted, Lyn had abandoned the boy who'd aroused her emotions, while Maddy was heading into a relationship. But both had chosen to move away from the confines of home for pastures new. Maybe they weren't so different after all.

*

Lyn had been a nervous wreck all day, though she'd tried to hide it from her mum. Now she was in her bedroom trying to decide what to wear. It shouldn't be difficult. It was only dinner with an old friend. But Lyn knew it was important to look her best. In the past, when she was about to face a difficult meeting with parents, staff or the school board, she'd known exactly how to dress for the occasion. But this was different. This was Ken. She wanted to look good but didn't want to look as if she was trying too hard.

Finally, after trying on and discarding several outfits, Lyn settled on a royal blue dress with a scoop neckline and a flowing skirt which reached to her calves. It was simple but had good lines and had cost the earth when she bought it for Christmas dinner with the family at Amy's over a year ago. Matched with her white cork wedge-heeled sandals it looked smart and feminine – at least Lyn hoped it did. She wasn't sure of anything these days. Her confidence seemed to have taken a plunge.

She twisted and turned in front of the mirror, trying to picture how she would appear to Ken, then gave up. If she delayed any longer, she'd be late. Gathering up the pile of rejected outfits still lying on the bed, Lyn returned them to the wardrobe, and walked out of the room.

'I'm off now,' she called to her mother, popping her head into Edith's room to be treated to a knowing grin.

From the outside, Pavarotti's Italian Restaurant looked surprisingly similar to one Lyn frequented in Brisbane. She loved Italian food, so it was a good choice of Ken's. Taking a deep breath, she pushed open the door.

Inside, to Lyn's surprise, the dining room was far from full. As her eyes gradually adjusted to the dim light, she spied Ken sitting on the far side of the room at a small table for two. He half-rose as he caught sight of her, and she was able to wave away the staff member who was offering to find her a table.

'Glad you could make it.' For a moment Ken hesitated as if he wasn't sure how to greet her. He looked good in the open-necked blue and white striped short-sleeved shirt. For a brief moment, Lyn almost wished she could turn back time, then common sense took over. Forty-five years had passed; they lived in different worlds; she knew almost nothing about the Ken Thompson of today, apart from the fact he was divorced, had a grown son, owned the town's biggest real estate firm. Maybe that was enough. Enough for what? Her mother would have known, been quick to offer her opinion.

'This looks nice,' she said primly, taking a seat opposite her old friend and seeing his eyes crinkle up with pleasure.

'We don't do too badly for a small country town,' he said, in the mocking manner she remembered.

Well, she'd asked for that. Did she really come across as the sort of derisive city-dweller she despised? 'I didn't mean...' she said.

'Forget it. I shouldn't be so defensive. What would you like to drink? They offer some good Australian and Italian wines, or would you prefer a beer?'

'A glass of red would be lovely.' Lyn gazed around the room to see a few groups of happy people. There was low music playing in the background and a delicious aroma of herbs and spices emanating from the kitchen each time the door swung open.

Once they'd ordered – Lyn choosing a seafood linguini and Ken the Pavarotti gnocchi which he said was their signature dish and his favourite – and two glasses were poured from a bottle of *Ciao Bella Sangiovese*, Lyn began to relax.

The meal was delicious, and Lyn enjoyed hearing how the town had evolved over the years, interested to discover Ken was now a town councillor. Who'd have thought her childhood companion would have developed into such a respected member of the community?

'We even have a university,' Ken said, when they were sharing servings of tiramisu and panna cotta.

'My granddaughter is coming to study there,' Lyn said. She paused, then continued, 'She's actually arriving tomorrow with a boy she met on a trip to the Philippines. They want to stay with Mum and me till they get settled. Her parents are furious – they blame me. But…' her forehead creased, '…I have a problem.' Lyn wondered how much to share with Ken, but he was an old friend, and a parent himself. 'I think they may expect to share a room and I'm not sure what to do. There's Mum to consider – and Amy and Chris. Maddy's parents,' she explained, seeing Ken's puzzled expression. 'Am I overthinking this?'

'Perhaps.' Ken laid down his fork and spoon. 'Maybe you should just ask them when they arrive. And I think your mother might surprise you.'

'Really?' Lyn took another spoonful of tiramisu while she considered Ken's reply. She'd always assumed her parents to be very conservative, strait-laced, out of touch with the younger generation – even her own. Growing up, she'd always been conscious of wanting their good opinion. What if she'd got it all wrong? 'Well, I suppose it can't hurt,' she said at last. 'But it is still Mum's house and she can determine how people behave in it. So, if she disapproves…'

She saw a wicked twinkle in Ken's eyes. He reached across the table to cover her hand with his. 'Trust me on this, Lynnie.'

Something inside Lyn melted at the sound of her old pet name. She felt a glow of pleasure. It had been a long time since anyone but her mother had called her that. When Edith did, it made Lyn feel like a child again, and she wanted to protest. But coming from Ken's lips, the name took on another significance entirely.

Ken must have had the same thought. 'What happened to us?' he asked, running his free hand through his hair. 'That night, the night of the school formal, we… Then you were gone. It didn't make sense. I couldn't believe it.' The blue eyes that had made her feel so confused on that long-ago night gazed into hers, and they were caught up in the bubble of their past. It was as if the rest of the room disappeared.

'Lynnie,' he urged in a voice thick with emotion, 'Can we try again?'

He couldn't be suggesting …. He was. Lyn's stomach lurched.

There hadn't been anyone since Glenn, and Lyn had missed the closeness of another human being. Would it be so wrong to give in to what she'd run from all those years ago? She wasn't a kid anymore. She knew she would be leaving again as soon as everything here was settled.

But was it fair to Ken? Did he want more than she was able to give him?

Twenty-one

Ken cursed his stupidity. He'd been too hasty. He'd rushed in where he should have taken his time. He saw the hesitation in Lyn's eyes. But the fact she hadn't removed her hand from below his gave him courage. 'Maybe we could start with dinner again. I'm not a bad cook, though I rarely bother these days. Neil and I…' He remembered Neil no longer shared his house.

'What's the matter?' Lyn asked, clearly seeing his eyes cloud over.

'Nothing…well, there is something. You met my son, Neil. He's been living with me since his wife left town – seven years ago. Now he's moved out of the house and left the office.'

Lyn's eyebrows went up. 'You had an argument?'

'Nothing like that. It's my sister-in-law. Alec's wife. She's just undergone surgery for breast cancer, and Neil's moved to Wooleton to help out.'

'Oh, I'm sorry. I remember Alec as a scrawny kid. It's difficult to imagine him with a wife and… children?'

'No children. That's why Neil…' It was good to unburden himself to Lyn, the way he always had when they were kids. 'As I think I told you, he was planning to move out there anyway, help Alec with the farm, take over when he and Judy are too old to manage. I was just beginning to get my head around it. With Judy getting sick, it's all happened a bit sooner than expected.'

'I'm so sorry, Ken. It must be hard for you. But what happened? How did Alec get Wooleton? I know how much you loved that place.'

Ken was aware Lyn had placed her free hand over his. The sensation of her slender fingers on his felt good. He knew Lyn would understand.

'Dad and me… you know how it was. Nothing was good enough for him if it wasn't done his way. Most of the time he was right and, what was worse, he knew it. Well, I came home from Ag College full of ideas of how we could improve Wooleton, bring in more profits. Everyone was going through a bad time. It would have helped us.'

'And, let me guess, your old man would have none of it?'

'Right.' Ken removed his hand and refilled their glasses before continuing. 'The joke is, now Neil and Alec are planning to do exactly what I suggested to Dad – combine sheep and cattle.'

'That must hurt.'

Ken saw the sympathy in Lyn's eyes. She always had understood him. 'Not as much as you might think. I've built up a good business with the real estate. I discovered I have a talent for it, and I enjoy the rewards of the industry – not only the financial ones. It was good to think Neil would be there to carry on when I decide to retire.'

'What'll you do now?'

'I've found a new guy to join me. It'll take some time for him to come up to speed. In the meantime, I'll be doing the work of two. Neil will be getting married soon, too, I expect. He's putting a house up on the property and his girlfriend is moving out there with him.'

'I think I saw her at Jo's barbecue – a tall, dark-haired girl.'

'Sally. Yes. She arrived in town out of the blue a couple of years ago and turned out to be Gordon Slater's by-blow. Caused quite a stir at the time. But she's a good girl, a nurse at the Base Hospital. I suppose that'll be a help for Judy,' he added as it occurred to him.

'Anything else, sir?'

Ken looked up at the waiter's question. 'Coffee, Lyn?' he asked.

Lyn shook her head. 'No thanks. I should be getting back. We have Maddy and her Zac arriving some time tomorrow and Mum's so excited. I want to make her a hot milky drink to help her sleep. I'll probably have one with her.' He saw a familiar twinkle in her eyes. 'And to answer your question, I'd love to.'

It took Ken a moment to realise to what she was referring.

'Dinner,' she said. 'I'm curious to discover just how good a cook you are.'

'Oh!' Ken felt faintly embarrassed, but pleased she was willing to give it a go – to give him a go.

They'd driven here separately, so had to say goodbye in the car park. It was rather public for any display of affection, and Ken wasn't sure how Lyn would respond if he tried to kiss her. He was so out of practice; he'd probably make a mess of it anyway. Instead, he slung an arm around her shoulder, gave her a squeeze, then a friendly peck on the cheek.

'I'll call you,' he said, holding Lyn's car door open for her, before closing it and waving her off.

That hadn't gone too badly. It had been good to rediscover his old companion. Maybe they hadn't changed so much after all.

Twenty-two

Lyn couldn't keep the smile from her face as she drove home. Who'd have thought Ken Thompson would have proved to be such good company. And the story of how he lost Wooleton, and now his son was there… it tugged at her heartstrings. The poor man. Things hadn't been easy for him.

'Is that you, Lynnie?' Edith's voice called out from the bedroom where Lyn had left her.

Lynnie… hearing her mother say it, didn't seem so bad suddenly. Oh, to be that child again.

Lyn called back, 'Be with you in a tick.' She wanted to have a quick check in the mirror before facing her mother's interrogation about her evening. Did she look different? Would her outfit pass muster? Lyn tugged at the neckline which suddenly seemed too low for a dinner at the Italian restaurant in Granite Springs on a weekday evening. She shrugged and peered into the mirror. Surely at sixty-two, she could make up her own mind what to wear? The face that stared back at her had a glow about it and her lips turned up in delight. Sluicing it in cold water and combing her tousled hair, Lyn took another look, before deciding she'd pass her mother's scrutiny.

'How did it go?' Edith wanted to know as soon as Lyn walked in. 'I'm glad you wore that nice dress from last Christmas. The colour suits you.'

'Let me fix us a hot drink first, then I'll tell you all about it,' Lyn said, though she intended to keep some aspects of the evening to herself.

She carried the two mugs of hot chocolate into her mother's bedroom and settled in a chair by the bed, waiting for Edith to begin. But to Lyn's surprise, all her mother said was, 'Did you have a nice time?'

'I did,' Lyn replied, taking a sip of the comforting chocolate drink. 'It's a really nice restaurant and Ken was good company.'

'Your dad and I often went there,' Edith said with a smile. 'He and old Marco Pavarotti were in the Rural Fire Brigade together. It was after you left. He's long gone, of course, but his son and grandson run the place these days. What did you have to eat?'

'Seafood linguini. Ken had the house gnocchi.'

Edith nodded. 'Good choices. Your dad always ordered the gnocchi. I found it a bit heavy, but I did love the spaghetti carbonara. Maybe...' She looked at Lyn with a pleading expression.

'We could go there for a meal,' Lyn said immediately, realising this was something that would please her mother. 'Maybe with Maddy and her guy. They're arriving tomorrow, remember?'

'How could I forget that? It'll be good to have some young people around the place – brighten us up.' She gave Lyn an assessing glance. 'You look quite radiant, dear. In fact, I'd say blooming. Usually when a woman looks like that, she's pregnant.' Her mother chuckled.

Lyn knew that was exactly how she felt, and now her face was burning up even more. 'Mother!'

'Oh, don't mind silly old me,' Edith said, catching her breath. 'Ken was good then?'

Good? What kind of question was that? 'Yes, Mother, Ken was really good.'

The old woman smiled with a glint in her eye. 'Then I'm good, too. Now, I think I'm ready to go to sleep.' She drank the last of her hot chocolate and handed the mug back to Lyn.

Back in the kitchen, Lyn replayed the evening in her mind. It had gone better than she anticipated. She remembered the thrill of excitement when Ken's hand covered hers, when he said they should try again. She wasn't eighteen anymore, wasn't afraid of her emotions. But the last thing she'd expected to find in Granite Springs was the reminder of her younger self.

*

Next morning passed in a flash. Still unsure about sleeping arrangements, Lyn made up the beds in both spare rooms. Then she tidied the already immaculate kitchen and living room, and, following her mother's instructions, prepared a traditional roast leg of lamb for dinner.

Maddy had texted again to say they were on schedule to arrive sometime in the afternoon, so Lyn had popped the meat into the slow cooker, and the aroma of rosemary and garlic filled the kitchen.

After a lunch of sandwiches so as – in Edith's words – not to spoil their appetites for dinner, Lyn's mother retired to bed. 'I'm feeling okay,' she said, in response to Lyn's concern. 'I just want to make sure I'm wide awake for Maddy and her friend. Maybe you should have a rest, too. You've been rushing around all morning.'

But, while Lyn thought her mother had a point, she wasn't ready for a nap just yet. She wandered into the living room and settled down with her book, hoping to manage a couple of hours reading before the young people arrived.

She read for a bit, but the tale of Second World War espionage failed to hold her interest. She had just closed her eyes when her phone rang. Seeing the number of Granite Springs Realty, Lyn became immediately alert. This time she was in no doubt as to who was calling her. It had to be Ken.

'Hello,' she said, her stomach giving the now familiar flip anticipating the sound of his voice.

'Hello to you, too. How are you today? I hope you slept well.'

'Yes thanks. And thanks again for last night. I really enjoyed it.'

'I'm glad.' There was a smile in his voice. It was funny how you could sense that on the phone. 'But that's not why I rang. I've just had a call from the Braithwaites – they're the couple I told you about who appeared interested in the house. They'd like to do another inspection and I wondered when would suit.'

'Oh!' Lyn thought quickly. Maddy and Zac were due soon, and she had no idea what their plans were. It wasn't going to be so easy to leave the house empty when there were four of them to consider.

Ken seemed to sense her hesitation. 'There's no need to feel you have to go out. They understand you might be there. They're keen, so it would be good to set something up soon.'

'Right...' Lyn bit the inside of her cheek as she tried to work out what would be best. 'Can I call you back once my granddaughter arrives?' she asked. 'I'm hesitant to set anything up without knowing how things stand with her. It's easy to keep the place tidy with only Mum and me, but with two nineteen-year-olds...'

'I understand. I remember what it was like when Neil was that age and had friends around. Can I expect a call from you tomorrow?'

'That should work. And maybe we can arrange something for the weekend?'

'Good.'

Lyn was about to end the call when Ken spoke again.

'Talking about arranging something for the weekend. I mentioned cooking dinner for you. Would Saturday work?'

Saturday? So soon? But Lyn heard the tension in Ken's voice. *Was he as nervous about their reconnecting as she was?* She wanted to agree, but the same concerns were there. Ken guessed right away.

'Maddy, huh?'

'Yes,' Lyn sighed. 'But I'm pretty sure she doesn't need me to be here to entertain her. Can I say yes for now, then if things change...?'

'Sure thing. We'll talk tomorrow anyway, so you may be in a position to confirm then. I hope you manage to resolve your problem.'

'My...? Oh, their sleeping arrangements. I've taken your advice. I prepared two rooms and I'll let them decide.'

'Good. Very wise. Until tomorrow, then.'

Lyn hung up, unable to subdue the tremor of excitement at the thought of having dinner with Ken again. While she was reminded so much of her childhood friend, the adult Ken was a completely different person. They had both made mistakes in their choice of partners and were older and wiser, but was the spark still there? Could they find what she'd thrown away in her youth?

*

Edith made her way through to the living room just as Lyn heard the sound of a car pulling up outside.

'Did I hear your phone?' the older woman asked, curious as ever.

'It was Ken. He has someone who wants to take a second look at the house,' she said dismissively. 'But I think that's Maddy, now.' Peeking out the window, Lyn saw a disreputable multicoloured campervan bearing the slogan *Bad Kids*. Seeing the size of the vehicle which Lyn assumed the pair had been camping in on their trip down from Brisbane, her question about sleeping arrangements was answered.

A young man emerged from the driver's side and a girl from the passenger side. She was a tanned, laughing young woman with legs that seemed to go on forever. Was this girl – wearing shorter shorts than Lyn remembered ever wearing herself and a tank top featuring a rainbow and the mantra *Good Vibes* – her granddaughter? Maddy had changed in the few weeks since Christmas. She wasn't the child Lyn remembered. No wonder Amy and Chris had been concerned. But she looked happy.

Lyn hurried to the door where she was greeted by Maddy and a young man. His hair, a dirty blond colour, was tied back in a ponytail, while Maddy's long blonde curls, which looked as if they needed a good wash, too, were hanging around her bare shoulders.

'Hi, Grandma,' Maddy said, giving Lyn a hug. 'This is Zac.' She turned to the embarrassed young man standing behind her.

'Welcome, Zac. Lovely to meet you. Your great grandma is eager to see you, Maddy. She's waiting in the living room.'

The two youngsters followed her through the house.

'Come here!' Edith said as soon as she saw Maddy walk in. 'And this must be Zac.' Her eyes raked the young man as if trying to decide whether or not he was good enough for her great granddaughter. 'Hmph. So, you're going to be studying here, too?'

'He already is, GG,' Maddy said, after she gave the older woman a warm hug. 'Zac is going into his second year at William Farrer. It was him that told me about the marvellous new School of Music and Drama that's starting there this year. It should be lit.' She gazed over at her companion, her eyes filled with adoration.

Lyn felt her heart contract. If only she could have been like this when she was Maddy's age. Why had she been so uptight and worried about giving in to her emotions? Look where it had got her!

'Why don't you two bring in your things and freshen up before dinner?' Lyn asked. 'I've prepared two rooms…?' She gave them a questioning glance and saw Maddy look towards Zac with a grin. '…or would you prefer to share?' Lyn hoped Ken was right and this suggestion wouldn't upset her mother.

Maddy tipped her head to one side. 'One will do, Gran,' she said. 'We can bring in my things, but…'

'I'm heading to Melbourne tomorrow,' Zac said. 'I need to catch up with my folks before semester starts, drop off the camper, and pick up my own car. I'll be back up in a week in time to find accommodation.'

Maddy and Zac headed out, his hand possessively around her shoulder.

'Well!' Lyn said, too surprised to say more.

'He seems a nice enough young man,' Edith said. 'And Maddy's obviously smitten. She has none of the inhibitions you had at that age. Maybe if…'

'Mum!' Lyn said, warningly. Sometimes her mother surprised her.

But Edith hadn't finished. 'Sometimes you remind me of Wyn,' she said. 'Like you, she kept everything bottled up. Reserved we called it in those days. It was a pity you chose her to run to when things threatened to get too much for you with young Ken. Al and I were afraid you'd end up like her. The poor soul has never known the love of a man. When you told us about Glenn, we were glad. Pity it ended the way it did. But maybe now you have a second chance.'

Lyn stared at her mother in amazement. Where had all that come from? Her parents had been worried she'd turn out like her Aunt Wyn, the woman she admired and wanted to emulate when she was eighteen? To Lyn, Wyn had been an elegant, independent, intelligent woman – the complete opposite of her mother who always appeared worn down by the daily routine of the farm and the demands of her husband. In comparison, to the young Lyn, Wyn's life held an element of glamour.

'Where shall we put these?' Maddy burst in carrying a rucksack, two enormous bags, and a large stuffed Pooh Bear. She laughed at Lyn's astonished expression. 'Mum thought I was mad, too. But I couldn't leave Pooh Bear at home. He'd have been sooo lonely.'

Suddenly Lyn relaxed and found herself grinning. Maddy might have a boyfriend, might be in the throes of first love, but at heart she was still a child – the child who had begged her grandmother to buy her this toy for her sixth birthday and who'd slept with him ever since.

'Take them into the room you shared with Sophie at Christmas,' Lyn said. 'Dinner will be at five. Your great grandmother likes to eat early.'

'Cool,' Zac said. 'I'm starved and something smells good.' He took one of the bags from Maddy and started to whistle as he followed her through to the bedroom.

'They'll be fine,' Edith said, as Lyn gazed after them. 'That one has her head screwed on the right way. Though I expect it was a blow to her parents when she decided to study in Granite Springs.'

'You're right. Amy thinks it's my fault. She, more than Chris I think, had counted on having Maddy at home until she finished her degree at least.'

'Well, Al and I knew what that was like when you took off for Sydney. It left a gap in our lives which we never managed to fill.'

'Oh, Mum!' Lyn felt a thickness in her throat. She had trouble meeting her mother's eyes. 'I didn't know.' It had never occurred to the younger Lyn, so intent on leading her own life, on putting Granite Springs and all it stood for behind her, what her departure would do to her parents. Now she realised how much she'd meant to them, how her leaving must have hurt them. 'I'm sorry. It never occurred to me to consider your feelings.'

'The young never do, and we didn't blame you for wanting more excitement than this town could offer, though we'd hoped…. But…' Edith's face brightened, '…you're here now, and so's Maddy. So, I intend to make the best of what life has to offer. Now, did I hear something about dinner? That lamb should be falling off the bone by now.'

Dinner went well. Maddy and Zac had lots of stories to tell of their travels and it was obvious Maddy was excited at the prospect of studying at William Farrer. 'The new head of school has a fantastic reputation,' she enthused, as she dug into the Mars Bar cheesecake Lyn had made from a recipe she found online. 'This is yummy, Gran.'

'I thought you'd like it.' Lyn was pleased her effort to satisfy her granddaughter's penchant for chocolate was a success. 'This head of school – how do you know about him?' Lyn asked.

'Oh, Mum actually remembered hearing about him years ago. He was in a band and was really chill. He was in Sydney before he came here. Dr Owen Larsen.'

'Doesn't ring a bell,' Lyn said. 'But I don't move in those circles. Well, I hope it all lives up to your expectations.'

'It will.'

Maddy gave Zac one of her adoring glances, leaving Lyn unsure whether Maddy was referring to the university or her companion. She hoped the girl didn't allow herself to be distracted from her studies by the thrill of being in love. She'd worked so hard to make this her career. It would be a tragedy to see it go up in flames on the altar of youthful passion.

But as she looked across the table at the two young people, so obviously in love, Lyn couldn't still a tinge of regret. Had she ever been so caught up in passion like that? Her feelings for Glenn had been strong, but not strong enough to take over her life. She loved her parents, her children and grandchildren, but that was a different sort of love. Lyn knew that, all her life, she'd shied away from any sort of all-encompassing emotions.

Had that been a mistake?

Was it too late to change?

Twenty-three

Ken hummed to himself as he prepared for dinner. He wanted it to be perfect, to prove to Lyn he wasn't a sad old has-been, and could serve up a gourmet meal. He'd taken out the old Margaret Fulton Cookbook his mother presented him with when he moved into town. He'd always suspected she disagreed with his father's decision, but was too much of the conventional country wife to voice any objection. She'd made do with helping Ken set up his new home, and the cookbook was one of her gifts. He'd enjoyed learning to cook and trying out new recipes, even though he rarely put his skills to use these days, preferring to snack or eat out.

Over the years, he'd added to his collection of cookbooks – much to Sheila's disgust. Now Margaret Fulton's famous tome sat alongside books by Jamie Oliver, Bill Granger, Peter Howard and, of course, Nigella Lawson. But, for a special occasion like this one, where he wanted to impress Lyn with an old favourite, it was to *his* old favourite he turned, and the food spattered page which held the recipe for the Vitello Tonnato.

Ken had sourced the veal from his local butcher earlier in the week and cooked it the night before. Now it sat chilling in the refrigerator. All he had to do was slice the veal thinly, arrange it on a platter with a little of the sauce, put it back in the fridge to chill again, and prepare the salad. He hoped Lyn would be impressed.

He'd taken the Braithwaites to have another view of the house the previous weekend and they were still interested but waiting for a building report and bank valuation. Lyn had confirmed his dinner invitation but delayed it a week to give her time to… what – pluck up courage? Was she as unsure about reigniting their friendship as he was, or was she just being polite to an old friend?

It seemed her granddaughter's boyfriend had gone to see his parents and, after a week spent in orientation at the university, the girl was happy to keep her great grandmother company, while the older woman was delighted with the arrangement. Ken almost laughed out loud when Lyn implied her mother still had hopes of her and Ken reconnecting on a more permanent basis. Lyn had made it seem like a joke, but Ken wasn't so sure. Edith Carter was a wily woman as he'd discovered over the years, and he knew how the Carters and his parents had been determined to make a match between the two of them. He could well believe Edith hadn't given up hope, even though there were no properties to combine this time around.

Everything ready, Ken checked the table he'd set on the patio before going upstairs to change. He selected a pale blue shirt from the closet and pulled on his dress jeans. Then he slid his feet into a pair of sandals, and brushed his hair. Almost completely white now, he realised with a sigh. Where had the young man with thick blond hair gone to? He saw him every time he looked at his son, but the face in the mirror was becoming more and more like a stranger. Would Lyn think he showed his age more than she did? They were both the same age, give or take a few months, so there was no hiding the years from each other, yet Lyn… she looked beautiful.

Downstairs again, he put on some music – an old album from their youth. Then, cringing after realising that might be too obvious, he changed it to one with more contemporary tracks. Taking a bottle of *Moondah Brook Verdelho* from the fridge, Ken poured himself a glass. It was a wine he'd developed a taste for after discovering it a few years ago. He was about to take a sip when the doorbell rang. He took a deep breath and went to answer it.

Lyn looked amazing. She was wearing one of those off-the-shoulder dresses which showed off her smooth, tanned skin. She stood there holding out a bottle of wine in one hand, the setting sun behind her forming a halo around her blonde hair. Ken was aware of his heart beating faster.

'Hi, Lyn,' he greeted her, hoping he didn't sound as nervous as he felt. It was as if he was eighteen again.

'I didn't know what you were cooking so I brought this.' She held up a bottle, identical to the one sitting on his kitchen bench.

'Great minds,' he said, holding up his hand with the glass which he hadn't taken time to put down. 'Come on in and I'll pour you a glass, too.'

As Lyn followed him through the hallway, past the living and dining rooms, Ken saw her glance around curiously.

'Lived here long?' she asked, as he ushered her into the kitchen and indicated she should take a seat on one of the barstools at the kitchen bench while he retrieved the wine from the fridge.

'Long as I can remember. I bought it when I got kicked out of Wooleton and have lived here ever since. Never seen any reason to move.' Though Ken had given it some thought more recently. Now he was alone again, with little chance of his circumstances changing in the near future, he had been considering downsizing. But he shuddered at the thought of going through a move and the whole process of starting again in a new place. It was easier to stick with what he knew.

'It's a nice place – spacious.'

Ken tried to see his home through Lyn's eyes. Over the years he and Sheila, then Ken by himself, had made a few changes, renovating to modernise the old seventies two-storey brick house that had proved to be a good family home. He poured Lyn's wine as he contemplated the now ten-year-old kitchen with its breakfast nook, large walk-in pantry and central cooktop. To his eyes it was nothing special, but it was home.

'I'm accustomed to living in an apartment which would probably fit into a quarter of this place,' she said with a laugh. 'And Mum's place is so old-fashioned.'

'I like it,' he said, 'though now Neil's gone, I'm not sure…' He gazed around the familiar setting. It would be hard to let it go. 'What'll you do when your mum's house sells?' he asked, to take the focus off him.

'I'll take up where I left off,' Lyn said. 'Before Dad died, I had plans to travel.'

But Ken detected a hesitation in her voice.

She was silent for a few seconds, twisting the glass in her hands.

'But I want to make sure Mum's all right first. I hate the idea of her going into a nursing home. It's her decision, but...'

'But?' Ken prompted.

'It's so hard.' Lyn took a gulp of wine, then put her glass down again, her fingers tracing invisible patterns on the surface of the benchtop. 'She doesn't want to be dependent on me, but I'm all she has left – me and Amy and the girls. And now Maddy has decided to study here. Half my family is in Granite Springs.' She spread her hands and gave a rueful grin.

'You're thinking of changing your mind?' Ken felt a leap of hope at the prospect of Lyn choosing to spend more time here.

'Not exactly. Oh, I don't know what I'm thinking, Ken. My mind veers from one thing to another. Right now, I just want to see the house sold and Mum settled somewhere – and it looks as if that's going to be Eden Gardens. Then there's Maddy.' She sighed.

'What's her fellow like?'

'Long-haired, though quite polite. He no doubt comes from a good family. I suppose they're all like that these days – students, I mean. He's studying to be a teacher, so he'll have to smarten himself up at some stage.'

'Wait till uni starts and you'll soon see,' Ken laughed. 'The main street will be full of long-haired students. They keep the shops and pubs in business. And I don't do too badly out of them, either. There are quite a number of rentals on our books which cater to students.'

'I suppose I should send Maddy and Zac your way, then,' she said, smiling. 'I expect they'll be house-hunting as soon as Zac gets back.'

'Not staying with you, then?'

'I think our company would soon pall. Though it's nice for Mum to have young company.'

'You too?'

Lyn nodded and picked up her glass again. 'Maddy's a great girl, and talented. She's going to be studying music. She's excited about the new school at William Farrer – someone called...' she thought for a moment, '...Larsen is heading it?'

'Owen Larsen. That's right. He's a good guy, if a little unconventional.' Ken chuckled. 'I think he was a bit of a shock to some people when he first arrived, and put a few noses out of joint, one in particular. Hopefully it'll all settle down once semester starts out there.'

Ken could see Lyn was curious, but he'd said enough. He wasn't one to gossip. If Lyn stuck around she'd soon find things out for herself. 'For what it's worth, I think she's come to the right place.'

'Her parents don't think so.'

'Parents don't know everything. I guess we were both a disappointment to our parents, too.'

'Hmm.'

Lyn shifted uneasily on her stool. Conscious he may have touched on a sore point, he asked, 'Ready for something to eat? It's a cold meal, so already prepared. I thought we could eat outside on the patio since it's a tad cooler tonight.'

Ken thought Lyn seemed relieved at the change in subject.

'Lovely,' she said.

'Let me give you a top up and maybe you could take the bottle while I bring out the food.'

'Can I do anything else to help?'

'No, all done.'

To Ken's delight, the meal was a success, Lyn even asking for the recipe. She seemed to relax after a few glasses of wine, and it was almost as if they were young again and the intervening years had never happened. But they had, and he knew they couldn't go back to the carefree friendship they'd enjoyed as children. But maybe, just maybe, they could forge another relationship, one more befitting their age and experience?

'Can we do this again?' he asked as they stood in the doorway, Lyn ready to leave. 'I enjoyed the company. It's been a long time.' Ken wasn't sure whether he was talking about Lyn and him, or his lack of female companionship.

'For me, too,' she replied with a smile. 'When I came back to Granite Springs, I never thought…'

Did she mean what he thought she meant? Was she talking about meeting him again? Deciding faint heart never won fair lady, Ken gently placed his hands on Lyn's shoulders and encouraged she didn't immediately move away, he kissed her.

Twenty-four

Lyn was glad to find the house in darkness when she returned home. She didn't think she could have borne her mother's questions, her hints, her hopes. Ken Thompson had kissed her! Finally, after all those years, she'd discovered what it was like to have his lips on hers, and she was still reeling from the experience.

Letting herself in quietly, Lyn tiptoed to the kitchen where she dropped onto a chair and gazed into space. The kiss had been unexpected. The evening had gone better than she'd anticipated. Ken had turned out to be a good cook, the cold veal dish with tuna sauce was new to her, and the discovery they'd both chosen the same wine got the evening off to a good start.

But it wasn't only the food and wine. Ken had been good company. If she'd been meeting him for the first time, Lyn would have been impressed. He was well-read, considerate – someone any woman would enjoy spending time with. And he was good-looking, too. The athletic eighteen-year-old had matured into a strong and attractive older man. Who was she kidding? Ken Thompson was sexy.

'Grandma?'

Startled, Lyn turned quickly to see Maddy standing in the doorway. She was barefoot and wearing an oversized grey tee shirt barely covering her, no doubt one belonging to Zac.

'I couldn't sleep, and I thought I heard you come in,' she said. 'GG said you were having dinner with an old boyfriend. Did you have a nice time?'

'I did. Did GG get to bed all right?'

'Yes. She wouldn't let me help her, but I followed her to make sure she was good. And Mum rang.' She sighed.

Lyn's heart went out to her. 'Did she give you a hard time?' She opened her arms and Maddy ran into them, just like she had as a little girl.

'Oh, Grandma. She sounded upset. I feel so guilty. It was okay when Zac was with me; it was easy to decide to change to William Farrer, and I love the campus. I even met Prof Larsen at the orientation this week. He's amazing! But what if Mum and Dad stay mad at me? There's Zac and…'

'There, there, honey.' Lyn patted Maddy's head. She remembered what it felt like to move away from home. Even if Maddy seemed more mature than Lyn had been at that age, it was still a big step. 'Let me tell you a story.'

Lyn recounted her own eighteen-year-old experience, stroking Maddy's hair all the time, while her granddaughter looked up into her eyes.

'And the man you had dinner with tonight is that boy?' she asked. 'That's so romantic! But what's it got to do with me and Mum?'

'Probably nothing,' Lyn said, allowing the young girl to sit up again. But she remembered her conversation with Ken and continued, 'I just want you to realise that, in order to grow, we may disappoint those who love us. It doesn't mean we love them any less. But you should appreciate there's no need to feel guilty if you want to make your own decisions about your life. Sometimes you may regret those decisions, but that doesn't make them any less important. It's part of growing up. And I'm proud of you.' She gave her granddaughter a hug. 'Now, I'm going to bed. Do you think you can get back to sleep again?'

'I think so.' Maddy yawned. 'Thanks, Gran. Does Mum know – about what you said?'

'No, honey. There was never any need to tell your mum my story. She never gave me a moment of worry. She always…'

'Did the right thing,' Maddy guessed. 'Not like us.' She gave a giggle and stretched up to kiss Lyn on the cheek. 'Thanks, Grandma,' she said, before disappearing.

Lyn sighed as she turned off the light and made her way into the bedroom, pausing en route to check on her mother, who was sleeping soundly. Shutting the door behind her, she closed her eyes to see Ken's face fresh in her mind. How could she dish out advice to Maddy, when she was so confused about her own life, her own feelings? It may not have been wise to spend the evening with Ken, but she didn't regret it. Her only regret was for the young girl who'd been too afraid to acknowledge her feelings and fled.

But was she really any wiser now? She still intended to leave town. What was she doing becoming attached to Ken Thompson, only to let him down again?

*

Two days had passed since her dinner with Ken, and Lyn was beginning to think she'd imagined the rapport they'd found. She'd managed to evade the majority of her mother's questions about the two of them, instead focusing on the style of his house and the meal he'd cooked.

It hadn't been so easy to fool Maddy, as her occasional sidelong glances and knowing grins testified. But the young girl had matters of her own to concern her now. Zac was due back from Melbourne, and Maddy was gearing up for the beginning of her first semester at uni.

'When does your young man get back?' Edith asked, as the three women sat together at breakfast.

'Today!' Maddy glowed with excitement. 'And we can start looking out for somewhere to live. There were several offers of accommodation on the notice board in the Mad House, but I thought I should wait till Zac gets here.'

'The Mad House?' Lyn asked, amused.

'That's what the students are calling the School of Music and Drama – cute don't you think?'

'What does your professor think of it?'

'I think he likes it. That's the sort of person he is. I'm really going to enjoy studying with him.'

Glad Maddy seemed to have recovered from her guilt feeling of the other night, Lyn asked, 'Have you spoken to your mum again?'

Maddy's face clouded over. 'Not yet. I don't…'

'Don't allow your feelings of guilt to get to you,' Lyn advised, having learned this to her own shame. 'It's important that you keep in touch, even more now you're becoming more independent of your parents. They are still supporting you.'

Maddy's cheeks burned. She dropped her head to her chest, then lifted her chin and met Lyn's eyes. 'I plan to find a job, just as soon as we have somewhere to live. I won't be a burden to my parents.'

'That's all well and good,' Edith said, surprising them by joining in the conversation. 'Your mum and dad won't stop worrying about you just because you're no longer a drain on their purse. In fact, it may cause them to worry all the more. Children are never a burden to their parents – they're a blessing, regardless how much they try to disregard them.' She sent a pointed look towards Lyn.

This time, it was Lyn's turn to redden. She knew she'd left without giving a thought to the worry she must have caused her parents.

Maddy appeared suitably chastened. 'Okay,' she said, 'I'll call Mum. Grandma, do you think your friend has rentals for students? If we're too late for the ones I've seen, we'll need to look elsewhere.'

'Yes, he mentioned that on Saturday.'

'And those people who came around last week. Is Ken still waiting to hear from them?' Edith asked. 'They seemed keen.'

'They're still collecting information,' Lyn said.

'And have we heard anything from Eden Gardens?' Edith plucked nervously at the edge of her shirt.

'Not yet.' Lyn reminded herself to contact them. She didn't want her mother to worry but, now they had a potential buyer in the offing, it was time to think of the future – her mother's future and her own. 'I'll call them today,' she said, to allay her mother's fears. 'We can always delay settlement till you're ready to move.' Lyn saw her mother tremble. Even though the sale and move had been all her idea, it was now obvious to Lyn that the older woman might not be completely happy with her decision.

The afternoon passed in a whirl of activity. Zac returned, his old bomb of a car overflowing with his belongings. Then he and Maddy left to check on their timetables on campus and to catch up with some of Zac's mates.

While her mother was having an afternoon nap, Lyn remembered to call Eden Gardens only to discover that while Edith's name had progressed up the queue, she was still on the waiting list. There was no call or message from Ken, and Lyn didn't want to call about the house sale lest she seem too needy. *Where did that come from? She'd never felt needy in her life.*

By the time the young couple returned, dinner was ready and, at Edith's urging, they sat down to a game of Scrabble afterwards, Edith enjoying showing off her prowess to the youngsters while Lyn looked on.

*

Lyn awakened next morning to the sound of the front door closing and a car driving off. Rising hurriedly, she drew on a towelling robe and headed to the kitchen. Maddy was sitting there, her head on her arms, sobbing uncontrollably.

'What's the matter?' Lyn sat down in the adjoining chair and reached an arm around her granddaughter's shoulders.

'Oh, Grandma,' Maddy sobbed, turning her face into Lyn's chest. 'It's Zac. He says…' she hiccupped, '…he's going to share with some mates. They've found a house out near the uni and… He says we'll still see each other and nothing's changed. But it won't be the same. I thought…'

Lyn leant her chin on Maddy's head. To think that in a moment of madness she'd imagined she envied the young couple, their love, their certainty. 'It may be for the best,' she said, knowing those were not the words Maddy wanted to hear.

'We've been living together ever since… He's the reason I came to Granite Springs. Now it's all spoiled. I don't know what to do.' She broke into heartrending sobs.

'What's all this?' Edith pushed her walker into the room. 'Is someone dead?'

Lyn stifled a smile. Trust her mother to put things into perspective. She allowed Maddy to answer.

'No, GG. It's Zac.'

'Where is the young fellow? I promised him a repeat game of Scrabble today.'

'He's gone!'

'Gone? You've broken up?'

'Not exactly, Mum.' Lyn thought it time to provide an explanation since Maddy clearly wasn't in the frame of mind to do so. 'He told Maddy he's already found somewhere to live – with a group of his mates.'

'That's all? You can stay here as long as…' Edith's voice trailed off as she no doubt remembered the house was about to be sold. 'Well, I'm sure you can find a nice group of girls to share with, and you can stay here until you do.'

'I suppose.' Maddy knuckled her now red eyes. 'He wants to pick me up later to go out to the campus.'

'Well, it's not the end of the world then, is it? Now, how about we have breakfast and you can tell us about those homes you saw on the board in that school of yours. Then, why don't you play something for us. You've been here over a week and I haven't seen you take out your flute once. Shouldn't you be practicing every day?'

Maddy brightened at once. 'Oh, yes, GG. I usually play every day. I even took Flavia – that's what I call her, my flute – to the Philippines. That's when Zac told me about the new school here.'

'Well, then. Why don't you fetch Flavia now?' Edith asked, giving Lyn a wink.

After half an hour with her beloved flute, Maddy seemed to regain her equilibrium and went off to get ready for Zac's return.

'They're so volatile at that age,' Edith said to Lyn. 'You were just the same. But you took it to extremes, didn't you? I don't know what happened between you and that boy…' she held up her hands, '…and I don't want to know. I only know it must have been something to make you leave in such a rush.'

Lyn couldn't meet her mother's eyes. What could she do to compensate for the silly behaviour of her younger self? 'I'm sorry, Mum. What can I say? Is there anything I can do to make up for my foolishness? I realise now how I overreacted. It was nothing. I guess at that age everything takes on monumental proportions. Aunt Wyn was good to me, and I enjoyed my time in Sydney. But I'm sorry I didn't come home more often. That was cruel of me. I wasn't aware how much I hurt you and Dad. I promise I'll visit more often from now on.'

And she would, Lyn vowed to herself. She'd come back to Granite Springs after her trip, book into a hotel for a couple of weeks, then schedule a visit every month. It wouldn't ease the guilt she felt at having neglected her parents for so long, but it was the best she could do.

'What do you think?' Maddy swept into the room and twirled to show off her outfit. She was wearing a white tee shirt under a pair of pink denim dungaree shorts. On her feet were a pair of gladiator sandals. Her hair was tied into a bun on top of her head.

'Very nice,' Edith approved.

'You look stunning, Maddy,' Lyn said.

'Eat your heart out, Zac Pender,' Maddy said as they heard his car return.

Oh, Lyn thought, *the resilience of youth.*

Twenty-five

There was a lightness in Ken's step as he entered the office on Monday morning. The kiss with Lyn on Saturday was enough in itself to put a spring in his step. She hadn't drawn away as he fully expected her to do. Instead, although he was out of practice, she seemed to enjoy it, may even have leant into him slightly. It was a good start, something to build on. But that wasn't the only thing affecting his mood.

He'd spent yesterday out at the farm. Judy seemed to be recovering well from the surgery. She'd be starting the chemo soon, and Alec was a bit worried as to how that would affect her – he'd heard stories of people becoming very sick after treatment. But Judy was optimistic. 'It's all to help me get well,' she told Ken. 'I'm willing to put up with anything for that.'

Ken admired her fortitude. She seemed to be coping with her illness better than Alec was. Maybe it was harder on the nearest and dearest.

Leaving Judy inside, Ken walked around the property with Alec and Neil, talking about their plans and what needed to be done. It was all very familiar to Ken. He offered to help out if needed, if Alec was caught up with Judy, and Neil needed a hand. It was good to be back there. Ken had a bond with the land he'd grown up on, and that had never left him.

His new employee, Ewan Prentice, was due to start today. It would no doubt take a few days to show him the ropes but would ease the burden he'd been carrying since Neil left. It had been a busy two weeks, maybe the busiest of the year. There had been a few sales, and the

Carter property looked as if it would go soon too. Ken wondered what Lyn would do then. She'd intimated her plans to leave, to continue on the trip she'd had to put on hold. But Ken thought he'd detected signs she regretted her decision, wanted to spend more time with her mother. He hoped she might want to spend more time with him, too.

His mind was still on Lyn, Wooleton, and his weekend, when Cathy knocked on his office door.

'There's a young man here – Ewan Prentice. He says he's the replacement for Neil. Do you want to see him?'

Ken pulled his thoughts back to his business. That was what he needed to concentrate on. 'Sure. Send him in.'

Time passed quickly as Ken filled Ewan in on their processes. It seemed he'd made a good choice. The young man appeared to pick things up quickly and showed he had the ability to think on his feet. Ken gave him a couple of matters to follow up on by phone and arranged for Ewan to join him on an inspection later in the day. Then he headed out to The Bean Sprout for his morning coffee.

'Your usual?' Frank asked, greeting Ken with a smile. 'And Marie has been baking white strawberry muffins this morning, or would you like something more substantial?'

Hearing Frank mention muffins made Ken realise he hadn't eaten since breakfast, which had been his customary slice of toast with vegemite. His stomach rumbled as he replied, 'A muffin sounds good. Marie not here this morning?'

'She had shopping to do,' Frank replied, 'and it's a slow morning. She'll be back for the lunch trade.'

'Thanks,' Ken said, when Frank delivered his large black coffee along with the delicious looking muffin. As he bit into the sweet confection and took a mouthful of coffee, Ken glanced across to where Frank was checking some paperwork. He wondered what had happened to these two. The Bean Sprout was a family business. Frank's family had owned it for several generations, and Marie had joined when she and Frank married, some years after he and Sheila. They'd never been close friends, bumping into each other at the usual community events: the picnic races, the midyear ball, the annual show day – back when Ken attended such gatherings. He hadn't bothered for years.

Frank and Marie had seemed to be a happy couple, always together

– until suddenly they weren't. They still ran the café together, but Ken knew Frank had moved out of the family home to live above the café. They hadn't made a song and dance about it. Ken only knew because, at the time, they'd asked him to value the house. He'd thought they were going to sell, but nothing had come of it. Ken guessed most of the town didn't even know the couple had broken up, unlike his own divorce which had almost been front-page news.

'Tell Marie she hasn't lost her touch. The muffin tasted as delicious as it looked,' Ken told Frank as he was walking to the door.

'She'll be sorry to have missed you,' Frank said, wiping down the countertop. 'She always says she can set the clock by your arrival.'

Was he so predictable? Ken guessed he was. His stomach asked for food around this time each morning and it broke up his day. Then, a terrible idea occurred to him. Marie didn't… She couldn't… She was at least ten years his junior. There was no way she could be interested in him as anything but a good and regular customer. But had there been something in Frank's tone? Ken shrugged off the thought. There were plenty of men in town more eligible than he was. And it was well known he'd never looked at another woman since Sheila left.

Until now.

'Mr Thompson,' Ewan greeted him as soon as he walked in.

'Call me Ken, please. Come in.' Ken led the way into his office and took his seat behind the desk. 'How did your calls go?'

'I got a mixed response.'

Ken frowned, puzzled. 'How so?'

'The first call went well. As you anticipated the Braithwaites are ready to put in an offer on the Carter house. They just have a few matters to sort out. I suggested they talk with you.' Ewan looked at Ken for confirmation.

Ken nodded. 'The other two?' He'd also asked Ewan to follow up on a couple of homes he'd inspected recently and hadn't heard back from.

'It was odd, but both gave me the same spiel – that they were offered a better deal and were still considering what to do. Have you heard of DNS?'

Ken had a vague memory of seeing signs with an unusual logo a few weeks earlier – were they For Sale notices? He tried to remember. 'I've seen a logo. What do you know about them?'

'I only came across them myself by accident. I think they're an offshoot of another company. They appear to be buying up land. I had no idea they were into real estate – houses.'

'Houses sit on land,' Ken said tersely. He should have paid more attention to those first notices he saw. 'I'll check them out.' He dragged a hand through his hair. One more thing on his already full agenda.

Ewan seemed to hesitate. 'Would you like me to, Mr... Ken? I can ask some of my old mates in construction. They might have heard something.'

'Would you? That would be a big help.'

'No problem.'

Ken watched the young man leave his office, go to his desk and pick up the phone. He leant his elbows on the desk, steepled his fingers and nodded to himself. This one would do well. It might take him a few weeks to get into the swing of things, but he'd been the right choice.

*

It had been a busy day. Ken couldn't face cooking dinner and the prospect of yet another takeaway wasn't inviting. He decided to spoil himself and have dinner at The Riverside restaurant. It was the best eatery in town.

It was a glorious evening, a light breeze ruffling the branches of the trees, the heat of the day beginning to disperse. As he walked across town, Ken reflected on how quickly things could change. In only a few months his own life had been turned around – Neil's decision, Judy's illness and, most importantly, Lyn's return. He wasn't sure what the future would hold, but he intended to face it with all the optimism he could muster.

As he'd anticipated, the restaurant was quiet this early in the week. Ken chose a table on the far side of the room, close to the window overlooking the river. He was gazing out into the growing darkness when a familiar voice broke through his thoughts. Looking up, he saw Col Ford and his wife.

'We don't usually see you here,' Jo said with a grin. 'Mind if we join you? I didn't feel like cooking tonight and managed to persuade Col to come into town.'

'Sure,' Ken said, not really certain if he wanted company, but feeling it would be rude to refuse. It was Jo's restaurant after all, and Col was a good friend.

'So, what's been going on with you?' Jo asked, when they'd been served glasses of the *Margaret River Cabernet Merlot* Col recommended. 'We haven't seen you since our birthday bash.'

Where he and Lyn got together, Ken thought.

'You heard about Judy?' he asked.

'I did,' Jo said. 'How is she? It must be difficult for both her and Alec. She's always taken such an active role on the farm, along with all her other community activities.'

'They're coping,' Ken said, rubbing his forehead. 'But it's rough. Judy's her usual philosophical self, but I've never seen Alec so worried. He seems to have aged overnight. Neil's there full-time now, and I'm helping out where I can. I started a new guy in the office today and looks like he'll work out well.'

'That's good to hear.'

'Business been good?' Col asked. 'I remember all the contracts we used to process at this time of year.'

'So, so. I think we have a buyer for the Carter house, but a few others seem to be hanging fire.' His forehead creased remembering the difficulties young Ewan had that morning, though their afternoon inspection had brought a more positive response. 'I don't suppose you've heard of a new company... DNS?'

He saw an odd look pass between Jo and Col. 'What? You have heard of them?'

'Are you having a problem with them?' Col asked, as Jo appeared about to reply.

'Not exactly.' Ken rubbed his chin. 'But several of our potential clients seem to have been approached by them and are undecided as to who to sign with. I hadn't heard of them till a couple of weeks ago.'

'It's Danny.' Jo said. 'My son, Danny. As you know, his real estate company has always focused on the development of villas – those hideous little boxes like the one he tried to force me into.' She shuddered, and Col placed a comforting hand on her arm. 'Now, he's gone into business with another guy with the intention of buying up land for high-density housing.'

'But these are in town,' Ken said in surprise. 'I thought Danny specialised in developments and small acreages on the outskirts. We've always got along well together as our activities didn't overlap.'

'He did.' Jo sighed. 'But this new venture…'

'What Jo isn't saying,' Col interrupted, 'is that Danny seems to have thrown his lot in with a shyster who's out to rip off people who want to put their houses on the market. From what we can judge, Danny's always been honest in his dealings, but we're not too sure about his new partner. It looks as if he offers more than he's willing to provide. He pulls the wool over people's eyes. I'm afraid a few are going to get badly burnt.'

'And I dread to think what it's going to do to some of those lovely old neighbourhoods, too,' Jo said, her eyes clouding over. 'My own son!'

'Hi, Mum, Col, Ken.' Jo's other son, Rob, appeared at the table with menus. 'Good to see you all here. Would you like to see the menu, or can I recommend the beef ragout?'

'I think I know the menu off by heart,' Jo laughed, her mood lifting. 'The ragout sounds good to me.'

The men agreed, and Col refilled their glasses.

Ken was glad of the interruption. The news about Danny and this other guy disturbed him. He needed time to think it over; he needed more information. Hopefully Ewan would be able to fill him in once he'd talked to his former colleagues.

'Have you seen any more of Lyn Carter?' Jo asked, when they'd finished eating and had asked Rob to pass on their compliments to his chef on a magnificent meal.

Ken wanted to squirm. He'd hoped this wouldn't come up. He should have known better. He wouldn't be surprised if Jo had deliberately tried to throw him and Lyn together. What was it about happily married people that made them want to matchmake their single friends?

'I'm selling her mother's house,' he said, hoping that would satisfy her.

'You said. But didn't I see you leave our barbecue together? You were pretty close at school, and you're both single again.'

'Jo!' Col warned.

'I know, I know,' Jo said. 'It's none of my business, and Lyn has told me she intends to leave as soon as she has everything settled here, but it seems such a pity. You're so well suited.'

'Our parents thought so too,' Ken couldn't help saying. 'And I think Lyn's mother still has hopes, but…' he hesitated, his own hopes in that direction forcing him to eat the words he was about to utter, '…it's not so easy at our age. We're both settled in our ways, have very different lives. Mine's here, hers is in Brisbane.'

'Don't let that stop you,' Jo said, giving Col a gentle nudge. 'We're all the same age and look at us.' She gave Col an adoring glance that filled Ken with envy. What would he give to have Lyn look at him like that?

'Leave the man alone,' Col said. 'Can't you see you're embarrassing him, Jo? Not everyone is ready for a relationship.'

'We weren't either. It can just creep up on you when you least expect it. I'm serious, Ken. You probably think I'm meddling in something that's none of my business. But I'm fond of you both, and life's too short to let love pass you by. That's all I have to say.'

She'd said quite enough. Ken couldn't wait to leave. Fortunately, Rob appeared again at that moment, wanting a word with his mother. While Jo was distracted, Ken rose to take his leave.

'Sorry,' Col said. 'Jo sometimes gets carried away. I'm sure you came in here for a quiet meal, not to be harangued about your personal life. But Jo does have a point. It must be lonely for you now Neil's gone.'

'Thanks, Col, but I can take care of myself.' Ken moved away, paid his bill and walked out with a sigh of relief.

But, as he walked home, he fingered the phone in his pocket, tempted to call Lyn. Was it too soon? Should he wait till he had an offer on the house? Would she expect him to call after their dinner on Saturday? He was so out of practice at this.

Maybe he shouldn't have been so abrupt with his old friend.

Maybe Col could have offered him advice.

Twenty-six

This business with Danny Slater was bothering Ken. He knew and liked the guy. He was the son of his old friend and had grown up with Neil. Ken thought he could trust him. The news he'd hooked up with some shonky developer was a facer, make no mistake. But he decided to wait to see what Ewan managed to dig up.

He'd thought about calling Lyn several times, but kept putting it off, unsure of her feelings. Aware how unpredictable she could be – had been in the past – he didn't want to spoil what might be the start of something. So he waited, not exactly sure what he was waiting for. It would be time enough when he had a definite offer on the house.

It was mid-week before Ewan knocked on his office door.

'Got a minute?'

'Come in.' Ken put aside the contract he'd been studying. 'Take a seat.'

'It's about that company you asked me to find more about – DNS.'

'Fire away!'

'Well, I checked with some of my mates in the trade. DNS seems to stand for the initials of two people – Danny Slater and Don Sherwood. Danny is a local man. Up till now he's been marketing villas and small acreages pretty successfully, from all accounts.'

'Yeah, yeah.' Ken knew this.

'It's the other guy who's interesting.'

Ken leant forward, elbows on his desk.

'Seems Don Sherwood is an out-of-towner. He hails from Queensland where he was suspected of using the purchase of land to launder drug money. Nothing could be proven but he wasn't able to continue doing business in that state. Late last year, he turned up here. He made representation to a number of the local guys, but they'd heard of him so knew to steer clear. This is where it becomes interesting.'

Ken picked up his pen and tapped on the desk. 'So, he's a crook?'

'Unconfirmed, but that's what they're saying.'

'And how did Danny get involved?'

'That's it. I remember Danny from school though we were never mates. But I've always considered him to be straight as a die. Weren't he and Neil…?'

'Yes. I know his parents, too. It's not like him to get involved with anything shady.'

Ewan scratched his head. 'It's not easy to figure out, but the guy I spoke with seemed to think Danny was looking to expand and this Sherwood came along at the right time, spun him some yarn, and Danny was fool enough to believe him.'

'Let's get this straight. Sherwood hit town, tried to connect with local contractors and was knocked back. Then he went fishing for other fools. He heard Danny was looking for a new scheme and managed to dupe him into joining him?'

'That's about it. He's splashing money around, offering to buy up old homes on good land, hoping to make a killing by working with Danny to build high-density housing – the type of villas Danny has experience in selling. It seems Danny is a gullible partner in all this. I don't think he has any idea where the money might be coming from.'

'Thanks, Ewan.' Ken leant back. 'Is there something else?' he asked, having expected the younger man to leave.

'It's just… My contact has his ear to the ground. He knew about the line of houses on Lark Street – the ones whose owners have been cagey with us. But he'd also heard Sherwood was planning to target Opal Street. Isn't that where the Carter house is? Have the Braithwaites made their offer yet?'

Ken felt his blood boil. It was bad enough this bastard had pulled the wool over Danny Slater's eyes – though he thought the lad would have had more sense – but to set his sights on the very street where Lyn and her mother were living! If word got out, if the Braithwaites got wind of it, if he succeeded in his plan, it would lower the value of their home. Or maybe that was the idea, maybe he'd approach the Carters with an offer to purchase. Ken needed to get his thoughts straight, put together a strategy, maybe even set up a meeting with Danny, Surely the boy would listen to him?

In the meantime, it would be best if he said nothing to Lyn.

Twenty-seven

'Didn't you say you were going out, Grandma?' Maddy asked, when they were clearing away the dinner dishes.

'Choir, wasn't it?' Edith asked.

Already Lyn was regretting the impulse that had made her agree to Jo's suggestion to attend the first meeting of the year for the Granite Springs Choristers. Jo wasn't a member herself, but it seemed Kay was, and Lyn remembered Kay well. She had a vague recollection of hearing about the choir when she was in high school. Back then, the choristers bore all the hallmarks of a group of fuddy-duddies who got together to sing equally boring stuff. Now, it seemed her old school friend had become one of them.

But when Jo called to remind her of the Tuesday evening meeting, Lyn had been hard-pressed to find an excuse without being downright rude. It was kind of Jo to think of her, to want to make her feel part of the community. And she didn't have anything else to do – except sit home and wait for the phone to ring.

After seeing Ken over a week ago now, enjoying his company, and after that kiss, she'd expected some sort of follow up – a call, or even a text. Wasn't that what people did these days?

'Are you sure you'll be okay on your own?' she asked Edith, knowing Maddy was going out too. Her annoyance with Zac had been short-lived. She'd spent most of her weekend with him in what she described as "a boy's own house straight out of the movie *Frat House*". Tonight they were going to a beginning-of-semester event out at the campus, and Maddy had dressed up in a short blue dress with a deep v-neckline Lyn knew Chris and Amy would disapprove of.

'I'm not in my dotage. It'll do you good to get out more. Jo's being a good friend to you, telling you about this after the way you treated everyone here.'

'I didn't…' Lyn began, then bit her lip. Her mother was right. She'd left town without saying goodbye, without a thought for anyone but herself. 'It is good of Jo,' she said instead. 'She always was a caring person. She hasn't changed.'

'And I remember how you used to love the school choir and those end-of-year performances. There was the time they did *West Side Story* and…'

Lyn remembered. She played Maria to Ken's Tony. It had been then, when they sang *Tonight* and *One Hand, One Heart* and gazed into each other's eyes, that she felt the first stirrings of something more than a childish friendship for Ken. Sure, she knew all the girls fancied him. But, until then, he'd just been the boy next door, the one she joked around with. Suddenly, she'd felt shy with him. Then he asked her to the formal, and her parents started dropping hints – his parents too. It all became too much. She wasn't ready for any sort of commitment. She didn't want to settle down. She was afraid of her own feelings, of the emotions Ken aroused in her.

But the performance had been a good one. She could still remember the surge of joy singing gave her. Lately the only singing she did was in the shower where no one could hear. Maybe it wouldn't be bad to see what the choir was like, even to go along to a few rehearsals. As long as nothing more was expected of her, and the director, conductor, or whatever he was called, didn't mind a temporary member.

'Lyn!'

Lyn sighed. 'Yes, Mum. I remember, too. It was a good production. But that was years ago.'

'You still have the same voice. As I said, it would do you good.'

'Okay.' Lyn could see her mother wasn't going to let up. 'I'll go this once, then I'll decide.'

That seemed to satisfy Edith who nodded to herself, before pushing herself up from where she'd been sitting at the table and, holding onto the furniture and door frames for support, managed to get herself to the living room and into the armchair by the window.

'Your walker is right there, Mum,' Lyn said, worried the old woman could fall when walking unaided.

'Can I have a ride, Grandma?' Maddy asked, appearing in the doorway, her mobile in her hand and a frown forming between her eyes. 'Zac's just texted to say he's taking his housemates in his car and asking if I can find my own way. Your choir thing's on campus, isn't it?'

Lyn saw there was no way she was going to get out of going, so decided to give in gracefully. 'Give me a minute,' she said, hurrying into her room to drag a comb through her hair and renew her lipstick. She checked herself in the mirror, before deciding the white pants and blue shirt she'd been wearing all day would have to do. She didn't see any need to change just to sit and listen to a choir practice. She'd sit quietly, make sure Kay could tell Jo she was there, and perhaps manage to slip away before they finished.

'Okay, Maddy. Let's go. See you later, Mum. Don't forget to call me if you need anything.'

'I've managed perfectly well for years without you to look after me,' Edith grumbled, but she softened and smiled when Lyn gave her a kiss on the cheek.

Maddy was very quiet on the trip out to campus.

'Want to talk about it, sweetheart?' Lyn asked, after suffering the silence for around ten minutes. She suspected she knew what the matter was. It was Zac. Now their holiday was over, he'd caught up again with his old mates and Maddy was no longer his top priority. Or, being charitable, he was having trouble freeing himself from the guys and their confused idea of mateship. But, for Maddy, he was still the most important person in her life.

Maddy started to cry, her eyes reddening and her shoulders heaving. 'It's not fair, Grandma,' she sobbed, accepting a tissue Lyn took from the box she kept in the well between the seats. 'We were a couple. I came to Granite Springs because I thought…'

Lyn had heard this before, but let Maddy go on.

'Am I being silly, Grandma? Was he just telling me what he thought I wanted to hear? But he didn't need to talk about all the advantages of my coming here, did he? We were sleeping together anyway. He didn't have to do it for that.'

Lyn swallowed hard. While she didn't need to know this, she was glad Maddy felt able to confide in her, doubting she'd be able to do the same with her parents. Somewhere along the line, Lyn had become more open in her views, perhaps as a result of her years of teaching. Her daughter had gone in the other direction, following Chris's view that their daughters should be shielded from what Lyn regarded as the real world.

'No, Maddy. I don't think you're being silly. But men and boys – Zac is still a boy, in my view – are different. They like to do things with their mates, at least most of them do.' Lyn thought of one who didn't, who'd preferred her company to that of his mates on many occasions. And she'd let him slip through her fingers – or more accurately run away from him, failed to see what was staring her in the face – that he was what her mother would call "a pearl beyond price". Unlike her, Maddy would never be tortured by her emotions. But giving into them didn't always lead to happiness.

'I know it's hard to accept,' Lyn said, 'but if he's the right one for you, it'll all work out. It may be that he encouraged you to come here before he'd thought through all the implications. Then, when he met them again, his mates convinced him he was mad to tie himself down to living with you. Maybe. I can't tell what he's thinking. But it seems to me he still wants you in his life. Tonight is an example of that. I suspect he's caught between a rock and a hard place. He wants to be with you, but there are his mates making demands on him too. The poor guy probably doesn't know which way to turn and, right now, is taking the easy way out.'

Lyn stole a sideways glance at Maddy who was sitting stock still, staring out the window with her lips pressed tightly together. She continued, 'You've said you like the school here, are impressed with the professor. That's a plus, and it's thanks to Zac you're here. Make the most of it. Make new friends. Find a place to live with other girls – or stay with GG and me for a bit till things settle down. See Zac, but don't let your life revolve around him. You're both very young. You're lucky to have found each other, to be so in tune with each other, to know what you want. I certainly didn't when I was your age – and I made lots of mistakes.'

One big one, I now realise.

'If Zac really loves you, he'll stick around, but don't be too available. You need to make a life for yourself that doesn't depend on him.'

Maddy didn't answer immediately, and Lyn wondered if she'd said too much. She'd brought up her own daughter, and been with girls every day as headmistress, but had never had to counsel someone like Maddy with issues like this. Lyn didn't know whether her advice was good or not. Who was she to offer advice to a lovelorn teenager?

'Thanks, Grandma.' Maddy dabbed at her eyes with the tissue and sat up straighter, before checking herself in the mirror on the back of the sun visor and taking out her comb and lipstick. Fortunately, she hadn't been wearing heavy eye makeup or mascara, so the damage inflicted by her weeping was easily repaired. 'I'll try to do what you said. You won't tell Mum and Dad?'

Not quite sure to which part of their conversation Maddy was referring, Lyn replied, 'My lips are sealed,' emphasising her words by lifting the fingers of one hand to her lips to simulate the action of turning a key in a lock.

'Thanks, Gran,' Maddy repeated. 'We're nearly there, now. Zac said he'd drive me home afterwards.'

'There, you see?' Lyn said, wondering if there had been any need for her lengthy advice. 'Have a lovely time.'

'You, too,' Maddy said as she leapt out of the car to where Lyn could see Zac and a couple of others waiting for her, near a crowd of students outside a large hall.

Glad she was no longer that age, though age didn't necessarily bring wisdom, Lyn drove around to the smaller building where Jo had told her the Granite Springs Choristers met.

Pushing open the door, Lyn entered a large room where groups of men and women, some her age, some younger, were chatting among themselves. She looked around. Her intention was to find a corner where she could be inconspicuous while enjoying the music. She noticed Kay standing with several other women chatting quietly as they waited for the rehearsal to begin. Then, as her eyes scanned the rest of the group, Lyn caught her breath. Ken was standing there among the other tenors.

Why had it never occurred to her he would be a member of this choir? She knew he had a good voice. It was only natural that, unlike her, he'd continued to enjoy singing. Seeing him standing there, oblivious to her presence, brought back their performance in *West*

Side Story even more forcibly than earlier. What if he thought she was stalking him? He hadn't seen her yet, neither had Kay. Maybe she could leave as surreptitiously as she'd entered. Lyn was about to turn tail when…

'You're new?' A wild-haired man dressed in torn jeans and a tee-shirt, wearing an old pair of trainers on his feet and holding a sheaf of papers greeted her. Shuffling the papers into one hand, he stretched out the other to shake hers. 'Owen Larsen. I conduct this motley band. You are?'

'Lyn,' she replied, too stunned to object. 'Lyn Hudson.' So, this was the Owen Larsen, Maddy raved about. He looked nothing like the professor Lyn had imagined. And he conducted the choir, too? Well, she supposed that made sense.

'You'd be a soprano? Good. We need another.' Owen held out a score and gestured to a spot in the choir. Too stunned to object, Lyn accepted the music and followed his pointing finger. Smiling a greeting to three strangers to be met with welcoming smiles, she could see Kay with the contraltos. Kay nodded across a welcome as Owen called for silence, and the chattering ceased.

'Hi, folks,' he said. 'Most of you met me last year when I joined the choir.' He gestured to an older man seated behind him who Lyn hadn't noticed. 'You know George asked me to take over from him. I'm honoured by his trust in me. I'm sure you'll all tell me if I mess up.'

Everyone laughed except, Lyn noticed, one man standing in the bass section.

'Right. Now, I don't intend to change everything George has put together during all his years with you, but he and I put our heads together over Christmas. The result is that, this being the start of a new year with a new conductor, I thought – and George agrees – we might try something new.'

There was a low muttering from which Lyn couldn't discern whether the group agreed or disagreed – probably a bit of both, she thought.

'So,' Owen continued, 'we're going to start the new year on a lighter note than usual. I was going through the score of *West Side Story* in preparation for our first batch of students arriving. It's going to be the first production in our new school,' he explained as Lyn saw a few puzzled looks. 'It made me realise it would be a great way to start the year, to re-energise the choristers. What do you think?'

Lyn felt her stomach lurch with a mixture of alarm and excitement. It seemed fate was not only pushing her into Ken's orbit, but forcing her to relive her past.

'Complete and utter madness. That's not who we are.' The voice of the man Lyn had noticed earlier boomed out, followed by Ken's, 'Sounds good, Owen. It's always been a favourite of mine.'

There was a murmured approval.

'Good!' Owen's eyes scanned the group, as if looking for any other dissenters. 'With some help from George, I've put together a few arrangements to enable us to get in the mood. They're in the scores I handed out as you came in. We'll start together with the Jet's rumble and see how we go.'

The evening passed more quickly than Lyn expected, and she enjoyed it much more than she could have imagined. Everything else seemed to fall away as her voice joined with the others soaring in unison. When Owen laid down his baton and said, 'Thanks, everyone. That's all for tonight. See you next week,' she couldn't believe two hours had passed.

As the two strangers on either side of her introduced themselves, Lyn saw Kay looking towards her, mouthing something and pointing to the doorway. Interpreting the signal as an invitation to meet outside, Lyn nodded and started to make her way towards the door.

As she passed Owen, he stopped her. 'Sorry I put you on the spot,' he said. 'I tend to act without thinking. You did come to join the choir, didn't you?'

'Well, I…'

'Didn't expect to see you here, Lyn.'

Lyn's heart almost stopped at the sound of Ken's voice. She turned abruptly.

'You know this lady, Ken?' Owen asked.

'I certainly do,' Ken said. 'You didn't tell me you intended to join the choir.'

'You didn't tell me you were a member,' Lyn retorted. 'But I didn't really intend to join. Jo suggested I come along to watch, then…' She gestured towards Owen who had been listening to them with amusement, his eyes moving from one to the other.

'*Mea culpa*,' Owen said, with a grin. 'I do it all the time. But you will join us, won't you? They're not all as mad as I am. Really!'

'I…'

'Of course she will,' Ken answered for her. 'We'll see you next week, Owen. Thanks for tonight. Brought back some lovely memories.' He took Lyn by the elbow and steered her out of the room, ignoring her feeble attempt to protest.

Once outside, Lyn saw Kay talking with another woman she didn't recognize. Kay started to wave to her then stopped when she saw Ken, and give a knowing smile before turning back to her friend.

'I'm glad you came,' Ken said, as they moved away from the other choir members. 'I've been meaning to call you, but didn't know if it was too soon. I'm out of practice.'

'Me, too.'

They walked slowly together towards the car park without speaking then, 'It was like being back in high school, wasn't it?' Ken said, when Lyn stopped at her car and pressed the control.

'You mean?'

'*West Side Story.* Tony and Maria. You and me. You haven't forgotten?'

'No.' Lyn felt her insides melt at the memory that had been tugging at her since her mother brought it up. She hadn't expected this trip to Granite Springs to evoke so many memories. She put her hand on the car door, ready to leave.

'Do you have to go straight home?' Ken asked. 'We could drop into the Italian for a coffee or a glass of something.'

Lyn hesitated. Her mother was on her own, but would approve of her having coffee with Ken. She'd more than approve, she'd be delighted. And it wasn't late. The noise coming from the hall on the other side of campus a sign that, for the students celebrating the beginning of the university year, the evening was far from over.

Ken looked at her pleadingly.

'Okay,' she said, 'but just a quick one.'

'I'll meet you there.' Ken stood for a moment, his eyes filled with something she didn't recognise. He appeared about to say more, then nodded and went to the black SUV she remembered from before. A man's car said a lot about him, and Ken's told her he was a confident businessman, a far cry from the callow youth who'd driven her to the school formal in his dad's old ute.

They met at the door of Pavarotti's. Ken pushed it open to allow them to enter. The restaurant was busier than when they were last there.

'They offer a special pasta deal on Tuesdays,' Ken said, as the same waiter as before showed them to one of the last free tables and offered them menus.

'Coffee or… how about a glass of prosecco? And they do a wonderful ricotta cannoli.' Ken raised one eyebrow.

'Prosecco sounds lovely and…' Lyn's mouth watered at the thought of the sweet, '…cannoli, too, please.'

As Lyn sipped the ice-cold prosecco and forked up a piece of the sweet pastry, she decided this was a good idea. Although Ken's presence in the choir had been unexpected, it shouldn't have been. They'd both loved to sing and had often sung along together on their way to and from school, when their friendship was just that.

'This is delicious,' she said. 'Good idea. Do you often come here after choir practice?' As soon as she said it, Lyn realised what a clichéd phrase it was, and blushed.

'Rarely. But Neil and I used to drop in for a late-night snack before he became caught up with Sally.'

'You've been in the choir long?'

'Long as I can remember. We usually do more classical stuff and, of course, The Messiah at Christmas. But now Owen's taken over, things may be different.' He rubbed his chin. 'He seems to be stirring them up out at the uni, too.'

'He's certainly different.' Lyn leant one elbow on the table and propped her chin on her fist. 'Maddy has been raving about him. He evidently took part in their orientation and wowed all the new students with his casual attitude.'

'How is your granddaughter? Is she still living with you and your mum?'

'Yes.' Lyn sighed and took a sip of her wine. 'Things haven't exactly worked out for her as she'd hoped. But she's young and has more sense than I did at her age.'

Ken didn't immediately react. Lyn could see him weighing up what to say. She forked up another piece of cannoli.

'I always did wonder why you left,' Ken said at last. It was as if he had to prise out the words. 'During *West Side Story* I thought… Then at the formal… you looked so beautiful. It was as if we were meant to be. I wanted to take you in my arms, to tell you… But it was as if you froze. Then you were gone with no explanation.'

Hell, Lyn had been expecting this. She knew Ken deserved an explanation. But it had been forty-five years ago – a lifetime. She took a gulp from her glass before replying, an empty feeling in the pit of her stomach despite having consumed an entire cannoli.

'I was scared.' Lyn met Ken's eyes, expecting to see blame but only seeing compassion. 'I was scared of how I felt. We'd always been together, played, fought, talked, laughed. You were my best friend. Then, suddenly, it was as if you'd changed, we'd changed. It started with *West Side Story* – those duets,' she laughed nervously. She could still remember the fluttery feeling in her stomach, how Ken seemed to have morphed from her childhood playmate to someone she didn't know.

'Then my parents started to hint how it would be so good for the two properties to be combined; how we made a great couple. It all came to a head for me at the formal. I could see our future stretching ahead – my life being just like my mother's and your mother's. It wasn't what I wanted. So, I ran.' Lyn paused and took another sip of wine. 'I'm sorry. I shouldn't have gone without telling you, but I was scared you'd make me change my mind.'

'Oh, Lynnie.' Ken put his hand on hers and squeezed it. 'I thought you mustn't care for me. That I'd done something wrong. That I was unlovable. I was lost for years, till Sheila came to town and seemed to like me.'

'Oh!' Lyn was devastated she'd hurt him so much. 'I know now it was selfish of me. I was selfish to you, and my parents – to everyone. I was only thinking of myself.'

'And now?'

'Now?' Lyn was puzzled.

'How do you feel now? Are you still scared? Does living in Granite Springs still seem like a fate worse than death?'

Lyn reddened. She hadn't uttered those words, but Ken knew her so well. She may even have said them all those years ago – a throwaway line he'd remembered. She thought for a few moments. 'No. I'm glad I came back.'

'Glad we met again?'

Lyn could see how much her answer meant to him. What should she say? How did she feel? All she knew was she regretted the impulse that had resulted in her hurting so many people. Yes, she'd had a good life, a successful career. She had a lovely family, even if Amy did annoy her at times – what families didn't have their upsets? And look what had happened to her plans for travel. Though she hadn't given up on them. Then she remembered his kiss.

She nodded slowly.

'I know it was a long time ago,' Ken said. 'We can't go back. But perhaps we can recapture the essence of that spark we had back then. What do you say, Lynnie? Are you willing to give it a go?'

Was this a chance to see if what was between them could lead to anything? What was she prepared to give up this time? What was she thinking? But she was curious to see what might still be between them.

'I don't intend to stay,' Lyn warned Ken. 'But I will be coming back more often, I owe Mum that, at least. It's not fair to you if...'

'Let me be the judge of that. I've never forgotten you.'

Lyn looked down at their hands. His were strong hands, hands she could trust. He wasn't like Glenn. Yes, he'd married and divorced, but so had she. And she'd never managed to forget him either, though she'd banished his memory to the back of her mind. He was waiting for her reply.

Lyn knew what he was asking, He wasn't talking about a few dinners, the odd drink. They were too old to pretend. She took a deep breath. 'If you're willing to take the risk then so am I.'

Twenty-eight

Lyn was glad her mother was asleep when she tiptoed into the house, her shoes in one hand. She went straight into the kitchen and, without turning on the light, poured herself a glass of water and drank it down. There was enough light from the moon shining in through the kitchen window for her to see what she was doing.

Lyn dropped her shoes on the floor and sat down at the table. She needed time to think. What had she done? Did she really intend to start a relationship with Ken Thompson – to have an affair? She had no intention of making it into anything serious, so that's what it would mean. But she'd agreed. Was she having second thoughts?

She touched her lips, bruised where he'd kissed her again, and let her imagination run riot. Could they really pick up where they left off forty-five years ago? Would Ken be willing to accept what she was prepared to give – the occasional trip to Granite Springs to visit her mother? And where would it end? For end it surely must.

It was all too much for this time of night. Lyn picked up her shoes and went into her bedroom. But she couldn't sleep. She heard the grandmother clock chime, ten, eleven, twelve. Then there was the sound of a car stopping, the door opening and closing gently, footsteps and giggling, before the door of the spare room squeaked and Lyn heard voices. It seemed Maddy and Zac had made up any differences they might have had. She turned over and, finally, fell into a troubled sleep.

*

'Good morning!' A dishevelled Maddy, followed by an embarrassed Zac, came into the kitchen as Lyn and her mother were eating breakfast. 'Is there any coffee?'

'There's water in the machine,' Lyn replied, musing how unembarrassed her granddaughter was. Though why should she be otherwise? Zac and she had been sharing a room here before he went to Melbourne. They were still a couple. The only difference was that now he was no longer living here, while she was. Only? It was quite a difference. But Lyn was glad they were still together. It was good to see Maddy happy again. Why couldn't she be less uptight about her own feelings for Ken?

'I guess the party was good,' she said, when the two youngsters had made themselves coffee and toast, liberally spread with vegemite. Zac was peeling a banana.

'Great,' Maddy replied, with more enthusiasm than she'd shown for days. 'Wasn't it, Zac?' She nudged him with her elbow.

Zac put an arm around her shoulder. 'Sure was.' He swallowed the last of his toast and knocked back his coffee. 'Gotta go, babe,' he said, kissing her on the cheek, before heading to the door. An adoring Maddy followed him.

Lyn heard an indistinct conversation before the door closed, and her granddaughter came wandering back, her shoulders drooping.

'Everything okay?' Lyn asked. 'Would you like more coffee?'

'No thanks, Gran. I think I'll shower, get dressed and go out to campus. I have a class today and I need to check out a few things, too. Maybe I should find some girls to share with. I don't want you to have to…' She grimaced and waved a hand in the air, before leaving. Lyn heard the bedroom door close.

'That poor girl,' Edith said. 'He's not treating her the way he should. She deserves better. I suppose you heard them come in last night. I heard you too. You were very quiet, but I don't sleep soundly these days, not since your dad died. I can't get used to sleeping alone. I miss him so much.' A tear slowly trickled down her mother's cheek.

'Oh, Mum!' Lyn hugged her mother. She couldn't imagine what it must be like to lose your partner of over seventy years.

'And what about you, young lady? Where were you last night? I'm sure the choir didn't go on till the hour you crept in.'

Lyn sighed. She sympathised with Maddy's desire to move out, to keep her private life just that – private. Unfortunately, Lyn didn't have the same option. She was here with her mother for as long as Edith needed her.

'Ken is in the choir. We went to Pavarotti's for a drink and cannoli afterwards.'

'You did?' Edith appeared surprised. 'But I could have told you he was a member of the Granite Springs Choristers if you'd asked. Has been for years. Your dad and I enjoyed going to their production of *The Messiah* every Christmas. I hear old George has retired now, and they have a new conductor. I hope he doesn't come with too many new-fangled ideas.'

'We sang several of the melodies from *West Side Story* tonight,' Lyn said without thinking. 'The new conductor is the professor Maddy has been raving on about – Owen Larsen.'

'That's right. I knew I recognised the name. *West Side Story*? I bet that brought back some memories for you and Ken.' Edith grinned and started to hum to the tune of *Tonight, tonight.*'

'That's enough, Mum. There's no need for you to rub it in. And, before you ask, I've agreed to see Ken again. But don't get your hopes up. We have no intention of getting any more involved than that,' Lyn lied. But how could she explain to her mother that what she and Ken intended to do was to behave exactly like Maddy and her Zac, though with more sense and insight than their younger counterparts, and hopefully with better judgement. How could she tell her mother that, after chickening out forty-five years ago, she was finally considering a physical relationship with her childhood sweetheart?

Lyn's stomach turned over at the thought. She wasn't young anymore; her body was no longer that of a teenager. But neither was Ken's and, if what he said was true, he was just as out of practice at this as she was.

'You never know,' her mother said. 'Sometimes those things have a way of creeping up on you when you least expect it. But he's a good man. I don't want you to mess him around.'

Had her mother read her mind?

'No chance of that. We're being honest with each other, Mum. He knows I'm not back for good.'

'I always felt he carried a torch for you,' Edith said, ignoring Lyn's remark. 'His marriage only lasted as long as it did because of the boy. Betty Thompson told me as much before she passed. She said you were the love of his life.'

Lyn stared at her mother, shocked. Ken's mother and hers had discussed them? But they'd been great buddies, so why should she be surprised?

After Maddy left, Lyn wandered around the house, trying to decide what to do next.

'You're getting bored, aren't you?' Edith asked, when Lyn had wiped down the kitchen surface for the third time. 'Why don't you go out for a walk and fetch me some books from the library? I don't feel like going out myself this morning.'

'Is something wrong?'

'No, but I feel like a rest today. It can be tiring having a houseful of people.'

'Sorry, Mum, I hadn't thought.' Lyn was assailed with guilt again. It hadn't occurred to her how unsettling it might be to have both Lyn and Maddy here – with the occasional addition of Zac. 'Of course, I can go to the library for you. I might pick up a few for myself, too.'

Armed with a list of her mother's favourite authors, Lyn headed off to the library. On the way, her attention was drawn to something she hadn't noticed before. Along the streets leading to the library were trees which looked as if they'd been wrapped in knitted woollen bands of wool or scarves. Some were ragged and torn as if they'd been there for some time, while others appeared more recent additions. Was this some sort of student prank? Lyn was amused to imagine groups of students wrapping the street at midnight, much the way they filled fountains with soap suds back home in Brisbane.

In the library, it didn't take her long to make her selection, finding several books to suit her mother and the latest Jane Harper for herself. Being back in the country whetted her taste buds for a book set in the Australian countryside. As she left, Lyn caught sight of the café where she'd met Jo and decided to stop in for a coffee.

She hadn't expected to meet Jo there today, but to her surprise she saw her friend sitting alone in the far corner. She hesitated for a moment, lest Jo didn't want company, but when Jo looked up and waved. Lyn walked over to join her.

'Good to see you, Lyn. I was just wishing I had some company. Col dropped me off earlier. He had a few matters to take care of. I expected him back by now, but I guess he got caught up. Been to the library?'

'Yes.' Lyn took a seat opposite and ordered a pot of lemon and ginger tea. 'Mum needed more reading matter and didn't feel up to the trip this morning. Good to see you, too. Thanks for suggesting the choir to me, though I had hoped to be an observer.'

'Yes, I heard Owen did rather throw you in at the deep end, didn't he? He can be pretty impulsive. The choir was long due for a shake up and he seems to be just the one to do it. George Turnbull knew what he was doing when he asked him to take over. Owen and Fran are our neighbours and there's never a dull moment.'

'Fran?'

'Oh, you wouldn't know her. She came to Granite Springs after your time. But, you and Ken left together?' Jo let the question hang, clearly expecting some sort of explanation.

News travelled fast.

Lyn felt herself redden, wishing she didn't show her emotions so clearly. 'Yes,' she said, fiddling with her teaspoon. 'We went to Pavarotti's for a drink.'

'And?'

'We talked over old times.' She shifted uncomfortably in her seat.

Jo raised an eyebrow. 'Far be it for me to interfere. But if you need someone to talk to… I promise anything you say will go no further – not even to Col.' She chuckled.

Lyn considered Jo's words. It would be good to unburden herself. She didn't have any other women friends here to talk to – not in Brisbane either. She'd never felt the need to confide in any of the women she worked or socialised with; never been close enough to anyone to bare her soul. Jo had always been honest. Lyn remembered how, as a child, Jo had been able to keep a secret. She hadn't changed.

Lyn made a decision.

'If you're sure?'

Jo nodded.

'It's so hard. I wonder if I'm making a mistake. Ken's ready to pick up where we left off. But, Jo, it was forty-five years ago. We were different people back then. I don't know…' Lyn twisted her hands together. 'Oh, hell. I don't know why I'm telling you this.'

'Back then… it's delicate I know, but we all wondered if you and Ken…?'

'No! Sorry, that didn't come out right. But, no, we didn't. I wanted to, but the thought of what it might lead to… that's why I left.' She gazed down into her tea.

'And now?' Jo asked gently.

Lyn raised her eyes. 'The attraction is still there – for both of us. But am I being fair to him to pursue it? As you know, I plan to leave again, and I'll only be back to visit Mum from time to time. Ken deserves better. He deserves someone who's willing to be here for him.' Lyn remembered her mother's warning.

'Maybe you should let Ken be the judge of that. What does he say? I do know he's never been interested in women since his wife left – and I don't think it was much of a marriage, from what I could see.'

'That's what he says. And of course, there's Mum, who would dearly love to see us get together. I don't want to raise her hopes either. You can see what a dilemma I have.'

'Only one of your own making. None of us knows what the future will bring. Look at me and Col. Who'd have thought we'd end up together? Yet here we are. You sometimes have to take what's on offer, take a chance and see what happens. But it's your decision.'

Lyn was silent while she digested Jo's words. Maybe she wasn't being selfish to want to spend time with Ken. She picked up her cup, took a sip, and decided to change the subject. 'I saw some of the trees in the street by the library seemed to have what looked like scarves around them. What's that all about?'

'Oh, the yarn bombing, you mean.' If Jo was surprised at the sudden change of subject, she didn't show it. 'That started a few years back. A group of women in the town decided streets around here looked too drab. It was a neighbour of mine – Magda – who'd read about it. A woman in the US – she was called Magda too – came up with the idea. Our Magda wrote an article about it for the Advertiser and, before we knew it, there were trees and lampposts being decorated with knitted and crocheted yarn. It's a bit like graffiti, though gentler and less offensive.'

'How weird.'

'It is, when you first see it. But we've grown used to it and even to expect new examples to appear. There are a lot of women in town with too much time on their hands. Producing those – and seeing them – takes people's minds off the drought. But the knitting groups have evolved into more than the yarn bombing they started out as. Now they put their skills to good use by knitting for a number of charities. Last I heard they were producing singlets for premmie babies and knitted knockers for women who've suffered from breast cancer and had a mastectomy.'

'I'd like to do that,' Lyn said, thinking of Judy, Ken's sister-in-law. She'd felt so helpless when she heard about her. Despite not knowing the woman, she wished there was something she could do.

'I can put you in touch with Donna, who works in the library as the heritage coordinator. She coordinates the knitting groups, too. I'm sure she'd be delighted to have another volunteer.'

'Thanks. I'd like that. Time is hanging heavy on my hands right now. There's only so much help Mum will allow and so many hours I can spend reading. The house is easy to keep, and Maddy is out all day and most evenings, though…'

'If you and Ken do get together that should fill a few of the evenings,' Jo finished for her.

'Maybe.' Lyn felt she'd said enough. Perhaps it had been unwise to confide in Jo, but the other woman hadn't been censorial. Quite the opposite. She'd helped Lyn see things more clearly. 'Thanks for listening, Jo. It's been a big help. I needed to talk it through. And thanks for the info about the yarn stuff, too. I'll check that out.'

'No worries.'

Col appeared just then, and the two women rose and embraced before leaving the café, Jo going with Col to their car, and Lyn making her way back to the library to have a word with Donna.

Back home again, Edith was pleased to see the selection of books Lyn had found. 'You took your time,' she said, once she'd examined them.

'I had a cup of tea with Jo Ford.'

'Good. It's about time you got out and spent time with your friends. She's a nice girl. I always thought so.'

'She was telling me about the yarn bombing and the local knitting groups. I asked about the wool I saw around the trees.'

'Of course. You wouldn't know about that. It only started up a few years ago. I thought of getting involved in the knitting myself, but…' Edith looked at her fingers, bent from arthritis. '…I'm not sure I could manage.'

'I went back to the library after I left Jo. I talked with Donna who seems to organise the groups.'

'That's right, Donna Burns. Your dad and I gave her some old documents and newspapers we found when we sold up the property. She looks after all the local history. And I heard she'd taken up the charity knitting groups, too.'

'Well, she'd pointed me in the right direction. I may not actually join one of the existing groups – I'm not much of a joiner.' Agreeing to join the choir was one thing, but Lyn didn't want to get involved in other local activities. 'It seems I can do my thing at home and deliver the end result to her at the library. Actually… she mentioned a number of women have found knitting helps relieve their arthritis if they warm up their hands first and take it easy. Maybe it's something we can do together.'

Lyn held her breath. It was an idea that occurred to her when she was speaking to Donna. When Lyn was growing up, Edith had always been knitting something, a pair of socks for her husband or a sweater for Lyn. Her hands had never been idle. It may have been the desire to assuage her guilt, but Lyn wanted the chance to share something with her mother, and this would provide the perfect opportunity.

She saw Edith's face brighten. 'Do you think I could? I can't remember when I last held a pair of knitting needles.' She looked down at her hands again and tried to flex her stiff fingers. 'But I haven't forgotten how.'

'I'm sure you haven't. We have to decide what to knit.' Lyn took a batch of A4 sheets from her bag. 'Donna said the options are little singlets for premmies, knockers for breast cancer survivors, or pouches for baby possums. They're all good causes. Ken's sister-in-law has breast cancer, so I'm going to register online for a kit to help breast cancer survivors. I feel it's something I can do to help. These are the patterns for the others. They're probably simpler.'

'Give them here.' Edith reached out for the patterns. 'I used to knit a lot of baby garments for the church fete after you left, but not since we came here. I'm not sure why I stopped.'

'You used to love your knitting. I remember how you taught me when I was only little. I can still hear you say, "In, over, through and out". But I never did much with it.'

'You were too much of a tomboy to sit inside for long.'

'Yes.' All those summer days wandering the paddocks with Ken. Life was so much simpler then. Lyn sighed.

'What do you have to sigh about? You have years ahead of you to sigh. You're still young.'

Yes, compared to her mother, Lyn was young, even if some days she felt as if life had passed her by. Where had that thought come from? She'd never considered herself to be old before. Maybe because she'd never taken time to think of herself. She'd always been too caught up in work. Was this what retirement was like? If so, maybe she'd made a mistake. But, she assured herself, everything would click into place once she started travelling.

Then what? The little voice she tried so hard to suppress was there again, reminding her she had no plans after her world trip.

Was that why she'd agreed to see more of Ken, to reignite the embers of their relationship? Was she afraid of growing old? Of being alone?

Twenty-nine

'What do I want with a dog?' Ken gazed at the wriggling black and white creature in his son's arms. Its little pink and white tongue was hanging out and it had a wicked gleam in its eyes. 'I suppose you'd better come in.'

Ken wasn't long home from the office. His hair was still damp from the shower, and his cream shirt was hanging open over his navy chinos. He was due to pick up Lyn in an hour's time. This was to be an important date – their first real one – and he'd booked a table at the prestigious Riverside Restaurant in the expectation of... well, in expectation.

'Going somewhere, Dad?' Neil asked with a wink. He set the pup down on the floor of the hallway and the tiny animal slithered around trying to get a grip on the tiles with his paws.

Ken couldn't help but smile at its antics. 'The dog?' he asked, ignoring Neil's question. His personal life was none of his son's business – not yet, anyway.

'Alec's Bess had pups, and this one is the runt of the litter. I remembered how you used to say you missed the farm dogs. You always make a fuss of Bess when we're at Wooleton. So, I thought...' he faltered, clearly seeing the baleful look in Ken's eyes. '...I thought he'd be company for you.'

'Company, is it?' Ken relented. and seeing the dog's struggles, picked him up. The animal immediately licked his face. 'Cheeky little blighter, isn't he? What's his name?' To his surprise, Ken felt drawn to the pup.

Bess was a good sheepdog and this offspring of hers already showed signs of her intelligence.

'Thought you'd take to him. He doesn't have a name yet. Judy and Alec were calling him Titch as he was the smallest of the litter, but that's hardly a name for a sheepdog.'

'Titch.'

Hearing the name, the pup wagged his tail, and snuggled into Ken's bare chest, the tiny claws scratching his skin.

'Well, it seems he's decided to answer to Titch. I guess we should find him a box or something until I have time to go to the shops.' Ken remembered a stash of empty cardboard boxes in the laundry. He'd intended to take them to the tip but, like many of his other good intentions, it was still waiting to be done.

Carrying the now excited pup, Ken led the way into the laundry where, after lining a box with an old towel, he deposited Titch in it. The dog immediately turned around and around before curling up and settling down happily.

'See, he's at home already,' Neil said, before opening the fridge and helping himself to a beer. 'Want one, Dad?'

'No. As you guessed, I am going out, and if I don't get a move on, I'll be late. Thanks for the dog. It's a kind thought. But this may not have been the best time to drop him off.'

It was probably the worst time, but Ken couldn't be angry with his son whose thoughtfulness brought a lump to his throat. He'd been feeling lonely since Neil left and there was no doubt this addition would fix that to some extent. His dad wouldn't have approved. Ken grimaced inwardly at the thought of what the old man would say about the idea of keeping a sheepdog as a pet. In Bill Thompson's mind, the only good dog was a work dog and all his animals lived outside. It was only after Alec and Judy took over at Wooleton that Ken ever saw the dogs – and cats – allowed into the house. He grinned. There were a few things about the farm these days that would annoy the old man.

'I won't keep you.' Neil grabbed a chair, turned it around and sat in it, elbows on the back, his eyes on the dog who was now falling asleep. 'Judy fed him before we left Wooleton. He'll be right till morning. You can get food for him then. Who's the lucky lady?' He grinned at Ken's discomfort.

'How do you know it's a lady?'

'You don't usually go to such trouble for a Friday night at the club, or to pick up a takeaway. Don't tell me…' Neil closed his eyes as if deep in thought. 'I'm not a betting man but I'd be willing to lay a bet it's that old childhood sweetheart of yours – Lyn Carter or Hudson. Am I right?'

Ken didn't answer.

'I knew it!' Neil drained his beer and tossed the empty can into the garbage. 'If I were you, I'd fasten my shirt and maybe comb your hair. You don't want to give her a shock.' He dodged out of the way of Ken's upraised fist. 'Don't worry. I'm off. Oh, and you might want to close the laundry door. Your Titch isn't completely housetrained yet.'

The slam of the back door signalled Neil's departure.

*

At the exact time he'd arranged, Ken arrived at Lyn's home. He nervously glanced in the rearview mirror before stepping out and heading to the front door. It was crazy, but Ken felt as nervous as he had before the school formal when he'd driven to the neighbouring property in his dad's old ute to pick up Lyn. It had been a magical night, one he'd imagined was the beginning of a future which he and Lyn would share, as he knew both sets of parents wanted them to marry and combine the two properties. But it wasn't to be. The playmate he'd come to love hadn't returned his affection and he'd been left wondering what had gone wrong.

It had never occurred to him Lyn might be afraid, but her explanation at Pavarotti's made sense, now he'd had time to think about it. They had been very young and very innocent.

The Lyn who answered the door was so different from the image in his head, it took Ken a few seconds to adjust to the woman he now knew.

'Something wrong?' she asked.

Ken shook his head. 'Sorry. I was remembering the evening of the formal. I think I was expecting to see eighteen-year-old Lyn Carter appear in a beautiful blue dress.'

Lyn chuckled and looked down at the white pants and loose flowery top she was wearing. 'I hope this'll do. And, I have to say, I think I prefer your current outfit to the maroon velvet one you wore that night.'

They both laughed.

'You've been looking at the old photo, too?'

'Guilty. Though it was Mum who dug it out. You'd better come in to say hello. She's been watching out the window for you for the past half hour.'

Sensing Lyn's embarrassment, Ken followed her into the living room where, sure enough, Edith Carter was installed in a chair by the window, a satisfied expression on her face.

'I'm glad you two have come to your senses,' she said. 'You're still a fine figure of a man. Your mum would have been proud to see this day.'

Ken squirmed. He hadn't expected this reception. It made him feel guilty, as if the expectations he'd harboured earlier had somehow been tarnished by this old woman's harmless remark.

Seeming to recognise his discomfort, she continued, 'Don't mind an old woman. Make sure you have a nice evening together. Lyn doesn't get out enough. She needs to see more people her own age. Don't make too much noise when you come in, Lynnie. I need my beauty sleep.'

Did Ken imagine it, or did the old woman give them a sly wink?

'My mother!' Lyn vented, when they were driving off. 'She has ears like a bat. I think she sleeps with one ear open. She can't bear to miss out on what's going on.'

'She's a wily old bird.'

'That's one way of putting it. But I think we're getting on better. We've started knitting together and I'm discovering it's very soothing. She uses the time to tell me stories about her and Dad – things I never knew. She could write a book about all the things that happened out on the property in the old days. Your folks probably could have, too.'

'They all had it tough in the early days,' Ken agreed. 'Alec has found some old notebooks of Dad's. I mean to go through them one day.'

'It's a pity they died so young. They were such good friends and neighbours – your folks and mine. Almost all of Mum's old friends are gone now. It must be dreadful to outlive all your peers.'

'And she's still determined to go into a nursing home?'

'I don't see an alternative. She's still as alert as ever, but she couldn't manage on her own. And I…'

Ken sent a sideways glance at Lyn.

'I can't stay around. I told you. She understands. I know she does. She'd never ask me to. But I can't help…'

Ken saw Lyn bite her lip, a frown creasing the smoothness of her forehead. 'You feel guilty?'

'I do.'

They reached the restaurant before Ken could say any more, but he sensed a weakening in Lyn's determination to leave Granite Springs. It gave him hope. While he was happy to take what he could get of her company, he knew it would never be enough.

'What a great place!' Lyn exclaimed, as they entered the large room overlooking the river. It was filled with chattering diners and a wonderful aroma of spices assailed their nostrils. 'How long has it been here?'

'A few years now. Jo Ford – Slater as she was then – set it up with her son, Rob. There he is now.'

'Evening, Ken.' A tall broad-shouldered man with spiky red hair came to greet them. 'You've booked?' He checked a folder lying on the table by the door.

'Sure did.'

'Let me show you to your table.' Rob led the way to a table for two by a floor-to-ceiling window overlooking the river.

'This is perfect.' Lyn smiled at Ken. 'Do you arrange this for all your dates?'

'Only the special ones.' Ken hoped his face didn't reveal just how special Lyn was. This was the first real date he'd been on since… he couldn't remember when.

After consulting Lyn's preference, Ken ordered a bottle of merlot and they both studied the menus. Finally, Lyn laid hers down.

'It's too hard. Everything looks delicious. What do you recommend?'

After barely a moment's hesitation, Ken said, 'I usually order one of the steak or lamb dishes, but I've heard the salmon is pretty good too. It comes fresh from the coast every day. What do you fancy?'

'Salmon for me, then. You?'

'I'll go for the lamb shanks. It's hard to change the habit of a lifetime.'

'The opposite to me. Growing up on a sheep property cured me of eating them. I keep thinking of all the baby lambs I helped rear.'

'There is that, but if everyone thought that way, the farmers would be in deep trouble.'

'I suppose.' Lyn realigned her cutlery and gazed out the window.

Hell, was this evening going to work, or be a complete disaster? Ken had been relying so much on it going well, on being able to reach out to Lyn, to forge a new relationship, one which might even encourage her to stay in town.

'Sir, madam.' A waiter appeared with the wine he'd ordered. Once they'd both taken their first sip, and Lyn had declared it wonderful, they began to relax, and the evening took a turn for the better.

They'd finished their meal, and were enjoying coffee when, looking around, Ken saw they were almost the last diners. 'I guess we should be leaving,' he said, glancing at his watch. Then he remembered the dog he'd left in the laundry. He hadn't intended to be gone for so long and had visions of the sort of destruction a small animal could create. He'd been asleep when Ken left, but that was hours ago. His consternation must have shown on his face.

'Something the matter?'

'No. I just remembered I have a dog waiting for me at home.'

'A dog?' Lyn appeared amused. 'That's a new one.'

'No, really. Just before I left to pick you up, Neil brought me a sheepdog pup. He's a cute little thing, but the timing couldn't have been worse. I left him asleep in the laundry, but by now…' He raked a hand through his hair. 'Sorry. What must you think of me? We've had a lovely evening and here I am, worried about a dog.'

Lyn stifled a laugh. 'Not at all, but I'd love to see this animal that can get you so perturbed.'

'You would?' Ken stared at her in amazement. He'd wondered if the evening might end in his inviting Lyn back to his place with an offer of coffee or a glass of something, but to have her actually invite herself…

She nodded.

'Okay.'

Back home, as soon as Ken turned on the light, he could hear a loud whining coming from behind the laundry door.

'The poor little thing's lonely,' Lyn said, opening the door. 'and he's weed on the floor.'

Ken was surprised when Lyn immediately picked up the pup who showed his pleasure by wagging his tail and sticking out his little pink tongue to try to lick her.

'Oh!' Lyn attempted unsuccessfully to move her face out of the dog's reach. 'Does he have a name?'

'Titch. He was the runt of the litter and it seems Judy called him that. It was a pity to change it,' Ken said, feeling he had to defend his choice of name.

'It suits him now, but he won't always be this size. Will you?' she asked the lively little creature. 'Let's see if you need another wee.' She opened the back door and placed the dog on his feet. A quick sniff outside and a cock of the leg against the veranda and he scurried back inside, practically leaping into Lyn's arms again.

Ken couldn't help but smile 'Now we're here, what about a nightcap?' he asked. He wasn't sure what to do next. He felt he'd lost control of the evening and the situation. This wasn't how he'd planned it to end.

Lyn looked up from the pup she was cuddling.

How Ken wished she'd show as much affection for him as she was for Titch. This was the first time he'd been jealous of a dog.

'What did you have in mind?' she asked, sounding distracted.

'Coffee? Hot chocolate? Brandy?' Ken tried to think what else he had to offer.

'Hot chocolate sounds good.' Lyn continued to stroke Titch who was clearly loving the attention. 'We never made time for pets when Amy was little and there's no room in my unit, even if I wanted one these days,' she said. 'And when I was growing up, Dad... I suppose yours was the same?'

'Working dogs only,' Ken agreed. 'It's all changed now on Wooleton. Alec and Judy run things differently, and Neil has a few new ideas, too. You wouldn't recognise the place. They're going to be running cattle.' Ken knew he'd already told Lyn that, but it still rankled with him that things had come the full circle and his ideas for the farm were about to be implemented.

'Mmm.' Lyn acted as if she hadn't heard him. She was so engrossed in the pup. But she had agreed to hot chocolate. Ken took the milk out of the fridge, put it on to heat and prepared two mugs, tipping in generous servings of chocolate.

'Shall we take it through to the lounge?' he asked, when the hot chocolate was ready, even though he wasn't sure about letting Titch loose in the rest of the house until he'd checked the dog's toilet habits, remembering Neil said he wasn't house-trained, although he'd done well earlier when Lyn set him outside.

He needn't have worried. Almost as soon as they sat down, Titch slipped off Lyn's lap, curled up in a corner, and went back to sleep. Ken joined Lyn on the sofa and, mug of chocolate in one hand, daringly reached an arm around her shoulder. To his surprise, she gave a satisfied sigh and snuggled into his embrace.

This felt different from the times he'd stolen kisses earlier. Ken could sense Lyn wanted to be here – in his house, in his arms. Carefully, he set his own mug down on the coffee table, before doing the same with Lyn's. Then, with both arms around Lyn, he drew her closer.

Thirty

Lyn lay staring at the unfamiliar ceiling in Ken's bedroom. She'd known it would be like this. Even when she was eighteen and innocent of love or passion, she'd sensed making love with Ken could be, would be, this overwhelming torrent of passion. What was she to do now?

When she agreed to see more of Ken, Lyn knew exactly what it meant, what she'd agreed to. The only surprise was how quickly they'd fallen into bed. If he hadn't mentioned the dog, would she have agreed to come home with him? It didn't matter now, but Lyn could imagine her mother's glee if she didn't arrive home till morning – had what Amy called a dirty stop out. Thinking of her daughter brought her down to earth.

Amy wouldn't approve of the mother she considered to be over the hill sleeping with an old boyfriend, sleeping with any man. And she was sure to find out. Lyn predicted that, as soon as Maddy discovered her grandmother's liaison – Lyn loved that word, it sounded much more exotic than relationship – Amy would be the first to hear.

'Hi there!' Ken's voice interrupted her thoughts.

Lyn turned to see him gazing at her with concern.

'Something wrong?'

'Nothing. I can't believe I… we…'

Ken drew her into his arms and kissed her hair. 'I've waited a lifetime for this, but you were worth waiting for. Lynnie…'

Lyn put a finger on his lips. She wasn't ready for any declaration of love, if that's what he had in mind. It was enough they'd shared a special moment, one she wanted to savour.

Ken took her finger and kissed it, before kissing her on the lips. 'Lynnie,' he said again, 'I didn't intend things to move this quickly. But we're not young any longer and I guess we need to take these things when we can. Hell, I'm not putting this well.' He stroked a strand of hair away from her face and gently caressed her forehead, his fingers moving down her cheek. 'I want you to know I'll never ask for anything you're not willing to give. I know this can't be forever. Nothing is. But I believe what we have together is something special, and…'

'It's special for me too, Ken.' A warm glow of pleasure spread through Lyn. She felt she could stay here forever. To think this was Ken Thompson, the man she'd known all her life. *If they'd made love back when they were both eighteen, would she have left?*

Deep down, Lyn suspected she'd always known the effect he had on her, even if she hadn't put it into words, hadn't allowed herself to imagine… But now she knew life was too short to spend it wondering. Her mother's words about Aunt Wyn came back to her.

Now she knew the thrill of making love with Ken, how was she going to walk away?

'I need to get back. Mum will…'

Ken laughed, a mocking laugh. 'How old are you?' he chuckled.

'I know, I know. But a mother never seems to give up worrying. I'd be the same with Amy. I know Mum won't rest till she hears me come home. She heard me the other night, even though I tiptoed in and didn't put on the light. I'm still getting used to it.' Lyn grimaced. 'I'm not a free agent. I sometimes feel I'm being treated like a teenager again.'

'Pity. But I understand. I hope it doesn't mean we can't do this again.' Ken drew her close and Lyn felt him bury his face in her hair.

'No.' She managed to rouse herself again. 'But maybe we need to plan things better next time. Tonight, I didn't expect to…'

'I didn't expect it either. I guess we have a lot to thank Titch for. Speaking of which, I should probably check on the little devil. I seem to recollect we left him asleep in the living room. He really should be in his box in the laundry. I'll get a proper basket for him tomorrow, and maybe we can…?' He raised an eyebrow.

'Tomorrow?'

'It that too soon?' Ken's mouth drooped. 'Sorry, as I said, I'm out of practice at this stuff, I have no blueprint to draw on.'

'Not too soon, no. But I need to check things at home. There's Maddy to consider, too.' Though Lyn knew quite well Maddy would have her own plans, plans which didn't include her grandmother. But she didn't want to rush things. It had been a long time since she was with a man, not since Glenn left. And, till now, she'd only known her ex-husband. She had a lot to think about. Was what she was feeling for Ken really something special, or the result of her having done without for so long? She needed time to digest what had just happened.

'What about lunch tomorrow, then? The club does a good weekend lunch. We can invite your Mum, too. She likes me.'

Lyn knew that was true. Her mother would be thrilled with the outing, but could Lyn bear to suffer her mother's innuendos all through the meal? 'Maybe,' she said. Then she had an idea. 'After we went to the Italian restaurant, Mum mentioned how much she and Dad had enjoyed going there, I promised to take her sometime, but haven't so far. Perhaps…?'

'Done! They're not usually busy at lunchtime, but I'll book a table, shall I?'

'Yes please.' Lyn knew it would delight her mother and it was a small thing. 'Now I really must go.'

Reluctantly, it seemed, Ken released Lyn from his grasp, and she slid out of bed and pulled on the clothes she'd discarded in such haste as their passion overtook them. Ken followed more slowly, merely pulling on a pair of pants before walking with her to the door. A quick glance into the living room on the way showed Titch was still fast asleep.

Lyn smiled.

*

'Grandma!'

Lyn blinked in the light that lit up the kitchen. Maddy and Zac were seated at the table drinking Coke and munching on doughnuts as if it was the middle of the day instead of… Lyn checked the kitchen clock …quarter past midnight. 'What…?'

'We just got home. We bought these yummy doughnuts from a van near the river. I checked on GG and she's asleep.'

Lyn could see Maddy was dying to know where Lyn had been till this time. 'I went out to dinner,' she said, adding, 'then for hot chocolate,' as she saw her granddaughter's eyes widening with disbelief. 'You guys are up pretty late, too.'

'There was a party at Zac's place. It got too boisterous, so we came back here.' Maddy rose and stretched. 'We were about to go to bed. Zac!'

With an apologetic grin, Zac joined her, and the pair disappeared in the direction of Maddy's room.

Lyn sighed. What it was to be young – or was she just too inhibited? But she couldn't imagine bringing Ken back here to face both her mother and Maddy over breakfast. Though why not? Neither would be shocked. Her mother might even be pleased. Was it a generational thing that made her want to keep her love life away from the prying eyes of her family?

Next morning, Lyn joined her mother in the kitchen, glad the younger pair were still asleep. Edith waited till they had both eaten and were on their second cup of tea before asking how Lyn's evening had been.

'I didn't hear you come in,' she said, her words sounding like an accusation.

'Maddy and Zac were here when I got back,' she said.

'I don't know why that young man bothers to pay rent in that place. He spends more time here.' Edith shook her head, but she was grinning. 'It's nice Maddy has someone. What about you?'

'I had a lovely evening. The Riverside is a big asset to the town. Did you know Jo Ford and her son own it?'

'Of course. Everyone knows. You've been away too long.'

'You're right, Mum. But I intend to rectify that. I won't wait so long before coming to visit next time.' As she spoke, Lyn wondered how her new relationship would survive her intention to only visit Granite Springs from time to time. It would be a bit like those people – mostly men, mostly in the mining industry – who lived a fly-in fly-out lifestyle. Could she really be considering having a relationship like that with Ken? How would he feel about it? But all that was in the future. She was here now. They'd only spent one night together. The whole thing might peter out in no time at all. Though somehow she didn't think so.

'Ken invited us both to lunch,' Lyn said. Seeing a look of surprise on her mother's face, she added, 'To that Italian restaurant.'

'Pavarotti's? That's kind of him. Whose idea was it?' she asked suspiciously.

'Lunch was his idea. I told him you wanted to go to Pavarotti's.'

'Hmm. I told you he was a good man. There's not many who would take pity on an old woman when he set out to court her daughter.'

Lyn, who was taking a sip of tea, almost choked. Court was such an old-fashioned word. It didn't have any bearing on what she and Ken had got up to last night. It reminded her of the Georgette Heyer books she'd enjoyed in her younger days, of times when a young man would ask a parent's permission to court their daughter with a view to marriage.

'I don't think that's what he has in mind,' Lyn said. 'I think the idea of courting went out with the ark. We're both far too old for that sort of thing anyway. He'll be picking us up at twelve.'

'Hmm,' Edith said again. 'So, how is he? His son's moved out to the farm, I think you said. Be lonely for him in that big house.'

'Yes, Mum.' Edith knew that perfectly well. 'Neil has given him a dog for company. It's a lovely little thing – a sheepdog pup called Titch.'

As soon as she said it, Lyn could have bitten her tongue out. She'd been so determined to keep quiet about her visit to Ken's house.

She saw her mother purse her lips, maybe at the idea of a sheepdog as a pet.

'You were at his house again?'

'He was worried about the dog.' Even though it was partially true, Lyn knew it was a lame excuse.

'I suppose one reason's as good as another. Did he say if those people have made an offer?'

'No. Sorry, I didn't ask.'

Why hadn't she? And why hadn't Ken mentioned it?

'I suppose nothing's happened, otherwise he'd have said.' But it was a bit odd. They'd had a building inspection and a valuer had come around last week. Surely they'd have made a decision by now? And hadn't Ken said something about expecting an offer when she had dinner at his place? Lyn tried to remember, but everything that had happened between them since seemed to have fried her brain.

*

'Here's Ken now!' Edith called from her vantage point by the window.

Maddy and Zac had emerged from her room barely an hour earlier and disappeared, allegedly to campus, Maddy muttering something about the library.

'Doesn't he have to work today?' Edith asked.

'I suppose he stops for lunch like most other people.' It hadn't occurred to Lyn it was a workday for Ken. It should have. She glanced down at the outfit she'd chosen. After discarding several others, she'd finally settled on a pair of dusky pink denim pants topped with a classic white shirt, rolling up the sleeves to create a more casual look. 'Ready?'

'I've been ready for some time. I had no need to primp and fuss, trying to decide on the most appropriate outfit.'

Was that what Lyn had done? But she did want to look good for Ken. Last night, something had shifted between them. It was more than the fact they'd made love – though that was an important step forward in their relationship. It was something intangible, something which left her with an ache she'd never experienced before.

'Ready, ladies?' Ken winked and looked past Lyn to where her mother was holding on to the doorframe.

'This is lovely of you, Ken. Your mother would be proud to see you taking an old woman out to lunch.' Edith stumbled forward, almost losing her footing.

'Maybe you should take your walker,' Lyn suggested, catching Edith by the arm.

'Nonsense. I have this young man to help. If you'll just give me your arm, Ken.' She brushed off Lyn's hand and beamed up at him, clearly enjoying every minute.

Without any further difficulty, the three managed to get into the car and were soon on their way.

Once at the restaurant, Lyn let Ken help her mother out of the car and into the building, where they were shown to a corner table.

'This is good of you, Ken. I've missed this place. Al and I often came here. Not latterly, when he became too frail. You may not remember old Marco who started it. He and Al went way back.'

Lyn settled back in her seat, prepared to hear a repeat of the story she'd heard several times already. But it was new to Ken and he listened avidly, interjecting from time to time with a question or an anecdote of his own. His father had been a member of the Rural Fire Brigade too, and so it seemed were Ken and his son.

Lyn was glad her mum was having such a good time, grateful to Ken for being such a willing listener. She knew there weren't many men who'd invite a woman's mother to lunch, never mind show such interest in her reminiscences.

They were halfway through the meal when Edith pointed a finger at Ken and asked, 'What's happening with these people who want to buy my house? I thought you indicated they were ready to make a decision.'

Lyn thought she saw a cloud pass over Ken's eyes, but it was gone in an instant.

Instead of answering immediately, Ken asked, 'Have you spoken to any of your neighbours recently, Mrs Carter?'

'My neighbours? What have they to do with it? I mind my own business and expect them to mind theirs. The street has changed over the years. All the old ones like me and Al have gone – died or moved away. That's another reason I'll be glad to get out. The younger ones don't care as much for the place. It's not like it used to be when we'd have street parties for Christmas and Australia Day, not at all.' Her eyes glazed over – something Lyn noticed happened a lot.

She put a hand on her mother's arm. This time Edith didn't shrug it off. 'Sorry, you must think I'm a silly old woman.' Her eyes cleared again. 'Have they changed their mind?' Her voice was as clear as ever.

'No, not yet. There are some odd things happening in town with real estate sales at the moment.' Ken paused then asked, 'You haven't been approached by anyone else about selling, have you?'

Lyn shook her head, surprised when her mother said, 'D'you mean that charlatan who wanted to talk to us before Al passed? We showed him the door quick smart. Al said he looked as if he was up to no good. He had a nose for such things.' She looked down at her plate, still half full of the spaghetti carbonara she'd ordered. 'I think I've had enough, dear. I'd forgotten how rich this is. But it was lovely.'

'You never said, Mum.'

'Why would I? There was nothing to say. Al told him what was what and sent him on his way. We'd decided to give Ken our business. We knew he'd get us a fair price. Al said you couldn't trust someone like that one. He looked as if he'd cheat his own grandmother.'

Lyn saw Ken try to stifle a grin. 'Do you know who Mum's talking about?' she asked him.

Ken became more serious. 'I'm afraid I do. I'm glad you decided not to do business with him.'

'Al took care of all that,' Edith declared. 'But I thought he looked a bit shifty. What does it have to do with the sale now?'

'Possibly nothing. I'm hoping to have an offer from the Braithwaites in the next few days. But thanks for that information. I need to do some checking up on a few things. Now,' he checked his watch, 'I'll need to be getting back to the office before much longer. Coffee?'

'No thanks, son. Lyn and I'll have a nice cup of tea when we get home. We've taken enough of your time. Thanks again. And see if you can persuade this one,' she nodded towards Lyn, 'to change her mind about Granite Springs. It's been good to us and it's not a bad place to retire.'

Lyn felt her mouth fall open. What was her mother trying to do? Hints and sly looks were one thing. She could cope with them – just about. But this was blatant, even for her.

'I'll see what I can do,' Ken chuckled, seemingly unfazed by her remark.

Ken helped Edith back into the house and, ignoring her protest she could manage perfectly well on her own, into her chair by the window.

'Thanks,' Lyn said to Ken as he was leaving. They were standing in the doorway out of sight and, hopefully, hearing of her mother. 'It meant a lot to Mum. I'm afraid she monopolised the conversation. I should take her out more, but she doesn't find it easy.'

'I think you're doing well.'

'Thanks.' Lyn's eyes softened. 'I'm trying. You do think the sale will go through?'

'Let's hope so. Any word from the nursing home?'

'Still on the waiting list. It's horrible waiting for a spot to become vacant – for someone to die.'

'And your granddaughter?'

'Maddy? She's still here, plus her boyfriend a lot of the time. But when it's sold…' Lyn clasped her arms around herself and turned to look at the house behind her. 'She tried to contact some share houses that were advertised on campus, but the places had all been taken.'

'I might be able to help. Ask her to give me a call.'

'I will.' What Maddy would do, where she would go when Edith was settled in Eden Gardens and Lyn left town, was something Lyn had been trying not to think about. It had even occurred to her to… But, she refused to consider the alternative that had popped into her head a few days ago.

'There's something else.' Ken shifted awkwardly on the spot. 'A friend – a client – has given me a travel voucher.' He avoided meeting Lyn's eyes. 'It's for a night at a new hotel on the lake in Canberra. I thought…' he paused. 'I wondered…' He cleared his throat. 'While you have your granddaughter here, maybe…'

He looked up and their eyes met.

Lyn's stomach started turning somersaults. Was he about to suggest what she thought he was?

'Maybe we could get away together for a weekend?' Ken didn't give Lyn time to reply. 'Think about it, will you? This Saturday I've promised to go out to Wooleton. Alec and Judy need a bit of a hand. Maybe the following weekend? I'll call you.'

Lyn's hand went unbidden to her throat as she watched him drive away. Her mother was right. He was a good man. Too good for her. What was she doing raising his hopes? But Lyn knew that, with Ken, for the first time in years, she was able to be herself without any artifice. He knew who she was, where she came from. He could immediately see through any defence she tried to put up. While this was comforting in a way, it was also threatening to feel so exposed.

'Lynnie, did you say you were making tea?' Edith's voice came from behind her.

'Coming, Mum.' Lyn closed the door and went into the kitchen. A cup of tea wouldn't solve her problems, but it might calm her confused thoughts.

Thirty-one

'There's someone here to see you.'

Ken looked up from his computer to see Cathy standing in the doorway to his office, a worried expression on her face. He gestured her to come in. 'Why the worried look?' he asked.

When she replied it was almost in a whisper, 'It's Danny Slater. You know, the man who...' Her eyes widened.

Danny? What did he want? Since discovering the identity of DNS, Ken had been doing a bit of research. It was all bad. So far, Danny's name hadn't been implicated in his partner's dealings, but it was only a matter of time. Ken had been in two minds about whether he should have a word with Danny or the boy's father, wondering if Gordon knew of his son's association with a suspected criminal. He'd decided it was none of his business, but wouldn't he want a friend to tell him, if it was Neil who might be in trouble?

'You'd better show him in.' Ken closed his computer and took off his glasses, rubbing the bridge of his nose. He rose as Danny entered looking sheepish.

'Danny! We don't often see you in here. How can I help you?'

The younger man's face had a greyish tinge and the bags under his eyes gave the impression he hadn't been sleeping well. Gone was the usually confident, ebullient Danny Slater Ken knew.

'Thanks for seeing me, Mr Thompson.'

'Ken,' Ken said automatically. 'Please sit.' He resumed his own seat, propped his elbows on the desk, and steepled his hands.

'I've got myself into a bit of a pickle. Dad said I should come to see you; that as a councillor, you might be able to help.'

'I'll help if I can, but first you need to tell me what's wrong. Would you find it easier with coffee?' he asked the now trembling young man.

Danny nodded, beads of sweat forming on his forehead.

Ken called through on the intercom for coffee and the two men waited silently till Cathy brought it in, closing the door behind her when she left.

'Now then, what do you need me to do and why?' Ken asked, pushing his coffee to one side and clasping his hands on the desktop.

'I've been a fool. I was doing all right with the villas and small acreages – more than all right, really. But Kylie wanted more. I'm not blaming her – she has a right to want the best of everything for her and the boys.' He shook his head. 'She got me into trouble before – with Mum – but I thought she was happy with our new house and…

'Anyway, this guy Sherwood approached me with a deal. I wasn't too sure about it, to be honest, but Kylie urged me to accept it. She had visions of…' he drew a hand through his hair '…I don't know what she was imagining. But it sounded okay, so I agreed. We formed this company, DNS – conveniently we share initials. He'd buy the land, arrange the development, and I'd market the homes – sounded simple and right up my alley. Kylie was all for it.' He grimaced slightly. 'Then, a few weeks ago, I began to smell a rat. I asked Dad to take a look at the contracts Doug was preparing. He said they were legit, but unfair. We were ripping people off. And…' he hesitated, '…Dad thought he – Sherwood – seemed to be throwing around a lot of money. It made him suspicious.'

'So how can I help?' All of this was confirming what Ken either already knew or suspected. But if the contracts were legal, there wasn't much he could do.

'Well, it seemed to Dad there was a loophole. The contracts are all subject to building approval. Dad thought that as a councillor, you were in a position to see that approval was denied, his proposals rejected.' He gave Ken a pleading look. 'I'd lose a bit of money in the deal if that happened, but it would give me an excuse to pull out of the partnership. I can't sell houses that aren't going to be built.' He gave an awkward laugh. 'I had no idea how he was going about the purchases. You have to believe me.'

Ken did. In his experience, and until now, Danny had always operated within the law, albeit a touch too exuberant for his liking. He leant back in his chair, one finger to his chin. He didn't normally take anything to do with council approvals for development. He wasn't on the sub-committee that dealt with such matters. But he did know the members of the committee. And it would be in his own interests to put a spoke in the wheel of this shyster who seemed to have pulled the wool over Danny's eyes.

'I'll have a word with your dad and see what I can do, Danny. But I can't promise anything. There are a lot of these horse traders around. You're a good businessman. You don't need to get yourself tied up with someone like that.'

'I know. Thanks, Mr… Ken. I appreciate your time.' Danny left, showing a bit more of his customary vigour than when he arrived.

Ken picked up his glasses and gazed into space. At another time, Danny Slater was a young man he'd have enjoyed doing business with himself. He'd shown poor judgement in this instance but had the sense to ask his dad for advice – and the courage to admit his mistake and to come to Ken for help. If he managed to come out of this unscathed, he'd go far.

Ken picked up the phone to call Gordon Slater.

Thirty-two

The phone rang as Lyn was loading the washing machine. 'Can you get that, Maddy?' she yelled, knowing Edith would try to get to it if it rang for long. Now her mother was feeling better, it was difficult to persuade her to take things easy.

'Will do, Gran,' Maddy called back.

She was a good kid. Lyn would miss her when she moved out. But she'd told her about Ken's offer and suggested the young girl pop into his office sometime this week. There was the sound of Maddy's voice, indistinct once the machine started its cycle, then her granddaughter appeared.

'It's for you. Ken Thompson.' Maddy winked. 'He says he has some news.' Her tone indicated she thought *news* was a private code word for something much more exciting.

Wearily, Lyn straightened up from where she'd been crouching by the front-loader her mother swore by. 'Okay, I'll get it.' Why was Ken ringing her today? They'd made arrangements to meet at choir that evening with the understanding they'd go back to his place afterwards. Surely he didn't want to change the plan? Normally confident, Lyn had discovered she was fragile where Ken was concerned. It troubled her to be so easily rattled.

'Ken? I didn't expect to hear from you today. Is anything wrong?'

'Far from it. We have an offer from the Braithwaites. A good one. Only two thousand below the asking price.'

'Oh!' Lyn fell into a nearby chair. So much had been happening, she'd almost given up hope on the offer they'd been expecting for over a week. Her mind immediately started to whirl with all the things they'd need to do now – her mother, Maddy, Lyn herself, the furniture…

'Are you still there?' Ken's voice broke into her rambling thoughts, and she realised he'd been talking all the time she'd been mentally making a list of what she needed to take care of.

'Sorry. I was thinking. An offer you said?'

'A good one,' he repeated, 'and they're willing to delay settlement till your mother has a place to go. I recommend you accept it. You won't get a better one.'

'Yes. That's good. I should check with Mum. Can I get back to you?'

'Of course. You can let me know tonight. Still okay?'

Lyn glowed at the way Ken's voice changed when he mentioned seeing her. It seemed to develop a softer and more intimate tone.

'Okay,' she murmured, her insides turning to jelly.

*

This time, Lyn was prepared to enjoy the choir, and the knowledge of what was to follow leant an extra vitality to her voice. Owen enthusiastically announced the program for their Easter production with the added instruction to everyone to ensure they attended every rehearsal until then.

But Easter was weeks away – almost a whole month. Lyn didn't know where she'd be by then. Now the house was sold, it all depended on the availability of a space for her mother at Eden Gardens. She stared down at her hands. Only a few weeks ago she'd have been glad to leave, eager to move on. But now…

'Ready everyone?' Owen called the group to order. They started to sing, and for the next hour everything else was forgotten in the joy of the music.

When they finished, with an apologetic smile to Ken, Lyn joined Kay, who was standing with another, younger, woman who was a stranger to her, but who she remembered seeing with Kay the week before.

'This is Fran,' Kay said. 'She's Owen's partner. She works at the uni with me and is Jo's neighbour.'

'Hi, Fran. I'm Lyn.'

'I've heard of you,' Fran said.

What had she heard?

'Jo tells me you and your mum have joined in the knitting frenzy that's hit town. I don't think I'd have the patience.'

'I'm finding it soothing,' Lyn said. 'I needed something to fill my time till everything's sorted out.'

'It seems to me your time is about to be filled quite nicely.' Kay gestured to where Ken was waiting patiently. 'I'm glad you two have got together. I always thought it was a pity…' She fell silent as Lyn flashed her an irritated look. 'See you next week?'

Not her, too?

'You will.' Lyn couldn't wait to get away. The trouble with friends was that they were too well-meaning, verging on the meddling. Though it was unkind to think that of Kay. Like Jo, her heart was in the right place. Lyn knew her friends just wanted everyone to be as happy as they were. But they'd been lucky with their lives, with their choices. Not everyone was as fortunate.

'I should go now,' she said. But she hesitated.

'Why don't you join us for coffee on Saturday morning?' Kay asked, seeing her indecision. 'Jo and I always meet at Mouthfuls. No need to decide now, but we'll be there if you feel the need for some feminine company.'

'Thanks.' With a smile, Lyn left them to join Ken.

'Ready?' he asked.

'Sorry. I felt I needed to catch up with Kay. She and Jo have been good to me.'

'No need to apologise. I was happy to wait. Enjoy this evening's session?'

'I did. Very much. Owen's a marvellous conductor. He seems able to get the best out of everyone, even that guy who looks so annoyed all the time.'

'There's a story there, but not for now. Shall we go straight back to my place tonight? Titch was on his own all day. I don't like to leave him too long.'

'How is he?' Lyn smiled up at Ken and linked her arm in his.

'He's a little devil,' Ken said, as they reached her car, 'chewing everything in sight. I may need to be more careful to avoid any further damage, though I'm afraid I'll have to throw out my good sandals. I was foolish enough to leave them on the floor in the kitchen.'

'He's only a pup. What did you expect?' Lyn laughed. Her car gave its familiar beep as she pressed the control. 'Shall I follow you?'

Ken gave her hand a squeeze. 'Yeah, I'll see you there.' He walked towards his car, and while Lyn waited for him to set off, her stomach fluttered with excitement.

'How's your sister-in-law?' Lyn asked, when they were settled on the sofa in Ken's living room, the little dog lying at their feet. He was asleep, occasionally emitting a faint snore, his nose twitching as he chased imaginary sheep in his dreams.

'She's getting there. But it's taken a lot out of her, and Alec has lost his carefree outlook. These days, with the worried look on his face, he reminds me of Dad. He's aged over the past few weeks. Despite all his setbacks in the past – having to leave uni, abandon his dream career, take over Wooleton – he always managed to make the best of things. But Jude's illness has knocked him for six. I think he might have gone under if they didn't have Neil. It's an ill wind...'

'You miss your son.' Lyn detected a note of regret in Ken's voice.

He sighed. 'I always thought he'd be there to carry on the business. But... it's the right thing for him, and for Alec. Dad would probably approve of him being there too, if not what they're doing with the place.'

'You still think of your dad a lot, don't you? Have you ever forgiven him?'

'For taking away my birthright?' Ken laughed, but it was forced.

'Is that how you still see it?'

'Is there another way? But Alec is glad of my help these days, and it's good to get my hand back in. I'd have been thinking of retiring by now, anyway. Farming's a young man's game.'

Lyn sipped the wine they'd been enjoying, before speaking again, wondering if she was about to press a hot button. 'Are you thinking of retiring now Neil's no longer around to take over? Or does it mean you'll soldier on regardless?' She tried to make it sound amusing, but it didn't come out the way she intended. Lyn bit her lip, hoping she hadn't put her foot in it. They were the same age. But the fact she'd chosen to take early retirement, was no reason for him to do the same. But, she thought, Jo and Col seemed to be enjoying theirs, though his other friend, Gordon, still appeared to be as busy as ever in his legal practice.

'It's not that easy.' Ken moved his arm from where it had been, around her shoulders, leant forward, his elbows on his knees, and peered into his wine glass. He sat like that for a few moments, before raising his head and meeting Lyn's eyes.

'I know Jo and Col are as happy as bugs in a rug out there on their acreage, but they have each other. Gordon's more like me. But he has Carol and a young child to take care of. There's no way he can give up work anytime soon – and I think it gets him out of the house.

'But what would I do with myself all day? There are only so many books I could read. I'm not one of those guys who like to spend my days on the golf course. I'd end up out at Wooleton getting in everyone's way. It's okay when Alec or Neil ask for my help – like now, with Jude sick – but most of the time they're fine on their own. And Neil and Sally will both be out there. I'd be intruding into their life. I know what that's like. Although...' He sighed again.

'What's the matter?' Lyn stroked the back of his neck, her fingers tangling in his hair, surprised how normal this felt.

'There's something going on, something I've been asked to take care of.' He took a gulp of wine and rolled his glass between his hands.

Lyn continued to stroke Ken's neck as he outlined his concerns about the new company, Danny's visit, and the request he try to influence the council. 'I don't know whether they'll listen to me,' he said, 'but I have to try. There's a council meeting on Thursday, and I can bend the ear of a few of them before that, but...' he shook his head, '...I'm not sure it will do much good. I'm sure to be accused of a conflict of interest. And it *would* be in my interest to stop this Sherwood guy.' He looked up at Lyn with a wry smile. 'We seem to be getting very serious. How about I refill our glasses and we think of something more pleasant?'

Lyn nodded and held out her now empty glass. Titch stirred as Ken stepped over him, but the little creature was sound asleep, looking so innocent lying there, head on his paws as if butter wouldn't melt in his mouth. But Lyn had seen the remains of Ken's sandals when they walked in. Titch might be little, but his teeth were very sharp and could wreak a lot of damage.

Ken put on a playlist of blues music on his way back, and the pair settled down cosily on the sofa, only stirring when the wine and music were finished. 'I think we should move to somewhere more comfortable,' Ken said thickly, unwinding his arms from around Lyn.

Then, to her surprise, he picked her up and carried her to the bedroom.

Thirty-three

It was the evening of the council meeting. Feeling nauseous, Ken checked himself in the mirror. Surely the grey pants teamed with a white business shirt and blue tie would give the right impression – make his fellow councillors take him seriously. It was too hot for the matching jacket, and many of the others would most likely turn up in the short-sleeved shirts they'd been wearing all day.

During the past couple of days, he'd found time to talk privately with those members of the development sub-committee he felt might be open to discussion. He'd been right on some counts, wrong on others. But at least he'd managed to get the proposal on the meeting agenda. This was no small feat as such matters were usually discussed – and decided – in the smaller sub-group.

As he'd expected, there were some who accused him of self-interest, of wanting to stifle competition. But he hoped to be able to sway the council tonight. One plus had been a call from Gordon.

'Thanks for agreeing to see my boy,' Gordon said. 'It means a lot. He's worried sick, and with good reason. If he can't extricate himself from this guy, he could end up being tarred by the same brush – maybe even with a criminal record. My Danny's no criminal. He's just a bit naïve when it comes to someone like Sherwood.'

More importantly, both Gordon and Col had stated their intention to attend the meeting. Granite Springs council meetings were renowned for permitting audience participation. It should make for a lively evening. Lyn had promised to be there too. While Ken was glad of her support, he might have preferred her to stay home. There was no guarantee he'd be successful in halting the development, and he didn't want her to see him suffer a public defeat.

At seven o'clock, the hall was buzzing with activity. It seemed word had got around about the unusual item on tonight's agenda. It was a warm night. The hall was airconditioned, and the television programmes left much to be desired. The council meeting would offer alternative entertainment.

Ken took his seat with the other councillors as the Mayor called the meeting to order and the general chattering gradually died away. He was glad to see his friends seated in the front of the audience, accompanied by Jo and Lyn. Lyn's hands were tightly clasped in her lap, an indication she understood how much this evening meant to him.

There was no sign of Danny, but over to one side was a burly man Ken recognised from the photo he'd found online when he googled DNS and Doug Sherwood. His lips tightened.

The first part of the meeting was taken up with regular reports and council business, tiresome but essential to the smooth running of the town. All proceeded without dissent. Finally, the item regarding development approval was tabled.

The chair of the sub-committee spoke forcibly on behalf of approving the application, then one of Ken's contacts spoke against. The debate went on for some time, till there were mutterings from the audience. The Mayor paused the discussion to ask for comments from the floor of the meeting, and Gordon stood up.

'Mr Mayor, councillors. Correct me if I'm wrong, but it seems to me that what we're discussing is high-density housing in an area designated for single dwellings. I believe the plan before council is for a number of apartment buildings.'

There was a rumbling from those councillors who'd indicated their support for the scheme, before the Mayor asked if the developer was present. Before he could reply, one of the audience stood up.

'That's him!' The man pointed to where Sherwood was seated. 'He wanted to buy our house, told us he was a new realtor in town and could give us a good deal. He never said nothing about apartments. We don't want none of those in Granite Springs.'

There was more muttering, and heads turned to look at the speaker.

'Thank you,' the Mayor said. 'Mr Sherwood, would you care to comment?'

Doug Sherwood lumbered to his feet, all eyes now on him. 'Mr Mayor, councillors. It's true my company plans to build several tasteful apartment blocks on the land in question. They will provide much-needed low-cost housing. The development will include a central garden area for the use of residents and...'

The muttering grew louder, drowning out the rest of what he had to say.

'Thank you, Mr Sherwood. It appears Mr Slater may be correct. I suggest this proposal be returned to the sub-committee for further consideration. If it is deemed appropriate for the zoning to be changed to allow for these apartments to be built, the matter will, of course, be available for public scrutiny and comment. I take it your partner isn't present here tonight?'

Sherwood looked around the room as if he could magically make Danny appear. He shook his head.

The meeting closed with the usual platitudes and pleasantries. Sherwood rushed out, phone in hand.

'Well done!' Lyn turned to Ken with a smile.

'I didn't do anything. It was Gordon who spoke up.' Ken turned to Gordon. 'Do people realise Danny's involved in this too?'

'Maybe, but they know Danny. Sherwood's the outsider. It's always easier to blame the guy you don't know. And Danny hasn't been the one going around trying to con people out of their homes.'

'What will happen now?' Jo asked. 'Will Danny be all right?'

Ken saw Lyn squeeze Jo's hand. She had a child, too. She must be thinking of her.

And he knew how he'd feel if Neil was involved in a shady deal.

'It's not over yet,' Gordon said. 'But I doubt the committee will let it go ahead. I suspect there'll be a public outcry if they try to change the zoning. It would open up a can of worms the council don't want in an election year.'

'Maybe you should stand this time,' Ken said with a grin.

'Carol would like that,' Gordon said. 'She'd be in her element as the wife of the mayor.'

Ken saw Jo roll her eyes. That was all Gordon needed. Sometimes he could be helpful – like tonight – but at others he was too pompous for his own good. Mayor!

'A drink?' Col looked at the others as the hall gradually emptied.

Gordon shook his head. 'I told Carol I'd come straight home – and I promised to let Danny know the result.'

'Sounds like a plan,' Ken said. 'Lyn?'

He saw her hesitate, check her watch, then, 'Maybe a quick one.'

Ken took Lyn's hand as the group walked along the road to the club, enjoying the peace of the evening till they reached the brightly lit building. He pushed open the door to be greeted with a cacophony of voices. It seemed the entire audience from the meeting had reconstituted itself here, plus the usual Thursday night revellers. There were a few waves from acquaintances but, thanks to Gordon's absence, no one knew the part Ken had played in the affair.

'I'm worried about Danny,' Jo said, repeating her earlier concern. All four were seated in a corner, the men with glasses of beer while the women had chosen white wine. 'I know he can be way too cocky, and he tried to take over Yarran a couple of years ago, but…

Ken saw Col pat her arm and give her shoulder a squeeze. How he wished he had the right to do that to Lyn. While affectionate in private, he wasn't sure how she'd react to demonstrations of affection in public. She could be very sensitive. He was still feeling his way with this new version of her.

'He'll be fine, Jo,' Col said. 'He has you and Gordon. And I'm sure Kylie will see sense.'

'I can have a word with him, too, Jo,' Ken offered. 'You do know Gordon sent him to me for advice. He's a good lad, someone I'd be happy to do business with myself if things were different.' Ken wasn't sure what he meant by that, but he remembered thinking it before, when Danny came to see him. He filed the thought away for future consideration.

As the evening progressed and one drink turned into two, the talk turned to the Easter picnic races.

'Why don't we make up a party this year?' Col suggested. 'I'm sure Kay and Nick would be in it, Owen and Fran too. How about it, you two?' He looked at Ken and Lyn.

Ken turned to see Lyn looking awkward. He felt her edge away.

'I don't know,' she said. 'Easter. It's a long way away. I may not be here.'

Ken's heart fell. He'd been trying to forget Lyn's imminent departure. Things had been progressing so well between them. There was the weekend in Canberra coming up – a whole weekend with just the two of them. He couldn't wait.

'Oh, you must stay,' Jo said. 'They're a lot of fun. More of a social occasion than a race meeting. And surely you're not going to leave before the choir's Easter production? You're all working so hard on it.'

Ken felt Lyn stiffen and placed his hand on her thigh under the table to be rewarded by a grateful smile.

'They both sound great, Jo. But it'll all depend of a number of things. I feel I've just been marking time in Granite Springs, lovely though it's been. But don't worry. If I'm still here, I'll be sure to get involved.' She gave what Ken recognised as a false smile.

'Let's hope,' Jo replied. 'I…'

This time it was Col who interrupted, 'It's getting late. We should all be making tracks.'

In the ensuing flurry of farewells, Ken lost connection with Lyn for a moment, only taking her arm as they left the club. When they were alone again, Col and Jo having gone to find their car, Ken asked, 'My place?' hoping Lyn would agree.

'Sorry, Ken. Not tonight. Maddy's out too, and I don't want to leave Mum on her own too often. We have the weekend to look forward to.' The look in Lyn's eyes said it all. It told him she was looking forward to their weekend together as much as he was.

Thirty-four

When Lyn opened her eyes, she knew today was going to be special. It took her only a few seconds to remember. It was Saturday. She was going to spend the weekend with Ken in a luxurious hotel on the banks of Lake Burley Griffin in Canberra. It hadn't taken much persuasion for Maddy to agree to be there for Edith. Lyn knew that probably meant Zac, too. And Edith had been delighted to hear Lyn and Ken's relationship was – in her words – *finally going somewhere.*

But while Lyn was eagerly looking forward to the time away, she still wondered if she was being fair to Ken. He said he was okay with knowing she intended to leave Granite Springs, satisfied that this time he would be prepared.

'Where is it Ken's taking you?' Edith asked, as Lyn was drinking her breakfast cup of lemon and ginger tea.

'I don't know the name of the place, but it's a new resort style hotel close to the lake. Ken was given a complimentary voucher.'

'Way to go, Grandma!' Maddy said, walking into the kitchen, her eyes glued to her phone as usual. 'Zac says he'll be over as soon as he can get away. How do you fancy a trip to the markets, GG?' she asked Edith.

'Are you sure you two young things want to be saddled with an old lady?' Edith asked, chuckling. 'I'll be perfectly okay here on my own.'

'But it'll be fun,' Maddy replied, waving her phone at the old woman. 'Zac says…'

Lyn didn't wait to hear what Zac had to say. She had no doubt

Maddy would prevail, and her mother would be well looked after. Zac was turning out to be a thoughtful young man regardless of his occasional lapses of judgement and his unkempt appearance. 'I'll leave you two to work it out. I need to get dressed and pack.'

Back in her bedroom, Lyn selected a pair of jeans, a shirt, and a floaty dress to pack in her overnight bag, before pulling on her favourite pink denim pants and matching tee-shirt. A quick glance in the mirror, a comb through her hair and she was ready. Hearing Ken's car stop outside, she took a deep breath to calm the butterflies in her stomach, picked up her bag, and headed out of the bedroom.

As she passed the kitchen, she popped in to give her mum a hug. Maddy had disappeared again. 'Remember, Mum. You can reach me on my mobile if anything…' Her voice faltered at the look in her mother's eyes. 'Sorry, I know you'll be fine with Maddy.'

'On you go. Don't keep your young man waiting. I'll see you tomorrow. I want to hear all about it.'

It was a relief to see Ken, to feel the clasp of his hand, his peck on her cheek. But Lyn couldn't help the niggle of worry in the back of her mind. What if something happened to her mum when she was off with Ken? She'd never forgive herself. But wasn't that just what she intended to do? Go off travelling, leave her mum in a nursing home where anything might happen. And she'd be far away.

'Penny for them.'

Lyn sighed. 'I'm worried about Mum.'

'I thought Maddy and Zac were on duty this weekend.'

'They are. They're taking her to the markets today and goodness knows what else they'll get up to. It's not that.' Lyn bit the inside of her cheek.

'Are you rethinking your plan to leave?'

Lyn's stomach lurched. Ken could read her mind so well. It had stunned her every time he did that when they were ten. She thought he'd have lost the knack.

'I keep remembering how I wasn't there for Dad when he… I don't think I could live with myself if I was traipsing about doing my tourist thing and something happened… if I couldn't get back in time.'

'How important is this trip to you?'

'It's something I've dreamt about all my life, but things have always got in the way.' She sighed again. 'Maybe it's just not meant to be. Maybe I need to rethink.'

'Is Granite Springs such a bad place?'

Lyn shot a glance at Ken. He was staring at the road ahead, his expression inscrutable. She thought about his words. She knew what her answer would have been forty-five years ago. The eighteen-year-old Lyn would have been quick to tell him the town and her parents made her feel claustrophobic, made her want to be free. There was a whole world out there to explore.

But was it still true? Did she still feel that way? Lyn remembered the warmth with which she was received by her old friends, the joy of singing with the choir, the satisfaction she found sharing the knitting program with her mother. And the town itself had changed. Granite Springs was now a thriving regional centre with restaurants rivalling any she knew in Brisbane. And Ken lived here.

'Maybe not,' she said slowly, seeing his expression change, his lips turning up in a grin. 'It's different to what I remember – not so... claustrophobic.'

'Maybe it's you that's changed.'

Lyn considered for a moment before replying. She supposed she had changed. A lot had happened in the intervening years. But she didn't belong here, did she? She was a big city person.

'Almost there.' Ken's voice cut into her musing, as they reached the outskirts of the city.

Seeing the high buildings, the swarms of people, Lyn felt a sudden and unexpected distaste for the familiar cityscape. Was this what she was yearning for? Suddenly, the peace of Granite Springs seemed to beckon her in a way she'd never imagined.

By the time they pulled up in the driveway of the hotel, Lyn had managed to control her thoughts and was again looking forward to their weekend. She decided to banish all her worries and enjoy what promised to be a romantic getaway.

*

The day flew past. After lunch in one of the many downtown cafes, they took in a visit to the art gallery followed by a leisurely stroll along the foreshore of the lake. Then it was back to their sumptuous room with the king-sized bed and the wonderful view.

Seated on the bed, waiting for Ken to come out of the shower, Lyn reflected that perhaps she'd found something that had been missing in her life, something she hadn't known she was looking for. Spending time with Ken was restful. It was like sinking into a warm bath. They knew each other inside out. The years apart had made not one jot of difference. But could she be content living in Granite Springs?

'That feels good.' Ken came out of the ensuite wearing a white towelling gown, courtesy of the hotel, and rubbing his hair with a towel. 'Your turn.' He entwined his fingers in Lyn's hair and kissed the top of her head as they passed.

As Lyn dropped her head back, allowing the water to cascade over her, she was struck by the realisation she was happy, happier than she'd been in years. Was it all due to Ken Thompson, or was there some other unseen force at work? Could it be that the change of scenery, coming back to Granite Springs, had been what she needed? Was the whole idea of travel, the dream she'd harboured for most of her life, nothing but a mirage?

Now wasn't the time for such speculation. She rinsed herself off and stepped out of the shower to find Ken standing there holding out a towel.

He wrapped it around her, his lips kissing the drops of water from her shoulders making her shiver with desire. His hands stroked her through the towel, then let it drop to the floor Standing before him, her body ached for his touch.

'You're so beautiful,' he murmured, his voice thick with desire.

Lyn felt something inside her melt. 'But we don't have time,' she began to object, trying to deny the overwhelming urge to feel his arms around her, to feel his...

'We have all the time in the world.' He stroked his fingers down her arm, his touch sending waves of longing through her, then picked her up and carried her to the bed. He laid her gently down, and their lips met in a deep kiss. Lyn's mind emptied of all other thoughts as she gave herself up to the sensation of Ken's mouth on hers, his warm touch on her nakedness, his strong body lifting her to heights of passion she'd never before experienced.

*

It was sometime later before they left the room to sample the delights the hotel had to offer.

They enjoyed drinks in the bar, followed by dinner in the dining room with a view across the lake. The fare here was Italian, reminding them of their dinner and late-night snack back home. As they slid into a corner booth, a waiter appeared with a complimentary antipasto platter and handed them menus.

True to form, Ken ordered the lamb dish – this time it was *casarecce* pasta and lamb ragout – while Lyn opted for the wood grilled swordfish served with eggplant and tomatoes. Ken ordered champagne to accompany the meal, adding to the sense of celebration.

Conversation during the meal was easy. They avoided anything controversial or any talk of previous partners. Ken expressed interest in what Lyn had been doing over the years, and she discovered more about the real estate business than she'd thought possible.

'What have you done with Titch this weekend?' Lyn asked, during a lull in the conversation.

'Neil took him out to Wooleton. Old Bess will be happy to see her offspring again and one more dog won't be noticed. I'm picking him up after work on Monday. Why don't you come out with me? I'm having dinner there. You've met Neil and will remember Alec, though he's no longer the toerag he was back then. I'm sure Judy would like to meet you. Neil's partner, Sally, might be there too. Would it be too much for you? It's about time you met my family.'

Lyn stared at Ken, her hand gripping the stem of her wine glass. This sounded too much like commitment. But Granite Springs was a small town. Ken's family were no doubt aware she and Ken were seeing each other. If they hadn't before now, this weekend would have clinched it. She supposed she'd have to meet them sometime and better at a family dinner than in the middle of Main Street.

'Maybe,' she said.

'It would mean a lot to me.' Ken's hand covered Lyn's on the table, sending shivers up her spine.

Perhaps it wouldn't be so bad. As he said, she already knew Neil and Alec. And she was curious to meet Judy who she'd heard good things about. 'Didn't you say this Sally is Gordon Slater's daughter?' she asked. 'Where does she fit in? I thought he and Jo married early.'

'It's quite a story. Seems Gordon had a roving eye and Sally turned up in Granite Springs looking for her father. Caused quite a stir at the time. I think I said. Her mother's dead, and she decided to make her life here. She'll make a good farm wife.'

Not like me. I'd never have fitted in, Lyn thought.

'Not like you,' Ken said, echoing her thoughts. 'I think I always knew you were destined for more than we had to offer, but I'd hoped what we had...'

More – yes, that's what she'd wanted. And she had been able to do more in Brisbane than she ever could in the town she'd grown up in. Lyn thought of all the young girls whose lives she'd impacted, the influence she'd managed to achieve in supporting and mentoring young teachers, the improvements she'd effected at Irene Longman College over the years.

But what did she want from life, now? Would the travel she planned give her the rewards she was searching for? Or could she find happiness by returning to her roots, trite though it sounded.

Back in their room, they turned to each other. The moonlight was shining through the window sending a streak of light across the thick carpet. The view over the lake was spectacular, but ignored as Ken's lips found hers, his hand pushed her flimsy dress from her shoulders, and they fell onto the bed.

Thirty-five

'What would you like to do today?' Ken asked. They were enjoying a breakfast of coffee and croissants in the hotel dining room. Outside they could see people walking and cycling along the foreshore and the Captain Cook Memorial water jet shooting high into the air. The sky was filled with colourful hot air balloons. From the distance came the peal of church bells.

'I don't know. You decide.' Unusually for her, Lyn was content to follow Ken's lead. She was feeling happy and relaxed after their early morning lovemaking. Waking in Ken's arms had been a revelation, one she was still coming to terms with. Despite having been married to Glenn for years, it wasn't something she remembered doing. Their mornings had always been busy, filled with activity. There had been no time to cosy up together, both so intent on the day's agenda.

Or had it been her who always leapt out of bed, avoiding anything that might delay her? Was Glenn right when he accused her of being too wrapped up in her career to spend time with him? Well, it was too late now. And Lyn was sure Glenn had never made her feel the way Ken did. His feet met hers under the table, catching them in a scissor hold. A flash of desire ran through her, forcing her to swallow quickly.

Ken grinned, seemingly aware of the effect he had on her. 'What do you say we go on a bushwalk this morning, maybe take a picnic lunch, then visit a couple of wineries before heading back home?'

'Sounds perfect.'

In no hurry to leave, the pair had another coffee before collecting their bags, loading them into the car, and setting off for a nearby national park. Glad she'd packed a pair of strong shoes, Lyn found she enjoyed walking along, her hand tightly clasped in Ken's. They completed a couple of the easy trails, managing to spy a koala hiding in the tall branches of a eucalypt, and were lucky enough to hear the melodious call of a lyrebird before deciding it was lunchtime.

The lunch, which they ate in one of several available picnic areas, comprised cold chicken, cheeses, sour dough bread, paté and fruit. The hotel had offered a packed picnic lunch which Ken carried in a small backpack he said he kept in the car boot for just such occasions.

'You do this often?' she asked.

'Not recently. But Neil and I used to take off for the day before he and Sally got together. I haven't had much use for it since then. Lucky I didn't toss it out.'

'Lucky,' Lyn murmured, wondering if he'd known about the picnic lunch deal. But it was a welcome respite after the exertions of the morning, and they washed the food down with bottles of ginger beer purchased at the visitor centre.

'Now for the wineries,' Ken said, as they cleared up the remains of their meal.

He'd come prepared. Once in the car, Ken handed Lyn a map of the neighbouring wineries, asking her to plot out a course, but stating they should leave the Pialligo Estate Winery till last as he had a surprise for her.

The afternoon passed in a leisurely fashion as Ken and Lyn sampled wines from a variety of estates. The car boot soon became filled with cartons, leading Lyn to joke that it looked as if Ken was planning to open his own wine business.

It was around five-thirty, and Lyn was becoming weary, when Ken said, 'I think it's time for our last stop.'

'Don't you think we've done enough? And where will you put any more wine?' Lyn was tired and hungry, though reluctant for the weekend to finish. It had been good to get away from Granite Springs, to pretend, just for two days, that she and Ken were like any other couple, out enjoying themselves without a care in the world.

'Bear with me. Just one more. I think you'll be surprised. I hope you'll enjoy it.'

Lyn's curiosity was piqued. 'One more,' she agreed.

But when they drove through the entrance to this winery, Lyn saw a line of cars ahead of them. 'What…?' she asked, twisting her head in an attempt to see what the attraction was.

'How does dinner followed by a performance of *A Midsummer Night's Dream* grab you?'

'You're joking!'

'Would I joke about something like that?'

Lyn should have known Ken would remember – her favourite Shakespearian play. When they'd studied it in year eight, she'd gone into raptures about it, much to Ken's disgust. He'd labelled it as *too girly for words*. It was one of the few things they'd argued about. 'You remembered?'

'Of course I remembered. When I was given the hotel voucher, I looked up events in Canberra – and there it was. It was a no-brainer. I booked right away.'

'But… how did you know I'd come with you this weekend?' Lyn was familiar with similar productions in Queensland and knew how quickly they were booked out.

'I didn't. You'd just arrived in town. We'd barely reconnected. But…' he said, with a wicked gleam in his eye, '…a man can hope. And you're here, aren't you?'

Lyn wasn't sure whether to be annoyed at Ken's assumption she'd fall in with his plans, or impressed he'd made such an effort to please her. She decided to say nothing.

'It'll be a late night,' she said after a long pause, her mind going to her mother who she was ashamed she hadn't thought of since leaving Granite Springs.

'Not a problem. I had a word with your mum and Maddy. They're not expecting you back till tomorrow morning.'

'Where…?' Damn the man. This was going too far. Lyn should have known he'd be like this. She realised Ken was laughing.

'What's so funny?'

'Your face. It's the same expression you always had when you thought I was getting one up on you. It's a very pretty face, but that expression!' He laughed again.

This time, Lyn couldn't help smiling. 'Oh, Ken Thompson. You'll never change. What did Mum say?'

'She told me to make sure you behaved yourself.'

Lyn was lost for words.

By this time, Ken had parked the car. With another laugh, Lyn got out and, taking his hand – something she was now becoming used to – allowed herself to be led into the restaurant.

Like the rest of the weekend, the evening passed too quickly. Lyn became lost in the performance, transported to the forest where the comedy of the four lovers played out. It ended all too soon. Lyn sighed as the actors took their final bow. She turned to Ken. 'Thanks so much. That was amazing!'

Ken just grinned and wrapped an arm around Lyn's shoulders as they made their way back to the car. She snuggled into his embrace, wishing the evening could go on forever.

Once back in the car, Lyn automatically checked her phone while Ken was backing out of the parking spot. To her surprise, there were at least three unanswered calls from Maddy and a text message.

Mum, was her first thought. Distraught she'd been enjoying herself while something had happened to her mother, Lyn hurriedly opened messenger and scanned Maddy's text.

Been trying to call U. GG fell. I called an ambulance. Am waiting at hospital. Call me. Mxx

Lyn gasped.

'What's the matter?' Ken asked, following the line of cars exiting the winery. 'Do you want me to stop?'

'Yes. No. I don't know.' Lyn was gripping her phone tightly. 'What time is it? I need to call Maddy.'

'Let me get out of this crush and I'll find a good stopping place.' Ken manoeuvred the car through the entrance and along the road, till they came to a wide section of shoulder where he stopped.

He turned to face Lyn. 'Now, what's up? What did Maddy say?'

'Oh, Ken! I knew I should have been there. It's Mum. She had another fall and…'

'Call Maddy and tell her we're on our way home.'

Tears were forming in Lyn's eyes as she pressed speed dial to connect with her granddaughter. This was exactly what she'd been afraid of when they drove to Canberra the day before. Had she had some sort of premonition? No. She didn't believe in such things. But, if she'd been there…?

'Maddy?'

'Oh, Grandma, Thank goodness. Where have you been?' Without waiting for a response, the girl continued, 'GG tripped coming into the kitchen. She was moving around without her walker and fell on the tiled floor. Zac called the ambulance and they were here in no time. I think she's damaged her other hip this time. She was very white. I was really worried. I…'

'We're on our way,' Lyn tried to reassure Maddy, though her own emotions were in turmoil. After a few more words of comfort, she hung up.

Ken drew her into his arms. 'Your mum will be fine. She's strong,' he said.

But Lyn knew he was only trying to reassure her, just as she had been with Maddy. 'She's ninety-four,' Lyn said. 'And last time, they warned us this could happen, that it was likely she could fall again. I told her to use her walker, but she's so damned independent.'

'A bit like someone else I know.'

Lyn was too upset to respond as she normally would. 'How long will it take us to get back?'

'The same time as usual. A couple of hours, as long as there's no holdup.'

Lyn took a few deep breaths in an attempt to calm herself. There was nothing she could do, no way they could speed up the journey. She wiped her eyes and tried to focus on the road ahead.

They drove along in silence, neither in the mood for the music station they'd enjoyed on the trip the day before. Outside, the darkness formed a velvet cloak, the road a ribbon of grey in the car's headlights as they sped along the deserted highway.

Suddenly, a shadow appeared to leap out in front of them, two bright eyes reflected in the headlights. Ken swerved. The kangaroo swerved, too – in the same direction – seemingly bent on self-destruction. He swerved again. The animal swerved, too. There was no way to avoid the collision that inevitably followed, the loud bump sending Lyn's heart into her mouth and her hand to her chest.

'Shit!' the expletive shot from Ken's lips as he pulled the car to a stop.

'You couldn't miss it.' Lyn opened the door and leapt out of the car, going to the injured animal. But it was too late. The impact had killed it.

Ken joined her and together they stared at what was either a small kangaroo or a wallaby. It looked even smaller, lying there on the tarmac. Still. Dead.

'The stupid creature,' Ken raged. 'Why did it have to follow the headlights?'

'It was as if it was mesmerised by the light.' Lyn bent down to take a closer look, to check the animal's pouch. It was empty. She stood up again. There was nothing they could do.

'We should try to get it off the road,' Ken said. 'Make sure it's not a hazard to other traffic.'

Lyn gazed up and down the road. There was nothing in sight. She thought of her mother, lying in hospital, of Maddy waiting anxiously for her arrival. But there was no way they could drive off and leave the dead animal lying there on the roadway. Since leaving Canberra they'd already passed several cases of roadkill. Now she understood how easily it could happen.

After helping Ken drag the animal onto the verge, Lyn started shivering. She wrapped her arms around her body, watching Ken inspect the car for damage.

'The headlight's broken and there's a huge dent in the bonnet, but I think we're safe to keep going. I'll just google who I need to call to report the incident, then we can be off. Sorry we've been delayed. I know how anxious you are to get home.'

'It can't be helped. You were driving carefully. It appeared from nowhere.' She shivered again. 'I hate to think we killed a native animal. They've suffered enough with all the bushfires.'

They continued on their way, though Lyn couldn't help thinking about the poor kangaroo they'd left by the side of the road. Life was so tenuous. First her dad, then this – and her mother was in hospital again. How could she go away and leave her, knowing it might happen again and again?

Lyn glanced at the strong profile of the man sitting beside her, a man who would always rise to meet a crisis. He was gazing fixedly through the windscreen. She knew he cared for her – and she cared for him. This weekend had confirmed that. But was it enough? She'd once thought she could make a life with Glenn. She shifted slightly in her seat. This was different. She knew Ken wasn't anything like her former husband. He was kind, genuine, honest and…

'Do you want to go straight to the hospital?'

Lyn answered immediately. 'Yes, please. Maddy's waiting. I really need to see Mum.'

'It'll be after midnight when we get in.'

'I know.' Lyn drew her knees up to her chin, hands clasped around them as if she could ward away her fear. She kept thinking, *what if…* But there was no guarantee her presence would have made any difference. The doctor had warned her second hip fractures were common, that when an elderly person had fallen once, she was likely to do it again. He'd also said the second one tended to be more serious.

The streets were quiet when they drove into town. In the early hours of Monday morning in Granite Springs, only a few revellers left over from Sunday night partying were making their way home.

Ken dropped Lyn off at the hospital. 'I'll park and meet you inside,' he said, as she jumped out of the car and dashed to the entrance, barely hearing his words.

At the ward, Lyn quickly spied Maddy and Zac. They were seated in chairs close to the nurses' station, the girl slumped against the boy's shoulder. Both had their eyes closed.

'Maddy!'

As soon as she heard Lyn's voice, Maddy became alert. She leapt up and hugged her grandmother. 'I'm so glad you're here,' she said. 'We didn't know what to do and didn't want to leave till you got here.'

'I'm here now.' Lyn stroked the young girl's hair, seeing her eyes red from crying. 'Where's GG?'

'She's in room six, but they wouldn't let us stay with her.'

Lyn looked around and, seeing a nurse at the desk, walked over. 'I'm Mrs Carter's daughter. I only just got here. Can I see her?'

The nurse gave Lyn a doubtful glance. 'I'll have to check. She's due for surgery first thing and we want her to have a good sleep.'

Lyn felt her heart sink. Another surgery!

'How is she?' Ken whispered, appearing from the lift in time to hear the nurse's words. Wordlessly, Lyn fell into his arms. It felt safe there, as if he'd protect her from all the ills of the world. But she knew he couldn't. No one could.

'I think it would be better if you came back in the morning,' the nurse said, returning to the station. 'Your mother's sleeping soundly and shouldn't be disturbed.'

'I won't…' Lyn began, only to feel Ken's hand on her arm.

'We'll come back in the morning,' he said. 'Thank you. Come on,' he said to Maddy and Zac. 'There's nothing we can do here. You two need a proper bed to sleep in. You did well to stay till now. Best we all go home and try to get some sleep.'

Still protesting, Lyn found herself travelling to the ground floor in the lift, accompanied by a determined Ken, and Maddy and Zac, who both looked half-asleep.

They all piled into Ken's car and soon reached Edith Carter's house. Maddy and Zac quickly disappeared inside. Ken and Lyn stood for a moment before he said, 'I think I should stay here with you for what's left of the night, if you've no objection.'

Objection? Lyn suddenly felt giddy as tears welled up behind her eyelids. The last thing she wanted was to be alone, alone with her thoughts. 'Thanks,' she said as he followed her inside.

*

At the hospital next morning, Lyn and Maddy were permitted to see Edith before she was whisked off to theatre. Zac had elected to go back to his share house, and Ken, after driving the women to hospital and ensuring all was well, had gone to his office.

'The operation may take a few hours,' the nurse told Lyn. 'Would you like us to call you when your mother's in recovery?'

'Please. I'll stay in the hospital.'

"Me too, Grandma,' Maddy said, linking her arm with Lyn's. 'I don't want to think of you waiting here on your own.'

'Thanks, sweetie.' Lyn knew she'd be glad of her granddaughter's company. She wouldn't be able to settle to anything till she knew her mother was out of danger. Although she was aware it was a routine operation, Edith was ninety-four and the fact they'd decided on surgery as a matter of urgency was cause for concern. She couldn't bear to lose her mother too, especially now they were becoming closer.

It was three hours and several cups of coffee later, before the anticipated call came to tell Lyn her mother was on her way back to the ward. During that time, Ken had called repeatedly offering to do anything Lyn needed. But there was nothing to do but wait.

They rushed up to the ward, where the nurse on duty said, 'Everything went according to plan. We were lucky Mr Vaughan, our orthopaedic consultant, had a free slot this morning. It's always best to have the surgery as soon as possible after the fracture occurs. It tends to provide the best outcome. Your mother's not a young woman.'

While grateful to hear all this, Lyn just wanted to see her mum. 'Can we go in now?

'You'll find Edith's still drowsy. Don't worry if she doesn't say much.'

With Maddy at her heels, Lyn hurried along the corridor, only slowing down when they arrived outside room six. Taking a deep breath and remembering how frail her mother had looked last time she was here, Lyn pushed open the door.

Edith was lying much as she had only a couple of months earlier. Her face was almost as white as the pillow it was resting on, her thin hair plastered to her head, her arms lying still on the coverlet. She looked…

Lyn drew a quick intake of breath.

As she watched, her mother's eyes slowly opened, releasing the tension which had been building up in Lyn. Although not considering herself religious, she uttered a silent prayer of gratitude, before moving forward to take her mother's hand in hers. She'd googled hip surgery in the early hours when she couldn't sleep. The mortality statistics frightened her. They weren't out of the woods yet. 'You gave us a scare,' she said, her voice unsteady.

'Gave myself one,' Edith replied in a quavering voice. 'But Maddy and Zac did all right by me. Got those paramedics there before you could wink. What a fuss about a small fall.'

'It was serious, Mum. You know that! Worse than last time. Lucky the surgeon was available to fix you so quickly. You should…' she started to say before stopping herself. Now wasn't the time to harass her mother about the need to use her walker.

'I'm sorry.' The nurse Lyn had spoken to appeared in the doorway. 'Your mother needs to rest. I must ask you to leave. Normal visiting hours are...' She proceeded to list the visiting times, much to Lyn's annoyance. She'd expected to be able to stay by her mother's side all day. 'Sorry,' the nurse said again, apologetically this time. 'It's Mr Vaughan's instructions.'

'We'll be back, Mum.' Lyn kissed her mother on the forehead and stroked her hair. 'See you later.'

'What shall we do now, Gran?' Maddy asked as they walked outside.

'I'm going home, then I'll call your mum to let her know about GG. But there's no point in her rushing down here,' she added, seeing Maddy's apprehensive expression. 'I'll walk. I feel like some fresh air. I might try to get some sleep. I don't think I got much last night. Do you have classes you should go to?'

Maddy scuffed her feet. 'I have a practice session with my tutor early afternoon, but if you think I should come back with you...'

'No, sweetie, you go ahead. I can come back on my own. You can visit another time. I don't expect there to be any change. I hate to see Mum lying there so helpless.' She brushed away a tear, grateful when Maddy hugged her tightly.

'Will GG be all right? I read about the dangers of falling at her age. And this was the second time.'

So Maddy had been consulting Dr Google too?

'I'm sure she'll make a good recovery,' Lyn said, being nothing of the sort. 'She's always been a feisty one.' But her mother didn't look very feisty in her hospital bed. Would she manage to recover from this, or would it be the beginning of a downward spiral?

Thirty-six

Ken couldn't settle to anything until he heard from Lyn that her mother was out of surgery and awake. What a thing to happen! As if the poor woman hadn't suffered enough. He wasn't clear in his own mind if he was referring to Lyn or her mother. Both deserved his concern. But, much as he liked and admired the older woman, it was Lyn who was constantly in his thoughts.

When he knew Lyn was returning home, Ken was tempted to join her. But what could he do other than hold and comfort her? Maybe that would be enough? They'd spent the night – or what had been left of it – in each other's arms. It wasn't a time for lovemaking. And he hoped he'd been able to offer some solace. He doubted Lyn had slept, though he knew he'd dropped off for a few hours, only wakening with a start when the sun peeked through the blinds they'd forgotten to close.

The computer screen in front of him was blurring, his mind busy elsewhere, when there was a knock on his office door.

'Danny Slater to see you, Ken.'

Ken cursed inwardly. He'd intended to call Danny today. He looked up to see the young man hovering behind Ewan. He'd regained his old confident manner and had a wide grin on his face. He walked toward Ken's desk, hand outstretched. Ken rose to greet him.

'I want to thank you, Ken. You've saved my life!'

Ken knew he'd done nothing of the sort, but he did have a hand in ensuring the development proposal hadn't been approved, not yet, anyway. 'Hardly.'

'Dad told me what you did. I'd never have been able to live it down if people found out I was involved with Sherwood, once it came out what he was up to. He's left town, by the way. So good riddance. I'm assuming his leaving means the council will abandon the proposal.'

'Glad to hear it Danny. And I only did what I'd hope someone else would do if Neil got involved in anything dodgy.' Ken doubted his upright son would ever give him cause for this kind of worry, but he meant what he said.

Danny knew Neil too. 'I think Neil would have more sense,' he said honestly. 'But Sherwood was so plausible. It looked too good to pass up.' He ran a hand through his hair. 'Dad thanks you too, and Mum.' For a moment his air of confidence slipped. 'I feel I've let them both down. I won't make the same mistake again.'

'I should hope not.' Ken eyed the young man standing opposite. He was a good lad. Ken had known him since he was in primary school. He'd been to school with his parents who were his good friends. It had been an honest mistake, and not one he'd forget in a hurry.

Ken shuffled a few papers on his desk, wondering if this was the right time to suggest something he'd been mulling over since the council meeting. 'Look, Danny. This probably isn't the time, but I'd like to have a chat with you once this has all blown over. There may be a few things we could work on together.' He tapped on the desk with his pen, hoping he wouldn't have cause to regret his words.

The young man's eyes lit up, then his face clouded over. 'I can take care of myself, Ken. But if you think you need someone to take on any new projects… I know you must be missing Neil.'

Damn the man! But Ken knew it was Danny's pride speaking – he was a lot like his dad in many respects. He couldn't hold that against him, and Danny was his mother's son, too. He must have inherited some of Jo's traits. 'As I said, when this blows over. It may not be finished yet. We'll have to wait to see what the council decides.'

'But you're on the council.'

'I'm only one of many. I hear your dad's thinking of standing next election,' he said, to take the heat off himself.

'Dad? I'm sure Carol would like that! And he'll do anything to get out of the house I expect. Thanks again, Ken. I look forward to hearing what you have in mind.'

Ken watched Danny jauntily walk out, smiling to Ewan and the two women in the office as he went. He shook his head, wondering how much was bravado and how much genuine confidence. He had the strong impression this debacle had dented Danny's self-assurance. He'd leave him to stew for a bit, before making the suggestion he had in mind.

Alone again, Ken's thoughts returned to Lyn. She had never given him an answer about dinner at Wooleton, but he guessed there was no way she'd be joining him there tonight. On an impulse, he picked up his phone to call Neil and ask if they could take care of Titch for a few days longer. Lyn would need his support. He wanted to be there for her.

Somehow, he made it through the rest of the day. Arriving home to the empty house, Ken was struck by how quickly he'd become accustomed to Titch's presence. The silence that met him when he opened the door only emphasised how much he'd come to depend on the little creature. The pup was someone to talk to. His inevitable snuffling and occasional barking bouts were something Ken now accepted as a normal part of the day. Without them, the place was like a morgue.

Ken dropped his overnight bag in the hallway, planning to take care of it later, and headed into the kitchen. He took a can of beer from the fridge and checked the frozen meals in the freezer. Nothing appealed. He took out his phone to call Lyn.

'How's your mum?' he asked, when she answered after only two rings. 'Are you still at the hospital?'

'We were sent home so Mum could rest, and instructed to stick to visiting hours. I'm about to go back now.'

'Have you eaten?'

'Maddy and I had something while Mum was in surgery. I can't face food right now.'

Ken understood. A meal together was out of the question.

'How about I meet you there?'

'Would you?'

Ken heard the relief in Lyn's voice.

'But what about your car?'

'In the garage. I picked up a courtesy car this morning. I'll be there. Seven?'

'Yes.'

That settled, Ken felt better and was able to eat a sandwich of cheese and tomato, grimacing a little when he realised the bread was close to being stale. He needed to make a trip to the shops.

*

Lyn was seated beside her mother's bed when Ken walked into the two-bed hospital room. The other bed was empty. The sight of the two women tore at his heart as he stood inside the door watching them.

Suddenly, as if aware of his presence, Lyn turned, her face transformed by a welcoming smile. 'Look who's come to see you, Mum,' she said.

Edith looked up, and Ken could see immediately how much frailer she was than when he last saw her. She seemed to have shrunk, to look her age. Whereas before, she'd retained her customary feisty attitude, she now looked like a sad old woman.

'What have you been getting up to when we were out of town?' he asked with a chuckle, taking a seat beside Lyn, the touch of her thigh on his making him start. 'Seems Lyn can't leave you alone for a day without you ending up back in here. I hope they're taking good care of you.'

'I'll be better when they let me out of here,' she said with a hint of her usual spirit. 'You can't get rid of me that easily. You had a good time in Canberra?'

Ken saw a pretty blush suffuse Lyn's cheeks. The old woman still knew how to stir her.

'That we did,' he said. 'Did Lyn tell you we hit a kangaroo on the road back?'

'She did not.' Edith glared at her daughter. 'I trust your car wasn't too damaged.'

'A dented bonnet, a bent bumper bar and a broken headlight,' Ken said. 'It's being repaired.'

'I hope you weren't hurrying back to see me?' Edith nodded to herself. 'Lyn said you both came straight here, but I had no idea. They gave me something to make me sleep.' Her eyes began to close as if talking about sleep had told her body it needed more of it.

'Thanks for coming. But I think it's time to leave,' Lyn said, before patting the hands lying clasped on the cover, and kissing her mother on the forehead.

As they both stood up, Ken automatically placed a hand on Lyn's back to help her out of the room. It felt the most natural thing in the world to be with her like this. Lyn had only been back in town for a few months, but already Ken couldn't contemplate what his life would be like when she left. He hoped it wouldn't come to that. But so far, he'd had little indication her plans had changed. Though with her mother having had a second fall...

'Oh, Ken!' Outside the ward, Lyn turned into Ken's arms with a sob. 'I hate to see her so helpless like this. Mum's normally so...' She buried her face in his chest, then lifted her head to meet his eyes. 'Sorry. What must you think?'

'I think you need something in your stomach and something stronger than tea or coffee to drink.'

Ken saw a weak smile appear amongst the tears trickling down Lyn's face. He gently wiped them away with one finger, pausing when he came to her lips.

'You may be right,' she said. 'Where did you have in mind?'

Ken hadn't thought that far ahead. He knew he had nothing to eat in his house and wasn't sure about Lyn's. The club or a restaurant were probably out as he knew Lyn wouldn't feel up to a crowd of people. 'Is there a café or something here in the hospital?' he asked, trying to remember if he'd seen one on his way through the entrance. It wasn't somewhere he'd ever had a reason to visit.

'There's one on the ground floor, but I'm not sure it'll be open at this time.'

'Let's find out.'

Thirty-seven

The café was about to close when Lyn and Ken reached it, but they were able to buy two of the four pita wraps which languished in the showcase and two bananas from the bowl on top of the counter. The espresso machine had been turned off.

'Seems it's juice, a soft drink or coffee from the vending machine,' Ken said with a wry grin.

Lyn opted for juice. Having sampled the coffee from the vending machine on a previous visit, she knew it bore little resemblance to the coffee she was accustomed to. Taking her advice, Ken chose a can of Sprite.

'Thanks again,' Lyn said, as they settled at a table in the deserted café. Fortunately, it wasn't closed off from the main entrance, so they were able to stay there as long as they wanted. They watched as the staff left, the only sounds the hum of the refrigerated cabinet of drinks, the distant buzz of people coming and going, and the even more distant thwup of the emergency helicopter coming in to land on the hospital roof.

'How do you think Mum looked?' Lyn asked. She'd been shocked by the change in her mother. When she left her on Saturday morning, Edith had been full of vigour, determined to be independent of the walker she despised. But the woman in the bed was a ghost of her former self. Lyn could hardly believe it was her mother lying so still in the bed upstairs.

Ken hesitated before saying, 'She doesn't look good, Lyn. This second fall seems to have taken it out of her. What does the doctor say?'

'Only that the surgery was successful.' She sighed and pushed her plate away. Her throat seemed to close up at the very thought of food. 'He says they'll know more in a few days. But the prognosis isn't so good. I've looked it up. The mortality rate for a second round of surgery… it increases.'

'So says Dr Google?' Ken raised an eyebrow.

'I know. But I couldn't sleep and…'

'Sorry. I should have been able to stay awake with you.' Ken took Lyn's hand in his and squeezed it.

'No. You drove all the way back. You were tired. You needed to sleep.' She twisted the straw in her juice with the fingers of her free hand.

'You're tired now. You should sleep tonight.'

'Is that an instruction, doctor?'

'I'm concerned about you, Lyn. I don't want you to get sick, too.'

'I'm all right.' But was she? What would she have done if Ken hadn't been here?

'Where's Maddy?' he asked.

'With Zac. She has assignments to complete. I told her there was no need for her to come tonight.'

'You shouldn't have come by yourself.'

'You're here.' Lyn couldn't describe how comforting she found his presence. She'd always considered herself to be self-sufficient, able to cope with anything life threw at her. But here she was, sitting in a deserted café in Granite Springs Base Hospital grateful for the company of the man she'd run from all those years ago. More than grateful.

'What'll you do?'

It was a simple question, but a loaded one. Lyn knew Ken wasn't asking what she would do that night, not even what she'd do when her mother was discharged from hospital. He was asking what she was going to do with the rest of her life. It was something she had been wondering too.

'I can't leave Mother.'

Lyn looked across at the familiar face, at the way his eyes crinkled when he smiled, his lips curling up on one side. She felt the warmth in the hand holding hers. A warm glow started in her toes and moved through her body.

And I can't leave you, either.

But the words remained unspoken.

'Let's get you home,' Ken said abruptly, almost as if he knew what she was thinking and was annoyed she hadn't said it aloud.

Entering the dark and deserted house, the tiredness she'd held at bay all day overwhelmed Lyn and she almost fell into Ken's arms. 'I'm sorry,' she said pushing herself away. 'I don't know what's happening to me.'

'You're exhausted. What you need is a sound night's sleep. Do you want me to stay or would you rather be on your own?'

'Please stay.' The last thing Lyn wanted was to lie in bed alone. She was sure her mind would spin the events of the past two days and the decisions she'd have to make when her mother was well enough to come home. One thing was clear. Edith would need a lot more care.

Ken helped the tired Lyn into the bedroom and into bed where she fell asleep as soon as her head hit the pillow. But, despite Ken's comforting presence, she tossed and turned, disturbed by dreams of falling, and of her mother.

*

'Awake?'

Lyn opened her eyes to see Ken standing by the bed with a cup of tea. She struggled to get up. 'What's the time?'

'Nearly nine. I need to pick up my car this morning, then get into the office and wanted to let you sleep as long as you could. You looked so peaceful lying there.'

'Nine?' Lyn tried to jump out of bed but found herself gently pushed back by Ken and a cup of lemon and ginger tea placed into her hand.

'It's okay, I called the hospital. Your mum had a restful night – probably more restful than you did. Visiting hours aren't till later. You'll be able to see her then.'

Lyn fell back against the pillows. He'd thought of everything.

'Thanks.' She seemed to be saying that a lot to Ken lately. Then she remembered. 'Maddy?'

'No sign of her.'

'Hell!' Lyn reached for her phone. One text message.

Staying at Zac's. Hope all is well with GG. Call later. Mxx

'She's at Zac's.'

'Of course she is. You don't need to worry about that one.'

'Did she come in to see about a rental?'

Ken rubbed his chin. 'She did. I let Cathy deal with it, but I don't think we were able to help. Sorry.'

'Oh!'

'Look, I must be off. Maybe we can have lunch? Call me.' He bent to kiss Lyn before leaving.

Lyn lay still for a few moments, holding her tea in both hands, contemplating the kindness Ken had shown over her mother's accident. There weren't many men who'd put her needs and her mother's above their own. She knew he'd intended to have dinner at Wooleton and pick up Titch the night before. Instead, he spent it with her at the hospital, then here. She assumed Titch was still at the farm.

As Lyn rose, showered, and made herself a breakfast of muesli and yoghurt, she felt disoriented. It was as if the life she knew, had planned, was disappearing to be replaced by one with which she was familiar, yet which had changed so much she almost didn't recognise it; as if she was caught up in a whirlwind over which she had no control – and she wasn't sure she liked it.

After breakfast, Lyn decided to do what she did best. She made a list – a list of everything she needed to take care of. Top of the list was her mother, then there was Maddy, this house, Eden Gardens, her travel plans, her unit in Brisbane, her future. The last item made her hesitate. Was her future still uncertain, something to be fixed? When she arrived in Granite Springs, Lyn had everything thought out, carefully planned. She hesitated again, before adding one more item to her list – Ken Thompson.

Lyn was still looking at his name, and picturing Ken, when her phone rang and she saw Maddy's face on the screen.

'Gran!' Maddy squealed into the phone before Lyn could speak. 'Great news! One of Zac's mates is moving out and I can have his room. Your friend Ken didn't come up with the goods, but this is even better. There's another girl moving in too – Hugo's girlfriend – so we'll be able to keep the guys in order. Isn't it great?'

Lyn didn't know what to say. Yes, it was good news Maddy had found a shared house, and Zac seemed to have come to his senses, but it was an unexpected turn of events. Amy and Chris had never been happy about their daughter's proposal to live with her boyfriend. Lyn thought they'd assumed she'd stay with Lyn and her mother. But the house sale had put paid to that idea. Well, Maddy was one item she could now cross off her list.

'You're sure about this, honey? You know you don't need to move out just yet.'

'Gran! You know it's what we planned before Zac's mates got his ear. It's a great place. Plenty of space and a big yard with a barbecue. We can have lots of parties.'

Lyn tried to remember what it was like to be Maddy's age, full of life and sure everything was going her way. She failed dismally. Life hadn't been like that for her. She'd spent her university years living with Aunt Wyn in a protected environment. A serious student, after denying her feelings for Ken, Lyn had eschewed boyfriends till Glenn came into her life. Although she'd been aware of the parties many of her peers held and attended, they'd never featured much in her own life, preferring as she did, to spend her time in study or in having political discussions with her aunt.

After a few more minutes, during which Lyn passed on news about Edith, assured Maddy she was pleased with her news, counselled her to let her parents know, and made arrangements for the girl to collect her belongings, Lyn hung up.

Arriving at the hospital later, Lyn hurried to the ward, pleased to see her mother appeared more alert. But the older woman was still clearly in pain.

'Mum!' Lyn bent down to kiss Edith who grasped her hand in both of hers.

'I think I've done it this time, Lynnie,' she said with a grimace. 'The doctor wants to talk with you, but he says I can't go back home. It's too much of a risk, and I don't want to put you in that position.'

Lyn's stomach churned. What were they going to suggest? Surely her mother couldn't stay here indefinitely. 'What's the alternative?' she asked in a trembling voice.

'I told them about Eden Gardens, that they didn't have a place for me yet. That consultant said he'd take care of it. I'm not sure what he meant. But I don't want to be a bother…'

'You could never be a bother, Mum. I'll talk with him today – find out what he meant. And, remember, I'm here for you.'

'Where's Ken today?' Edith asked, peering behind Lyn.

'He has work to do, Mum. But he's concerned about you, I'm having lunch with him so I can let him know how you are this morning.'

'Hmph. I'll be bound that's not the only reason,' Edith said with some of her old bounce. 'Nothing wrong with my mind, Lynnie. It's just my damned hips letting me down.' She chuckled as if cracking a joke.

'I'm glad to see you haven't lost your sense of humour.'

'Mrs Hudson?'

Lyn turned to see Mr Vaughan standing behind her.

'A word.' He gestured to the corridor.

'You can say what you have to say in front of me,' Edith said. 'I don't hold with secrets and it's me you're going to be discussing.'

'Very well.' The tall, silver-haired man walked in. He remained standing at the foot of the bed. 'Mrs Carter, your mother,' he gestured to Edith, 'has informed me she plans to move to Eden Gardens when a place becomes available – that she is, in fact, waiting for word. It so happens I – we – have contact with the director and have been able to pull a few strings.'

'Get on with it,' Edith said. 'stop beating around the bush.'

'Are you trying to say you can have her moved up the waiting list?' Lyn asked.

'Just so. It appears there will be a spot available which will enable Mrs Carter to go there directly from the hospital when she's discharged. It could be as soon as Thursday.' Having delivered this bombshell, he swept out again.

Left stunned, Lyn and her mother stared at each other, the latter's eyes beginning to fill with tears.

'It's good news, Mum,' Lyn said at last, though it was a shock to think her mother wouldn't be coming home again.

'It's what I wanted,' Edith said, her voice breaking. 'Though I did think to see my own place again. You'll have to take care of things, Lynnie.' Then she seemed to recover, her voice strengthening. 'I have a list of the things I want to take with me to Eden Gardens. I made it some time ago. There's my favourite chair, my bureau, a bookcase, a few odds and ends. The rooms aren't large, but I can have a few of my own things about me.'

This time it was Lyn's eyes that started to fill. 'Oh, Mum. It's such a big step. Are you sure?' She realised this was almost exactly what she'd asked Maddy only a few hours earlier. Maybe it was Lyn who wasn't sure of what her future held.

'It'll all work out, you'll see,' Edith said enigmatically. 'Now, if you're meeting your young man for lunch, hadn't you better go? I'll be all right here. You might want to check with Eden Gardens just to make sure he's got things right. You'll find my list in the top drawer of the bureau in my bedroom. You can bring it in with you tonight and we'll go over it.'

Lyn was bemused when she walked out of the hospital. Her mother seemed to be coping with this better than she was. She remembered what Ken had said about Alec and his wife, how Judy was coping with her cancer better than Alec and how Lyn had counselled him that was often the case. But she hadn't expected it to refer to her mother and herself. She breathed a heavy sigh.

*

Ken was already seated at a table at the back of The Bean Sprout when Lyn walked in. He rose to greet her with a kiss and she immediately felt better. It was as if, by just being there, Ken had lifted a weight from her shoulders.

'What's up?' His eyebrows drew together. 'Has your mother taken a turn for the worse?'

'No, nothing like that. Mum's looking and sounding a lot better. But she won't be coming back home.' Lyn felt her eyes moisten again. She knuckled away the incipient tears. 'Sorry. I knew it would happen, but it seems so final. The consultant has managed to arrange a place for her in Eden Gardens. She'll go there straight from hospital. She won't be coming home,' she repeated.

'That's good news, isn't it? You knew she'd be going there.'

'Yes, it is,' Lyn sniffed. 'It's just… Sorry.' She drew out a tissue and blew her nose. 'Of course, it's good news. She'll likely be moved as early as Thursday. I presume she'll need rehab this time, too,' she added.

'She'll be in the right place. It's one of the best around.'

'I know, and it's her choice.' Lyn took a deep breath. 'She's made a list of what she wants to take there. I've to bring it in tonight.'

'Would you like me to come with you again?'

'Would you? What about Titch?'

'He's right for another night or so.'

'Then please. Why don't you come around for a bite to eat first? Six o'clock?'

Lyn found her mother's list without any trouble, reading through the items with surprise. Edith had thought this through carefully. She must have been planning her move for some time. The discovery should have made Lyn feel better, but it didn't. By the time Maddy called around with Zac and a borrowed ute to pick up her belongings, Lyn was wandering around the house touching those pieces of furniture and ornaments she remembered from her childhood. She supposed they'd all have to be sold.

'Is GG really not coming back home?' Maddy was all packed but seemed reluctant to leave. 'What will happen to all of this?' She waved her hand around the kitchen where Lyn was preparing a quiche for dinner.

'I expect it'll be sold or go to charities. GG will have worked it all out. She's done that for everything else.' Lyn hadn't looked any further in the bureau, but had no doubt there were more lists, lists of items to be sold or given away. The wonder was that her mother hadn't made a list for what Lyn was to do with herself once the house was settled and the keys were handed over.

'Do you think I could have a few things for Zac's place? It's a bit bare.'

'I'm sure you could. Why don't you ask her next time you visit?'

'Thanks, Gran. I'll go tomorrow morning. I don't have any classes. I'll be busy settling in tonight, and the guys want us to go out for a celebration dinner – to celebrate Cass and I moving in. You don't mind, do you?'

'No, Ken's going to come to the hospital with me tonight.' She saw a gleam appear in her granddaughter's eyes. She knew what Maddy was thinking. But she was wrong. There would be no place for Lyn here once everything was settled.

Her life was in Brisbane. She was happy there. She could fulfil her dream of travel. So why did her heart sink at the thought of leaving Granite Springs?

Thirty-eight

'Would you like me to finalise the house sale?' Ken asked. They were at her mother's house, after walking back from the hospital leaving Edith asleep. 'The Braithwaites are keen to settle and now your Mum has a place…' He allowed his voice to trail off, seeing Lyn's stricken expression. 'They won't wait forever,' he added hesitantly.

'No, you're right,' Lyn said with a sigh. She picked up the glass of wine she'd poured when they arrived back, but barely touched, then put it down again. 'I don't know what I'm going to do, Ken. I had it all worked out – get Mum settled, go back to Brisbane, rebook my flights. But I hadn't counted on this happening.'

'Maybe you can stay?' Ken suggested, his heart in his mouth. It was something he'd been wanting to say to Lyn ever since she walked into his office. Until now, he'd kept his feelings to himself, fearful of being rejected. But now it wasn't about him. It was about her mother. 'Did the doctor…?'

'He didn't give any indication how long she might have, if that's what you're asking. But I know Mum would hate me to turn my life upside down for her, even though…' Ken saw her bite on the inside of her cheek. He remembered her doing that as a child when she had a difficult decision to make. But, back then, the decision might be whether to order a Golden Gaytime or a Sunny Boy Razz.

'Would it be so bad?' Ken dared to ask. He could see she was undecided but didn't want to press his luck. He wanted her to stay so much it hurt. If she did decide to leave, only to visit occasionally, how could he live with it? He'd lived without her for the past forty-five years. But that had been before…

Lyn didn't reply. 'When are you picking up Titch?' she asked instead.

Ken sighed inwardly. The moment had gone. 'Later in the week. Neil says he's enjoying being back on the farm, and old Bess is knocking him into shape. It's amazing how bitches manage to train their young with no help from us humans. But Judy starts her first round of chemo next week, and Alec is worried how she might react to it. I'll need to get Titch before that. Would you still be interested in coming out to Wooleton with me?' he asked, without much hope of her accepting.

'I'd like to, depending on how things are with Mum. When exactly were you planning to go?'

'Towards the end of the week. Your Mum gets discharged on Thursday?'

'All going to plan, then she'll have to settle into her new home. Oh, Ken, I can't bear to think of her being there. It's like the beginning of the end.' Her eyes began to fill with tears.

Ken joined Lyn on the sofa and drew her head to his chest. 'It's the best place for her. You couldn't provide the sort of care she's going to need. And she'd already decided this house was too big for her to manage. Remember?'

'You're right, of course. As usual.' She raised her head and gave a watery smile.

'Now, finish that wine and let me take you to bed. All this has been emotionally draining for you. What you need is a warm cuddle and a good night's sleep.'

'Right, again.' Lyn did as she was bid and, Ken's arm around her shoulders, she allowed herself to be led into the bedroom.

*

All day Thursday, Ken was on tenterhooks waiting to hear from Lyn. She'd refused his offer to keep her company while she participated in the transfer of Edith from the hospital to the nursing home. He knew she'd find it traumatic and wanted to be there for her. But, independent as ever, Lyn told him she'd be fine, reluctantly agreeing to have dinner with him if all went well.

It was four in the afternoon before the highly anticipated call came. He'd almost given up hope.

'She's settled in well.'

Ken could hear the relief in Lyn's voice.

'The staff are all very nice there, making her feel welcome, and she has the room set up just as she wants it. It was a good idea of yours to arrange to have her bits and pieces delivered before she arrived.'

Ken grinned to himself. He'd done something right. It had been easy for him to have a removalist he knew pick up the few items and boxes from Edith home and transport them to Eden Gardens – the work of barely an hour. It was the least he could do for the mother of the woman he loved, and who had been his own mother's best friend.

'You're feeling better about her move, then?'

'I think so. She sent me off with a flea in my ear and instructions not to come visit till Saturday. I think she wants to get more of a feel for the place before I go there again. It's not like visiting her in hospital.'

'So, we're still on for dinner?'

'Yes. I'm looking forward to it. I feel I've been on a roller coaster since we got back from Canberra. Now, maybe I can begin to relax. Maddy's settled. Mum's settled.' She paused.

Ken didn't want to hear what Lyn planned to say next. Perhaps she was going to tell him she was preparing to leave town. He rushed in, 'How about we go out to Wooleton tonight for dinner, then?'

'Tonight? Isn't that rather sudden? What about Alec and Judy?'

'They won't mind. I'll give Alec a call. Judy starts her chemo on Monday, so meeting you might help take their minds off it.' He doubted it, but wanted to set Lyn's mind at ease and was eager for her to meet his family.

'Okay, if you're sure.'

'I should be finished here by half five. I can pick you up at six.'

'See you then.'

Ken returned to the task he'd been engaged with when Lyn rang. Coincidentally, he'd been finalising the settlement details for the Braithwaites' purchase of the Carter house. Now Edith had moved into Eden Gardens, there was nothing to hold it up, and the new owners were keen to take possession. The only question he had was, what was going to happen to Lyn when she no longer had a place to stay?

Ken knew what he would like to happen, but he hadn't dared to voice his wish that she move into his house, the house which echoed with emptiness, the house which desperately needed a woman's touch. His king-sized bed figured in his thoughts, too.

*

'It's been a long time,' Alec greeted Lyn as she and Ken climbed the steps to the veranda surrounding the old farmhouse. 'But you still look the same.'

Lyn laughed, the first genuine laugh Ken had heard from her since their Canberra trip. 'Well, I can't say the same about you, Alec.'

Alec patted his thinning hair and thickened waist. 'We can't all be like my big brother,' he said. 'Come inside and meet Judy. Neil's out in the paddock but should be back soon. Sally couldn't make it tonight – she's working.'

They walked into the house, Ken's hand on Lyn's back – he could sense her nervousness. Seeing her here brought back so many memories of times they'd snuck into his mother's pantry to feast on the glace cherries and slabs of cooking chocolate she stored there for her baking.

'Ken!' A short, plump, dark-haired woman came to meet them, arms outstretched. 'And you must be Lyn. I've heard so much about you,' Judy said, hugging them both. 'It's about time you brought her to meet us,' she chastised Ken, with a smile. 'I was sorry about your dad. He was a fine man. And I hear your mum's had a bad time of it, too?'

'Thanks. Yes. We got her settled into Eden Gardens today. I don't know...'

Ken saw Lyn begin to wilt.

'She had it all arranged, Judy,' he said. 'This last fall just brought it forward a bit.'

'Fancy that! I wish we could persuade my mum to take that step. It would put my mind at rest to know she was being cared for. I've heard good reports about Eden Gardens.'

'Mmm.' Lyn murmured, but seemed to brighten a little at Judy's words.

'Here's trouble,' Alec said as Neil entered the kitchen, towering over Alec and Judy, but eye-to-eye with his dad. 'You've met Neil?' he asked Lyn.

She nodded.

'Dad, Lyn,' Neil said, giving Ken a slap on the shoulder. 'I'll just get cleaned up. Pour me a beer, Uncle Alec? Won't be long.'

For a few moments, Ken was beset with a trace of his old resentment that his brother had taken his place here on Wooleton, and his son was now treating it like home. Then he looked at Alec and Judy, remembered what they were going through, and any bitterness drained away.

'Beer for you, too, Ken?' Alec asked, going to the fridge. 'What's your poison, Lyn? I think we have a bottle of white wine in here somewhere.'

'That'll be fine,' Lyn said. 'Is there anything I can do to help?' she asked Judy, turning towards her after Alec had poured a glass of chardonnay.

'You can stay here and talk to me,' Judy replied. 'Alec has the barbecue going on the back veranda. The men'll be going out there.'

'You've changed the place a lot since I was here last,' Ken heard Lyn say as he took the can of beer his brother was offering and followed him out to the veranda. A top-of-the-range barbecue was waiting for the steaks which sat marinating on a covered platter.

'Looking good,' Alec said.

Ken knew his brother wasn't talking about him. 'It's been a while,' he replied.

'Forty-five years by my reckoning. I was just a kid in Year Ten, but I remember how you swooned over her, and that suit you wore to your formal... Oh boy!' he chuckled.

'Yeah, it was a bit much,' Ken agreed. 'And it was a long time ago, another lifetime.'

'Is she back for good this time?'

'You don't beat about the bush, do you?'

'Only thinking of you, big brother. I remember how cut up you were last time when she disappeared. Wouldn't like to think of that happening to you again.'

'Yes. Well.' Ken took a gulp of beer, shuffled his feet and gazed out across the paddock to where the sheep were making short work of the feed Neil had been spreading. 'As you say, it's been a while. We're not the same people we were back then. We...'

'No need to go into the gory details, mate. I just don't want to see you getting hurt. This family has enough on its plate without that.' He threw five steaks onto the grill and prodded them with the barbecue fork, avoiding Ken's eyes.

'Thanks, but no need to worry about me. I'm a big boy. I can take care of myself.' Ken was aware of his brother sending him a sidelong glance.

'See you do.'

'Judy's chemo starts next week?'

'Monday. We have to drive to Canberra. Might stay a couple of days. They've been trying to get a set up at the Base, but it hasn't happened yet.'

'If you need me to help out...'

'Thanks. Up to Neil. He says he can manage. But you might want to keep in touch. He has a mountain of energy – like you were at his age – but he can't do everything himself. It's good to know he can call on you if it all gets too much for him.'

'Right.' Ken took another long draught of beer, thinking how things changed. When what he saw as his birthright had been given to his brother, he vowed never to set foot on Wooleton again. But, over the years, he'd mellowed. Age did that to a man. Then there was Neil's defection which brought it all back. But now, the way things were with Alec and Judy, there was no way he could fail to offer to help in any way he could.

By the time Neil and the two women joined them, Lyn helping Judy carry out two bowls of salad, and Neil bringing the wine bottle and more cans of beer, the conversation had changed. Ken and Alec were debating the comparative benefits of wind and solar power.

Attracted by the smell of meat cooking, Bess and Titch appeared seemingly from nowhere and began to sniff around the men's ankles.

'Nothing for you two here,' Neil said. 'I'll feed them inside, then they won't bother us.'

'Want a bet?' Alec asked, but watched as Titch received a fondling from Ken and a cuddle from Lyn, before following Bess and Neil inside.

'He's a natural with animals,' Alec said, when the door swung shut behind them. 'Jude and I are grateful you didn't make a fuss about him coming here.'

'No point in standing in his way once he'd made up his mind,' Ken said. 'But it was a tough call. I won't say I was pleased about it. I'd thought… Hell, you knew I thought he'd be there to take over from me, Alec.' A touch of his old anger threatened to erupt, before he shrugged it off. 'I guess this place is in his blood.' *And mine.*

The business of serving out the steaks and settling down to their meal helped Ken regain his equilibrium. He didn't want Lyn to see the frustration that still wasn't far from the surface, and Alec and Judy had enough on their minds at the moment without his adding to it.

Over dinner, Judy was interested in hearing what Lyn had done with her life and her travel plans.

'You still intend to go ahead with them?' Judy asked, when Lyn explained how they'd been put on hold when her mother suffered her first fall.

Ken saw Lyn's eyes cloud over. 'I've been wanting to do this all my life,' she said. 'And something has always happened to stop me. This time, I was determined nothing would, then Mum…' She bit her lip. 'But now she's settled, and the house is sold, maybe I can finally realise my dream.'

Ken was vaguely conscious of the sympathetic glances of Alec, Judy and Neil, but he was watching Lyn, and what he saw from the expressions which flitted across her face was someone who was conflicted, who wasn't sure what she wanted.

It gave him hope.

Thirty-nine

Lyn fell quiet on the drive back into town. Judy's question had hit home as nothing else had. Since she and Ken had reconnected, since she'd discovered the passion she knew had been smouldering in the background all of her life, she'd managed to stifle any thoughts of what to do next.

But now she knew she had to decide. She was faced with a choice – to remain here in Granite Springs, be here for her mother and spend time with Ken, or go back to the life she knew. Whichever she chose, Lyn knew she'd regret it. The easier route would be to return to Brisbane, continue with her travel plans and make occasional forays back to Granite Springs. But would that be enough – enough for her mother; enough for Ken; enough for her?

Lyn knew her troubles were insignificant compared to Ken's – she saw how frustrated he still was regarding the farm, and she knew he was worried about the future of his business – but they were real to her. It was all too hard.

Titch gave a small bark from where he was tethered in the back seat. She reached back to fondle his ears, wishing her life was as simple as this little dog's.

'Okay if we go to my place?' Ken asked. 'I need to get Titch settled.'

'Sure.' Lyn didn't care where they spent the night. She wondered how many nights they'd have left to spend together, knowing the choice was all down to her.

Once there, Titch raced around as if checking nothing had changed since he left, then, fed and watered, settled down in his basket in the laundry.

Ken closed the door behind him and turned to Lyn. 'Thanks for coming to Wooleton with me.'

'You still don't find it easy, do you?'

'You noticed? No...' His eyes dropped to the floor and he scuffed his feet. 'There was a time when I couldn't bear to be there. It eased over the years, better after Dad died. Mum liked to see me. But special occasions like Christmas were always difficult. Then when Neil...' His eyes met hers, and she could see the hurt. 'It almost broke me. I'd never let him know. The lad has a right to make his own decisions. And it's his birthright.'

'It was yours, too,' she said, gently.

'Not a life you wanted to share.' He gave a wry smile.

'I'd never have been happy on the farm, Ken. I'm not like Judy. Alec chose a good one there.'

Ken nodded. 'I suppose I always knew you were destined for more than Granite Springs had to offer. Yet here you are. Here we are.'

Suddenly Lyn felt claustrophobic. It was as if the town closed in on her, reminding her of why she'd left, why she'd stayed away. Had she really changed, or was it just a case of circumstances conspiring to fool her into believing she had?

'Hold me,' she said.

In Ken's arms, she could forget everything, she could pretend yet again. It would be time for decision making soon enough.

*

Two days later and back home after another night of torrid lovemaking, Lyn tried to get things into perspective. What she'd found here with Ken was good – more than good – but was it enough for her to completely change her plans, change her life? She tussled with the question while she consumed the two cups of coffee it took for her to summon up the energy to start on the tasks she knew she had to do. Ken said the house sale would settle at the end of next week. She had a houseful of furniture to get rid of before then and a thorough clean of the place to arrange. Then she needed to find somewhere to stay if she was going to spend any more time here – maybe book into a motel.

First, however, she would visit her mother to check all was well.

Eden Gardens looked good as Lyn drove into the circular driveway and parked in the visitor's car park. The gardens were well maintained, and the large white-painted house rose impressively from the paved courtyard. As she walked towards the entrance, Lyn could see Edith seated by a window in her favourite chair.

'Mum!' Lyn gave her a warm hug. 'How are you?'

'I'm just fine. You didn't need to come running in here today. The staff are lovely. I have everything I want. It's like staying in a hotel, except I have my own things around me. And, before you ask, I'm using that wretched thing.' She pointed to the walker standing by her chair.

'That's good. I worry about you.'

'No need to worry. I assume the house sale will be able to be finalised now. What do you intend to do with all the furniture?'

'That's for you to say. I thought you'd have worked it out.'

Her mother grinned and produced a sheet of paper which Lyn could see contained two lists.

'I have,' Edith said. 'Some of it should fetch a good price at Morton's auctions, while the rest can go to charity. I've listed them here. Of course, you, Amy and Maddy can have first pick, but I'm not sure any of them would suit you. You'd probably consider them too old-fashioned for your taste.' Her lips turned down.

'It's not that.' Lyn thought of her mother's heavy wooden furniture and her tiny waterfront apartment. 'My unit is pretty small, and Amy and Chris don't have much more room either. But Maddy did ask if she could pick out a few pieces.'

'Bless her. Of course she can have her pick.'

'She'll be pleased. And I'm sure she'll visit you soon.'

'She'll be welcome. But tell her I don't expect her to take time from her uni studies to visit an old woman. It's enough to know she's happy. She is, isn't she?'

'She seems to be, now she's moved in with Zac, but they're young and...'

'He's a nice lad. And not everyone's like you, Lynnie. Some recognise the right one early in life and stick to them. Your dad and I met when we were both just eighteen and neither of us ever looked at anyone else.'

Lyn felt her level of exasperation rise. Her mother was at it again, implying she should have stuck with Ken, that he was *the right one*. 'Not everyone is as lucky,' she said, only to see her mother raise her eyebrows.

They were interrupted by one of the staff knocking on the door to ask if they'd like tea, and in the ensuing fussing with the arrival of tea with an accompanying plate of biscuits, Lyn's irritation was forgotten.

Edith showed off the tiny garments she'd been knitting and asked about Lyn's. To her embarrassment, Lyn was forced to admit she'd made little progress since her Canberra trip, but it prompted her to tell her mother about meeting Judy who might be one of the recipients of knitted knockers. To her relief, Edith didn't take this as an opportunity to promote Ken, but listened attentively as Lyn described the changes Alec and his wife had made to the old farmhouse, with which the older woman was very familiar.

'The old order changeth,' she said at last with a sigh. 'And how does Ken feel about all of this – his son out there, too? It can't be easy for him,' she said, repeating Lyn's own words.

'It's not. Neil seems to love it there. I think Ken's finding it difficult to accept, and then there's his real estate business. It's a disappointment for him his son's not going to be there to take it over.'

'He's had a few obstacles to overcome but always managed to make a go of it. I'm sure he'll do the same with this. He's a strong man. But even strong men have their weaknesses.' She gave Lyn a piercing stare. 'Don't hurt him any more than you have to. I know you have your own life – you've told me that many times – but you'll not find a better man.'

Lyn knew her mother was right, but now wasn't the time for this discussion. The time might never be right. She left her mother, feeling no further forward in her decision making. But she now knew how to deal with the furniture. She'd make that her first priority.

*

A week. That was all the time she had. Lyn's gaze travelled around the room, filled with the collections of a lifetime. She wondered how her mother had been able to leave it. Every piece held memories for her – what must it be like for her mother? There was the table where she'd done her homework every night, the chair where she'd sat on her mother's knee to read her first primer, the footstool that had been just the right size for her five-year-old legs. It was sad to think of them all going to strangers. But, despite the memories, there was no place for them in Lyn's life nor, anymore, in her mother's.

Maddy had promised to come around that afternoon with Zac to pick up the few items she wanted, so Lyn started to make the calls she knew had to be done. First to the auction house where she discovered they held auctions every Thursday and would pick up from her on Monday, then the charity nominated by her mother who also offered to pick up. She asked them to do it later in the week, but still allowing her time to have the place cleaned before the keys were handed over to the new owners on the weekend. Then she'd be homeless.

It was an odd thought, but not completely true. Lyn had her unit in Brisbane, even though it was rented out for another month. She needed to do something about extending the lease if she wanted to travel, she reminded herself.

Lyn was having a cup of lemon and ginger tea and browsing through her emails as she waited for Maddy's arrival, when one caught her eye, forcing her to pause. It was from the group of property managers that had arranged the lease for her Brisbane home.

Hello Ms Hudson.

We wish to inform you that your tenant, Ms Wilson, has given notice she will be vacating the unit on Russell Street at the end of next week. She understands that, as she is breaking the lease, she may be liable for rent for the remainder of the period, should we be unable to relet. Given the current demand rate for rentals in the area, we believe it will not be difficult to find another tenant. We require your approval to set this in motion and advertise the property for rent. We also require you to inform us of the rental period you wish to nominate.

Yours faithfully,
Peter Rowlings
Property Manager

Lyn re-read the email, as if by doing so, she could change its content. Damn! One more thing to deal with! But was it? Only a moment ago, she'd considered herself homeless when this house was handed over. This news could prove to be a godsend. It could be a sign, a sign for her to return to Brisbane, pick up her life there, and continue with her plans.

Why did the thought not bring her relief?

Instead, she felt more confused than ever.

Forty

Ken decided to make his approach to Danny Slater outside of the office. He'd sounded out Gordon first to ensure his idea wasn't completely mad, and his friend had been delighted. Gordon's actual words had been, 'He doesn't deserve this. But if you're sure about it and you can see your way to working out something, you have my blessing. It'll put Jo's mind at rest and probably manage to please Kylie, too.'

It was all Neil's doing, thought Ken, as he closed up the office and headed for the club where he'd arranged to meet Danny. If Neil hadn't made the deal with Alec, there would have been no need for any of this. But, like his brother, Ken was acutely aware of the need to retire sooner rather than later and he didn't want to see the business going to a complete stranger. He checked his watch. Lyn would be expecting him in just over an hour. That should give him enough time. Then he could enjoy his weekend.

The club was beginning to fill up with the usual Saturday night crowd when Ken pushed open the door and walked in. As arranged, Danny was waiting for him in the foyer.

'What's this all about, Ken?' he asked. 'You were very mysterious on the phone. I could have come into the office again.'

'Let's get a drink, first, Danny, then I'll fill you in. I wanted to meet here rather than the office to keep it more confidential.' Though, looking around the crowded room, Ken wondered if he'd made the right decision. Maybe the office would have been better. But he hadn't wanted to risk any of his staff overhearing, in case it didn't go down well.

The pair headed to the bar where Ken ordered a couple of beers before finding a quiet corner booth. But, once there, the words eluded him. It wasn't till he caught Danny looking at his watch, that he started to speak, reciting the speech he'd prepared.

'It's like this, Danny,' he began. 'We're both in the business of real estate in Granite Springs. We've never stepped on each other's toes, and I respect the reputation you've built up.' He saw the other man flinch slightly. 'I know you almost ruined it recently, but you saw the light in time. That's the main thing. The point is, I know where you come from. Your dad and I go way back. Bear with me,' he said, seeing Danny begin to fidget. 'You're a good man. You're honest. You know the real estate market.'

Ken drew breath and took a sip of his beer. 'As you probably know, I always intended Neil to take over Granite Springs Realty when I decided to retire. You probably also know he chose differently and has moved out to work our family property with my brother, his uncle.' It still hurt Ken to refer to Wooleton as *the family property*, knowing he no longer had any stake in it, but he couldn't think of it in any other way.

'Sorry, I seem to be being longwinded about this. I've given it a lot of thought, and I've come to the conclusion that...' he took a deep breath, '...rather than see the business going to a stranger, I'd like to propose we form a partnership.'

Ken saw the other man's eyes widen and his mouth open to speak. He held up one hand. 'I don't intend to muscle in on your successful enterprise. This would be a partnership in Granite Springs Realty. It would enable you to take over when I decide to retire – I'm not ready to do that for some time yet, but I want things in place for when I do. Your dad will draw up the agreement to ensure it's fair to all parties. I've already spoken with him.'

'You've spoken with Dad?' Danny seemed stunned.

'Wanted to make sure it was all possible before approaching you. No need to decide now. You'll want to think it over, discuss it with your wife, maybe your dad? I realise this may come as a surprise. You probably have a few questions.'

'Yes. No. Sorry, Ken. This is a shock. I don't know what to say. It takes a bit of thinking about. Coming on the back of the Sherwood affair. I'm flattered you'd even consider working with me after I got involved in that debacle.'

'That's partly what brought me to this conclusion,' Ken said. 'It showed me you know the difference between right and wrong and that you're keen to expand – both valuable attributes in our business. I think Granite Springs Realty could benefit from a fresh point of view, and I need someone who can predict a future direction for the business. I admit I'm pretty set in my ways.'

'Well! When do you need an answer?'

'I don't have a deadline. I just wanted to float the idea before you got caught up in some other scheme.' Ken chuckled, eliciting a smile from his companion.

'Thanks again, Ken. I'll do as you say. I'm honoured at your faith in me. It's not something I'd ever expected or considered, but…' Ken could see a gleam of anticipation in Danny's eyes. 'I'll get back to you when I've had time to think it through – and I'll talk with Kylie and Dad.' He checked his watch again. 'Sorry, I need to go now.' He drained his beer, shook Ken's hand, and left.

Ken relaxed. That was one part of his plan done. He had no doubt Danny would agree, once he'd taken time to consider the proposition. He knew Gordon would encourage him and, from what he'd heard of Danny's wife, the partnership in and eventual takeover of Granite Springs Realty would feed her ambition.

Now, if he could be as successful with the proposition he intended to put to Lyn…

*

Ken was whistling when he pushed open the gate to the Carter house, seeing Lyn's head silhouetted in the living room window. He felt good. He'd got over Neil's defection, had found a successor. Now, everything depended on Lyn's decision.

She greeted him at the door with a hug, her now familiar body leaning into his in a way that made him confident all would be well. Their lips met and held.

'Hey,' he said when they finally moved apart. 'What did I do to deserve that? How was your day?'

'Don't ask.' But she proceeded to tell him. 'I visited Mum and she seems to be settling in well. The staff are very good. We had tea and talked.' A cloud flitted across her face seeming to indicate not all of the conversation had been to her liking. 'Then I came back here. Maddy picked up a few pieces of furniture she wanted, I called the auction house and a local charity Mum nominated then...' she hesitated, making Ken feel there was something else, something she wasn't saying, '... then here you are. Dinner will be ready shortly. Would you like a glass of wine first?'

Why did Ken get the impression her cheerfulness was forced?

'Sure. I brought a bottle.' He produced the bottle of merlot he'd been carrying in one hand while hugging her.

'Thanks.' Lyn fetched a couple of glasses and placed them on the kitchen table. Ken took a seat, poured the wine, then held up his full glass. 'To us,' he said.

Lyn didn't return the toast, merely taking a sip of wine before turning away to fuss with the stove where a pot was simmering. 'I only made a spag bol,' she said. 'Hope that's okay.'

'Of course.' Ken was now surer than ever she was keeping something from him. Now might not be the time to make the suggestion he'd been mulling over all day.

'How was *your* day?' Lyn asked, when she'd served up the familiar dish, accompanied by salad and crusty sour dough bread.

'Interesting.' Ken proceeded to tell her about his conversation with Danny, explaining how he was sure the younger man would accept and put to rest his fears for the future. 'I'm not planning to retire anytime soon,' he said. 'But I want to know the business will be in good hands when I do.'

'You trust him? After all that funny business?'

'I do. He's learned from his mistake and won't make the same one again. I'm sure about that. And he had the sense to speak to Gordon and me before it got out of hand.'

'You're really planning for the future.' There was a wistful note in Lyn's voice that gave Ken the courage to say what was on his mind.

Before he lost his nerve, he blurted out, 'I hope you're going to be part of that future, too, Lyn. I know you were scared when you left Granite Springs all those years ago. But things are different now.

We're different. Even Granite Springs is different. Surely you can see that? There's no chance of your turning into your mother – if there ever was. What do you say?' He held his breath, looking across the table at the only woman he'd ever loved.

Ken's heart plummeted when Lyn didn't answer immediately. Instead she avoided his gaze, focussing instead on the half full glass of wine which she was gripping so firmly by the stem, he thought it might shatter.

It must have been only a few seconds, but to Ken it seemed as if the silence went on for ever.

'I'm sorry, Ken,' Lyn said at last. 'I got an email from Brisbane today. The tenant in my unit is moving out. I'll be going back at the end of next week.'

Forty-one

Lyn wakened alone next morning. She rolled over to touch the pillow where Ken's head should have been and cursed her own stupid pride that had sent him away.

The disappointment on Ken's face when she told him of her decision to return to Brisbane had almost made her change her mind – almost, but not quite.

Then they'd argued.

Lyn wanted to hide her head under the covers when she remembered the insults they'd thrown at each other. They'd behaved like eight-year-olds. Now, in the cold light of day, she regretted her wild accusations. But she still intended to leave Granite Springs. What would she do here if she stayed?

She rose, showered and dressed in a daze, then brewed the coffee she knew she'd need to see her through the day. It wasn't a morning for herbal tea. She stood gazing out the window where the weather reflected her mood. It was raining. The farmers would be pleased.

Maddy called as Lyn was going through her mother's belongings to determine what could be donated to the local charities Edith had nominated and what was only fit for the tip. She was so full of the joys of life, Lyn didn't have the heart to spoil things for her by sharing her own dark mood. Instead she made all the right noises, but she did tell her granddaughter she was returning to Brisbane at the end of the following week.

'What?' Maddy yelled. 'But I thought you and Ken Thompson… GG said…'

Lyn winced. Her mother again! She'd have to tell her the news, too, and wasn't looking forward to it. Why did everyone want to see her and Ken together? She tried to stifle the little voice at the back of her head that whispered it was what she wanted, too.

*

Everything was ready. Most of the furniture had gone, her bag was packed. All Lyn needed to do was make a final trip to Eden Gardens to visit her mother, then she'd arranged to have lunch with Maddy before her plane left late afternoon. Maddy had agreed to see to the removal of the last few pieces of furniture and drop the house keys into Ken. Lyn couldn't bear to face him. Her heart ached at the realisation she might never see him again, unless they met accidentally when she came to town to visit her mother. It wasn't how she planned it. But she'd known deep down, her idea of a fly-in fly-out relationship would never work. Not with Ken. With a man who cared less, it might have. But Ken wasn't like that. He wanted commitment, a commitment she wasn't ready to give. He'd made that clear.

Suddenly, her phone rang, the sound echoing through the empty rooms. Lyn didn't recognise the number. She picked it up.

'Mrs Hudson, Lyn? Is that you?' The man's voice was vaguely familiar, but the words so garbled she could barely understand him.

'Neil?' she asked, finally recognising the caller and wondering why he wanted to speak to her. Surely he wasn't going to plead his dad's case?

'It's Dad. There's been an accident.'

Lyn felt the breath leave her body. Her hand went to her chest. 'How bad? What happened?'

'It was my fault. It should have been me who took feed out to the sheep. Uncle Alec and Aunt Judy are in Canberra, at the hospital. She had a bad reaction to the chemo. Dad came out to help. He was on the quad bike when it… Hell!'

Lyn could picture the young man's anguish, but she needed to know the extent of Ken's injuries. 'How bad?' she asked again, her heart thumping wildly.

'They took him to Base Hospital. They said it could be worse, but...'

'I'm going there now.' Her trip, her plans, everything else flew out of Lyn's mind at the thought of Ken suffering in hospital. She just knew she had to see him, be with him.

The trip to the hospital seemed to take forever. Lyn parked in the now familiar car park and raced into the building, drawing to a halt only when she came to the bank of lifts as she tried to remember what Neil had told her. Orthopaedics, Level 3, Ward 2. She entered, pressed three and let out the breath she'd been holding. What was she going to find when she reached the ward? Was he conscious? Lyn had been so traumatised by Neil's news, she'd barely heard his explanation. It had something to do with Ken helping out at the farm because Alec had gone to Canberra with Judy, a quad bike and... The lift pinged to indicate she'd arrived.

Now she was here, Lyn hesitated. Would Ken want to see her? She'd rushed here without thinking, only knowing she had to see him, she couldn't bear it if...

'Are you all right?'

Lyn looked up to see a nurse gazing at her with concern. She realised she'd been leaning against the wall, tears streaming down her cheeks, imagining what might have happened to Ken.

'Yes.' She tried to knuckle the tears away. 'Sorry, I don't know what came over me.'

'Why don't you take a seat and I'll bring you a glass of water?'

'No, I'll be fine. I need to...'

'Lyn!' Neil Thompson came striding down the corridor – a living image of the young Ken Lyn remembered so well.

'Neil! Is he...?' Lyn tried to gauge the young man's expression.

'He'll live.'

Lyn swayed, about to faint.

'Hey, steady on. Dad's not in any danger. He was a touch delirious when I found him and was repeating your name. I thought I should call you. I don't know what went down between you two. But he's been like a bear with a sore head all week. Thanks for coming.'

Lyn tried to pull herself together. 'Can I see him?'

'Don't see why not. He's in a single room. Doesn't look too hot. His right leg got crushed. He has some broken ribs and what they call soft tissue injuries. They say there may be some concussion. He was lucky. He could have been killed.'

Lyn could hear her heartbeat hammering loudly in her ears. The words *he could have been killed* echoing around in her head. In an instant, she knew how much Ken meant to her. She loved him. She'd always loved him. How could she have been so stupid as to think her life in Brisbane, her plans to travel, were more important than her feelings, the feelings she'd tried so hard to suppress?

Stumbling, she followed Neil into the room where Ken was lying so still that, for a brief moment, she imagined Neil had lied to her. The man in the bed turned his eyes towards them and his lips turned into a faint smile, before changing to a grimace of pain.

'Lyn!' Ken whispered, then his eyes closed again.

'I'm here,' Lyn said, moving to sit by the bed and taking a limp hand in hers. 'I'm not going anywhere,' she added, despite knowing Ken couldn't hear her. She was telling herself as much as him. There would be a lot to work out, plans to change, an entire life to unpick, but Lyn knew what she'd found here in Granite Springs was worth all the disruption that might entail.

*

'Is it really you?' Ken asked. 'What day is it? How long have I been here?'

It was three days later, and the worst of Ken's injuries seemed to be over. He'd undergone surgery for the broken leg, but the doctors said the only thing for the broken ribs and tissue injuries were rest.

'It's Monday. You've been here for three days. I'm so glad to see you looking brighter – more like yourself,' Lyn said.

'The doc says you can go home in a couple of days if you continue to improve,' Neil said from where he was standing behind Lyn. 'But you'll need to rest. No more tearing around the paddock on the quad bike like a mad thing. And you can't be on your own.'

Ken tried to grin. 'How's Judy?' he asked.

'Coping. The first lot of chemo took a lot out of her, but she's coming good. She has a week before her next treatment. Uncle Alec says we can manage till you're back on top of things.'

Ken turned back to Lyn. 'You were going to Brisbane.'

'I changed my plans.'

Their eyes met, the message passing between them saying more than words.

Neil shifted uncomfortably. 'I'll leave you two. You have things to say.'

Lyn looked down at her hands till she heard the door close behind him.

'I hope you didn't change your plans for me,' Ken said, trying to hoist himself up in the bed. 'As you told me, you have your life, and neither I nor Granite Springs have a part to play in it.'

'Did I really say that?' But Lyn had. She remembered. 'I spoke in the heat of the moment. We both said a lot of things we didn't mean. I didn't know… When Neil rang to tell me… I realised what I was throwing away. Can you forgive me?' Lyn's voice caught, seeing an expression she didn't recognise on Ken's face.

He reached for her hand and squeezed it. Then he slowly said, 'I have to be sure you mean it, that you won't disappear on me again. I can't go through that at my age. You're not just taking pity on a sick old man?'

'Old? If you're old, I'm old, too. And I'd forcibly deny it to anyone who tried to say that about me. But, no, Ken, it's not pity. When I heard about your accident, I felt as if I couldn't breathe. I hadn't realised how much…' Lyn faltered, then continued, '…how much you mean to me. Nothing else matters, not my life in Brisbane, not my travel plans. You're the most important thing to me. And that means Granite Springs, too. Since coming back here, I've found a degree of peace and contentment I didn't know existed. It took me a long time to realise it. You're part of that, you and this town. When Dad died, I came back under protest, eager to get it all over and leave again. But… I found you. I found a way of life I'd forgotten.'

'You were going to leave again,' he reminded her.

Lyn blanched, thinking how close she'd come to giving all this up. 'It was a moment of madness,' she admitted. 'I thought my tenant leaving was a sign. I was so confused. I didn't want to love you. I knew you'd be hurt if I left, but I thought…'

She was stopped by Ken leaning over towards her. She felt his breath on her cheek. She shivered with anticipation. Then, 'I can't reach you,' he said, falling back on the pillow. 'Can you…?'

Lyn stood up, bent over him, their lips met and his arms encircled her, pulling her down towards him. It was like coming home. *How could she ever have imagined she could leave this man?*

Minutes later, when, breathless, she'd returned to her seat, their hands now tightly clasped, Ken asked, 'Did the house settle? Where are you staying?'

Lyn blushed and bit her lip. 'I… Neil suggested… I moved into your house – just till I find somewhere. I'm looking after Titch. He misses you.'

'That's good. I'm sorry. I think I'm falling asleep. Stay…' Lyn saw his eyes close and felt his hands loosen their grasp. She sat in silence watching him sleep, wondering what he meant. Did he mean for her to stay here or to stay in the house?

A nurse appeared to tell her to leave, and reluctantly, with one last glance at the sleeping Ken and, dropping a kiss on his brow, Lyn did as she was bid.

*

Exactly a week after she'd been startled with the news of his accident, Lyn waited with an equally impatient Titch for Neil to bring Ken home. During her visits in the intervening days they'd talked a lot, resolving for Lyn any qualms she had about staying in Ken's home. It was a nice house, or would be with a few feminine touches. There were no remnants of his ex-wife's presence. She'd been gone too long for any to remain. Lyn guessed they'd gradually disappeared over the years as the place turned into a bachelor pad for Ken and Neil.

Ken had asked her to stay – that's what he had meant – but Lyn still wasn't sure about giving up her independence. What if Ken hadn't meant what he said in the hospital, what if it was all a pipe dream? However, it was close to Eden Gardens, so made it easy for her to visit her mother on a regular basis. Maddy had dropped around a couple of times too, complaining about her tutors and raving about the professor and the production of *West Side Story* she was involved in. She and Zac seemed to be as close as ever.

Suddenly, Titch began to bark furiously and, peering out of the window, Lyn saw a car draw up and Neil helping Ken out. She watched, her heart in her mouth as the man she now admitted she loved, struggled to manage a pair of crutches, waving away Neil's attempts to help. She hurried to the door, Titch at her heels.

'I'll be right now, Neil,' Ken said, as soon as Lyn opened the door. 'I'm sure you're needed back at the farm. Give my love to Judy.'

'If you're sure…' Neil looked at Lyn and shrugged.

Ken slowly made his way to the door where, balancing precariously on one crutch, he managed to put an arm around Lyn and kiss her – a kiss that left her dizzy and fighting for breath.

'Are you…?' she managed to say as they wrestled their way into the living room where they ended up together on the sofa, Titch attempting to leap up to join them, his tongue hanging out in delight at having his special person back.

'I'm fine, particularly fine now I'm with you. It was worth falling off that damned thing to get you here. You will stay, won't you? You won't run away again? This house has been like a morgue since Neil left. I need you, Lynnie. I need you more than I can say.'

'To fill up the house?' she joked, but she knew it was more than that, much more. She needed him too. The realisation took her by surprise. She'd admitted she loved him – to herself at least. But she'd never admitted she needed anyone before now.

At last, after forty-five years, here in Granite Springs, she'd found something many people never find at all. She'd been given a second chance. It had been waiting for her right here in Granite Springs. Ken had been waiting for her. She'd found a new life.

Epilogue

The crowd chanted the countdown. Snowflakes coated their eyelashes as Lyn and Ken gazed upwards to see the sparkling crystal ball drop in Times Square to herald the start of another year. The air was filled with music and cheers and they were almost blinded in a blizzard of colour as confetti sprayed down on them. The noise was so loud, Lyn thought her eardrums were going to burst.

It had been Lyn's dream for so long to be in New York on New Year's Eve. She had to pinch herself that she was finally here. The noise, the colour – it was all so much more exciting than she could ever have imagined. As if sensing her exhilaration, Ken squeezed her hand tightly. She turned her face towards him, seeing the familiar way his eyes crinkled, his pleasure mirroring her delight.

Despite the roll-neck sweater and the puffer jacket she was wearing, plus the woollen beanie pulled down over her ears, Lyn shivered as the extreme cold and frost made her face tingle and her eyes water. It was so different from the Australian summer they'd left behind. Ken's arm immediately went around her, pulling her close.

'Happy?'

'Blissful. Can't you tell?'

Ken grinned and held her tighter, keeping her safe from the crowds surrounding them. Lyn closed her eyes for a moment reflecting on her good fortune, on her decision to stay in Granite Springs with this wonderful man.

The time was right as it hadn't been when they were both eighteen.

It had taken her forty-five years, a failed marriage, the loss of her father, her mother's two falls, and Ken's accident for Lyn to appreciate what she'd thrown away. But now she knew she'd made the right decision. Even Amy approved of her move to Granite Springs, vowing to visit regularly now that her mother, grandmother, and her daughter all lived there.

Maddy was about to enter her second year of study and she and Zac were still together, making plans to move into a studio apartment in one of Danny's new developments early in the year. They were housesitting while Lyn and Ken were gone, taking care of both the house and Titch.

Meanwhile Danny proved himself as the perfect partner in Granite Springs Realty, filling the gap Neil left, while still managing his own business. Ken had no hesitation leaving him in charge while they were gone.

As the crowds surged around them, Lyn felt her feet begin to slip. Ken's arm tightened around her. 'Let's get out of here,' he mouthed, the sound of his words muffled by the clamour of over a million voices.

Lyn nodded and allowed herself to be led through the noisy crowd to a spot where she could draw breath.

By the time they managed to make it back to their hotel, they were both ready for a celebratory glass of champagne and the smoked salmon and cream cheese bagels they'd purchased earlier. Lying back on the bed which surely must be larger than king-sized, they could still hear the festivities still going on in the street below. It seemed as if all of New York was celebrating.

They had one more week here before heading off to Colorado for two weeks skiing in Dillon then returning to Granite Springs in time for Neil and Sally's wedding on Valentine's Day. To Ken's delight, Neil had finally *done the right thing* by Sally. They were to be married at Wooleton, and young Daisy was going to get her wish to be a flower girl.

Christmas had been a big family affair, with Amy, Chris and the girls arriving at Ken's home two days before Christmas. Edith joined them there on Christmas Eve, and they picked her up on Christmas morning when they were all invited out to Wooleton. Judy seemed to be on the road to recovery, though much of the preparations had been done by Neil and Sally who were proud of the new home they moved into a couple of months earlier. The young couple chose Christmas Day to announce their engagement.

'Not before time,' was Ken's comment before hugging them both and raising his glass in a toast.

By the time they returned to Granite Springs, the granny flat Ken had planned would be finished, and Edith could move into the family room in Ken's house which had been renovated and extended for her. If only she would agree.

Although Edith said she was happy in Eden Gardens, and Lyn knew the staff were treating her well, Lyn felt bad each time she left her there. There was plenty of room in Ken's house –Lyn still had trouble calling it hers, even though she'd been living there since Ken was in hospital. As he told anyone who'd listen, she'd come to take care of him and forgotten to leave.

On her occasional visits, Titch had taken Edith to his heart and she'd developed an attachment to the little creature. It surprised Lyn, given Edith's former dictum regarding a dog's place being outside and sheepdogs being working dogs. But Titch had managed to charm her into changing her mind. Lyn hoped that, when Edith saw the renovated section of the house, she'd change her mind about that too.

Lyn's aunt Wyn had agreed to step in to care for Edith while they were gone on their travels – the next trip to Britain over Easter to fulfil Lyn's desire to visit all the places she'd read about, then to Egypt for a cruise down the Nile. It would take them a few years to get through her list, but they had plenty of time. And Lyn knew it would be more fun to travel with Ken than the solitary trip she'd planned the year before.

Everything was falling into place as if it had been meant. Who'd have thought at this time last year that Lyn's life was going to take such an about turn, that she'd find love and a future in Granite Springs?

THE END

Look out for the next Granite Springs novel, *The Life She Imagines*, which is Marie's story.

Marie Cunningham's life falls into disarray when she is suddenly thrust into caring for her teenage niece. After operating The Bean Sprout Café with her former partner, becoming a single parent is not a life she ever imagined.

Drew Hamilton has arrived in Granite Springs to take up the position of principal at the local high school. Recently divorced, he is struggling with the unfamiliar role of single father to his unsettled teenage daughter.

When an unexpected incident brings the two together, the chemistry between them is not immediately apparent. Forced to associate as their teenage charges become best friends, they gradually lower their defences to discover they have a lot in common.

But when a ghost from the past threatens to derail her new life, who should Marie turn to for support – the new man in her life, or the ex-partner who's always been there for her?

Can Marie and Drew find their happy ending, or will the past threaten to pull them apart?

From the Author

Dear Reader,

First, I'd like to thank you for choosing to read *The Life She Finds*. Having spent seven years teaching university and living in an Australian country town, I've enjoyed writing a series with a rural setting and drawing on my experience of living in the country – with goats – and teaching in university. This is the fourth book in the series set in the fictional country town of Granite Springs and I'm thrilled by the response of you, my readers, to this series, how you tell me my characters are real people you'd love to have as friends. I feel they're my friends too, and they've become a part of my life. I hope you've enjoyed meeting Lyn and Ken.

If you'd like to stay up to date with my new releases and special offers you can sign up to my reader's group.

You can sign up here
https://mailchi.mp/f5cbde96a5e6/maggiechristensensreadersgroup

I'll never share your email address, and you can unsubscribe at any time. You can also contact me via Facebook Twitter or by email. I love hearing from my readers and will always reply.

Thanks again.

Acknowledgements

As always, this book could not have been written without the help and advice of a number of people.

Firstly, my husband Jim for listening to my plotlines without complaint, for his patience and insights as I discuss my characters and storyline with him, for his patience and help with difficult passages and advice on my male dialogue, and for being there when I need him.

John Hudspith, editor extraordinaire for his ideas, suggestions, encouragement and attention to detail.

Jane Dixon-Smith for her patience and for working her magic on my beautiful cover and interior.

My thanks also to early readers of this book –Helen, Maggie and Louise, for their helpful comments and advice. Also to Annie of *Annie's books at Peregian* for her ongoing support.

And to all of my readers. Your support and comments make it all worthwhile. I'm thrilled you enjoy my more mature characters.

Apologies to those of you familiar with events at the Pialligo Estate Winery. While the winery has hosted an event called *A Midsummer Night's Dream – Shakespeare by the Vines*, I've taken liberties with the timing of it.

About the Author

After a career in education, Maggie Christensen began writing contemporary women's fiction portraying mature women facing life-changing situations. Her travels inspire her writing, be it her frequent visits to family in Oregon, USA or her home on Queensland's beautiful Sunshine Coast. Maggie writes of mature heroines coming to terms with changes in their lives and the heroes worthy of them. Her writing has been described by one reviewer as *like a nice warm cup of tea. It is warm, nourishing, comforting and embracing.*

From her native Glasgow, Scotland, Maggie was lured by the call 'Come and teach in the sun' to Australia, where she worked as a primary school teacher, university lecturer and in educational management. Now living with her husband of over thirty years on Queensland's Sunshine Coast, she loves walking on the deserted beach in the early mornings and having coffee by the river on weekends. Her days are spent surrounded by books, either reading or writing them – her idea of heaven!

She continues her love of books as a volunteer with her local library where she selects and delivers books to the housebound.

Maggie can be found on Facebook, Twitter, Goodreads, Instagram or on her website.

www.facebook.com/maggiechristensenauthor
www.twitter.com/MaggieChriste33
www.goodreads.com/author/show/8120020.Maggie_Christensen
www.instagram.com/maggiechriste33/
maggiechristensenauthor.com/

Made in the USA
Middletown, DE
15 June 2022

67207913R00161